The THORNE at My Side

ERIN MARIE BASSETT

Published by EMB PUB LLC

Copyright 2024, Revisions 2026

Developmental and Line editing by Liza Illuzzi @editz_by_liza

Front Cover Illustration by Priti Das @priti_designs

Wrap Cover Design by Erin Marie Bassett

é

Hot people vote.
(That's you.)

Trigger Warnings

None.

The Politics of It All

I AM A WILDLY open-minded person (Aquarius, hi) and pride myself on my ability to see things from multiple points of view. I've voted for candidates of both major political parties at the federal level and do my best to support local individuals who I believe are driven to make our city a better place.

In this story I have purposely not assigned political parties to the characters because I want them to exist in an ideological world where voters can choose between people who understand that their job involves a lot of grey area. The task of running a country as diverse and as expansive as the United States is not a small one and yet I feel like our options as voters are rather limited.

You'll probably figure out where my current opinions reside as you get into the story but I promise you, like Elizabeth Bennet herself, I am a person who can have her mind changed.

I did not write this book to start a political debate. I wrote it because I thought "what if *You've Got Mail* happened through texts in Washington DC?" and this story is the one that unfolded as I tried to answer that question.

All I'll say on politics today is that we as citizens are responsible for making informed decisions and expecting more of our elected officials. We have much, *much*, more in common than we don't. At the end of the day we are humans and as anyone in a relationship will tell you; there is more than one way to load the dishwasher but if we work together we won't have to eat off of paper plates again tonight.

Take care, talk soon -

Erin

The THORNE at My Side

The Playlist

The THORNE at My Side

MAGGIE

@MenInSuitsDC

PROLOGUE

"Damnit, what now?" I mutter to myself as my phone starts ringing.

I never understood the expression "dead on your feet" until this moment right here. And, can I just ask the universe; why is it that your phone falls to the absolute bottom of your bag anytime it rings? Oh, and why does it ring exactly when you're trying to open your door after a grueling five day, eight state, campaign swing? When all you want to do is curl up in your chair, eat your frozen dinner, and watch Jake Gyllenhaal do something combative on your laptop.

"Yeah?" I answer after seeing my little sister's name on the caller ID. If it had been a colleague, I would have masked my annoyance and tried to pull an ounce of professionalism out of the depths of my reserves. But it's a Monday night, and it's Liz, so I know she's having girls night with her friends and if I don't answer now she'll just call back in a few hours and be more buzzed than she might already be.

"Whoa, you talk to your mother with that tone?" She jokes. "Actually, strike that, I know you do!" She laughs.

"What do you need, Liz?"

"Can't a girl just call her sister?" Liz asks innocently. She's anything but. When I don't respond she fills in the blank for me. "Okay, fine, I'm calling because I want to know if you follow this account MenIn-SuitsDC?"

"You know I'm not on social media. So, no I don't." I huff as I drop my bag on the floor and slide out of my heels. I shouldn't have answered this call, I don't have the energy for this.

"Phew! You should! The girls and I are drooling over some of these guys."

"Aren't the three of you in committed relationships?" Liz is engaged to be married on New Year's Eve later this year. Her best friend Nora got married last month. Their other friend, Angie just started dating her older brother's best friend. I only know these things because Liz shares. Mom too for that matter.

"Yeah, what does that have to do with anything?"

"You're looking at an account that creates content with the purpose of objectifying men."

"So you have seen it?" She accuses.

"No, I'm guessing."

"Well, you're not wrong. But we're just looking. Since when is it a crime to appreciate the male form in finely tailored three piece suits?"

"Jimmy owned one dress shirt when I met him, I need a hit of the financial district every so often," Nora chimes in from the background.

"Kyle doesn't dress in suits anymore either and I kind of miss it." Liz says and I can hear her mind drift off to the summer she and her fiancé met at work in the city.

"Holden still does," Angie says with a lit of a smirk to her voice.

"Okay, as much fun as this is, I had a good but long day and I need to veg out," I say and kind of let the sentence fade away hoping Liz will pick up the hint and hang up.

"Have you hired a second in command yet?" She asks instead. In February, I got the job as head speech writer for Senator Melissa Quinn's presidential campaign. I spent the year before that submitting samples to her team and doing everything I could to get on her radar. I knew I'd be able to grow her campaign and take things to the next level.

And I have, but I've been doing the work of two, if not three people, for months and it's wearing me down.

"Not yet, but I've been reviewing resumes." It's not a lie, but no one has inspired me to call them. It just feels easier to do it myself instead of explaining my vision to someone else.

"Is Senator Quinn as cool in person as she seems on social media?" Angie asks.

"Believe it or not, she's even cooler. Especially if you're into women-centered domestic policy like I am." I look up at my whiteboard and see the post-its I used to pitch myself as her next speech writer. Colorful squares of notes about maternal health, paid leave, childcare, abortion rights, Title IX, and digital safety of minors.

"How does she deal with the comments about her being a single woman?"

"Honestly, she ignores it or makes a joke about it behind the scenes. But you can't tell anyone I told you that." The long day is clearly getting to me if I'm sharing behind-the-scenes insights on the record. And yes, I know my sister and her friends aren't reporters but these days citizen accounts are everywhere. But the number of times Senator Quinn's single-childless status has come up and has been used against her in this campaign drives me even further towards wanting a relationship before I seek office.

It'll just be easier.

"Meet any cuties out on the road?" Liz asks like she's reading my mind.

"No, I was working."

"You know, wild idea here, but you could meet someone at work."

"I could, but I honestly don't have time for dating. I'm working constantly." Even when I'm sleeping I hear Senator Quinn delivering her stump speech.

"It's not healthy to work all the time, you need something else in your life." Liz says.

"Are you a therapist now or something?" I challenge.

"No, but I have lived experience and years of inspirational quotes from social media wisdom to share with the people."

The girls continue talking on their end like I"m not here as I undo the button at the top of my pants and feel my body take up a little more space with the freedom.

"Oo, look at this one," Liz gasps and I hear the phone muffle as she passes it to one of the other girls in the room.

"Holy shit!"

"That can't be real."

I'll never admit it but my interest is piqued and I am tempted to ask Liz to send it to me.

"Maybe you should just camp out near the hockey arena? Athletes in suits? It's unfair."

"I'd never date an athlete." I say, a professional athlete doesn't fit the Ideal Partner profile I've created.

"Wait, that guy isn't an athlete, but you can't tell by looking at him, it says down here in the caption." Liz starts reading, "DC Renegades Captain Felix Fournier pictured leaving opening night at The Ned with long time off-ice buddy, Au–"

"Liz, I don't really care, I'm not going to use a random social media account to find a date."

"Feels like a missed opportunity." She mutters.

"Be that as it may, I'm going to make dinner and go to bed. I'll talk to you later."

"The account is MenInSuitsDC if you need something to look at in bed later!" The girls start giggling and I roll my eyes.

"Bye Lizzard," I say quietly.

"Bye Maybe." She says gently and the call ends.

I hang up and sink into my chair. My studio apartment is maybe 400 square feet total but the distance from this side of the room to my kitchen where a microwavable dinner waits in the freezer feels like an impossible journey. Every bone in my body is tired. Traveling is always exhausting because of the extra planning I have to put in before I leave. I close my eyes and mentally replay the last week.

The thousands of people at the rallies to see her speaking, endless small towns like the one I grew up in, the motorcade of cars that snakes down country highways, the campaign team who make sure that everything is set up and ready to go. And then when she starts speaking, everything fades away and I can only focus on the words I crafted.

At this point she has the stump speech memorized, but with only a few months until the election I'll need to revise it and create new versions that go deeper into detail. There will be debates and in depth interviews as I get America to believe in her. I'll get up in a minute, microwave dinner, and start working on outlining the variations I'll need to draft.

But I don't get up, instead I fall asleep in my work clothes in the oversized chair in the corner of my apartment.

Chapter One
MAGGIE

"Are you high?"

"Maggie I don't care how good your date was last night, you need to focus." Sam Gibson, my second in command, scolds over the phone.

"Trust me, I was not thinking about Mike," I report. Mike, who was beige in every way. So beige that I didn't even consider taking him home. Another date to add to the growing list of men that won't get a second date with me. Little does Sam know, but my mind is stuck on the vague and ever-evolving image of a mystery man. My ideal man. The man I have yet to meet but after years of looking I feel closer to meeting than ever before.

Sam sighs and repeats herself. "This article says, over half, 54%, of students surveyed said they think using AI for school work is cheating."

"Well that's encouraging, I suppose," I say around a yawn as I hold the phone between my shoulder and my ear while I slip my running shoes on. Sam likes to call me first thing in the morning with whatever article kept her up the night before. We stumbled into this pattern when she learned that I went to bed early and woke up to run. She, on the other hand, burns the candle at both ends. "But then further down it says that 56% of students surveyed said they've used AI tools for coursework."

"Oh, that's just sad." I say as I stand and go to my white board. We're working on a speech for an event at a technical college in Michigan next week. My boss, Senator Melissa Quinn, is running for president from the lovely state of Kentucky, and if you're wondering if that's easy or not, let me be the first to tell you; it's not.

"This technology is the end of the world as we know it. People aren't going to think for themselves anymore. Our young people, who will run this country someday, will not be able to tell a machine generated news story from a human written one. It's almost like we need to include typos to prove we're real!"

"I love that idea, gosh it would save us so much time in editing!" I joke as I write "AI Issue" on a post-it and stick it on the board.

"So, tell me why Mike won't make the cut." Sam transitions as I sit down and tie my running shoes. This is the other part of the routine we've fallen into, a few minutes of non-work small talk. Relationships, recipes, funny things we saw people do on the metro.

I give Sam the rundown. How I met Mike at a workshop for political writers a few weeks ago. How we hit it off and after a few rounds of drinks we set up the date last night. I tell her that the conversation was really good, because it was. He believes in the same things I do. He might even be more passionate about the good old days, a true luddite.

I didn't believe him when he told me he only uses four apps so I looked. He has his email app, with the elusive inbox zero, a podcast app, and the news app. Then in one folder he's got everything else that comes preloaded on your phone and a weather app. I was impressed.

But in that placating a toddler way.

I took a minute when Mike went to the bathroom to envision him as my partner. He'd be fine enough in pictures, but I could easily see myself getting annoyed with him at the end of the day. He has a righteous tone to him like he wants me to think he's smart.

Sam points out that he never gave me a chance to show off how smart I am either. She's a good hype woman to have in your corner. We end the call and I finish getting ready for my run.

When I was hired as head speech writer for the campaign, I almost passed out. I'd been pitching her team for over a year because writing speeches for a national campaign was the last item on this phase of my career plan. So to be able to do it, and for a woman, is a dream come true.

My pitch was simple; focus on the issues, stick to your guns, rise above the criticism, and make your policies accessible.

Since I've been on the team her numbers have consistently grown with more and more independents coming on board. That will be the key to winning this election, getting people who identify with policies from both major parties to vote Quinn.

I'm excited about my job. It has been the opportunity of a lifetime, and one I've been working my lifetime for.

Two years in the prosecutor's office after law school, then three years as an assistant district attorney, two years clerking for the New York Supreme Court and then one year on staff as a press secretary for a House of Representatives member. Each step bringing me closer to this. And from here I'll take the steps to become a candidate myself.

Maggie Collins, the right leader for you.

I just need to nail down Mr. Collins because watching Senator Quinn do it as a single woman confirmed I don't want to do this alone.

Before I leave, I open up my bedside table drawer and pick up the little e-ink, text only, phone from SMS Connect.

SMS Connect is the latest craze for single Washingtonians. When you enroll you pay a fee, fill out a lengthy personality test, and then their service sends you a basic phone with one contact in it. You can't send pictures, you can't send links, and they suggest you don't meet until you've been texting for at least twelve weeks. Or you don't have to meet at all and you can send the device back. They even take care of telling your correspondent that you've terminated your service agreement.

The ads started appearing everywhere around the holidays. Their message was simple; now is the time to start a relationship because then you could go home and tell your parents you were seeing someone. I braved my way through Christmas, letting my mom focus on my sister's engagement, and didn't sign up until July when I completed my semi-annual progress review. With my 15 year plan in hand I noted that everything in the career section was moving along well. Everything in my health and wellness section was on track. But the relationship column was woefully behind schedule.

By 32, I was supposed to be dating someone seriously, with an engagement planned for my 33rd year and a wedding before my 35th.

I'm 36 and have had less than seven, but more than five, second dates in the last three years. Even fewer third dates.

But I didn't need to review the numbers to know my dating life was pitiful. It's not for a lack of trying! I date, I meet guys, I seek them out. I have hope, I have optimism, I have regular waxing appointments.

My mom thinks I'm too picky, not that I've asked for her input. It's not even trust issues or problems with intimacy. I want to be in a relationship. I'm just looking for something specific.

Enter; SMS Connect.

With my second glass of wine in hand after my self-reflection, I snuggled up in the corner of my big chair and watched a couple walk hand-in-hand down my street. I felt jealous of their smiling faces, their comfortable laughter, and the affection in their eyes.

I slammed back the rest of my wine, hissed as it burned its path to my stomach, and visited meetyourmmc.com. I might have signed up in a fit of passion but when I got home from my run a week later and the little device was waiting at my door for me, it felt like Christmas morning.

I powered it up and sat on the edge of my bed wondering who I was matched with. The e-ink screen popped to life and I heard a quiet ping telling me a message was already there. I held my breath and read the first note. Laughing when he admitted to looking up questions to ask on a first date before writing to me.

And now, like there has been every morning since this little phone arrived, there's a message waiting for me from DCFox.

DCFOX: My cat Brinkley keeps getting calls from UFC to join the circuit. He's got a fierce left hook that he bops me with at least twice a day. But every time they call, he simply turns his tail on them and says he'd rather stay here and lounge in the windowsill watching the birds in the tree behind my apartment. I can't say I blame him, it's a pretty good life.

When I was out tonight, the air was starting to turn crisp. The humid summer mornings are hopefully behind us. Don't you hate that humidity? Although, maybe you don't, maybe you're one of those people who loves feeling like you're breathing in hot pasta vapors. And I bet your hair never gets poofy. But, if it does, let me know and I'll send you a bottle of the spray my sister swears by; just let me know your name and address.

I'm kidding! It hits me every so often how strange this arrangement is, but not knowing has its advantages. I find myself looking twice at women and wondering if by chance they're you. Do you do the same?

I find myself nodding along as I read, and giggling quietly as I bite my bottom lip. The messages from DCFox turn me into a bumbling school girl.

It's been that way for nine weeks. Three more to go until we can meet.

I slide the little phone into the drawer and head out the door for my run. The air is cooler and I smile as I take a quick turn to the heart of Adams Morgan. When I moved to DC, I was immediately drawn to the neighborhood's colorful buildings, the bustling restaurant scene, and how there seemed to be little parks tucked away around every corner.

I lift my hand in a wave to Joanne at Sunrise, the local coffee shop and bakery, who is putting out her sidewalk sign. She smiles back before I turn again towards the wide paths in Kalorama Park. My Upbeat Morning Music playlist powers me past the playground where parents and nannies are unloading their strollers and guzzling caffeine. Past the basketball court where a group of guys are playing shirts and skins. I can't help but slow down a little bit for a quick peruse. It's been a while since I've had any skin-to-skin contact and watching their pecs and shoulders glisten revs me up. The final corner of the park takes me back to Belmont Road where it's a straight shot home by way of Sunrise Bakery.

I jog up the steps of the bright blue painted brick building and order my coffee and pastry to-go and pull out my phone while I wait.

An email from my favorite meal prep blogger with new recipes for the week catches my eye. I take a look at the baked chicken breasts that are served with charred broccoli and quinoa. Each ingredient can be made in a big batch and it makes enough to feed me all week.

Back in law school I skipped dinner more often than I ate it. The most I'd do when I did have dinner was to eat a bag of microwave popcorn and chug a diet coke. Then one day, I was on the phone with my mom as she was getting back from grocery shopping. It reminded me of the routines the Collins family stuck to each week.

I hung up with my mom, made a list, and put together my first week of meal prep that same day. It worked best for me to have dinner ready, breakfast was often grab and go, lunch was on campus or in between meetings. The travel schedule of the campaign makes things tricky but I've stuck with it and have started to use my freezer more so food doesn't go bad.

Sunrise is only a few doors away but my croissant is down to its last bite by the time I open my apartment door. I finish it, take a drag of my coffee, and get ready for work.

I've got my routine down to a science. Dry shampoo and a shower cap, body shower, dry off, skincare, body lotion, get dressed. I don't lay my clothes out the night before because picking an outfit doesn't take much mental effort. I've curated a professional wardrobe of whites, creams, browns, and light blues. Tight fitting top or bodysuit, wide leg pant or pencil skirt, and a blazer. Nude or black pumps. Done.

After my makeup I pull my hair back into a low bun or claw clip if it's a humid day. Again, the choice is already made for me so I work on autopilot while I listen to NPR.

I developed this system years ago when I realized how draining it was to pick an outfit every morning. One Labor Day Weekend I donated all but four items from my closet and restocked on basics. Now that I stand behind a woman running for president the clothing choices I make get commented on too. It isn't as frequent as hers, you should have seen the stink people made about her sneakers, but the first time it happened I felt exposed on a level I wasn't ready for. Now everything I wear is neutral. Designed not to draw attention.

I slide my notebook into my bag and check my phone before leaving. I find a text waiting for me from Sam. It'll be easier to just chat with her while I walk so I dial her number.

"Hello again Sam!" I cheer after I hear her quick hey. "Are you feeling as amazing as I am?"

"Are you high?" She asks seriously.

"On life!" I joke as I lock up behind me. "I had an exhilarating run, a perfectly flaky croissant for breakfast, and I've been thinking about the best products for frizzy hair all morning."

"What?"

Oh, right, that was just the text from DCFox.

"What happened to you in the last hour? Did you manage to sneak in some morning bedroom funtime?" She asks as I reach the sidewalk.

"No! Just a run and feeling the sun on my face. And running past a group of guys playing pickup basketball without shirts on. I might have slowed my pace and tried to perk up my tits a bit as I passed. "

"I've told you before Maggie, I know you're hard up right now and you're a smoke show but I won't date my boss."

I laugh. This is a running joke since I received her resume. It was the only one out of the bunch for deputy speech writer that got me excited but I was upset that it was a man. I had this idea of an all female writing team. I was mistaken because instead of putting Samantha down as her name, she wrote Sam. When she walked into the office for her interview Jorge, Senator Quinn's assistant, called my office saying "Sam was here for an interview" and his voice had this teasing tone to it. I was expecting a wildly attractive man that Jorge and I could gossip about later but instead, in walked this feisty woman.

When I asked, she said it was a social experiment to see if she'd get more call backs as a man than as a woman. I laughed and said "marry me" in response because I am passionate about women's rights and try to surround myself with kindred spirits. And if I was going to trust someone to craft messages for the senator's campaign I want someone who believes in the same things I do.

"I know and it kills me a little bit every time you tell me no." We share a laugh. "How am I supposed to find someone who gets me like you do?" I ask her with fake exasperation.

"You could try SMS Connect," Sam suggests. "I wonder if it really works."

"I mean, it's a pretty solid system." I say with a physical shrug she can't see.

"Wait, did you sign up for it?"

"Yes," I admit quietly even though the other people on the sidewalk with me have headphones in and can't hear me or Sam's question for that matter. Something about needing to use the service makes me feel like a failure.

"You did? Ohmygod, Maggie. What do you think?" Sam asks and I can picture her sitting on the edge of her seat.

"Well the guy I'm talking to is great, but it's also confusing because I don't actually know him. And I hit it off with Mike and he was fine so maybe I should just end the SMS Connect thing and go with Mike."

"You hear yourself right? Don't settle for fine because it's in front of you."

"Yeah, okay, you're right."

"So what do you and Text Man talk about?"

"Oh it's nothing, we talk about D.C., podcasts, music, sports, hair products," I chuckle. "He's got a cat named Brinkley."

"So he's into pussy?"

I bark out a laugh as I reach the metro station. "I mean, a girl can only hope. Okay, meet you at the office in 30."

"See you then."

Chapter Two
AUSTIN

"Dude, where is your head at?"

"Up and at 'em!" My sister calls out as she flips the switch on the automatic blinds in my bedroom.

"Elle, when are you moving out? I can't handle you and your morning person tendencies." I grumble as I roll away from the light.

"Austin, I'm barely a morning person, you're just nocturnal. It's seven, normal people don't call this early."

"Is The Morning Show still on?" I know it is because I hear Showbiz Scoop in the background. It's a segment I've been featured on from time to time so I have to fight the urge to throw the TV out the window when I hear the jingle. "Because that, by definition, is still the morning."

"Yes but you know I have to be up to open the studio for the 5:30 class."

"But why do I have to be up for that?"

"You're lucky I waited to wake you up until I got home. Plus, Dad wants to see me be responsible and getting you to the office before 10:00 is one way I can show him that."

She cheerfully knocks out a beat on my door. When I let my little sister Eloise move in with me, I didn't know she'd try to use me as her ticket to prove to Dad she's responsible. The piece I'm missing is how turning *me* into a morning person proves that *she* has hit the trust inheritance requirement. Had I known, I would have told her it's not worth the effort. Dad only cares about one thing, making money. He doesn't care what time of day it happens or really where it comes from as long as it hits the bank account.

I hear Elle out in the front of the condo talking to Brinkley. As I head to the shower I check the little gray rectangle I've become overly attached to. I turn it off at night, after I send my message to TalkShopGirl because if I don't, I'll sleep with one ear open hoping to hear the ping indicating her response. Which means the only way to tell if TalkShopGirl has responded is to turn it on.

I brace myself for not hearing back from her. It hasn't happened yet, but the last thing I wrote to her was about a hair product Elle wouldn't shut up about yesterday so I'm concerned.

But also, these conversations as DCFox are the most genuine words I've ever exchanged with a woman. Because TalkShopGirl has no idea that I am Austin Thorne, media conglomerate heir and tabloid darling.

Most women date me for my bank account or access to the company's broadcast and gossip channels and my verified status on social media. And, while I'm certainly not complaining because those women are usually an appealing combination of attractive and inattentive, the texts I exchange with TalkShopGirl make me feel like a teenager. The pimply kid who is too tall for his muscle mass, too nervous to approach his crush, looking for anything to say to her.

Like a full paragraph on his sister's hair products.

The little phone comes to life and I lean against the counter in my bathroom as I brush my teeth and read her latest note.

TalkShopGirl: I like thinking that our texts are this ongoing conversation. One where our messages don't have a beginning or an end. And, I love waking up to your notes. I open my eyes and try to avoid this little device as long as possible before I finally give in and check because I am desperate to know what DCFox has to say.

As soon as I start reading your words the rest of the world fades away. I don't hear the hustle and bustle of my neighborhood. I don't hear the notifications on my team's slack channel. I only hear the rhythm of my own heart as I read my note, from you.

A wide smile spreads across my face. It's ridiculous because we don't know each other but she sounds as invested in this relationship as I am.

When I walk into the corporate headquarters of Thorne Media Corp an hour later, I head straight through the lobby to the back patio that overlooks the river.

This is where my project manager, Kevin Young, prefers to work. He'll sit outside when the weather allows or inside with his back against the marble lobby wall, laptop propped on his legs.

"Austin, good morning," he says when he sees me. I smile at him and nod towards the walking path. He snaps his laptop closed and falls into step beside me.

"I just got off the phone with the team in India and there's been a power outage so they're not going to complete their tasks for today."

"Excellent," I mutter.

"And we got a call from the guys over at Alpha. They want to figure out how we can adapt this project for them to control the content their users are seeing."

"Alrighty," I slow my steps and look out over the river, the soft glow of the autumn sunshine washes the city in a golden hue. "And what's the status of the offshore work?"

"Dude, where is your head at?" Kevin says with a laugh.

"Sorry," I laugh at myself quietly. TalkShopGirl's words float through my head.

I only hear the rhythm of my own heart.

"You get laid last night? Is Allegra back in town?"

"What? No. No way. I mean, she's fine and all but, no."

I clear my throat because while Kevin and I are close we don't need to be talking about my sex life a few hundred feet from the office. "So are we still on schedule?" I regroup.

"It'll be tight but we should be ready for launch next week, which is three full weeks before the election."

"We should probably announce ourselves; tell people we're coming. We're going to dominate the news cycle once we're live."

"I'm hesitant to do it too soon. With the talk of lawsuits and the anti-trust environment our current congress wears like a badge of honor..." Kevin speaks with concern in his voice.

"You think people will be lining up to picket the big, bad, AI Media company?"

"The one that destroys everything these politicos hold dear?"

I laugh. "We'll just have to win them over with our sheer volume of content and high powered search engine. Until then, let's start running ads, coming soon, a TMC AI Media initiative so stock your doomsday cellars today."

Kevin and I share a laugh. We might joke about it but we both understand the reality. This project has been four years in the making and when it goes live, it'll revolutionize the way people receive their information.

The AI database we built is powered by an algorithm that factors in just about everything the user does on their device. And as soon as it's live it will deliver personalized news to users eight times a day. The articles will be written specifically for them so they find them interesting and helpful.

That's the public facing side of the project. Then there is my pet project, a version of the tool that will write speeches, responses, and talking points for politicians based on what their backers, followers, and opponents have said in the last 24 hours.

Their content will be customized to address trending topics and our technology's ability to match the candidate's tone of voice will ensure a natural sounding script. We'll be able to draft digital content as well. And the speed at which we'll do so will put all the trolls to shame.

It's an expensive product to develop but like how the first AIDS pill cost a billion to produce and the second only cost a dollar, this thing will have a low operating cost and the profits will turn almost immediately. And those profits will grow exponentially when we add in sponsored, in-line content and more obvious ads.

And like Kevin said, the government is not in our corner on this one. There are already laws in the E.U. that protect user generated content from AI scrubbing and I bet the U.S. will follow. Especially if Senator Quinn is elected. Digital safety and privacy are key to her platform.

There is a TMC marketing coordinator assigned to AI Media and they'll get the word out as soon as we give the green light. I've had a few promising meetings about the speech writing side of the business and should get those contracts closed this week.

My biggest worry at this point is the final pitch to Dad. He doesn't care about the innovation of the product. He doesn't care about the user projections. He only cares about the bottom line. In fact, my "presentation" could be as simple as it cost A to make, we'll make B from advertising and as long as Dad feels like it's enough we're good to go. He's going to ask for my numbers and then jot them down on his notepad.

Where all those notes go remains a mystery.

I've heard the outgoing president leaves a note in his desk for the next guy, maybe when Dad transitions the company to me next year I'll get access to the notes archive.

When the elevator doors open on the 24th floor I head straight into my dad's office. I see my grandfather is in the office today which will make this pitch more entertaining. He likes to hear more than numbers.

Alfred Thorne is the patriarch of Thorne Media Corp. He started this company with money he saved cutting lawns in ritzy neighborhoods around D.C. He'd overhear discussions and started to write them down and soon realized he was sitting on a wealth of information because no one took him seriously. He published a one-page flier with a salacious headline but an all true story from what he overheard in the backyard of the Secretary of State and soon the royalties were pouring in.

He, of course, lost his access as a lawn boy but he quickly organized a team of rag-tag reporters who would follow important people around and pick up whatever they could.

He basically invented the paparazzi.

My dad took over when he turned 35 and he expanded the Thorne reach into every type of media you can imagine. He started buying up radio stations and later podcast production studios. He bought up flailing social media apps at bottom of the barrel prices. He even got into the streaming service game.

Now it's my turn to take the company to the next level with my AI driven news product.

Dad sits behind his desk and my grandfather sits in one of the chairs in front. I take the other. I remember grandad's office being wood furniture and wingback chairs. A smog of cigar smoke was always present.

Dad, of course, redecorated when he assumed the CEO position. He hired a trendy 80s designer who delivered the epitome of office decor at the time with red desks, light gray chairs with chrome legs, and a curved sofa.

"Austin, glad you could join us," Dad greets as he continues to read something on his computer. "Your grandfather and I were discussing the AI project."

"I spoke with Kevin before coming up here, we're on track but we're a little worried about the launch."

"How so?" My grandfather asks.

"Well, we're concerned about the current congress's affinity for regulating user generated content apps, the EU is already ahead of the US with restrictions on AI combing social media, and the speech writing component will not be well received by anyone employed in D.C. to write speeches."

"Speech writers are a dime a dozen," my father says dismissively.

"Well there certainly are dozens of them, especially in an election year."

"Don't do that son, don't aggrandize them. You give them too much power and it'll come back to bite you."

"Who are you most concerned about?" My grandfather asks.

"The marketing team mentioned two earlier this week. One, Miles Frick is working on the Goeglier campaign down in Florida and getting a good response. Another is Maggie Collins who is working on the Quinn campaign here in D.C.. Apparently she has really taken them to the next level."

After we discuss a few more specifics, including the numbers I knew Dad would want to jot down, I head back to my office. I need to decompress after meetings with my dad.

Only a few more hours until I can get home, change into loungewear, mix a cocktail, and respond to TalkShopGirl. By far, my favorite part of the day.

Chapter Three
MAGGIE

"Who died?"

DCFox: My grandfather is buying another boat. He took me out to see it being built last weekend and I have to admit, there wasn't much to see that you haven't seen before. A yacht is a yacht. He insists it is all state of the art, but I just see a bunch of anchors and knots.

I laugh as I read his message. Considering I've only been on pontoon boats back in my hometown in upstate New York I can't even imagine what the interior of a yacht looks like. But my mom has embraced our town's annual pontoon decorating contest which makes me think I might have a few ideas for sprucing things up that I could pass along.

It was a long day at the office but a good one. The senator is gearing up for her second debate which is focused on domestic policy. These are the issues voters really care about. The things that impact their daily lives.

My mind is racing with all the snippets we need to write. Two minutes on each with a list of bullet points for the rebuttals. I pull out my trusty pack of post-it notes and felt tip pen and get to work. We won't know who will speak first but there are ways to word responses so it doesn't matter.

"My opponent will suggest," I start to speak out loud as I jot down ideas and slap the colored squares on my white board.

After an hour, I boil water and pour it into the mason jar ramen I prepped on Sunday and take the meal with me to my bed. My studio apartment doesn't have room for a dining table so I either eat at my desk, on the floor, in my overstuffed chair, or on my bed. Right now the chair is covered in my clothes, so, bed it is.

I cue up *She's The Man* on my laptop, my comfort movie of choice, and press play right before I wake up my SMS Connect phone. DC-Fox's message about the yachts make me chuckle. Sometimes our conversations are back-and-forth, get-to-know you exchanges. But other times we simply put our thoughts out there and let the other person into our consciousness a bit.

When Viola decides to take matters into her own hands after the girl's team gets cut, I write a note back.

TalkShopGirl: I have watched She's The Man 200 times. When it came out I was the student council president fighting for additional funding for after school activities so I saw a lot of myself in Viola.

Not that I've ever tried to pass myself off as a man, but her commitment to what she believed in resonated with me.

And, I remember falling hard for Channing. And getting caught up in how cute Amanda Bynes looks as Sebastian and then how hot she looks as Viola at the fair. Truly a masterpiece of early 2000s pop culture. I hate to love all the moments that Duke should figure it out but doesn't.

Watch it, you'll love it.

***

My alarm sounds at 5:15. Waking up early was a habit I nurtured during law school. So many of my friends would stay up late trying to study and I had a few late nights but learned that if I went to bed by 11:00 I could be up by 6:00 to get a jump on the day. When I graduated I kept adding to my morning routine and had to add another 10 minutes when the SMS phone arrived.

Speaking of...I roll over and poke the sleep out of the corners of my eyes with one hand while the other hand pulls out the little phone. I press the power button and wait.

Ping.

DCFox: She's The Man huh? I think it is brave of you to admit that your favorite movie is about a girl who dresses up to pretend to be a boy and falls for her roommate. But then again, my favorite movie is Angels In The Outfield and we probably don't need to psychoanalyze me for that.

I was surprised to get your note tonight, I always pictured you writing to me with morning hair and hot coffee. For the record I'm writing mine before bed. I was up working later than I wanted to because there's a lot going on with my job at the moment. I know we can't share details but I'm excited for what is in the works, and where it'll lead me.

***

A few hours later I am smiling as I carry my Sunrise Bakery breakfast with me to the senator's office. Sam has been eerily quiet so far this morning. Usually I'll have heard from her at least twice by now. She's my morning news source. When I first started this role I would wake up and read every headline myself and that would determine the tasks for the day. Now Sam takes the first pass and flags things for me before I go in and read everything myself when I get to the office.

My smile disappears as I walk into the conference room and see Sam's expression.

"Who died?" I ask assuming we'll be rescheduling our week around some senator's memorial.

"Our jobs." Sam says stoically.

"What are you talking about?" I ask with a laugh as I sit down next to her at the table.

"She doesn't know?" Jorge asks as he comes in with a tray of muffins and fruit and sets it on the table.

"Know what? Seriously, what has gotten into you two?"

With the drama of a made-for-tv movie both Sam and Jorge slowly turn their attention to me.

"Maggie," Sam starts.

"Stay seated while we tell you this," Jorge cautions.

"There's been some news."

"If this is all some prank to tell me that we're like seventy points ahead in the polls I'm going to kick both of you in the shins." I say as I rip a piece of my croissant off and pop it in my mouth.

They both pause and then flash eyes at each other.

"I'm not gonna tell her," Jorge insists but he makes no move to leave the room.

"Ugh, fine," Sam pouts, turns back to me, "I'm just going to say it. Quickly. Rip the bandage off." She inhales and exhales. "Go time."

"Sam?"

"Okay, Thorne Media Corp announced a new AI Media app that will create custom news content for its users." She rushes through the sentence then gasps for breath.

"What?" I ask, blinking hard and squeezing my hands into fists. It is nearly impossible to stay on top of the 24 hour news cycle as it is. Then add in social media and it becomes exactly impossible. How am I supposed to do my job effectively if a robot is writing news too?

"TMC, is set to release, "AIM" their calling it, but it's an app that will deliver custom news stories to consumers all day long." Sam repeats slowly.

"That's," I stutter, "that's," I throw my hands up in the air, one still clutching my now decimated croissant.

"It's something, alright." Sam mutters.

"Impossible!" I finally spit out.

The election is three weeks away. The debate is next week. My news alert listserv gets updated every 15 minutes and there's always something new about the senator. My position has always been that she shouldn't care about news but Ben, the campaign manager sees things differently. I slump back down in my chair and toss my mangled pastry onto the table.

"I'm glad I was here to see that." Jorge says before he turns and steps out of the room. "Oh," he pops his head back in with a saccharine smile on his face, "remember the seminar starts at 2:00 and you'll be in this room so clean up any crumbs, thanks."

I turn to look at Sam who is watching me with observant eyes, trying, I'm sure, to figure out what is going through my mind. I'd tell her if I could. It is hard enough as it is to keep track of all the news mentions, to adapt to the rapidly shifting trends and opinions. One commencement speech can go viral and start a national conversation on child care and we not only have to know the ins and outs of the speech but we need to have a response ready to go because reporters are everywhere and the first thing they do is ask a "relevant" question.

I would argue, and I've tried, that whatever conversation has spun up on social media isn't always relevant. It might be timely, and some are truly important, but more often than not when an important figure like Senator Quinn comments on it, the issue gains credibility. She's a person who can *make* a discussion happen. And her silence can speak volumes.

Maybe this is a thing that we can be silent about.

My brain registers the lie but I'm going with it.

"It's going to be fine," I finally say to Sam after my mental pep rally. "We're making a mountain out of a molehill that hasn't even been built yet." I am not sure who needs to hear this more; me or Sam. She is well aware of my frustration with writing reactionary content.

"Okay," Sam stretches the word out into four syllables. "So the official campaign line is "it's going to be fine?"

"We might need to wordsmith it a bit." I smile and then busy myself cleaning up flakes of pastry that have fallen on the table, the floor, and on my top. Classic writer move, cleaning when there are mountains of other things to do.

"This is a nightmare come true. A night terror come true. This is literally the worst case scenario!" Sam spits back at me.

"Stop spiraling," I tell her, "this has nothing to do with us. It's a computer trying to do the job of intelligent people and it won't go anywhere. People want to hear from experts with insight."

"Well now I know you've lost it because that's an outright lie. They're going to customize news for every user," Sam says as she scrolls further down the article.

"That's basically impossible so really they're just going to be feeding the same story to different people and the consumers are going to think they're getting something custom. It's a sham."

I can't look at Sam because she'll know immediately that I'm lying. She'll be able to see on my face how worried I am about this.

First of all, the speed with which AI could produce articles is scary. And if a news source, like Thorne, is behind it they'll be publishing the content far and wide almost immediately.

There's no way for our team to keep up with everything that is said about the senator online. But I made it a point to identify key drivers of content and keep tabs on the general consensus. I have a dashboard that tracks certain hashtags and skims comments on our posts. The secret service does too so we don't have to worry about any of the threatening ones.

And trust me, as a single woman running for president, the senator receives plenty of them. The shit people (read: pencil dick men) think they can say from behind a screen is atrocious.

"Plus," I add as I walk my scraps over to the trash can, desperate for a change of subject, "we have to get ready for this afternoon."

Senator Quinn is co-hosting a Young People in D.C. day alongside her most public opposition, Senator Williams. In an attempt to show bipartisanship, she and Senator Williams will be giving PolySci majors and Senate interns tours of the Capitol Building and our offices. Then, they're invited in for small workshop sessions with people on their teams. I'm hosting one with Sam on the art of speech writing in the modern age.

"Good morning!" Senator Quinn comes in and takes a seat at the table. I shoot eyes at Sam and she hurries to her seat as Jorge strides in to take notes. "I'm glad you're all here. I'm excited to bring people in through the office today and I wanted to talk with you for a moment before I get started."

"What's on your mind Senator?" I ask.

"I wanted to let you know that I'll be bringing in a new AI writing solution to support you. We're closing in on this thing and I expect you to do everything you can to keep my momentum going!"

"Absolutely," I cheer with a smile on my face. I can hear the way my voice is climbing as the predicament I'm in starts racing through my mind. My heart rate sky rockets as I try to envision how this will actually work.

I can feel Sam looking at me, waiting for a tirade of some sort on how AI will be the end of the original thought. And while I've gone deep on the subject after a glass of wine, or two, now isn't the time.

"This could be really good for us, the best of both worlds!" I continue. I'm head speech writer. I am the person people rely on. I'm the one who is going to get this done and I set the tone for the team.

"I'm so glad to hear your support for this, Maggie." Senator Quinn says, "there will be more information in the next few days but in the meantime, keep up the good work."

With that, the Senator stands and leaves the room with Jorge on her heels.

"So, are you really okay with this?" Sam asks wide eyed with concern.

"It's not like she gave me a choice." I roll my shoulders back as my foot starts to bounce under the table. "But it could be good. It's going to be good. We'll make sure it's good."

"That's a lot of 'goods'. As a professional writer I've got to intervene here."

"Fair, right, yes, okay. Umm, just give me a minute?" I throw my thumb over my shoulder and Sam nods. I turn and head out of the office, down the stairs at the end of the hall, and past my favorite security guard, before striding out onto the steps for some fresh air.

What I didn't admit upstairs was that we are already having trouble keeping up with the volume of content that hits the internet everyday. Factor in the 24-hour news channels, network news, and local coverage, and it is essentially impossible.

I can feel the stress creeping across my body. My jaw already feels tight so I work it around for a minute and then roll my head a few times. I knew the last three weeks before the election would be demanding but the addition of an AI co-worker is going to only make matters worse.

But I need to get a handle on this if I ever want to run for office myself. I need to learn how to toughen up, how to deal with the pressure of being in the game as the clock winds down.

If my right eye starts twitching that's when I'll know it's bad. That's always the sign of impending doom.

I take a seat on the steps and lean forward to rub my temples, a tension headache starting and it's only 9:45 am. It's going to be a long day.

Chapter Four
AUSTIN

"Consider this goodbye for now."

"How did you swing this?" Elizabeth Johnson, my assistant, asks me over the phone as I hold the door open for the two TMC interns I've got in tow with me today.

"Senator Williams wanted something scrubbed about his kid at a frat party. I did it for him with the expectation of access to his office for exclusives."

"You're the best in the biz." She says. Elizabeth has been with Thorne Media Corp for forty-three years. She started as a typist in the newspaper division and quickly rose in the ranks to the secretarial corps. She was the first woman at the company to hold the title of Executive Assistant because she appealed to HR for an updated role description when she worked for Dad.

When I joined the company after grad school, Dad had me in a middle management position for the first six months. I enjoyed that position, I learned a lot about how the work actually gets done around here. After those six months, I was basically Dad's shadow for the next year. I attended all his meetings, sat in his office all day, and would even commute with him.

One early October commute, I slid into his car and Dad lowered his newspaper and said, "Today you'll start as the head of the Business Development division. I'll need to see a plan for a new revenue initiative by the end of the week."

Then he flicked the paper back up in front of his face and we drove to the office in silence. Elizabeth was waiting for me in the lobby to show me to my office.

She got me settled, asked me a litany of questions ranging from my preferred brands of snacks and how I take my coffee, to my clothing sizes and my social media login credentials. Then she stood, told me I'd have lunch delivered at noon and that I had a meeting with my senior manager of business development, Kevin Young, in five.

"What else is there for me?" I ask as I stand with the two interns.

"There's been a podcast interview request. Actually it's a panel. But it came on the heels of the announcement this morning."

"What podcast?"

"For The Record," Elizabeth says. "You've been on it before."

"I remember. What time?"

"They want to start at 6:30 and it's a 90 minute session."

"Okay, book it. Is it in person?"

"Yes. I will have Greg ready with the car at 6:00."

"Thank you, Elizabeth."

She hangs up so I put my air pods into their case and turn to Annabel and Matt, the interns. I was able to schedule this tour during a Young People on the Hill event so we'll blend in. I wanted to give them a chance to see how the sausage gets made since they'll be assisting editors and writers with intel from the Senate and House of Representatives. It feels a little odd to be here though; usually Thorne employees are only invited to the capitol building when under subpoena.

After a lifetime spent in D.C., and in the media world, the whole thing has lost its luster. I'm only thirty four but I've witnessed countless people cycle through this city. I've seen many more get chewed up and spat back out to whatever up or down state small town they're from. The turnover rate in Washington is high and it doesn't pay off to connect deeply or go all-in with anyone.

That thought brings TalkShopGirl to mind. She said she comes from a small town but it doesn't feel like she got off the train in D.C. holding a suitcase and sporting wide open eyes, hoping to make it in the big city. But maybe she's acclimated in her time here. D.C. can do that to a person.

After I've taken my two interns around to the offices our news magazine is friendly with, we turn a corner and I see a poster on an easel announcing a speech writing workshop as part of the event. I notice that it's being hosted by Maggie Collins who was on the list of speech writers to watch. I'll admit I haven't looked closely into her, or any of the others, since AI Media is going to blow any human writing out of the water.

All the past speech writers or campaign managers I've met are old white guys so it's interesting that Maggie Collins has made her way in this space. I guess with a female candidate it's more likely. I don't want that to sound misogynistic, it's just how the world of politics works. It's an old mens club.

Maybe Maggie is a college or law school friend of the senator's. Maybe she pulled her up to the big leagues when she got the lead in the primaries. The poster says this event is co-hosted with a Sam Gibson, who I haven't heard of, but I'd bet money he's an old white guy.

It starts in a few minutes so we head inside and I find a spot along the back wall. There is chatter throughout the room as the kids around the table settle in. I would not consider myself old by any stretch of the imagination but being in a room with 20 year olds makes me feel ancient. When the room quiets down, I look up from my phone.

My world stutters to a halt and proceeds like a stop motion film. I watch, unblinking, as the most beautiful woman I've ever seen strides into the room. Her blonde hair shines around her face like a halo and I am hypnotized by the movement of her hand as she tucks one loose strand behind her ear. The rest of her hair is pulled back at the base of her head. Sleek, proper, and super fucking sexy.

She bends slightly to set a stack of notepads on the table and I get a peek at the perfect bubble of her ass under the pair of wide leg pants that fall from her hips like a waterfall.

Her piercing blue eyes start to scan the room as she begins her presentation. I don't hear the words she's speaking, all I can focus on is the pink heart shape of her lips as they move. And I start to devise ways to taste them.

I subtly check that my suit is in place. A quick little tug on my shirt sleeve confirms that, yes, it is still tailored to perfection by the team at Hugo Boss themselves. I check that my shoes are scuff free and I pass my fingers over my mouth and jaw to make sure everything is in order. The final piece is adjusting my glasses on my face so she is in perfect focus.

It has been a long time since I've seen a woman I want to impress. She hasn't paid me any extra attention, in fact she seems to be avoiding eye contact with me. I hope that means she is flustered by me.

On instinct I scan the room again to make sure that none of these dweeby post-teens pose an actual threat. None detected. They're all wearing suits that are just a little too big or too small and their hair is a half inch on the long side. The young women in the room are glued to Maggie's words and she seems to spare them a few more eye contact moments than the guys.

I am wholly focused on the visual of Maggie. I don't process a word she says because I am thinking of the different ways I want to have her and where I would start. She seems like the type that likes to ride on top but I'd like to see her bent over with me holding her wrists behind her back.

"So, to answer your question, no, the Thorne announcement doesn't worry me."

My attention snaps and I try to piece together what she might have been saying at the start of that sentence, or even if there was a question before it.

The intern standing to my left, Matt, looks at me and I give a quick shake of my head. She didn't look at me when she called out Thorne so there's a chance she doesn't know who I am. My dad is still primarily the face of the company and since I've been focused on the AI Media project for the last three years I haven't been making appearances for the company besides at our private holiday parties and fundraisers.

"Thank you everyone for coming today, if you want to grab a business card on your way out you can email me and my team for anything. Networking is the way of the world in D.C. so it's best to start getting comfortable introducing yourself to strangers!"

She laughs a little and I feel the sound in my chest. It settles there and then slowly radiates through me like rays of sunshine.

The room starts to come back to life as twenty-somethings filter out, take cards, and shake her hand. I hang back to be one of the last ones out and hopefully catch a minute of her time so I can introduce myself. Not sure how I'll handle it when she learns my last name but I'll cross that bridge when I get there. I'm good in a pinch.

"Oh that's really exciting," she says to Annabel who just said she's in the editorial division at Thorne for this semester. "News magazines and news production is serious and important work. It's wonderful to see that Thorne is also investing in people, not just algorithms."

I step up and Annabel gets the clue to leave. The stunning blonde turns her sapphire blue eyes at me and extends her hand.

"Maggie Collins, thanks for coming to the workshop."

"Hi Maggie, I'm Austin, thanks so much for putting it together."

We're the last two in the room so I step back as she starts to gather up her papers. "I noticed you weren't really engaged with the discussion today." She says as she stands back up and meets my eye.

"I'll admit I was more interested in the woman leading the discussion," I take a step forward, clearly on the prowl, and instead of flirting back or giving me bedroom eyes of her own, she pauses and then snorts out a laugh. I straighten and nervously rake my hand through my hair. That is not the reaction I was expecting and I'm unsure what to do next.

"Sorry. I'm sorry." She says as she gathers herself. "That's just such an awful line!" She presses a hand into my chest as if to give my heart a condescending pat on the head. Instead of making me feel chastised, a current of electricity shoots through my body. I want to pile my own hand on top of it and trap her there to keep the energy flowing. "I run a successful political communications team and my looks aren't a part of that skill set. I'd much rather be known for my body of work."

"Fair enough," I smile as I stick a hand in my pocket. I hear her, I do, and if she caught the attention of my research team then her body of work must be as impressive as her figure. "I do recall you saying you weren't worried about the Thorne announcement today, is that true?"

"Of course it's true. I know this is D.C. but I'm not in the habit of lying to a group of people. Sure it'll be an adjustment but there's no way a computer can replicate what I do."

I'll admit one of our selling points is the potential for staff reductions but when I'm staring in the face of a beautiful woman who might lose her job because of mine, it hits differently.

"Is there anything else? I need to get back to work," she says with a quick glance over my shoulder. I turn and the other woman from the presentation is standing behind me. Her eyes snap up to my face after clearly enjoying the fruits of leg day.

"Oh, no, I'm good. Thanks again," I pick up one of her business cards. It's thick with a QR code embossed on one side, her name clearly printed on the other. "These are nice."

I swipe the card against my palm and I take a step backwards towards the door. "Consider this goodbye for now." I say as I step past her coworker and out to the hallway where the interns are waiting for me.

We head back to the office where I'm able to put the beautiful blonde, Maggie Collins, out of my mind while I handle change orders and an afternoon stand-up meeting. However, she floats back into my thoughts as I step into the car on my way to the podcast recording.

As we pull into traffic I search her name in AI Media's database and the first return is her headshot paired with an article written by TMC's top competitor, The Chronicle.

My thumb hovers over the image before I open the article as my mind returns to the electricity we generated between us this afternoon.

I wish I had paid more attention during her workshop instead of worrying about my appearance and enjoying hers. Even though I'm creating a product that will be her direct competition, I want to know more about what she does, and how she thinks. Not only because it could make the product better but her wit and sense of humor put me on my toes. My ego might not be used to getting turned down but he's definitely ready to play.

Greg, my driver, navigates us through Dupont Circle. My eyes dart from car to car as it passes by. Everyone was up in arms when the first self-driving technology hit the road but that turned out okay. Well, as long as there is still a human there to intervene.

I shake my head to clear the small spark of doubt that snuck in over the course of the day. My news article technology isn't going to put people's lives in danger like a self-driving car would. They're just words. What harm could they do?

Chapter Five
MAGGIE
For The Record

"That's nice of you to say Mike, I appreciate it."

Mike, my lackluster date from last week, called me because he wanted to talk about the Thorne announcement. One of the things we bonded over when we met was the prevalence of AI in content creation.

"I'm serious Maggie, you are in the perfect position to document the downfall caused by this technology."

He's been on and on now for most of my Uber ride to the podcast studio. He wants me to start collecting evidence. I can't tell if it's for a book or a criminal case.

"I'll think about it Mike." I placate. "It's going to be interesting that's for sure. Listen, I just pulled up, I gotta go."

"Okay, I'll talk to you later."

I hang up without responding instead of lying. The last thing I want to do is talk to him again. As I step out and thank the driver, a matte black Tesla Model X, with those obnoxious wing doors, pulls up behind me. I roll my eyes because all the possible good will points this jerk could earn by driving an electric car get wiped away by the wing doors. I jump on the elevator and head up to the third floor. In the reception area there is a table with green apples and cucumber slices. I put a few on a napkin before stepping back and taking a seat.

I bring the apple to my lips but pause when the door opens.

Austin.

Sam and I took a full fifteen minutes after watching him walk away earlier to discuss his physical attributes. I haven't been that thirsty ever in my life. I spotted him the moment I walked into the room, my eyes drawn like magnets to where he was standing at the back. I'm not even sure what caught my attention first?

Was it his chestnut hair that looked like he styled it by running his fingers through it?

Or his broad chest and shoulders that filled the jacket he wore like a second skin?

Maybe it was the way he confidently slid his glasses back into place before burrowing into my soul with his iron ore eyes?

I struggled for the rest of the presentation to keep my eyes off of him but I felt his gaze on me the whole time.

I definitely noticed his ass and thick thighs as he walked out. Sam and I could have used a cigarette to calm us down after the way we oogled him.

I admired his suit when he was at the workshop earlier and it's still as sharp now. He smooths his hand down the front of the navy blue wool with a small monochrome plaid woven throughout and my eyes follow the movement. His shirt is crisp and he still isn't wearing a tie so I can see the dip at the bottom of his throat under an Adam's apple that bobs when he lifts his gaze and lays eyes on me.

Two earthy eyes sparkle behind his round framed tortoise shell glasses and you'd think that would make them more difficult to connect with but you'd be wrong. It's like the glasses serve as spotlights and all I can focus on is the way his eyes slightly widen as he recognizes me.

"Hello again," I say with a smile as I lower the apple back to the napkin in my lap, wishing I had taken the time to reapply my lipstick before coming in here. I couldn't believe that my snarky side got the best of me and that my professionalism slipped into almost flirting. Maybe this is my opportunity to redeem myself, play nice.

"Well, what a small world," he says as he steps over and takes an apple for himself. I watch him settle into the chair across from me. He sits back and slings one leg over the other and balances his ankle on his knee. I watch, transfixed as he pulls his phone from his pocket and begins typing something. I find myself swallowing air when he parts his full lips to sink his teeth into the apple. The crack of his bite ripping through the flesh of the fruit echoes through the room and my mouth waters.

I am laser focused on the droplet of juice stuck to the corner of his mouth. The urge to stand up, walk over to him, and lick it clean hits me like a freight train.

"Oh good, you're both here!" A woman says with a clap that startles me out of my lusty haze. "I'm Jenna, your producer today. Did you introduce yourselves? Maggie Collins, speech writer and campaign communications expert," she waves towards me, "and Austin Thorne, senior executive at Thorne Media Corp and lead on the new AI Media project that was announced today."

What now?

He's *who*?

How did I not know who he was?

After dropping that bomb Jenna walks out of the room and I am left shell shocked. My eyes are unfocused and the room around me blurs. Austin Thorne threatens everything I hold dear. My job, my profession, my intelligence. The product he invented challenges my livelihood and I won't be able to ignore it. I feel, more than see, Austin stand and start to move past me. I snap out of my trance and grab him on the, unfortunately firm, bicep.

"You're Austin Thorne?" I accuse.

"The one and only," he says as he spins slowly in my direction. I hate to be drawn in by his dangerously dark eyes but I am. They're captivating.

"Why were you at my workshop today?" I ask as the heat returns to my body, and I feel the flush climbing up my neck. It's unclear if it is umbrage, frustration, or craving. My breathing is shallow. I'm not sure if I'm going to fight, flight, freeze, or fawn. When the next words come out of my mouth I learn that snark is my defense mechanism. "You needed to size up the competition?"

"You're not my competition, Maggie."

"Yes, I am."

He laughs. He has the fucking nerve to laugh. Shock and indignation roll through my chest. He is standing here mocking everything I have worked for. Everything I have built over the last twelve years. "You're not. There isn't any competition for the product I'm about to bring to market. People are going to love having their news spoon fed to them in a tone and language they understand. I'm not responsible for the American public being too self-absorbed for their own good. I'm going to dish out what they want to hear, revolutionize the news industry, and make a ton of money while I do it."

He looks at me like I might have a response for that.

Unfortunately, I don't.

Speaking impulsively, off the cuff, has never been a strength of mine. I learned that the hard way when I tried to wing a response in my student council president debate in high school that I couldn't think on my feet. I do much better when my statements can be prepared, edited, and revised before going out into the world. It's why I'm so good at speech writing, I love crafting a well thought out message. One that ebbs and flows and brings people along for the ride on the waves of the spoken word.

"Ready?" Jenna calls from down the hallway. Austin cocks an eyebrow, taunting me for a response, and when I don't give him one he holds out a hand indicating ladies first. I step down the hall and shoot a text to Sam.

> Get me everything you can on Thorne Media Corp - who pays them for stories, for advertisements, annual revenue. Anything.

Sure thing boss!

I put my phone on silent but keep it on the table in front of me as I settle into my chair and put on the headphones. Sam is an incredible opposition researcher. She'll be able to find me something. I simply have to hope that Austin Thorne is as ill prepared to meet me as I am to meet him.

***

"Well, let's take a moment to consider the alternative."

It physically hurts to contain my eye roll as I mark another tally on the top of my notes. It's the sixth time Austin has said "consider" since we sat down to record. I started keeping track after the second time he said it.

"Maggie? Any response to Austin's point there?" The host asks with an animated shift of his shoulders in my direction.

I blink, hard. I was so caught up in being annoyed by my brutally handsome but irritating opponent slash co-guest that I totally missed the point he made.

"I'll save my breath on that one," I say with a snarky smile and as much deadpan sarcasm as I can muster. Maybe some political blogger will read between the lines and come up with a point for me.

It's happened before.

This interview is not going as well as I hoped it would before I learned that Hot Austin was Austin Thorne. Sam has sent a few texts but nothing useful. I was hoping she'd find an exposé saying he accepted money from fur traders to cover up a story about clubbing baby seals. Or some connection to oil companies. Or the mafia. Or a fringe political group that believes our next president should be a goat.

A girl can dream.

Instead she sent a few articles about the Thorne gossip outlet which I am familiar with because of a run-in my sister's best friend had with them last summer.

It was an insider tell-all style article about Liz's friend Nora and her boyfriend, the rising home improvement TV star, Jimmy Lewis. It said terrible things and could have been considered libel if Nora had wanted to press charges. I was able to track down the anonymous source for them and confirmed she was paid.

Considering, as Austin would say, this article was small potatoes on the celebrity scale, I can only imagine how much they shell out for good stuff.

"Ha, alright, fair enough, I wanted to move on anyway." Charlie, the host, says as he flips to his next page of notes. "A lot of our listeners are outside of the D.C. area and they message us asking what it's really like to live and work in politics. We posted your headshots just before recording and, well, I'll be honest, they're getting quite the response."

"I'm not surprised Charlie, I tried to use it as my state department photo but no luck," Austin chimes in, oozing charm, and I feel a small tremor under my right eye. I press my fingers into it because I do not want to go full twitchy eye with Austin two feet in front of me. "What'dya think Maggie? Would you consider pulling some strings from the Senator's office and get these headshots on our passports?" And when his smile turns on me I hate that I blush as much as I hate the twitch that triggers again.

"No, sorry Austin, we use our connections at the State Department to address global crises." I sneer as I add another tally to my Consider Tracker.

"I want to get back to that," Charlie says quickly, "but first, Maggie, what is it like dating in D.C.?"

"Your listeners want to know about my dating life?"

"Well, kinda. They're interested in the politics but also the lives of the *people* in politics."

"Let's consider the subject here for a minute," Austin chimes in and I snap my head toward him unsure where this is going. "Maggie here is one of the hardest working people in D.C., I doubt she even has time to go on dates."

I don't catch my reaction quickly enough and I tuck my chin into my neck as I try to decipher if that was a compliment or a dig or a passive-aggressive combination of the two.

"That's certainly true, both of you are dedicated to your high-profile jobs, so how do you find time to date?" Charlie asks Austin.

"My latest relationship ended recently so considering that, I've been taking it slow. Keeping my options open." Austin says as he insecurely looks down at his fingernails. If I was in a better headspace and not feeling like I'm on a tilt-a-whirl I'd pounce on this moment of vulnerability. But also I'm wondering who would date this guy? Besides being sexy as hell, and richer than sin, he's cruel and mean and aloof.

Instead of kicking him when he's down I add another tally at the top of my notebook. It's like he's doing it on purpose.

"Have either of you heard of SMS Connect? For our listeners, it's a new service in D.C. where young professionals sign a contract that says they're willing to text with a match, words only, no pictures, for three months before they even suggest meeting each other. The idea is the matchmaker knows what you need in a relationship and doesn't want physical attributes to interfere."

"I've heard of it," I say while trying to keep the crimson from running rampant across my face. "It seems like an interesting concept."

"Are you on it?" The host asks me and my mouth goes completely dry. Like I just stuck a handful of saltines in it.

"From what I understand," Austin jumps in, "if she was, she wouldn't be able to say. This matchmaking business is more secretive than the freemasons." He throws me a wink and my stomach trips over itself while my brain flicks me between the eyebrows.

We manage to get back onto political topics but I'm continuously distracted by Austin. By his presence, his eyes, his "considerings". And by the fact that he has out-talked me this entire time.

I made a comment about wildlife being negatively impacted by the oil industry. He spat back about how farm land displaced native species populations and I didn't have a response or a redirect.

Then we got into early education. The senator has been working to make PreKindergarten mandatory for public school districts. Getting kids in school as four year olds immensely benefits the child and their family. But Austin had a stat from a not-yet-released study saying kids who started phonics at age five read just as well, if not better, than those who started earlier.

The volleying went back and forth after that. I got him on microplastic pollution in the water supply. He got me on the senator's flip-flopping opinion on tax reform.

I've learned that saying anything nuanced is best left to newspaper editorials. It's immensely easier not to misspeak or get misquoted when you've had time to draft, edit, revise, and revise again before printing.

We wrap up and promise to do it again sometime. I said I'd "consider it" and gave Austin a pointed look.

He didn't respond and I enjoyed a moment of pride for being snarkier than him.

But maybe having jokes that are so inside they only exist in my head is a red flag.

The final "considering" tally was seventeen in an hour and a half. Way too many.

With my phone in hand, I leave the recording studio and walk towards the elevator. I can hear the door brush along the carpet as it swings open behind me and I can feel the way Austin closes the distance between us. I don't want to talk to him. The anger I was feeling before, the fire that was lit in my belly has died off. I'm exhausted. I want to go home and eat something sweet while watching an action movie.

Sometimes you're just in the mood for Daniel Craig.

"I'm surprised you didn't try to throw me under the bus back there." Austin says as he reaches my side at the elevator.

"That's not nearly high tech enough of a way to take you out." I mutter as I open up the ride share app.

"Oh, c'mon, MC, all those brains of yours couldn't come up with something?" He laughs as he steps forward and holds the doors back while I step through. He presses the lobby button and it almost feels like we're being shut in a barometric chamber. All the air has been sucked out of this small space and I've never been claustrophobic until this moment.

I stare straight ahead as an instrumental version of a Black Eyed Peas song plays over the speakers. I can feel Austin's gaze on me like my skin is being scanned by a laser. I'm not ready to know why I feel so attuned to his presence.

"Shark attack," Austin says and I whip my head around to look at him.

"What?" And why isn't he respecting elevator etiquette? The rules of polite society say you should just stare straight ahead and not speak when in an enclosed space with another human.

"A shark attack death would be poetic don't you think? As long as I was doing something awesome like surfing or wakeboarding when it happened."

"Maybe you're taken out by a disgruntled employee, but they give you some weird disease when they sneeze on your salad and you die slowly as your teeth turn to dust and you choke on it."

"Cruel but that's closer to what I expected from you," he says with a wink as the elevator lands in the lobby and he holds his hand in front of the doors for me again.

His long strides bring him next to me as I reach the front door. Sam always complains about how fast I walk. I'm 5'9", she's 5'4" and Austin is even taller than I am, 6'2" I'd guess. Again he opens the door for me and holds it as I walk through. It's this weird waltz we've done now three times as he holds the door, lets me pass, and then slides up to my side.

The ridiculous Tesla is still idling at the curb so I'm assuming it's his.

"Although, with your speech writing capabilities maybe you could go a little more realistic. Snot-borne diseases rarely cause dental issues." He leans close to make sure I hear him as he passes me and I catch his scent. Salty, and fresh, with a musk like olive oil or something. I feel an awareness turn on in my chest and have to stop myself from inhaling deeply.

And while I am wondering if that scent is sold as a candle I could burn in my studio apartment, my brain registers his words. And how his tone is this infuriating combination of teasing, smug, and confident. And how I don't want to stop sparring with him.

"My speech writing brain power is better spent trying to solve political problems than debating nonsense with you." He spins around on his heel and strides back to face me. "AI isn't nonsense. This is going to change the world."

"But not for the better," I ground out as my clenched fist finds my hip.

"It's going to be the best thing since sliced bread. People are going to flock to it for its convenience even though it's laden with preservatives. People are lemmings and don't want to think for themselves. They want to sit back and be told what to think. They want to know that they're thinking what their friends are thinking. They want dumb dance videos and marriage pranks."

"No, people want more than that." I reply but even I can hear how empty my argument is.

"Maggie, c'mon." He stands up a little taller and I only realize how close we have gotten to each other when I have to lift my chin to maintain contact with his graphite eyes. "You're a smart person so tell me, why do videos of people doing something nice for a stranger out perform nearly anything else on the internet?"

"Umm, I ah," I mumble.

"I'll tell you, they go viral because the people on their phones don't realize that humans can interact with each other. They've completely forgotten that positive, real life, interactions exist. They're living in their algorithm and not thinking for themselves. They're sending memes to their friends instead of meeting them for coffee and talking to them. They're following GPS directions in their hometowns because they've forgotten how to think for themselves. Most people think they're political because they know the words to *Hamilton* or watched *The West Wing* with their parents but have never canvassed for a candidate or connected with their representatives."

I won't admit it but he just described half of the frustration I experience at my job. It is sexy to be on the side of the young female candidate. But while I'm going to take the backing from people who are voting for her because she's a woman, a part of me wishes they'd pay attention to the issues and understand what the policies mean.

"So your solution is if you can't beat 'em join 'em?"

"More or less. It's too much work to right the ship; we're headed straight for the iceberg, but I can play some lovely music while the boat sinks."

My ride share pulls up and rolls down the window, "Ride for Maggie?"

I'm still stunned that Austin wants to be the string quartet conductor on the Titanic while the rest of us fight for our lives.

"Time to go," Austin says and then he leans closer and I can feel the heat of his breath on the shell of my ear as he whispers, "next time I'd be happy to give you a ride."

He slowly pulls back and his eyes rake over my body. Lava pools in my center under his gaze and I make my way to the gray sedan on wobbly knees.

Chapter Six
AUSTIN
Put it all on the line.

"How'd the podcast go?" Elle asks as she gives Brinkley a little chin scratch and tosses her bag on the island.

"Good," I say as I sip my beer and try to refocus on the baseball game on TV.

"Just good?" Elle prompts as she comes and sits down next to me. "I would think there was quite a lot of action between you and Maggie Collins."

My head whips towards her, "how do you know about Maggie Collins?"

Is she reading my mind? Because my eyes might be pointed at the TV but they're seeing Maggie. No woman has distracted me like this before.

"She was all over the show's social media, geesh, chill out. Elle walks into the kitchen and continues talking to me, "When I saw her headshot I knew you'd be a bumbling mess because blonde hair and blue eyes are the epitome of beauty to you. Plus I can't imagine a speech writer whose livelihood depends on creating content would like the idea of AI Media coming into her space. I bet she was pissed." She says with a laugh as she plops down in the corner seat of the sofa with a bag of popcorn.

I look at her with side-eyes and confirm she's in a position to keep talking to me instead of watching the TV the sofa is pointed at.

"She's beautiful, there's no arguing that. But she's so," I pause looking for the right word to describe how I wanted to be near to her while at the same time wanted to yell at her for her naiveté. How I had to get close enough to smell her perfume while feeling the wall of resistance between us. "Frustrating."

"Frustrating?" Elle repeats around a mouth of popcorn.

"Yeah, she's incredibly smart, I've read some of her speeches and the op-eds she's written in every publication but ours, but she barely engaged with me on the podcast and afterwa-"

"What happened afterwards?" Elle asks, leaning closer to me with interest in her tone.

"We argued on the sidewalk but she didn't say much so I was basically arguing with her facial expressions which can't hide her thoughts at all. I hope she never plays poker."

"Interesting," Elle says as she leans back into the corner.

"Tell me about your day." I ask in a not-so-subtle attempt to change the subject.

"Smooth," she laughs and then sighs, "Dad introduced me to Carly, his latest girlfriend. He asked me to meet him for dinner and I should have known she was coming because he said to," she develops a mocking baritone, "wear something suitable and not your hippie dippy costume.""

"Aww, but I like you in sustainably farmed organic hemp." I whine. She throws a handful of popcorn at me and we share a laugh. Elle spent her first two years after college in the Peace Corps in Cambodia. Then a year teaching English in Japan. Then she decided to spend another two years traveling through Eastern and Western Asia where she joined a non profit organization that was monitoring textile factories. Her "hippie dippy costume" as Dad called it, is actually a collection of ethically made pieces that she doesn't buy too many of. She still carries around designer handbags though because, as she says, nothing beats Italian leather.

Last year, she called me after being off the grid for three months to say that she just landed at Dulles. While I was still trying to wrap my head around her sudden arrival she asked if she could crash for a night or two.

It was a wild time, the first few days all she wanted was to eat American junk food. Then the switch flipped. She woke me up at 5:00 am and told me she was going to yoga.

She has been working as a yoga instructor and using her business degree to help them manage the studio. I'm not in a rush to push her out because it's been fun to have her around but the early wake ups and forced introspection is getting old.

"So, how'd it go? Do you think Carly is going to be our new step-mother?" I ask as I pick up the kernels she tossed at me and eat them.

"Well, considering she's the right age to be my step-sister, I hope not. But who knows. Who cares really? It's like Dad's hobby is marrying women."

I laugh because she's not wrong. Elle is five years younger than me. My mother was Dad's second wife, who got pregnant with me while he was still married to his first wife. Elle is the daughter of my nanny, Laura, and my mom figured she'd be as good as anyone to raise me so she got her settlement and left. She moved out to LA and we exchange emails twice a year on her birthday and mine to stay in contact.

Elle's mom, Laura, who I also call Mom, raised both of us. For about four years it was as Dad's wife and then it was as his ex-wife but she never left us kids. Laura still lives in the Colonial she shared with Dad in Spring Valley and hosts us for brunch every so often.

Dad has gone through a few more wives in the twenty years since they split. The longest stretch was when he married the daughter of his business rival, then bought her father's company. Without that acquisition we wouldn't have expanded into video and podcast production which is now our most profitable media sector. Well, for now. The January earnings report will include AI Media's profits and I'm expecting to impress Dad and hear his succession announcement in the same meeting. Maybe he'll marry this new girl and start his retirement.

"He does seem to try and collect them all doesn't he," I say.

Elle picks some lint off the knee of her sweat pants. "Do you think we'll be like that?"

"Like what?"

"I dunno, it's not like he's a commitmentphobe, he will marry anyone with legs, but he doesn't seem to be long term focused."

"Because he also wants to fuck anyone with legs," I mumble into my beer bottle.

"Right? And he's not ugly, but he's old! Do these women go for him because he's rich and influential and sort of famous?"

"Yeah," I trail off because I've been pursued by women thinking I'm going to offer them the same thing as my dad. But when they find out that I don't inform the media when I'm headed to an event, they tend to lose interest. Or when they find out that I won't buy them their own apartment, like Dad has been known to do for his mistresses, they back away.

"So, do you think we're like him?"

I look over at Elle who is still pulling at the loose string,. I can see the vulnerability clear as day on her face even though she refuses to turn and face me.

Dad doesn't keep marriage as an investment opportunity to himself. No, he's always making strategic introductions. I think that is part of why she disappeared for three years.

"The fact that you're even asking tells me that you're not. I know I'm not. Otherwise I would be on my third wife by now, not rooming with my sister." I reach over and punch her in the thigh. She lets her legs fall over and then laughs.

"I promise to get a place soon, I just don't know where I want to settle yet."

"You can stay as long as you want."

Because as annoying as she can be, I've gotten used to her being around. Her presence makes me feel less lonely.

****

I settle into bed and take out my SMS Connect phone. TalkShopGirl and I have exchanged so many different messages over the last two months and I really love ending my day with her. Her emotional presence soothes my frayed edges.

I think back over the course of today's events. The AI Media announcement, the workshop where I first saw Maggie, then feeling sparks fly during the podcast recording. I'm definitely attracted to her but I don't think it's mutual. After all, she's the one who hypothesized killing me slowly with poison.

Plus the whole point of signing up for SMS Connect is to form an emotional bond, not a physical one. I enrolled because I want to truly connect with someone. I'd be tossing all these messages off a cliff if I focused only on how attracted to Maggie I am. I want to find a person who will be a true partner to me.

When Elle and I were talking earlier I started thinking about Dad's wives over the years. He has made jokes that by my age he was already on his third wife and I need to get my first one out of the way. Like marriage is the same as getting a flu shot. I didn't take the time to explain that I want more than a pretty face and hot body. There is a small and petty part of me that hopes TalkShopGirl isn't hot. Just to show everyone that I truly connect with a woman for reasons besides her looks.

I already know I'll find her beautiful no matter what she looks like.

I don't know why Mom, Laura, stayed around. She could have pushed us kids away on some nanny or to boarding schools but she didn't. She raised us and made sure that our dad was in the picture. She never talked badly about him, well in front of us at least.

Mom never remarried either. I'm not sure why. Did she still love my dad? Was it just more challenging with a daughter and step-son around?

She is the best woman I've ever met, besides her daughter, and she deserves so much more than what my dad gave her.

I huff out a breath and decide to go for broke.

DCFox: I've been thinking, which might be a dangerous endeavor, but my mind keeps playing out the different scenarios for this relationship. My parents, well it's pretty complicated, but my dad is a relationship junkie. He goes all in with every new woman he meets. My step-mom, who raised me alongside my half-sister, has only been in a relationship with my dad. She jokes that he's got so many personalities that she has really been married to at least eight different men in her lifetime.

I bring this up because my sister and I were talking tonight and she asked if we'd be like him. Neither of us have been successful in romantic relationships thus far but we both agreed that we're still hopeful. So, I wanted to tell you, even if what we are doing here doesn't lead to ever-lasting love, it's teaching me how I want to be in a relationship.

How I want to be honest, and authentic. How I want to anticipate hearing from the other person. How I want to think about them throughout the day. How I want them to see the best version of me, believe in that version of me, even when I'm at my worst.

Maggie's face flashes in my mind and I set the phone down for a second. I really hate the person I became with her today. I felt compelled to be right, to win, to make her understand my point of view. It was too easy to let the condescending side of me loose. I hate that in my pursuit of winning, I made her feel small.

While I appreciate that this text-only format lets me plan my words to you, I worry that the off-the-cuff me, the one who is driven by competitiveness and pride, is wildly different. That if we meet in person I won't be able to separate the two.

And, maybe I'm putting the cart before the horse assuming that we'll meet someday, but after the day I've had, I needed to share the side of me that isn't as charming and light-hearted. Maybe this device is making me feel braver than I really am. I'm not sure I would ever say this face to face to a woman I'm wooing. But who knows, maybe, hopefully, once I see your face I'll feel differently.

I send her the message and quickly power off the phone. I face the window and stare at the drawn curtains waiting for any drowsiness to come. It doesn't. My mind only races with the events of the day.

Brinkley rolls over and settles in next to my calves and the microdose of connection to another living creature settles me. I close my eyes and focus on the warmth of him and slowly drift off to sleep.

***

I wake up to the sounds of Elle making breakfast. The blender whirrs with some greens and protein concoction she always makes. When I pull back the covers the SMS Connect phone slides to the floor. I wince as I hear the device crash on the hardwood.

Shit.

I quickly pick it up and turn it over in my hands. It's fine. With an inhale I perch on the edge of my bed and read the message from TalkShopGirl.

TalkShopGirl: It's amazing that we were both in a melancholy mood yesterday. Maybe that's the wrong word but I got home after a long day and wanted to talk to you but also felt strange bringing my troubles to our exchange. I have to admit that while I feel bad you were feeling blue, it brought a smile to my face that we can now be more open with each other in this way.

Before I got your message, I looked at this little gray rectangle for a while and imagined who you might be, what you might have been doing.

I wanted to ask you if you've ever been so flustered that you couldn't think straight. This happened to me yesterday. I had every opportunity to put this jerk in his place but whenever I tried to respond the words just weren't there.

So as I sat in my comfy spot last night watching James Bond, I wanted to know how you would have responded. I wanted to know what you thought of this problem I'm facing. I wanted to know, well, you.

And without knowing who you are I still feel like I know you, and I am glad to know another part of you. There is a lot of pressure to perform when you first meet someone and that isn't my comfort zone. I like to be prepared. I like to know what's going to happen. And when I'm faced with uncertainty I freeze.

But in these messages I get the chance to write out what I'm thinking, what I'm feeling, and it feels less risky. But maybe this is the biggest risk I've taken yet.

I smile as I read, pride and confidence shining through, because it feels like TalkShopGirl and I jumped off the cliff together, hand-in-hand.

Chapter Seven
MAGGIE

Not the worst idea.

I BITE MY BOTTOM lip as I reread the message from DCFox last night and my response. I feel like a teenager trying to mind-meld my crush into kissing me. But instead of sitting across from Cole MacDonald in some musty basement, I'm standing in my 370 square foot studio apartment, alone, and staring down at a phone.

Sam and I exchanged some texts last night and agreed to get an early start at the office this morning. She's going to meet me at Sunrise and then we're going to get on the metro together. The Senator has asked us to come in for a meeting at 10 and we're not sure what it's about.

"So, how are things going with the SMS Connect guy?" Sam asks as we reach the station.

"Good, really good, I feel like we had a breakthrough."

"Really? What kind?"

"We both admitted to having bad days," I say over my shoulder as I pass through the turnstile.

"And that was a breakthrough? You know everyone has bad days."

"Yes Sam, I know that, but so far we've only exchanged positive things or neutral things like our favorite movies. And I realized I was always editing out any negative tone. I'd put a positive spin on everything. But we also haven't shared personal stuff so if I was talking about work it was always in general statements."

"And your last message was negative?"

"I mean, no not really, but I got the sense from his message last night that he'd had a bad day, or that he was in his head about something so I admitted that I was feeling the same."

"And what are you in your head about? The AI stuff?"

"Yes, and the fact that Austin Thorne was in my orbit not once but twice on the day that he announced AI Media. That feels like an omen."

"I did some reading about it, and it's a pretty smart set up." Sam says as we step onto the train.

"How so?"

"Well, they're going to leverage the reach of their media side to put out messages and news. And then they'll create shorts and content that will be related to news but not exactly news."

"What do you mean?"

"Let's say something goes viral, something about a man dismissing women's sports."

"I'm annoyed already but go on."

"The AI software will pull quotes and responses by following hashtags and the trail of shares. Their product will write articles and make videos to post to social media."

"Are they whipping up fake accounts to post these on?"

Sam levels me with a knowing look. "They could pay one person to post it and then hope people make it their own. Hope that people stitch it or share it. And by the time it's made the rounds no one will care that AI generated the content."

"I hate that it's true, but it is." I admit.

"But that's not all of it. There's an application of the software they're selling on a private basis. It wasn't highly publicized yesterday."

"What is it?" I knew her opposition research skills were top notch.

"It's a personalized content generation tool. Basically they will create a database of a public figure's past speeches and public comments and then the software will create new speeches and responses based on a simple prompt. The tool can be set to factor in the audience too so the message it produces will really hit home."

We slip into silence because neither of us needs to say it out-loud. She just described our jobs. And there's the chance AIM can do it better than we can because it bypasses all the human emotional trap-falls we face when writing impassioned speeches.

"Is your eye okay?" Sam asks.

I reach up and press along my eye socket that still twitches under the pressure.

"Yeah, just the physical manifestation of my stress."

"You need to bang it out."

"What?"

"Bang it out? Have sex? The horizontal tango? Doing it? Getting laid? Shagging, nailing, boning? Buttering the biscuit?"

"Ew, I hate food ones."

"You shouldn't, sex can be a feast if it's done right." Sam explains as she gets a far off wistful look in her eyes. "I don't care what you call it but you should be banging regularly. Especially between now and the election when *tensions* are high."

"There is no way I have the time or the mental capacity to date anyone right now."

"I'm not saying date, I'm saying doin'. Get yourself a fuck buddy. No strings, just sex." She pauses. "Unless getting tied up is your thing then all the strings but no feelings."

"I don't know." I say with a shake of my head. I've never been one for sex for the hell of it. I've had long term boyfriends in the past and even though I knew they wouldn't last, I liked the consistency of a relationship. For now, my hand seems to be doing fine enough.

"Well I do. Just try it and see if it helps."

Both of us spend the rest of our commute in our own thoughts.

I'm trying to figure out how I can stay employed if a computer is gunning for my job and can customize a message as well as I can.

So much of what I do early on with a politician is establish their voice. Work with them on their tone. Advise them on the differences in a campaign rally crowd and a trade group assembly. How their messages are going to be received in each arena.

While my professional future hangs in the balance, I can't seem to get Sam's sex-for-stress-relief idea out of my head. In fact, every time my eye twitches I've done a quick kegel which seems to help a little bit but it's a short-term solution.

When we surface at Union Station we make our way towards the Dirksen building. I decide to shake off my defeated mindset because I'm not out of the game yet. The dreaded AI Media hasn't even launched. There's nothing to be afraid of. The senator has a debate coming up and we've got a lot of work to do.

***

"Are you out of your mind?"

"Maggie!" Sam whisper-scolds from my left.

"I'm sorry Ma'am, but with all due respect, what were you thinking? I know you said yesterday you were bringing in some support but I didn't think it would be this!"

"I understand this is a surprise Maggie, but it is an opportunity I can't pass up." Senator Quinn says calmly. Too calmly. Like maybe the deep state has something on her and they're forcing her into this. I'm tempted to ask her to blink twice if she needs help.

"So, to clarify, you've contracted with AI Media on custom content for the rest of the campaign?"

"Yes, starting with the debate next week." She folds her hands on the table in front of her. I don't think that's a universal distress signal.

"Why?" The senator blinks at my candor. I've never been this blunt with her, or anyone.

"Maggie, I can see that you're having trouble with this information but the AI Media team is coming in tomorrow to start the background work. They've promised me they can get everything into the system by next Tuesday and they'll be able to craft real-time responses for me during the debate."

"You're going to use them during the debate?"

"Yes, along with your prepared statements and rebuttals, I'll have a tablet with me and they'll be sending me lines to use based on audience response and who is tuned in."

"I, umm, okay." I can feel myself blinking hard but the nightmare I find myself in isn't ending.

"Thank you Senator," Sam says.

"Yes, thanks." I say on an exhale. With a nod, Senator Quinn dismisses us from her office and we step out into the hall and close her door.

Sam and I trudge to the office we share in silence.

"This is about as bad as it could get." Sam says as she sits down across from me.

This is the first time in my entire career that I've felt well and truly lost. There have been challenges and setbacks of course but my mind has always spun up solutions immediately. A next step appears and I move towards it. In the courtroom you can hit pause if something unexpected comes to light. In politics? The hurricane keeps coming and the eye of the storm is a false sense of security.

And I've never been up against a computer.

Or a man as charming as Austin Thorne.

C'mon Maggie, regroup.

I've worked too hard to get where I am to give up now. I'll come through stronger. I'll make my name being the woman who bested AI and *considering* how white male biased AI is, my victory will be one for all womankind.

I pace back and forth, amping myself up. I've got this. I've been training for this my entire career. I'm the best damn speech writer this town has ever seen. It's time to get to work.

***

Sam and I spend the rest of the day working on the senator's opening remarks for the debate. She'll have three minutes and we need to grab attention, make people fall in love with her, and get her policy ideas across. It's a tough assignment but together we are making good progress.

After a thirty minute debate over whether "change" or "reform" was the best word to use, we decided to call it a day. Sam met up with some friends and I went straight home and changed into my workout clothes.

Usually I run in the morning but I know if I don't hit the pavement now I'll be restless all night.

I put my headphones in and head for the river. It's further than my usual route but I need a change of pace.

Chapter Eight
AUSTIN

Cat-like reflexes.

"HE'S NOT TAKING MEETINGS right now sir," I look up as Elizabeth tries to run interference.

"He'll take one with me," my back stiffens as my dad says this and appears in my door. He continues walking in and stands in front of my desk. "Good to see you working late. What are the AIM numbers?"

I share the report that I had gotten from Kevin fifteen minutes ago.

"That's fine for the first day, but you better 20x that by Friday."

"Yes sir," I reply and then I stop myself from asking him how he'd do it.

The outcomes of this project are riding on me. And me alone. His expectation is that I will blow this away.

I had thought joining the company would improve my relationship with Dad. That he'd enjoy taking me under his wing.

It's been the opposite experience. I shadowed him and then he threw me into the deep end and set huge revenue targets. He's in his sixties and I expect him to retire soon. He hasn't talked about it but I don't see why he wouldn't start transitioning responsibility to me next year and then fully step back the year after that. He's the same age as Grandpa when he stepped down.

After Dad leaves my office without so much as a goodbye, Elizabeth sticks her head in checks on me. I give her a reassuring smile and she nods.

"Greg is waiting to take you to yoga. I have a change of clothes for you and your mat."

"Thank you Elizabeth."

I change in the bathroom in my office and sit quietly while Greg drives me across town to the yoga studio. The evening class is a hot, isometric hold focused class where we move slowly but hold each pose for a full minute.

It sounds simple but it is a brutal workout. And it is exactly what I need after a surprise meeting with Dad.

***

I'm wiping sweat from my brow when I spot Maggie Collins across the street. I almost didn't recognize her in leggings and a cropped hoodie with her hair pulled back into a high ponytail, but my attention was magnetically pulled to her form. She's jogging along the river path that will pass my condo building. Does she live nearby? It's funny how she was a stranger no more than two days ago but now I seem to see her everywhere. And when we got the contract signed with the senator's office this morning I realized I'll be spending much more time with her.

Without thinking, I make my way to the corner and start to cross. I've got the walk signal as I move towards her. She isn't slowing down or looking to the left or right as she approaches the bike path crossing and I can see a group of riders on road bikes headed straight for her.

I pick up my pace and get to her just as she's about to find herself in the middle of the peloton. I sling my arm around her waist and pull her back against my chest.

My body ignites at the contact. Warmth and electricity race through my bloodstream and instinctively I flex and hold her even closer.

"The fuck!" She yells right before pain radiates up from my foot to my leg, followed by a sharp sting at my ribcage. I stumble backwards, grabbing my side as she spins around and pulls her leg back.

"Back off asshole!" She grunts as she lands her sneaker to the side of my knee.

I collapse, my yoga mat unrolls, and I reach up to grasp anything to help me win this fight against gravity. As I fall, I latch onto something soft and I open my eyes to find I'm pulling Maggie by the hip down on top of me.

Her arms flail out to the sides as she tries to catch herself but it's too little too late. My face is sandwiched between the sidewalk and her ass.

Maggie scrambles up, rights her clothing, and stares down at me. She's pulling her leg back to kick me while I'm down and thankfully my brain kicks in.

"Maggie, whoa, stop!" I beg as I curl up into the fetal position and place my hands up in the air. "It's me, Austin."

"Why are you attacking me, Austin Thorne? Is this why you wouldn't share dating advice? Because your advice is to grab women from behind and try to pull their pants down?"

"Hey now. No. *No.* That's not what happened." I grunt as I stand up. My left leg is in serious pain. I look up at her and see the hurricane brewing in her ocean blue eyes. The crossed arms. The hip popped out to the side. I can still feel her on my palm but that's probably not wise to dwell on at the moment. "It was an accident."

"Grabbing me was an accident?" She asks with an eyebrow raised.

"No, that was to prevent you from getting run over by a bunch of middle aged men in lycra. The almost pulling your pants down part was the accident. I'm sorry."

"Oh," she says quietly as she looks at the pack of bikes that are almost out of sight, "well, okay," she says quietly. I brush my hands off on my shorts and when I take a step, I immediately limp. My knee is already swollen.

"If you ever want to change jobs, I hear the Secret Service is hiring." I say as I start to rub my knee.

"I took a self defense class when I first moved to D.C. and I watch a lot of action movies. You are lucky I didn't go full S.I.N.G. on your ass like Sandra Bullock taught the women of America in *Miss Congeniality.*"

"Well watch out *Kill Bill.* You did a number on me."

"Sorry," she winces as she looks down at my knee. "That looks bad."

I take a step to retrieve my yoga mat and inhale sharply with the movement to try and sooth the sting.

"Here," she says as she steps next to me and picks up my mat. "Were you at yoga?"

"Yep," I point across the street to the studio. "I practice there and when I came out I saw you trying to play real-life frogger and thought I could come to your rescue."

"I usually pay better attention," she admits. "But I was distracted by the fact that I'm going to have to compete with a computer to do my job for the next four weeks."

"Ah, yes, big bad technology," I tease as she hands me the rolled up mat.

"You know what, I can't with this." She waves a hand in my general direction. "I can't go another ten rounds with you only to hear that the human brain is trash. Some of us try to make the world a better place and that requires some bravery and putting our neck on the line."

At the mention of her neck I immediately drop my gaze to it. The slender column holds her head strongly and the nook of the hoodie looks like a place I could get lost in.

"Do you need help or can I go now?" She asks, drawing my attention up to her face. Her jaw is clenched but her blush betrays her. She caught me looking and liked it.

"Where are you headed?" I ask, not answering her question and standing at my full height. Her gaze follows and I like the view of her looking up at me.

"I've gotta make my way home."

"Shame, I figured you would at least buy me a drink to make up for the fact that you've sent me to physical therapy with your attack tonight."

"I did not attack you," she shrieks and I can't hold back the smile that breaks across my face after riling her up. She sees it and narrows her gaze at me. I want to keep sparring with her. "You'll be fine," she says after a deep breath. "Big strong man like you can handle a little kick to the side of the knee."

"You think I'm big and strong?"

"That's what your pretty little brain heard?"

"You think I'm pretty?"

"Fuck off Austin," she says but I can hear the laughter in her tone. She locks eyes with me for one last beat before turning, checking for traffic, and jogging off.

***

The soft curve of Maggie Collins' hip is my first thought as I wake up. I've positioned a pillow next to me in my sleep and even though I can't remember my dream, I am guessing it featured a tight blonde who filled my world with feeling.

Pain in my knee, but energy everywhere else.

I wonder if she is thinking about me this morning. We're set to meet at nine to begin working on Senator Quinn's private database. I'm bringing a few team members along since they understand the tech much better than I do. I'm more than a pretty face, but not when it comes to programming.

After my shower, I carefully dry my hair, shave closely, and moisturize. When I'm done, I like what I see. Maggie will too. I stand at my closet with my towel slung low on my hips and Brinkley struts in. His big cat on the prowl energy is contagious. I select a dark olive, almost gray, suit and a crisp white shirt, classic but the modern cut turns heads.

"Whoa, hot stuff!" Elle says as I head to the kitchen and pour myself a coffee. "You're all dressed up?"

"Am not, I wear a suit everyday."

"True, but you don't spend extra time primping in the mirror and working pomade through your hair."

She has a point but hell if I'm going to admit it's for a girl. One who I might put out of business and who, rightfully, hates me because of it.

This is the thought loop I'm caught up in on the drive to the Dirksen building. And no matter which way I look at it, I can't solve for the fact that I find Maggie Collins attractive. I want her in a way I can't describe. But she hates me because of who I am and the business I run. We're destined to be enemies no matter how much I want her.

***

"Mr. Thorne, welcome, right this way." The receptionist at Senator Quinn's office leads me, Kevin, Javé, and Tyler, into a conference room. I had Elizabeth send over a breakfast spread so the table is covered with trays of pastries and cut fruit. There is a carafe of cold brew and a box of hot coffee on a little table along the wall. We don't wait long for Maggie and her team to walk in.

Maggie is back in her power suit and I miss the sliver of skin I could see under her cropped hoodie last night. Her hair is pulled up in one of those claw clips and there's a wayward line of ink on her jaw. I want to reach out and rub it off.

"Did anyone see you come in?" Maggie asks as she sets down a stack of three binders, two legal pads, and a notebook.

"Well we tried to lose the photographers on motorbikes but it was difficult," I respond and I catch Kevin's smirk.

"Funny Austin, I'm serious. I'm still not convinced this partnership is a good idea and I'm not even close to admitting that the senator is using this technology on her campaign. I don't want this information getting out."

"Well TMC and AI Media want this partnership announced as soon as possible."

"Well Senator Quinn wants to win the presidency," she retorts and I see the eyebrows of everyone else in the room shoot up.

"Let's see what we can come up with," I say with a wide grin I know is grating on her nerves.

***

"Well if we *consider*," Maggie sneers, "the fact that the presidential debate is next week I think we need to wait to announce the partnership. I don't want the news cycle to be dominated by this story."

"It'll be dominated by this story no matter what. It's best to get it out now and let everyone ask their questions before the debate," I reason as I pull my glasses off and pinch the bridge of my nose. We've been going around in circles for 45 minutes. We haven't even begun to work on the content we need to. "Let's take a break," I say as I stand up from my chair and slide my glasses back on.

The rest of the room files out to the reception area leaving Maggie and me in the room together.

"Maggie," I interrupt her frantic scribbling on a legal pad. "Do you want to announce this partnership at all?"

"No! I don't!" She practically yells. "I cannot for the life of me understand why Melissa wants to do this and I cannot see how this could be anything but bad for her."

She stands and starts pacing the short wall of the conference room. Maggie reminds me of a caged animal. She's backed up against the wall and using all her restraint to stay composed. What I wouldn't give to see her unravel.

"Senator Quinn is running for president of the United States and we have worked, I have worked, tirelessly to make the fact that she's a single woman irrelevant. To make the fact that she can think for herself her top asset as the leader of the free world. Now she's gone and hired an AI service backed by the sleaziest media company in the country that is well known to steal from peter to pay paul and pocketing plenty in between."

"Nice alliteration," I joke and she storms over and gets in my face.

"Are you going to keep making jokes or are you going to help me figure out how to tell the American public, tell the whole fucking world, that my boss is using a computer to write her speeches and that it won't effect her political decisions?"

Maggie's chest is rising and falling and there are only inches between us. The air crackles and before it can explode, I grab her face in my hands and pull her mouth to mine.

My fingers curl around the back of her head and I hold her there as she opens her mouth to me. Everything else fades away as I taste her. The bitter tang of her iced coffee softened by a hint of vanilla floods my senses and I crave more. My body hums when her hands dig into my ribcage holding me to her.

I spin us and prop her ass against the table and she lifts her leg to hook it around my hips. I grind my growing erection into the space between us and swallow her moan in my kiss.

Before I completely lose my mind I break us apart and rest my forehead against hers. Slowly she slides her leg back down to the floor and her hands grip the side of the table instead of me. Both of our chests are heaving like we just raced the 100m.

That kiss was pure passion, energy, connection. I don't know what to do with this newfound craving. I roll my head and peck one last kiss to her lips before stepping back and walking out of the room.

I rake my hands through my hair as I walk down the hallway to the elevators. Kissing Maggie Collins was not on my agenda today but fuck me, that was incredible. As I step into the elevator I turn around and look back toward the office. Maggie is standing in the doorway watching me. Her arms are crossed but one hand is up near her face and her thumb is brushing across her soft pink lips as she studies me. The doors close leaving me with the image of her and her mouth.

Impulsive physical interactions are not my M.O.. Usually PDA is limited to a hand on the small of a girl's back as we walk into or out of an event. And that is less about wanting to be connected with my date and more about the optics. It's polite.

As the elevator descends my entire body pulses with energy. Maggie's lips, her soft core, her taste, her sounds are imprinting themselves on my brain. I savor each for a moment before I start to plot ways to kiss her again.

Chapter Nine
MAGGIE

A fake date is better than none.

THE ELEVATOR DOORS CLOSE across Austin's face and I see the questions racing through my mind in his eyes.

What the hell just happened?

Who is this man?

When can we kiss again?

I have never done anything that uninhibited in my life. It was like my sex drive took over.

I got increasingly wound up all morning. Every stress-laden thought about work was met with two lust-laden ones about Austin.

When his hands bracketed my face, the word "finally" flashed in my mind. Our crash landing of a kiss made all the previous turbulence worth it.

That was, without a doubt, the best damn kiss I've ever experienced. It was intense and wet and I melted into his solid body. It has awoken something in me. A wild kind of hunger.

I don't rely on guys to meet my needs. I can do it all by myself. That kiss tells me Austin would know how to meet my needs and then some.

I followed him out to the hall expecting to confront him about the kiss that both shook and steadied my world but when I saw him comb his hair back with his fingers like he regretted it, I froze. Then he turned and I watched feelings dance through his expression as he took me in. The look in his eyes made me doubt he was feeling remorseful.

My lips are still buzzing twenty minutes later when he and his team walk back into the conference room. I bite down hard on my lip to stop myself from smiling at him like a schoolgirl with a crush. As much as my body might want to engage with Austin again, I need to stay focused. He's charming, attractive, and kisses like a Marine returning from deployment, but I have a job to do.

"We've got an idea for a joint statement," Javé, his teammate, says as they file into the room. I actively look anywhere besides at Austin.

"Let's hear it," Sam says.

"While unexpected, Senator Quinn has always been a leader when it comes to embracing change. Her use of AI technology in her campaign will elevate the conversation," I scoff and everyone turns to look at me.

"Sorry, go on," I mutter through clenched teeth and look down at my notes. Sam kicks me under the table and then scribbles something in her notebook.

Get it together, be professional.

As a man would say "calm down."

I snort a laugh and cover it as a cough as Javé picks back up.

"And provide an example for those who follow." Javé finishes.

There's a pause while we all look around the room at each other.

"It's a start," Austin says, drawing my attention to him where he stands at the back of the room with his hands in his pockets. He shrugs and I watch the fabric of his perfectly tailored jacket fall back into place against his body. My hormone addled brain wants to rip that jacket off and get my hands on the muscles I saw on display last night in the fading light.

"Yeah," I finally agree. "Why don't we work on that a little bit more, it's almost there." I pause and find Austin's pewter eyes fixed on me. I stumble into my next sentence. "I, umm, would like to have a few minutes of Austin's time to discuss the, umm, timeline."

"Can we do it in your office?" He asks and I choke on air before nodding and start to pick up my things. Sam mouths "be nice" to me as I stand. If only she knew.

Austin lets me lead the way out of the conference room. It's a short walk to my office but my thoughts race like a bat outta hell.

Are we going to kiss again?

Does he want to?

Are we going to fight over that pitiful excuse for a press release?

Can I just stare at him for a minute?

What if I punch him in the throat and *then* kiss him?

I let Austin step past me before I close the door behind us, careful not to look in his eyes as he walks by. In the last twenty minutes I've developed a serious weakness for the heat in his charcoal gaze and I don't want to get burned.

As I turn to him I start, "What the hell was tha-"

I trail off as my eyes connect with Austin's for a split second. It's not even enough time to measure before his gaze drops to my mouth and my body alights.

"I don't know," he gruffs before grabbing my face again and searing me with his lips. I lose my balance and one of his strong arms loops down to my waist to support me.

I fist his dress shirt under his jacket and join him in the kiss. He tastes like strong coffee, and cowboys, and he smells a little bit like Christmas.

I inhale deeply through my nose and he grips my nape a little tighter. My head spins with the dreamy feeling of being kissed senseless. My body moves itself closer to him because it feels so good in his arms. I feel sturdy on my feet but also secure that he'd catch me if I fell.

One of his fingers loops into the waistband of my pants and it's enough to make my knees wobble. I break the kiss and come up for air but Austin's hold on me doesn't relent. I flatten my hands against his chest and can feel how quickly his heart is beating.

"Let's get to work," I say quietly as I step back.

He lets me go and takes a seat in a chair across from my desk. Maybe Austin can spend his days in endless makeout sessions but I have work to do.

"Senator Quinn will get a lot of shit for having AI Media write her speeches. I'm not sure I'm comfortable defending her statements if they've been computer generated. I also will not be a robot's editor. How is TMC going to handle the commentary?"

"I'm not worried about it," Austin says.

"How can you not be worried about it?" I ask.

"Because, Maggie, despite the little statement our teams are writing right now, there's no way anyone will be able to tell she's using AI. There's really no point in even announcing it." I see the mask he wears for work slide into place. It's a blank expression that almost makes him look plain. I wouldn't see the difference if I hadn't seen the fire in his eyes after our kiss.

I lean back in my chair and cross my arms. I might have been flustered and tongue tied at the podcast but I've had time to process this partnership and I'm fired up. "Well, since Thorne Media Corp is motivated by money and a lack of regard for original thought, I can see how you'd think that. But I, and the senator for that matter, believe in the American people. We believe in respecting them and treating them like adults. Even with AI, the senator is driven by her moral compass."

"Which is currently pointed at TMC's money and lack of regard for original thought." Austin states matter-of-factly.

"Unbelievable," I mumble.

"What is, that I can engage in a professional discussion while thinking about slipping those pants off your hips and confirming that our kiss did the same things to you as it did to me?"

I stare at him. It was hard enough to concentrate around him but now it seems like he's going to keep throwing these kisses in my face. And while I'm infuriated by his comment the lust train is also leaving the station and if he did what he promised he'd find a pair of ruined panties. But I can't let him win that easily. "I knew when we met that you're all talk but I never expected you to be a frat-boy idiot too."

"Well, considering I was the president of my business fraternity, I'm the most frat-boy idiot of them all."

He laughs at himself and I just stare back at him wide eyed. Even when I'm mustering all my professionalism I'm unable to get through a conversation with him.

He drives me insane with frustration.

With annoyance.

With desire.

The man pushes *all* of my buttons.

"Maggie?"

"What?" I ask as I blink up from where my eyes were fixed on his hands. The image of them all over me disappearing in a cloud of smoke. He smirks because he caught me looking.

"What are your plans tonight?" He asks doing a complete 180 from what we were just discussing.

"I've got a date." I lie.

In fact, my plans are to head home, drink a gallon of ginger turmeric tea to calm my nervous system, and take a bath with my favorite vibrator to give those nerves an outlet.

"That's fun, with who?" Austin asks as he leans back in his chair.

"You don't know him," I say as I lift my chin to muster as much truth to this lie as I can.

Those mesmerizing, gray-brown eyes, that I've pictured with alarming frequency since we met, twinkle with amusement. He's looking at me like I'm the prey he's toying with before going in for the kill.

"Try me, I know everybody in this town," he adds a wink at the end to really grind my gears.

"Ehrlich Gramblespock," I say slowly, basically chewing each syllable, before smiling because, holy crap, that's a gem of a name to pull out of nowhere.

"Uptight Ehrlich?" Austin repeats like we just discovered that his first cousin was my younger sister's college roommate.

I can't help myself. I laugh.

"Yes, Uptight Eurlich, I'm looking forward to it," I say as I bring the straw of my iced coffee to my lips. I take a sip to mask my smile. I like playing with him.

"Austin?"

"Mhmm?" he says while staring at my lips. I know what he's thinking and I like it. Is it okay that I like it? I should be focused completely on the campaign. And the work ahead of me in the next three weeks. The debate, the final campaign stops, Election Night itself.

So much of my job happens in my own head. I figure out what words to string together. I research; I revise. I debate internally if the speech is ready before handing it in.

I don't know if I can trust Austin but he's here and the question bouncing around in my head spills out. "Is this a good idea for the senator?"

He looks at me and tilts his head to the side slightly, like he's considering my question. It's endearing, like a puppy.

"You and I might disagree but I think it is. It'll get results, that's for damn sure."

"And you think results are everything?"

"I think there are a lot of people in this town who talk big and deliver small."

Somehow that sounds like an insult.

"Not me of course," he says with a teasing smirk and a slight roll of his hips. My eyes flick down to the inseam of his pants and, okay, he's probably right, but I'm still feeling insulted.

"It is a lot more difficult than most people think to get a majority of legislators to agree on something that impacts the entire US population," I huff out, defensively. I uncross my legs and lean closer over my desk. Austin's cologne hits my system and I have to blink hard to refocus. "Sometimes you have to start big, over promise, and then work backwards." I tell him.

"Wouldn't it make more sense to under-promise and over-deliver?"

"Under-promising isn't going to win elections."

"True," he concedes. "I guess you think results are everything too." The eyebrow he raises at me is begging to be punched. I feel my hand curl into a fist.

"So just to wrap this up, you were asking if the computer program I built would be smart enough to fool the American people. I think I just proved it could."

Before I can say anything he winks, stands, and leaves the office.

***

Later that night, after my highly satisfying bath where I let my mind wander to Austin and our kiss as my hands wandered my body, I'm staring at my SMS Connect phone. It was a long day and I was dealing with the AI Media project when I expected to be doing debate prep. By the end of the day we had most of the senator's speeches from the last six months uploaded onto their servers. The debate is in a week and they promised we'd have a version of her personalized chatbot to try using during debate prep on Monday.

I'm wondering if they're under-promising and over-delivering like Austin seems to be so fond of.

My head hits the pillow and I think about DCFox and unbidden, Austin's face appears. Then I laugh because I could not imagine him being at the other end of these messages. There is heart and warmth in DCFox's messages and while kissing Austin was certainly hot, he's as cold as they come.

I roll to my back and think about how I got here. I'm ten years into my fifteen year plan and everything has fallen into place. I want to run for office and have focused all my effort on gaining the necessary experience and making contacts throughout D.C.

While I admire the senator's drive to become president I don't think that is the path for me. I'd rather serve as a House rep, maybe a senator. I want to be someone who represents a small, relatively speaking, group of people and can be their leader at a federal level.

I'll need to find a place to move in the next few years because I need residency before I can run for office. I always figured I'd either buy a home in my hometown in upstate New York or buy a home wherever my partner is from.

But to do that I'd need to find a partner. The credentials for my future plus one are clear to me but I've found it difficult to explain it to others, especially my mom. I usually tell her about the dates I've gone on and why I won't be pursuing a second date with any of them.

Her favorite one to tease me about is when the guy showed up with noticeable nose hair. I couldn't stop staring at it. He might have been perfect in every other way but that single, long, thick nose hair?

Woof.

I tried to explain to her that it shows he lacks the basic grooming skills someone in the public eye must possess. If he could look at himself in the mirror and think "yep, good to go" with visible nostril fringe then he wouldn't be able to learn the skills either.

I'm looking for someone who is willing to support my career. My parents had an incredibly supportive relationship where each was free to pursue their ambitions while they worked together for the family.

It took me a while to see that my mom's neurotic habits were to make sure all five humans she was responsible for, herself, my dad, my two siblings, and myself, were fed and watered and had enough clean clothes.

Laundry was her wheelhouse. She created a system where each of us had an assigned laundry day and the spare two days were for sheets on one day and towels on the other.

It never stopped her from relying on me for help though. Liz is seven years younger than me and my mom had me change most of her diapers and washing bottles after school. I distinctly remember my parents getting exasperated with her toddler antics. Some of those moments became long lasting family jokes but most of them live in my brain as a reason to keep myself together. I love my little sister, but it took a long time for her not to be the dependent baby of the family.

I haven't been home for anything besides the 24 hours of Thanksgiving or Christmas in a long time. It isn't that I don't want to go, exactly, it's that I can never find the time. I'm always working to further my career and the careers of the influential people I work for. And when the senator wins I'll be even busier as she prepares to take office.

For the quickest of seconds my mind asks "what if she doesn't win?" and darkness seeps into the edges of my thoughts because I'd be back at square one if she loses. I have tied my ship to hers and without the presidency, we'd both be unemployed. I'll be scrambling to find a new politician to back.

People won't be hiring because they'll be bringing the team that got them into office with them.

And I'd still be alone.

Maybe it'd be easier to reinvent myself again without a partner. Maybe having someone else's expectations in the mix would hold me back. But I think of the way my parents supported each other and my chest aches at the idea of being alone.

My mind wanders to working with Austin today. Yes, he was snarky, and confident, but he listened and kept the work moving whenever he could. Partnering with AI Media and TMC is miles outside my comfort zone. I never expected to makeout with Austin Thorne in my office either.

The decision has been made for me, we have to work together, but how hard do I want to fight it? Can I stay true to myself while getting the job done alongside AI Media?

I don't think I feel brave enough to quit but am I strong enough to work through this alone?

I glance at the clock and realize that I need to get to sleep. But I know I won't be able to settle down until some of these thoughts are out of my head. Part of me was waiting to get a message from DCFox, but when have I ever waited around for a man?

Before I drift off to sleep I send a note to DCFox.

TalkShopGirl: I'm a pretty risk averse person. I play it safe. But I also follow my intuition. I'm at a crossroads at work. I could continue down the path I'm on, stick to what I believe, double down. Or I could pivot and travel down a road I haven't been before. One that challenges my long-held beliefs.

I know without specifics it is difficult for you to weigh in but I wanted your take. I wanted to see what you'd say. What do you do when you have a life-altering choice to make?

Chapter Ten
AUSTIN
Daddy Issues

WHAT DO I DO when I have a choice to make? Well, I'm not sure. I haven't had a lot of choices in my life. Not major ones anyway. College was pretty much picked for me, my condo was recommended to me by my family's real estate agent. My job was mine before I even graduated thanks to nepotism in the name of legacy.

I guess starting the AI Media project was a choice I made. But at the end of the day, Dad told me to build something new that would make the company money and I did.

What if you have to choose between TalkShopGirl and whatever is happening with Maggie Collins?

I shake my head to clear the thought. Maggie and I collided and put our work frustration into those kisses. That's all. It was just two incredibly hot kisses. And it doesn't matter that she felt fucking perfect in my hands. And the fact that I'm thickening now just thinking about it is irrelevant.

DCFox: Honestly my life has been pretty well plotted out. You'll understand more once my secret identity is revealed.

I'm envious of the fork in the road you're facing. Knowing how predictable my life is I'd tell you to take the path unknown but I also understand the apprehension that brings.

I turn the phone off after sending the message and slide it onto my nightstand. TalkShopGirl has texted me at night a few times recently. I like that she's thinking of me before bed. It feels intimate. I stare at my ceiling and imagine her awake now, lying in bed. I don't fight the image of Maggie Collins as it appears. I drift off remembering how her body felt lined up to mine.

***

As I walk up to my dad's office I adjust my shirtsleeves and try to shake off the no response from TalkShopGirl that I woke up to. I won't deny that it has put me in a sour mood all morning.

"Good morning Austin. He's ready for you," Darlene, my dad's assistant, says as she steps out of his office. "I'll bring breakfast soon."

"Thanks Darlene," I tell her with a warm smile. Darlene has known me for more than half my life and I love seeing her familiar face around the office. She may be the longest female relationship my dad has ever had. Probably because she comes equipped with a highly sensitive bullshit detector and doesn't let him get away scott free.

"Take a seat, son," Dad says as he finishes writing something on a slip of paper before folding it and setting it to the side. "I was just on the phone with Stan III. As you know he's the chairman of the board over at The Chronicle and he was calling to share some news."

"That sounds ominous," I say as I settle into the chair on the other side of his desk.

"Mhmm," Dad murmurs, "He was telling me something interesting about this AI Media business."

"What did he have to say?" I ask as I try to hide my nerves. I'm still developing my shrewd business sense but it is pretty clear this is a threat.

"He's preparing to sue all these *little* AI companies that have popped up lately for copyright infringement." Dad finally looks me cold in the eyes.

"What?" I demand as my crossed leg falls to the floor. A lawsuit could ruin AI Media.

"After talking to a buddy in the justice department he got to thinking. He claims his newspaper didn't give permission to have the robot read everything they published and spit it back out, without sources, to users. It's going to be a class action lawsuit with three other national papers."

Fuck. That argument is clear enough for the general public to understand it and form their own opinions. They wouldn't need a lawyer or an influencer to explain it to them and they'd stop downloading AIM as a result. But, on the other hand, in the age of social media reporting do people, everyday people, really care about properly attributing sources?

"What does this mean for us? Are you going to sue as well?"

"I want to join this lawsuit because it's a smart move for the future of traditional news but it means we're buck naked and bent over because of your little experiment. "

"Understood, sir." I reply, feeling like 10-year-old me wearing a suit that's too big. Like I'm being scolded for something I've poured all my energy into for the last three years. A project I believe in. And in one fell swoop it feels like a total waste of time.

And I can tell my dad feels the same way.

"They're preparing the suit for the end of the month. You'll need to make sure we aren't at risk by then."

"I'll pull the team together today." I mentally prepare the war cry I'll use for the team. I'm going to need their best ideas. I need them to understand the importance of solving this and protecting our work. When AIM is successful, I will be too. Finally proving to Dad I'm ready to take over the company.

***

"Ok, let's try another," Maggie is paging through a legal pad looking for her next debate question. "Ah yes, here we are," she clears her throat. "The cost of childcare is rising faster than any other family expense across the country. In fact, in most states it exceeds the median cost of housing. How do you plan to address this crisis American families face every day?"

Maggie looks at me and cocks an eyebrow. She thinks she's got us stumped. That our software won't come up with the perfect answer to this question. I just smile at her and place a hand on Tyler's shoulder. I know we've got this. The team and I met before coming over, we talked through the lawsuit solutions and then we ran through a few practice questions. If the answers didn't impress me we went back and improved the prompt.

"There isn't a clear answer to this issue," I start to read when Ty tilts the screen towards me.

"Ha!" Maggie scoffs as she leans back in her chair and crosses her arms.

"But I understand how important solving it is to every family. I propose a multi-faceted approach that includes paid leave for parents, preschool for every four year old, and the development of publicly subsidized early childhood centers for infants and toddlers."

"And how are you going to pay for all that?" Maggie asks as Tyler types her question into the computer.

"I'll work alongside the brilliant minds in the senate, the house, and in local government across the country. I'll work with nonprofits, schools, and houses of worship to brainstorm solutions. I won't pretend to have the answer tonight but I can't pretend there isn't a problem to solve."

The room goes quiet and I can see Maggie fighting with herself. It's the perfect political non-answer answer. The crowd will eat it up and only later will they realize she never said exactly how she'd do it.

We all know the answer is that she'd have to raise taxes but a political candidate would be finished if they said that out loud.

"Fine, let's try another one," Maggie says with a sigh.

***

When I get back upstairs to the conference room I can feel the tension rolling off the shoulders of everyone there.

"What's going on?" I ask and Maggie looks up in my direction with an angry heat in her eyes.

"Senator Quinn came out against the bill that would have supported the expansion of tech company data rights."

"Just now?" I ask, because it seems like a pretty big thing to do out of the blue.

"No, eighteen months ago," Maggie sneers.

"So, what's the problem?"

"Well now she's hired one of those tech companies to use all her data and the data of unsuspecting individuals to write her campaign messages!" Maggie gets more and more angry as she continues. Halfway through it she stands and her shoulders nearly touch her ears as she starts to pace.

"And?" I ask with a smirk on my face, I know where she's going, she's going to say it's a conflict of interest.

"How is this not a conflict of interest?! How are we supposed to answer the questions that will come our way when this comes out?!" she basically screams at me.

"They're not sleeping together," I tell her. "She's making a smart decision to use the best technology available to her."

"Of course they're not *sleeping together*," she scoffs. "Is that really-" She stops abruptly and looks at me. I can see questions rolling through her head.

"Austin, will you join me in my office for a moment?" Maggie says through gritted teeth and a less than friendly smile.

"Of course," I cheer and watch the rest of the people in the room look at each other with confusion. When I reach the door, I turn back, "Javé, why don't you work on a response to this perceived issue so when Maggie's eye stops twitching we can share it with her."

I find Maggie in her office. She is pacing three steps in one direction, pivoting, and pacing back.

"Maggie?"

She stops and turns to me. "Close the door."

I like where this is going.

"Hi." She says nervously.

"Hi Maggie." I smirk.

"Okay, so, oh god," she looks up at the ceiling and takes a deep inhale. "Have you ever had a fuck buddies arrangement?" She blurts out. Her face looks just as surprised as I feel, like she heard her words for the first time when she said them out loud.

I freeze where I am and watch her chest rise and fall with her breath.

"Have you?" I ask, not answering her question.

"No," she admits, "but I can see the value."

Can she?

"Why are you asking, Maggie?"

"I think you know why."

I can't help the smile that spreads across my face. I have wanted to get my hands and lips back onto Maggie since they first experienced her. I've been doing everything in my power to get to know her, to get closer to her, to be in her orbit since we met.

"How do you propose we start?" I ask.

I watch her eyelashes bat up and down and she inhales sharply.

"Not like that Maggie, I mean boundaries, rules. Clear lines drawn."

"Oh," she says with a flutter of a laugh and her hand comes up against her throat. "How about between now and the election?"

"Okay, and how often?"

"I'll be traveling for the campaign and not on a regular schedule the next three weeks, so how about we give the other person a twelve hour heads up?"

"Via text?"

"Sure."

"Done," I agree and I hold out my hand to shake. She laughs and shakes it. I hand her my phone to enter her contact info.

"Is that really how you want to seal this deal?" She asks with an eyebrow raised in challenge and she puts her name in.

She holds the phone out for me and I see that she's entered just her initials.

M.C.

"Not giving me your full name huh?"

"Austin the less people who know about this or have the opportunity to find out about it, the better. I didn't go full code name but I think we can K.I.S.S."

"We already did."

"Keep It Simple Stupid."

I laugh, and then lean in to press a kiss to her cheek.

"Consider this your twelve hour heads up, MC." I check my watch. "Well, more like a sixteen hour heads up, but text me your address and I'll be there in the morning."

Chapter Eleven
MAGGIE

"So, we're just going t–"

I WOKE UP BRIGHT eyed before my alarm at 5:02 am. Austin is supposed to be here at 6:00 am. Do I shower? I definitely need to brush my teeth. What about make-up? Should I make breakfast for him? Coffee?

I've never been in a situation like this before. But as soon as Austin said the words "sleeping together" I realized that I wanted him. I wanted the stress release of no strings attached sex. And I know I won't catch feelings because he's the opposite of what I want in a partner.

I mean, not in the looks department, he's definitely nice to look at, but I am interested in making a name for myself based on my positive influence on people. He's from an influential family, he runs a giant company, and believes in profit over people. Yuck.

He gets driven around town in a space car by a freaking driver. I doubt he's ever really had to work for anything in his entire silver spoon life.

Nope, not for me.

After I brush my teeth and work on my hair so it looks like I just woke up when really it's been manipulated by brushes and dry shampoo, I slide back into bed. To soothe my nerves I pull my SMS Connect phone out of the drawer in my nightstand. I exhale a shaky breath. There's a message from DCFox.

DCFox: Have you ever thought to yourself "I know this is a bad idea but I'm going to do it anyway"?

And then later when the consequences hit, all you can do is just nod your head and think, yep, saw this coming a mile away.

I got some bad news at work this morning but it was followed by some really good news. Some plans that I can get behind even if they're not the best strategic move.

I think this new venture got me excited because I'm tired of having to make the smart choice. Of having to out-perform everyone around me. Of having to be the best.

Today I just want to show up as me and have that be enough.

Gosh, he just gets me! There's something about his words that make it feel like he's in my head. He soothes concerns and anxieties in me that I wasn't even sure I had.

I'm smiling contentedly with the little device pressed to my heart when there's a knock on my door.

I squeak in surprise and toss the phone in the drawer. Tipping over to perk up my boobs in my bralette before reaching for the knob.

Austin is leaning against the doorframe in gray joggers and a slate blue t-shirt. The intimacy dials up to a thousand because of his casual outfit. His suit yesterday was drool inducing but it made me want to admire him from afar and let my eyes drink him in.

These joggers? These I want to get my hands on and, more importantly, use my hands to take them off.

When I move on from the flood of lust his outfit produced in me, I see that in one hand he's got two coffees and in the other a bag of pastries from Sunrise. I feel my eyebrows wrinkle, "Why did you bring me coffee?"

"And, good morning to you, too," Austin says as he steps into my apartment. He leans over, pecks me on the cheek and hands me the pastry bag. "I figured it would satisfy the buddies part of our arrangement. I want to hold up both ends of the bargain," he says with a wink.

"Oh, okay." I mumble as the shock of this greeting falls away. I step past him to the kitchen.

"I like your place," Austin says.

"Yeah, well, it's not much and I'm sure nothing compared to wherever you live but, I like it."

When I step back out of the kitchen Austin is staring at me. He laughs to himself and closes his eyes in a heavy blink as he goes to set the coffees down on the little table in front of my beloved oversized chair.

"What? What's funny about where I live?"

"Nothing." He says but I don't believe him for one second.

I cross my arms and jut a hip out to the side, "C'mon Thorne, I can take it. I already know, on so many levels, that this is a bad idea. So you might as well insult the studio hovel that takes up much more of my monthly income than it should."

He looks up to me and I feel his eye contact in my solar plexus. "Maggie, I like your place. Real estate in DC is ridiculous and you've turned this apartment into a warm and inviting live/work space. The giant whiteboard really pulls the whole place together." He smirks and my thighs clench. "But seriously, I can see how you would enjoy coming home here at the end of the day and waking up here in the morning. Take the compliment."

"Oh," is all I can manage to get out. I blink a few times and shake my head before admitting, "I don't know what to do with you being nice to me."

"Would you rather I be mean?" He asks with a laugh. "I'm not that kind of lover."

"Ew, don't say lover."

"Don't say ew."

"Ugh! You're so annoying."

"This turning you on Maggie?"

Yes.

His presence alone elevates my heart rate. Our verbal sparring takes it even higher. And it continues to beat at a furious pace as the rest of me freezes. Austin steps closer and brushes the fingers of his right hand along the hem of my tank. When he makes contact with my skin, goosebumps explode across my abdomen. When he drags his fingers up my stomach, lifting my shirt with it, my knees almost buckle.

"So, we're just going t–"

Austin answers my unfinished question by pressing his lips to mine. The hand that was under my shirt splays wide and his fingers slide under my breast leaving a trail of sparks in its wake. His other hand cradles the back of my head and his fingers tangle in my hair and icicles spill down my spine.

Instantly my body tries to wrap itself around him. My hands rake through the short strands at the back of his head as our mouths open to each other. One leg slides up around his hip and he cradles my thigh in his palm. I can feel him pressing up against my center and unlike at the office, we don't have to stop.

I drop my leg and push him back a step. The kiss breaks loudly and both of us freeze for a moment, chests heaving with inhales, my eyes stay focused on Austin to the point that everything else around me fades away. I can see how his muscles are tense but not with stress, with restraint, and I feel the same tension in my limbs.

We could still stop this, we haven't gone past the point of no return. We could scrap this whole thing and go back to being work enemies. I'm trying to make the case for not going any further but my logic processing center is flooded with hormones signaling sex is exactly what I need. And that Austin is the man for the job.

With his eyes still on me, Austin pulls his glasses off and sets them on the table next to the coffees. My chemical fogged brain hears his message loud and clear. Game on! I whip my shirt off and when my head is free of the fabric, I see Austin doing the same. There's an unspoken race that's begun to get naked first. Soon shirts, shorts, pants, socks litter the floor.

I unhook the front clasp of my bralette and before the lace slides off my arms Austin has my breasts in his hands. His mouth descends as he pushes them together and my nails dig into his scalp.

"Austin," I breathe out and he responds with a nip to the tender skin of my chest. He soothes it with an open mouth kiss and my head falls back in pleasure.

"Fuck, Maggie, thank god you're so stressed."

I grip the short strands of his hair and pull his head back so he looks up at me. His hands fall to my waist and the way he holds me toes the line between harsh and supportive.

"Every word out of your mouth annoys me," I say as he laughs against my neck. I rake my fingers down his chest, abs that ripple under my touch, and when I cup him he hisses sharply. "But maybe I know how to shut you up."

"Do your worst Maggie Collins," he says as he walks us backwards to the bed. I push him down as I climb up and straddle him. There is no way I'm giving him the power here. As I reach to my bedside table for condoms I also see the SMS Connect phone and my brain asks me one more time if I'm sure.

Sleeping with Austin is just for the physical benefits, I tell myself. This is scratching an itch. Scheduling it will keep us from interacting inappropriately at work. I'll be able to focus and do my job better.

When I straighten on top of Austin again he's looking up at me, inquisitively. Is he reading my thoughts? But as I slide the condom down his length his eyes widen and all logistical thinking leaves my mind.

"You sure you're ready for me, MC?" He asks as his thumb presses into my clit and my toes curl.

"Are you sure you're ready for me?"

He laughs. "There's no way in hell I'm ready for you, Maggie."

I line him up at my entrance, with an inhale I sink down on top of him and watch as his head presses back into the mattress.

His hands come around to hold my ass and I tilt forward over him.

Together, without speaking, we move in tandem. Riding each other toward our peaks. I hear myself grunting with each thrust and it matches his sharp exhales. We're volleying back and forth together and I realize we've moved up my bed when I reach up and can grip the headboard. His hand splays wide across my pubic bone and his thumb circles my clit again and I feel zaps of electricity in my arms and legs. This sex is fast, exhilarating, no time to feel nervous. It's exactly what I didn't know I needed.

"Fuck Austin, yes," I growl out and he presses harder.

"Good girl Maggie, ride me, use me," he whispers, almost reverently, and I jerk my hips harder. My stomach bottoms out and as he toys with my mound I feel my insides flutter and my head free falls from tension to bliss.

"Yes, oh fuck, yes!" I breathe out and start to slow my pace as my pussy contracts around Austin's cock and I bring my hands down to his chest. With his heart pounding under my palm, I feel a smile creep across my face and I almost laugh as the tension leaves my body. Austin grabs my wrists and pushes up into me as my orgasm fades and then he moves my hands to one side and slides out from under me.

"Turn around," he commands and post-orgasm Maggie is willing to follow directions. "Hello old friend," he says to my ass as he kneads the flesh.

My mind is battling between the desire that's ramping up again and how much I want him to stop talking. I need him to stop reminding me that he's Austin Thorne, and potentially the thing standing between me and career success.

Right now he's standing between me and another orgasm. "Shut up and finish already," I say, breathlessly.

"You sure about that? You've only had one but I can give you more." He tells me as he leans over and I feel his cock slide through my folds. Involuntarily my head falls as his head brushes against my clit. I inhale as he pulls back.

"I can give myself as many orgasms as I damn well please."

"Like this?" He asks as he swirls two fingers over my clit before sliding them inside me. They curl forward and rub along my g-spot.

"Oh fuck," I exhale and fall forward to my elbows. The tension is back but this is a stress I could get used to.

"Is that a request, Maggie?"

"Yes, please, fuck me." I hear myself whine and I can't even spare myself the time to lament needing him as much as I do at the moment because he thrusts forward and fills me. He sets a relentless pace and with each push my tits brush against the comforter and I'm quickly back at the threshold of another orgasm.

"Shit Austin, I'm gonna come again."

"That's a good thing MC," he grunts out and with a light smack to my butt, my insides are convulsing again. "That's it," he coaches and then he holds my hips hard and jerks inside me. "Fuck Maggie." he growls.

I fall forward to the bed, unable to hold myself up and his hand caresses my back. I'm on fire but his touch chills me. The chills continue as he pulls out and guides my hips down to the mattress. My eyes follow his bare ass as he walks to the bathroom. I have to bite the tip of my thumb to hide my smile.

I owe Sam flowers or a lifetime supply of coffee for this idea.

I don't know how I'm going to continue to work with him knowing we could be spending time together doing this. Like the kisses we shared, this feels like an out-of-body experience.

It felt like he was made for me. Like he knew exactly what I needed. How did he know to push me a little harder? A little further? How did he know that I needed to be in charge but have his efforts match mine?

Usually when I climb on top, guys lean back and let me ride them. Which feels good and I can definitely get there like that but when Austin was pushing up into me and meeting me thrust for thrust my orgasm hit me harder than ever before.

I slip my robe on and tie the belt. Austin steps out of the bathroom and I take in his naked glory. He is lean and strong, and the way every muscle moves his body towards me makes my brain fuzzy. He steps into his boxers, then pants, and then he picks up his shirt and slides it over his shoulders. I'm mesmerized and when his eyes find mine my stomach flips and he grins. Not a smirk, a full blown smile. The kind of smile I could become attached to.

If I didn't hate him, and what he stands for, so much.

Austin picks up his socks and then sits in my chair to put them on. I realize I'm staring so I step into the kitchen and pull the pastries out of the bag. I put them on a plate, wondering if we're supposed to eat breakfast together now, and when I step back into the room, Austin stands and claps loudly which startles me.

"Well, *friend*," he accentuates the word as he grabs his glasses and sexily slides them back on his face; how is that even a thing? But now all I want him to do is take them off again. "I guess I'll be going."

"Guess so," I say quickly and slide the plate back onto the counter behind me. Just sex Maggie. Just sex. "I believe we have a meeting later today." I say as I fiddle with my hands, not sure what to do with them.

"I believe you're correct," he says with a laugh as he picks up one of the coffee cups. "These got cold, next time I'll use insulated cups."

He tips the drink in my direction as he reaches the door. I glance at the clock and see that it's almost 7:00 a.m.

"Can I give a 12 hour notice in person?" I blurt out.

"Are you giving me a 12 hour notice in person?" He asks instead of answering my question.

"Ugh! Why are you like this? Just, fine, yes, can we hook up again, tonight?"

"Yes, we can Maggie, but I'd like to hear you ask nicely," and I want to smack the smirk off his face. Instead I give him two middle fingers as I brush past him into my bathroom for a shower. I hear him chuckle as my door opens and closes behind him.

I have a feeling it's going to be a long day.

Chapter Twelve
MAGGIE

"Prove it."

"You're looking exceptionally well today," Senator Quinn cheers as she joins us in the conference room. I see Austin grin out of the corner of my eye but I do not allow myself to look at him.

Even though I've been sneaking looks at him since he walked in because my mind won't quit the slide show of this morning.

The coffee and pastries and quick kiss hello.

The absolute rush on both our parts to get naked.

The first orgasm.

The sound of his voice behind me.

The second orgasm.

The mix of feelings afterwards of wanting him to stay in bed so I could cling to him and trail my nails up and down his back as we snuggled while also wanting to claw his eyes out.

Maybe I was a cat in a past life.

"Thank you, Senator," I say and leave it at that because what am I supposed to say? I got railed and it released a lot of my stress? That I'm counting down the hours until 7:00 tonight because that's when Austin is getting back in my pants?

Or pencil skirt as it were.

We practice a few debate questions and the AI Media answers are good. The senator knows how to adjust her rehearsed responses with the new lines she's given. Part of being in politics is performing and when you're a woman all eyes are on you, expecting nothing short of perfection.

The thought makes me question whether I really want to run for office. I'm not good at thinking on my toes. I get flustered and nervous and rarely experience the flow state I achieve when I'm writing. I've known this ever since I ran for student council.

I remember what my dad said when I told him I wanted to run and bring back after-school programs that had been cancelled because of budget cuts. He told me that I was the girl who could get it done and that the students could count on me.

Those sentiments stuck with me as my mom helped me make glitter paint campaign signs. I spent every spare moment I had figuring out how I would find the money for the programs.

"No one else was going to do it" became my motto.

By the end of the school year, I had secured enough funding to bring back all the original programs and add two more. And I was the first student to be invited to sit on the county-wide school board.

And thus, a future public servant was born.

I've been backing people and causes I believe in my entire adult life. That track record is part of why cooperating with the TMC team is especially difficult for me. I don't believe in AI generated content being the future. I don't think it's smart to rely so heavily on technology. I understand the advantage of being an early adapter but shouldn't we wait to see if the app works first?

Austin and his team leave after lunch and I barely get my butt in my desk chair when Sam starts.

"Who did you hook up with last night?"

"What?" I laugh and keep my eyes down at my desk fearful that she'll figure it out just by looking at me.

"C'mon Maggie, I know you were seeing that Mike guy but you were not this relaxed after your date with him."

"You're right, Mike is nice, like really nice, and I like talking with him, he's smart."

"Buuuut..." then Sam gasps. "Oh my god! Did you meet your SMS Connect friend?"

"Ha, no. He's still just writing incredible text messages every night."

"So, who turned you into this Sex On The Beach version of Maggie Collins today?"

"Can't say."

"Ew Maggie," Sam gags, "you hired an escort?!"

"NO!" I yell out and then, after double checking the door is closed, I whisper to confirm it, "No. I did not hire an escort. *I* know who it was but I'm not going to tell *you* who it was."

"Can I guess?"

"Sure, but I'm not going to give it away."

"You'll just give it up!" Sam whoops and lifts her hands for a high five.

I laugh as I clap my hand with hers. It feels very locker room to high five over sex but since I feel like I unlocked the secret to my sanity I want to celebrate.

"Twenty questions style?" Sam asks.

"Sure," I agree as I rearrange the items on my desk to avoid eye contact with her.

"Is he someone we know?"

"Yes."

"Dang, that doesn't narrow it down much. Umm," she starts rolling her nails on the desktop. "I'm going to Guess Who this... does he wear glasses?"

"Yes."

"Really?" She readjusts in her seat, energized by her good guess. "Someone we know who wears glasses..."

I know that if I look at her she'll somehow pick up on the name through telepathic channels. Instead I open one of my desk drawers and start thumbing through files.

"This is crazy but the only guy I can think of when you said glasses was Austin Thorne."

I slam the drawer shut so forcefully that my pen cup topples over.

"No. Way." Sam says before she presses her lips together between her teeth and I see them starting to turn white. Her eyes double in size and I think they might explode.

"Sammy, breathe."

"Holy shit," she exhales dramatically. "Austin Thorne? But you hate him? He hates you? Right? How did you pull this off?"

"It all started when we kissed a few days ago, and then I got your sex-as-a-stress-release idea in my head, and asked him to be my fuck buddy."

"Wait you kissed?!"

"Twice." I grimace because maybe this is information I should have told my closest colleague slash only friend that's forced to hang out with me because of our jobs.

"I don't believe it." Sam says, astonished.

"Well, believe it because, oh my god Sam, it was so worth it."

"Yeah?" Sam smiles slyly and leans forward towards my desk. I scootch forward too.

"He brought coffee and pastries but the coffee got cold while we got after it."

"And, it was good?"

"More than good. Like maybe the best I've ever had. I mean, I was so annoyed with him every time he spoke," except when he was talking dirty, "but he met me stride for stride and it just, worked."

"But you're not dating right? I can't imagine that being good for either of you from a publicity standpoint."

"No, it's just sex, pre-arranged, and only until the election."

"This feels like such a good and bad idea all at the same time."

"I can't say I disagree."

"Wow, okay," Sam is quiet for a second as she leans back in her chair. "That's not what I expected when I came in here, but I like it." She shakes her head. "Anyway, I wanted to talk about the timeline of releasing the partnership statement."

"I'm still not convinced we should." I say as I flip open my notebook.

"Well, if the senator does really well at the debate because of the AI responses, I expect Austin will want the credit."

"I expect he will. But the whole point is that there isn't a way to tell if it's the AI or if it's the rehearsed statements we've been working on for months," I say as I flip aimlessly through my notes. "And, what if the AI answers are terrible and she tanks? I don't want anyone to know that we relied so heavily on this new technology."

"I guess we'll just have to see how it goes."

With that Sam stands and leaves me alone with my thoughts. It's difficult to concentrate knowing the hours are ticking down until my evening with Austin. I need to put him out of my mind so I can get some work done.

***

I was able to focus on work after Ben, our campaign manager, stopped in my office and asked for a speech for a newly scheduled stop in the morning. Senator Quinn is meeting with the new cohort of political science students at George Washington University and has been asked to talk about innovative solutions to age-old issues.

I got lost in writing about funding models that are successful in other democracies across the world. I researched team building theories so members of our federal government could see each other as allies more than enemies. It was an accident that I looked up and caught the clock thirty five minutes ago, instantly remembering Austin was meeting me at my place at 7:00.

I threw my things in my bag and rushed out to the Metro. Thankfully, I caught a train almost as soon as I descended to the platform.

I'm home for only a few minutes, enough time to drop my bag, kick my heels into the closet, and pee, before there's a knock at my door.

I open it and find Austin on the other side with a bouquet of flowers. He's changed out of his suit and has a pair of jeans and a navy blue t-shirt on.

"Have you had dinner yet?" He asks as he steps into my apartment and kisses my cheek again. I'm stunned into silence as I take the flowers from him, stare at them, and then up at his back moving into my kitchen.

"No, I just got home, have you?" I ask blinking a couple extra times in confusion. I'm new to the whole fuck buddies thing but wouldn't having dinner together be more like dating?

"No, not yet," he says as I step into the kitchen. He turns to me and crosses his arms over his chest. The material around his biceps strains and my insides clench but then I catch the look on his face. He's frustrated.

"What?" I challenge and watch as his eyes flick down my body before meeting mine.

"I just can't believe you are doing everything in your power to thwart my business."

I laugh. "What are you talking about?"

"Why won't you approve the statement about the partnership? The senator says she's waiting for your approval."

"I'm doing what's best for the senator." I say as I set the bouquet down on the counter and cross my arms, mirroring him.

"No, you're doing what's best for you. You're so afraid of this technology you're not even willing to admit it works. That it could be helpful to you."

"Is this about work or is this about *this*?" I ask, flicking a finger indicating the two of us. "Because if you're expecting me to fess up—"

"No, believe me, I'm not telling anyone."

Ouch but, yes. My thoughts exactly. I decide on the spot that telling Sam doesn't count because she essentially figured it out all on her own. I just added a couple details.

"I can't even begin to explain how bad it would be if the news of our arrangement got out while we're also not telling people about working together." I pull down a vase and put the flowers into it. My actions break the tether between us and the air shifts. Austin turns to my fridge and pulls out a beer. He wags it at me and I nod so he goes back for a second. I finish putting the flowers away as he walks back into my studio and leans against my desk, propping one leg over the other at the ankle.

"Okay," he takes a sip of his beer. "Tell me again why she can't go public? I feel like I'm missing something."

"You're missing the genitalia required to understand it."

He laughs as I take my beer and sit down in my preferred corner of the oversized chair. "So if I had tits I'd understand?"

"More or less," I answer with a smile as I take a sip. "Did you know that 75% of high school valedictorian's are young women? And that most people getting bachelor degrees are women? So adjusting for that we should see at least 50% of the leaders in the country being women.

"But they're not. Not by a long shot. It's because work is designed for women to fail when they become mothers, and make it nearly impossible to succeed at work because school ends at 3:00. Senator Quinn got a bunch of flack for being a childless cat lady but part of me is convinced she wouldn't have been as successful as a professional and a politician if she had a family.

"There are women who have made it work, probably by hiring other women to manage their children and household. And there is compelling data saying that companies under a woman's leadership grow faster and stronger than under a man's. Investment portfolios managed by women perform an average of 5% better."

I can tell Austin is paying attention. His eyes are focused and with each new little fact I drop they widen slightly behind his frames. I know I'm bordering on unhinged but now that I've started I'm going to keep going. I've got a point to make. And if it means he walks away and we don't hook up tonight then fine, I'll at least have released some stress by ranting.

"There's a feedback issue for these high performing women too. Like 75% of them receive negative feedback from their bosses when their male peers get like 2% and most of what they hear is about their personalities. *Smile more, be more cooperative.* That's inactionable criticism which, news flash, demotivates them! And then they perform worse which, spoiler alert, leads to more negative feedback at their next review. So even though more women are in powerful positions in corporate America, it's still not a great place to be.

"Now, in politics it's undeniably a man's world. Senator Quinn has the opportunity to do something unprecedented here and the negative side of things will be insane if people spin it like she's cheating. If there is any type of story line of *she couldn't do this on her own, she needed AI* or something, I'm not sure she'd come back from that."

"But wouldn't she be seen as innovative?"

"Maybe, but I'm more realistic about the general population's opinion of women."

I take another sip of my beer and wait for Austin to argue but he doesn't say anything.

"Let's say she was a 47 year old single man with the same career, credentials, voting history,"

"But no tits," Austin provides and I glare at him while laughter bubbles in my chest.

"Correct, no tits," I say and he smiles proudly for getting the answer right and a little laugh sneaks out of me. "If she were a man the trending headlines about him wouldn't be about his wardrobe, or his skincare routine, or his diet. It would be about policy, his vision. It has taken us months of consistent messaging to have the press focus on her policies first. It's still a delicate balance. I'm afraid of doing anything that could send the narrative off in a direction I can't control."

"I think you need to have a little more faith in the media and the general public."

"Ugh! You would say that! Did you know that for every three articles or posts about her policies there are seventeen about her clothes, makeup and hair? You know as well as I do that reasonable headlines don't sell so media outlets spin things up to be sexier and in the world of the male gaze a woman's clothing choices are sexy."

I'm wound up. I have shifted forward in the chair and crossed my arms. Realization hits me that while Austin is in charge of this AI project he still works for a media company. I curl into myself a little more when I realize that he could turn around and report all of this to a gossip columnist at Thorne.

"Maybe we shouldn't do this anymore," I say as I stand up and walk to the kitchen. I set my beer down and let my head hang as I brace both hands on the counter. It felt good to get all that off my chest but what good does it do?

I gasp quietly as I feel Austin slide up behind me and press his wide chest into my back.

"You're an incredibly sexy woman Maggie," he whispers into the shell of my ear and my knees tingle in response, "and hearing your passion for your job, for your candidate, it makes me want to be on your team." His fingers squeeze to release my claw clip before he brushes my hair off my shoulder and lands his mouth there. My head lolls back to fall on his shoulder. "But you need to learn how to trust people," he whispers against my skin.

"What? I trust people just fine," I protest and when I try to turn around he presses me into the counter harder. I can feel his cock on my ass through my skirt and his jeans.

"Prove it," he says quietly in my ear as his fingers pull the zipper of my pencil skirt down. He drags it down my legs and helps me step out of it while I'm still hooked at the hips against the counter. Both of his hands run up the back of my legs before he grips my thong and pulls that down too.

His hands on my hips twist me before he gently lifts me onto the counter. He pulls his glasses off and sets them right next to his beer. My stomach flutters with excitement. That little movement is a promise of what's to come.

The windows are open behind him and I can see people walking down the street. "Austin, the window," I start before he kneels in front of me, runs his hands up my thighs to part my legs, and his mouth descends to my pussy.

The walls come crashing down around me as he works my center with his mouth. My heart was racing when I started to share my thoughts on women in politics. I believe women are more capable than men in most things. But right now, my heart beats wildly to fuel the blood sprinting through my veins because a mouth on me is not something I can do on my own.

Austin latches onto my clit which sends my body into a tailspin. My toes tingle and my stomach clenches as I grind down to meet the movements of his tongue. The sensation is moving up through my body. I am not ready to let go. He feels so good. How does he know exactly what I need? I come undone as he slides a finger in me and I incant his name in praise.

He lifts his head and licks his lips. His dark eyes connect with mine as he takes a sip of his beer and sets the bottle back down before he grabs his glasses and slides them onto his face. Every small movement of his sends heat to my core and radiates out to my already melted legs. I don't know what to make of the look in his ashen eyes. I slide off the counter and start to think about how we're going to continue our activities when he just gives me a curt nod and walks to the door. He opens it and leaves without looking back and I'm left standing half naked feeling sexually satisfied but mentally frustrated.

This thing between us is just sex I remind myself. I shouldn't care about his feelings. Or his mood. Or why our encounter just now felt like a turning point.

Chapter Thirteen
AUSTIN

Sisters and Situations

I AM SO FUCKED.

When her taste, smell, the fucking beautiful sounds she made, flooded my senses, my chest pinched and I struggled to breathe. The sip of beer after going down on her only washed her more deeply into me.

I don't hate Maggie Collins.

Not even a little.

I admire her. I like her. I want to give her things. I want to take care of her. My painful erection is testament to my physical desire, but I could enjoy myself just as much if we spent the night talking.

So, I bailed. I'm not supposed to feel things for Maggie Collins. My feelings are reserved for TalkShopGirl, the woman I've developed a connection to through words alone.

I limp as quickly as I can to my bedroom and pull out the SMS Connect phone.

DCFOX: I know we still have a few weeks before we meet, and that we can't send pictures, but I have an idea.

Please message me back if you see this tonight. I silently beg her, hoping the universe will deliver the plea.

I slide out of my clothes and then into bed with only my boxer briefs on. The ceiling swims in my vision as the blood courses away from my brain.

If TalkShopGirl doesn't reply in a few minutes I'll need to take a shower. I squeeze my eyes shut to try and avoid seeing Maggie as her orgasm climbs to its peak.

It doesn't work.

The passion in her crystal blue eyes as she shared what she believes in is only slightly less sexy.

Everything about her drives me wild.

Ping.

My head whips to the phone.

TalkShopGirl: What is your idea?

Fuck. Yes. I need to play this right.

DCFox: There's something to be said for chemistry, right?
TalkShopGirl: There is...

That's my girl.

DCFox: Could we test our chemistry tonight?

I pull myself out past the waistband while I wait for her to respond. Usually when I jack off in the shower it's to a mental collection of body parts, waves of hair, feminine curves, painted lips.

Tonight, I'm going to picture a woman holding a phone. Maybe another toy.

TalkShopGirl: How would we do that?

I sit up straight and type quickly.

DCFox: I'd like to exchange texts while we masturbate. I want to feel as physically connected to you as I do to your words.
TalkShopGirl: I'm in.

I sigh with relief. This is insane, to feel proud of myself that she's put her trust in me. I'm a faceless set of words on a screen to her. But she's somehow full of life to me.

DCFox: Start by getting comfortable.
TalkShopGirl: Done.
DCFox: I'm lying in bed, fisting my cock. It's already hard.

She could get scared off at any moment, but if I'm not myself here, we have no chance of a future together.

TalkShopGirl: I'm naked in bed, too.
TalkShopGirl: And I'm wet.

Fuck me.

DCFox: Are you going to use your fingers? Or a toy?
TalkShopGirl: Fingers.
DCFox: Lick them and run your hand down your body. Circle your nipples. I bet they're fucking perfect, aren't they?
TalkShopGirl: What are you going to do?
DCFox: Try not to come, yet.
TalkShopGirl: Circle your nipples too.
DCFox: Yes ma'am.

I'm not worried about our chemistry anymore. Not one bit. TalkShop-Girl is right there with me.

TalkShopGirl: Would we fuck slowly in bed or hard and fast over a desk?

Stars dance in my vision as I try to catch up.

DCFox: Whatever my dirty girl wants, she gets.
TalkShopGirl: Desk.
DCFox: You're perched on the edge for me.

I fist my cock roughly and after a few strokes of self-loathing I give in. All I picture is Maggie. She's sitting on her desk with her legs open for me. Leaning back on her elbows and the smile on her face is powerful and dirty.

I'll never tell TalkShopGirl that I pictured another woman while we shared this. It isn't cheating but it doesn't feel exactly right either.

TalkShopGirl: In nothing but my black heels.

I groan out loud.

DCFox: I'd sling those heels over my shoulder and taste you.
DCFox: A long lick stopping right at your clit.
TalkShopGirl: Yes.
DCFox: Where are your hands?
TalkShopGirl: On my tits, scraping through your hair.
TalkShopGirl: Right now? I'm two knuckles deep inside myself.
DCFox: One finger or two?
TalkShopGirl: One

DCFox: Add another.

I stroke myself as I picture Maggie going two fingers deep on herself. I can feel her heat on my own hand as I force myself to breathe. The intensity of this moment we're sharing is overwhelming.

TalkShopGirl: I'm close.

DCFox: Me too.

TalkShopGirl: I'm going to set the phone down on my chest to finish.

DCFox: Think of me pinning you to the desk.

DCFox: Driving my cock into you.

DCFox: Giving you everything you need while taking what I want.

I close my eyes and squeeze myself as the Maggie in my mind shifts to her knees and is below me. I hold my dick out for her and my knees shake as I imagine her swallowing me. A sweat breaks out across my back.

I inhale, my dick swells, and the image changes. Maggie is back on the desk, naked except for the black heels propped on the edge.

Imagination Austin steps between her thighs and she reaches up to grasp me by the shoulders. I pump myself aggressively as I imagine sinking into her bare. Holding her by the crook of her neck and slinging her heels over my shoulder. Roughly returning everything she gives me. Watching her face splinter with building tension.

Her ocean blue eyes widen under me as I fuck my hand and explode my release as her head falls back in my imagination.

DCFox: TalkShopGirl, are you still with me?

TalkShopGirl: Yes. I'm here. Just breathing. Smiling. Satisfied.

I slowly glide over my deflating erection before letting it hang heavy between my legs. I'll shower in a minute but for now I want to imagine snuggling up with a woman. Maggie.

DCFox: I think we're killing this SMS Connect thing.
TalkShopGirl: I agree.
DCFox: Good night, TalkShopGirl.
TalkShopGirl: Good night, DCFox. ;)

I smile to myself before sliding out of bed. I was wound up after being at Maggie's but this impromptu session confirmed that TalkShopGirl and I are compatible beyond the words we exchange.

Did we just cross a line? Will we be able to go back to our normal exchanges? I can't even fathom what it'll be like to meet her for the first time.

I let out a deep exhale before swinging my legs over the side of the bed. For one moment I allow myself to worry that meeting TalkShopGirl will leave me wanting.

Wanting someone like Maggie Collins.

***

Even after a satisfying shower, I couldn't get Maggie's impassioned words out of my head. I channeled her influence into some research. Sure as shit, she was right. Not that I'm surprised. She hardly seems like the type to say things that aren't true. Especially about something she's so passionate about.

And all this women empowerment research has me walking into my sister's room.

"Elle, did you know that women do business better than men?" I ask as I sit down on the stool she has next to her closet so she can reach the top shelf.

"No shit they do, but why are you suddenly discovering this?"

"I just heard some stats tonight that got me thinking."

"Yeah?"

"Yeah, it's not a big deal."

"Does it have something to do with why you came home and got in the shower right away?" She snickers as she tilts her head inquisitively.

"You weren't home, how'd you know I went to the shower right away?"

"Austin, I was sitting at the dining table. I said hello. You just marched awkwardly to your room without noticing me at all." I don't appreciate the look Elle is giving me.

"I had a lot on my mind."

"Or your head?"

"Okay, this is not what I came in here to talk about."

"Let's move on to why you were up and out of the apartment before I got home from class this morning. Is that what you *came* in here to talk about?"

"Why does everything sound sexual with you?"

"Answer the question."

"I was motivated to get up this morning."

"Get *it* up! Whooha!" Elle bellows and holds up her hand for a high-five. I leave her hanging. "Oh c'mon! That was funny."

"Moving on, I know you don't work there but I figured you might know anyway. How many women are in management at Thorne?"

"Not many, why?"

"I'm reading stuff on women-run companies who outperform male-run peers."

"There's evidence?"

"Yeah, a few different articles."

"Any posted by Thorne?"

I stop to think about it. I used the AI Media search tool to start my research. It is designed to pull Thorne articles first but there weren't many.

"A few, not many. I'd have to check the sources of the others."

"That doesn't surprise me. I feel like a lot of our articles take a traditional white male point of view."

"They do?"

She laughs, "yeah, of course you haven't seen it." She tsks like I should know better.

"Hey, that's not fair," I start but she might be right.

"How many women helped you write the code for AIM?"

"I'm not sure. Why?"

"Because if you're writing for women there's a different tone, different words you can use to be more effective. It might be worth looking into so that you make the most of your fancy new technology."

"Hm," I say and then I lift myself off the stool and head back to my room. I email Elizabeth with questions and ask her to set up a call with Tyler so I can ask him the questions Elle asked me. She responds within a few minutes reporting that we only had a few women on the project and they didn't work on the whole code, just sections of it. She attached the HR assignments for the project as evidence.

My sleep wasn't restful. I tossed and turned and each time I slipped into consciousness my mind would turn to fixing this. The next day dawns and I feel a storm cloud settle in around my shoulders. It brewed as I got ready for work. As Greg drove me across town to the office. As I said a quiet good morning to Elizabeth who eyed me sideways for my lack of usual enthusiasm.

The day has been full of meetings and brainstorming solutions to our inclusion problem and the looming lawsuit. Not helping me focus is the fact that Maggie is in my mind anytime I'm not actively working. And she might be there when I am actively working because I find myself asking very Maggie-like questions.

Her voice is in my head as she asks me, "Are there biases in your recruitment process that might deter female candidates?"

And, "What strategies can be implemented to foster allyship and support from male colleagues once women have been hired?"

Or, "When are you going to make a woman the leader of the project?"

I slide my glasses off and flip them to my desk. Overcoming decades of gender bias is not for the faint of heart. As I lean back and press the heels of my hands into my eye sockets, Elizabeth knocks lightly at my door.

"Mr. Thorne," she says clearly.

"Austin, Elizabeth, call me Austin."

"Yes sir, I wanted to remind you of your appointment with Allegra Sinclair this evening. I've scheduled you a table at The Ned for 8:00."

I slide my glasses back on and notice that it is 7:30 already. "Thank you Elizabeth, you should have gone home hours ago."

"My hours are your hours, sir." She says with a little glance over the top of her glasses at me.

She's been invaluable to me over the last several years. Elizabeth has seen me through a few failed relationships, helped our team clean up my social media presence and get me untagged from posts that past girlfriends have tried to burn me with, in fact, she's my best line of defense. I screen my calls through her and once she knows I don't want to talk to someone she shuts it down.

Except when it comes to Allegra Sinclair.

Even if I told Elizabeth that I didn't want to talk to Allegra anymore she'd have to keep answering the calls; Al is on Dad's *"approved list"*.

The Thornes and The Sinclairs have a long-standing family friendship. The kind that meant we "summered" together and would spend major holidays together over catered meals after getting professional family photos taken.

Allegra is a year younger than me and we've had an on-again, off-again thing going since high school. On when we're in the same room. Off as soon as we're not.

I've never scheduled a date with her, I've never taken her out to dinner. I've never even spent the night. A couple of years ago she left D.C. and moved up to New York to start a clothing line.

When she left she asked me if I'd come and visit her and I laughed. Then when I saw the look on her face I realized that she was serious and I tried to back track. I didn't mean to hurt her feelings, but I thought we were on the same this-is-just-sex page.

The few times we've seen each other since her move, we've enjoyed the on-again aspects of our "friendship" but she has also tried to be more public about it. She'll ask to meet for drinks or dinner. Or she'll be waiting for me in the lobby of the office.

The last time she was in town, five months ago, she clung to my arm as we left dinner and when our picture was taken as she moved to get into the car she stopped, turned, and spelled her name for them. I asked her why she did that and she slid her hand up my thigh and said, "they should know who I am, don't you think?"

It was at that moment I realized she expected me to propose to her. I spent the night considering it. Playing out a life with Allegra Sinclair as my wife. Even when I went back to her hotel room and we slid into bed together I pictured doing that with her every night for the rest of my life.

Sex with her that night felt like a death march. Like I was going through the motions. Like I was obligated to fuck her.

The next morning I signed up for SMS Connect.

And after that exchange with TalkShopGirl last night I have no regrets about it at all.

Except maybe that I pictured Maggie.

And, I hope for etiquette's sake, I can keep her particular shade of blue eyes from my mind when I meet Allegra tonight.

***

"The designing is going really well. I've got a runway show set up for London which is exciting and it's all hands on deck to get that going now."

"That's great Al."

She curls her shoulders in, which does make her chest smoosh together as she slowly stirs her martini. Allegra is beautiful, all American, charming. All her charm is pointed at me but it's ineffective. I think it's because she isn't Maggie Collins. I bite back a laugh because I cannot imagine Maggie ever acting this way. Blatantly hitting on me. No, her personal brand of flirting is to tell me I'm dumb.

That's fine, I'm hot for teacher.

"So, are you taking me back to your place?" She asks as she drags a manicured red nail across the back of my hand.

"Ah, no, Elle is there."

"Why is your half-sister living with you?" Allegra scrunches up her nose in disgust and pulls her hand back.

"Because she's my sister." I reply gruffly and then I signal the waitress for our check. I don't need to be here any longer. And I don't need to defend my decisions to support family or Elle's life choices.

Allegra reaches across the table again and skates her long nails up my hand. A shiver starts to rock me. I try to suppress it because I do not want any bodily responses associated with Allegra anymore.

"Maybe you can come back to mine then?"

"I'm sorry, Allegra, I've got an early morning so I'm going to head back."

She sits up straight and scoffs.

"Seriously Austin? Why did I even come here tonight? You've barely made conversation, you're not excited about my business," she pauses and her eyes widen. "Is that because you don't want your wife to work?"

"What?" I cough out with a laugh.

"I asked if you're being dismissive of my clothing line because you don't want to marry a woman with a job. You want a little housewife. A country club darling to just sit and drink long island iced teas in tennis whites while gossiping about all the other little wifeys they're friends with."

"You paint a pretty clear picture there Allegra but no, I'm not thinking that."

"Sure you're not," she replies indignantly.

"Allegra, I can assure you, I was not thinking about marrying you. When I do get married I want a partner, a teammate, someone who is interested in me, not just my last name." I stand and watch her face turn to surprise at my outburst. I button my suit jacket and lean in. "And she will be the one to decide if she continues to work or not."

I puff up my chest and walk away. It feels like TalkShopGirl would be proud of me for walking away and not engaging further. I slip the hostess my card and tell her to call Elizabeth to pay the bill and then I push myself out the door to the slightly chilly night air.

As I climb into the car my mind switches gears to Maggie. My body comes alive as I'm thinking about her lips. Then I picture her eyes and remember her impassioned speech that compelled me to get down on my knees in front of her. The way she got fired up about women running businesses got me harder than any foreplay has before. Maybe it's the work adversaries dynamic but she calls me on my shit and makes me think. No woman has done that before. My palms itch to press into her soft curves. Instead I pick up my phone.

> We didn't establish this but is our arrangement exclusive?

Not that I'm considering sleeping with anyone else. Actually, I'm more concerned she might be. Senator Quinn's team is traveling tomorrow, does she have someone to help relieve her stress on the road?

> It absolutely is Austin. I'm not okay being one of many.

What a cute, and quick, response. I smirk as I reply.

> I love when you get jealous.

> Shut up.

> Don't worry MC, my physical therapy services are all yours.

> I'm like a ginormous Theragun that also brings treats.

I laugh as I picture Maggie's eye roll. She's too easy to rile up.

The shock in her voice when she asked why I brought coffee was worth the stop. I don't know exactly what prompted me to bring coffee and flowers but it was probably Mom's insistence that you never show up empty handed.

And I've had to show up to a lot of places over the years. It started when I was a star swimmer in high school and Dad realized having me at his side at parties humanized him. People saw him as a doting father when I can count on one hand the number of meets he came to. Mom and I started being his plus ones at backyard BBQs or informal lunches. Then in college he invited me to cocktail parties and business lunches. I realize now what I didn't at the time, he was grooming me to be just like him.

By the time I graduated I could walk into a room of his colleagues and be recognized.

That's one downside to being a Thorne. There are many, but the one that bothers me the most is that people only seem to want me for my last name. They only want to know me to get closer to Dad. A lot of women only want the attention that comes with being seen with me. That dynamic becomes abundantly clear when I would rather stay home from a party and they say "well I'm going and it'll look bad if you're not with me".

It's in those moments that I get dressed, go to the event because I'm polite, get pictured with her on my arm, and then within a few days make sure Elizabeth has arranged for all of the little things girls leave around my apartment to be packed and left in the lobby.

It was fortuitous that I saw an ad for SMS Connect the morning after Allegra brought up the prospect of marriage. I remember feeling relief that finally I'd have the chance to meet someone who was interested in everything besides my face and last name.

As I let myself into my apartment I see that the lights are off which means Elle is either not home or already in bed. I make my way to my room and after changing into my Ron Dorff sweats, I pull out my SMS Connect phone.

With an arm propped up behind my head I start to scroll through the messages TalkShopGirl and I have exchanged.

Arousal spikes as last night's notes dance across the screen.

But I keep going back into our history, all there in front of me. I find myself laughing quietly when she's describing how she has a love-hate relationship with dairy.

How she describes her family as "so small town they don't even know it" because they've never seen any other way. How she immediately wrote another message telling me she felt bad for saying that, and she really loves her mom and dad, and her sister is a lot younger, and ended up at home for good reasons while her brother doesn't even live around there anymore so he doesn't really count.

I shared frustrations about my family too. I talked about Brinkley who I'm realizing has taken quite a liking to Elle and hasn't been hanging around me as much lately.

I scroll back to the most recent message and take the phone in both hands to start writing my next.

DCFox: Hey TalkShopGirl, I've been thinking of you all day. Not just because last night was, in a word, hot, but because you've become a moral compass to me.

Do you ever become the worst version of yourself? The one that you hate but feel like it's such an ingrained part of you that you'll always be that way a little bit.

I got annoyed with someone tonight and I lashed out. It wasn't their fault what they said hit at the most insecure parts of me. But in the moment, I couldn't control that the hurt part of me was who responded. I hope I wasn't too harsh with this person but I'm also so frustrated by their lack of understanding.

As I walked away I felt proud of myself for not going further. For getting myself out of that dynamic. And I wanted you to be proud of me too.

I'm lying here realizing that you don't know me but you might know me better than anyone else.

Chapter Fourteen
MAGGIE

Flirting on All Fronts

"I'M LYING HERE REALIZING that you don't know me but you might know me better than anyone else."

I reread the last line of DCFox's message out loud. It expresses exactly how I feel about him. After our sexting session, which I was primed for after Austin's visit, I woke up scared that everything would change between us. I wasn't sure if he'd go back to sharing the little things about his day or emotional things with me. I can get orgasms from Austin, he's not where I turn for emotional support. That's DCFox's job. It felt too good to be true that DCFox could be both. Turns out the day I spent nervous that we'd ruined things was for nothing.

TalkShopGirl: I completely understand what you mean. I feel like sometimes I act as a version of myself I don't like just because I think that's what the other person expects from me.

I become quiet or I swear more often depending on who I am with. When, in reality, I'm a loud person who doesn't like to curse.

Well, maybe that's not exactly true because a well placed cuss word can have a profound impact, but there are definitely people who bring it out in me.

I hate feeling so malleable. So flexible. I do have convictions and strong values and sometimes it's too easy to set them aside if they're not the same as the person I'm with.

And, I couldn't agree more about being strangers but knowing each other deeply. I have a feeling that you are beginning to know me better than I know myself.

I slide the phone back into my nightstand and stretch my arms overhead. Today we are traveling with Senator Quinn. She has seven events in three different states and when I was leaving the office yesterday I heard Jorge confirming something back in D.C. at 7:00 pm. Travel days stress me out but I've learned to try and stick to as much of my routine as I can to help me manage the disruption. That means I start my day with a run but instead of going to the office at 9, I'm headed to the airport.

My feet hit the pavement on beat with the music in my headphones. I get lost in the lyrics and the feel of my steps ricocheting through my body. My mind hasn't been this clear in months. I feel energized. Maybe my multiple orgasms in 72 hours is the magic sauce.

At a stoplight I pull out my phone to text him. The texts last night surprised me. I didn't think he'd care about being exclusive but I'm glad it's been established. He probably texted me to ask because he got propositioned by some beautiful woman last night. I felt his arousal in the kitchen before he left. And then greedily I brought myself to the edge with DCFox's words before falling over into bliss. Maybe Austin is suffering from some serious blue balls. The idea makes me happy on a feminist level but also sad for him on a personal one.

> I'm finding it's harder to start my day today. You?

Things are plenty hard over here.

I bite my smile when his response comes in immediately. Almost like he had my text thread open at the time.

These ripples of excitement are totally new and when the light changes and I start to run again, I realize that the arrangement with Austin is something new. Something I've never done before. It is a change in my routine and maybe the novelty is energizing me as much as anything.

***

"You're smiling a lot today," Sam says as we sit down for lunch. "And, you're never happy on travel days."

I simply shrug in response.

"And, it's been a day where we were in the air as long as we were on the ground. The worst kind of travel day, where if we didn't have Jorge telling us when exactly to get on the bus we'd surely have missed one of these flights."

"I guess I'm getting used to it." I say although that's a lie. I'm feeling good because I had sex with Austin Thorne and then was able to walk away with no strings attached. It's the ideal set up.

"Wait," Sam pivots towards me in her seat. "Did you do the dirty again?"

I cough on a piece of kale.

"Wow, nice job." Sam turns back to her sandwich and nods like she's impressed with me. "I honestly didn't expect you to take my advice seriously but I'm so glad you did. You're a new woman."

"Well, I don't know about that but some of the stress certainly has lifted."

Not having to worry about Austin's feelings or what his expectations are is freeing. For the first time I'm enjoying myself with a man and not worrying about the future or if he's as invested in the relationship as I am.

Eventually, the man at my side will need to be a teammate. Almost like a coworker. So it might be best if we're not madly in love.

Love can lead to mistakes. It's a distraction. And I'm sensible enough to know that the partner I need might not come with passion. That's fine. I'll need someone attractive, at a minimum without visible nostril hair, since I'm learning how good sex is for my stress levels. And I think I do want kids someday. Although there are ways to have kids without the sex part. But I was able to get off just from DCFox's words so unless he has a 152mm goiter coming off of his neck I think we're good.

"Maggie, can we look at the remarks for the game tonight?" The senator calls from her cluster of seats a few rows behind Sam and me.

"Of course, be right there," I call over my shoulder and I busy myself putting my salad away. Once it's cleaned up I pick up my notebook and walk to her seat.

"You're actually not going to have to say anything during the puck drop, you're just shaking hands with the charity recipient, Alice, and the team captain. Felix, I believe is his name. His foundation provides housing for the family members of patients and your research legislation helped with the treatment for the cancer Alice just beat. You'll be interviewed during the first period by the TV announcers and that's where our remarks are going to come into play."

"Makes sense, what is it, a three minute interview?"

"That sounds about right," I reply as I flip around the various topics in my notebook. "This could be a good opportunity to talk about your healthcare work since you're next to a cancer survivor."

"Okay, let's ask AIM for something." The senator says casually like she isn't insulting my intelligence.

"We can have their team put something together," I say hesitantly. "You sure?"

"Of course I'm sure. And we can use the stump speech lines too, I know those by heart, but it could be good to have a fresh perspective."

"Okay, will do. Is there anything else?"

"No, I'll see you when we land."

With that I close my notebook and move back to the seat by Sam. Thankfully she's got her nose in a pile of briefing memos that I asked her to summarize. I give her a quick smile when she looks up to tell her that I'm good, but in reality I'm spiraling.

For the last six months I have been the person to write all of the senator's blurbs and talking points. Every time she was on TV or speaking in front of a crowd it was my words coming out of her mouth. Now? Now she wants to use AIM. I guess since we loaded her speeches into their database it will still be her words, my words, but it feels wrong.

Like we're cheating.

Any sense of relaxation or calm that I felt earlier was just erased. All it took was one sentence to remind me how Austin's product could put me out of a job.

I sit down and write my points for her on-air comments tonight and then send an email to Tyler on Austin's team with the prompt. I figured I'd add in that it is a hockey game since the demographics of the audience tend to be of the famed white male variety. Let's see what his computer comes up with.

****

"And that is why I fought so hard for this research legislation. Access to cures shouldn't rely on your connections or status, it is a right."

"Thank you Senator Quinn, well said." The announcer wraps up before going back to game analysis.

The senator walks off camera to the small group of us who came with her tonight. We're going up to the owners suite now to watch the rest of the game. I thought the senator would want to leave after her appearance but she told us in the car on the way over from the airport that after talking to the team owner, Tom O'Callahan, she wanted to stay for the whole game.

Jorge even secured her a DC Renegades jersey to wear.

"Did you see the puppies?" Sam asks as we start walking down the concourse.

"Puppies? No."

"Oh that's too bad, they were really cute. I guess they do an adoption night with a local shelter and they just got a litter of pit bull puppies. I might go back and adopt one," she looks longingly over her shoulder and steps sideways into me. "Oh sorry, yeah, do you need me? If not, I'm going to go check things out."

"You're just going to adopt a puppy on a whim? Isn't that a big decision?" I ask before she walks away.

"I'm just going to go and ask questions, I probably won't adopt one tonight."

I laugh and roll my eyes because that "probably" tells me that she will definitely be doing it if it's an option.

I catch up to the senator as we get in an elevator to the top level of the Kofee Center.

The suite is at center ice so I've got a view of the full arena. Fans line the stands and cheers erupt when a fight breaks out on the ice. I settle into a seat at the front of the box and Jorge brings over a plate of chicken fingers for us to share.

The first period ends scoreless, the second does too, but in the opening minutes of the third period the Northern Knights score and the arena goes quiet.

Somehow 20,000 DC Renegades fans all agreed to be nervous at the same time. It's a political writer's dream to get a crowd all on the same page that way. To be able to rile them up and calm them down and energize them behind a common cause.

And political campaigns are kind of like sporting events but there are fewer rules and the race takes too long.

The thought makes me yawn. It has been a long day. The energy burst from my run has definitely worn off over the course of seven campaign stops and now a late night sporting event.

"We're going to head down to the locker room at the end of the game. Tom says it's a must see." The senator wiggles her eyebrows and I roll my eyes with a smile.

Halfway through the third period the Renegades get a power play and they score just before it expires. A few minutes later, Felix Fournier somehow loops the puck from behind the net over the goalie's shoulder to put them ahead. The entire arena is on their feet for the final three minutes.

They're quiet but the tone is optimistic this time. I don't know how I can tell the difference but I can.

Time runs out and the Renegades bring home the win. We gather up our things in the suite and head down the elevator to the basement of the arena. Upstairs, the suite and the hallways were carpeted and filled with artwork and photographs of the achievements of the teams over the years.

Down here the walls are made of cinderblock and the floors are concrete. There are golf carts driving back and forth with employees wearing matching polos saying things into walkie talkies.

I've been backstage at speeches and conferences before but something about the cold simplicity of the space strikes me as odd when these guys were just under flashing lights and skating to the sounds of thousands of people cheering for an hour.

We're directed to an area that is between the locker room and the player's parking lot. The senator and Jorge go but I opt to stay in the hallway. I don't really want to see half naked athletes right now, I'm too tired to fully appreciate the splendor.

"Are you following me, Collins?"

I snap my head up at the sound of Austin Thorne's voice. He's standing in front of me wearing jeans and a cream crewneck sweater under a blue wool blazer. He's got a DC Renegades scarf wrapped around his neck. I drink him in and get caught on the way his burnt wood eyes twinkle behind his dark frame glasses.

Goosebumps explode on my arms with him this close as I'm remembering the way he slid his glasses off and set them on the table before we fucked. Or how he removed them before going down on me in epic fashion. Mentally I'm begging him to slide them off again now. Or, even better, I'll take them off for him.

"What are you doing here?" I ask because I cannot think of anything else to say. He is the last person I expected to see. He laughs and the sound vibrates through me.

"I'm waiting for my buddy. He and I are going out to celebrate the win."

"He's on the team?"

Again Austin laughs and it's a breathy sound that makes the backs of my knees tingle.

"He is, he's the captain."

"Felix? The senator was here for the puck drop."

"I know, I saw."

"Oh."

We're quiet for a beat before he shifts to one side and leans his elbow against the wall. One foot kicks up over the other and it is such an outrageously planned but casual pose that even my stiff limbs react. The air around us changes and I feel a buzz of energy. A spark of competition lights again because how dare he try to use the prop-one-arm-above-my-head move?

I mimic him and cross my arms and throw a shoulder into the wall. Except I'm a little too far away and I have to readjust my footing after a harder landing than I'd planned.

"Did that hurt?" He asks.

"No," I reply even though, yeah it did a little bit.

He just smiles knowingly and asks, "How was the rest of your day after the *hard* start?"

"Fine," I reply quickly.

"And what do you have to say about the senator using our language for her interview?"

My jaw tightens so hard I'm afraid my molars might crack.

"I appreciate that she had the option." *But I didn't need the reminder, thank you very much,* is what I don't say.

"Of course, choice is everything."

"It is."

"So can I choose to set up our next sex date?" He asks as he leans his head down a little closer to me.

"Yes, but I'll need a heads up."

"Oh, the head's up Maggie," and his eyes flick down to his pants where things do look a little fuller. I realize that with my arms crossed I've pushed my boobs together and even though I'm seething with anger around Austin I think I might be smiling a little bit too.

"You're obnoxious." I say as I stand up and look over my shoulder to see the senator walking with a player.

Before I can step away Austin places his fingertips, splayed wide, on my stomach and I freeze at the contact.

"I'll be at your place in the morning."

I sneak one last look at Austin before we turn the corner for the car and trip over my own feet when I catch him looking at me.

Chapter Fifteen
AUSTIN
Shifting Focus

TalkShopGirl: It's brave of you to admit that you don't like doing the dishes. I can't say I blame you but tidying up after myself has been engrained since childhood.

Doing dishes for just one person does get annoying. I'll give you that. When I'm cooking or meal prepping I challenge myself to use the least number of utensils, bowls, pots, pans, or measuring cups as I can. It's a little game. It was an exciting day when I found a set of measuring cups that have smaller measurements marked on the inside. So the 1 cup has ¾, ½, and ¼ lines too.

It is a victory to only use that measuring cup for multiple ingredients as I prep my meals.

I laugh as I finish reading TalkShopGirl's message. I bet she packs efficiently for the TSA screening process too. If we do meet in person and hit it off she'll have to get used to flying private.

The idea of flying around the world with TalkShopGirl is a distracting one and I've got Maggie Collins to focus on this morning. After I brush my teeth and splash my face with cold water I get dressed and head out the door.

It doesn't take me long to get to her apartment. We're not in the exact same neighborhood but D.C. is small once you get to know it.

I lean my skateboard against the wall outside of Maggie's apartment. This is the way to go. I didn't realize how awkward it would be to climb into the backseat and have Greg know exactly what I was up to. He's seen me through a lot over the years but nothing quite like this.

My ride over was necessary this morning. Since I ran into Maggie last night I've been half hard and the exercise got blood flowing everywhere else. Fuck, I wanted to push her up against the wall last night. Put my hands on her curves. I felt her electricity when I touched her stomach to stop her from running away. Felix caught it, and then he caught me staring at her as she left, and I had to dodge questions all night long about who she was.

I run one hand through my hair and then raise it to knock on her door, but I pause because I can hear her talking.

"Sam, I don't know what you want to hear! I took a page out of your playbook and got a fuck buddy." She pauses. "That's besides the point. He's hot and the things he did with his mouth the other day still send tremors through me."

I puff my chest up a bit.

"You asked!"

With a smile I rap my knuckle on the door.

"Shit, he's here, okay, bye."

I school my features as I hear her walk up to the door.

"You think I'm hot," I answer as she opens it and I can't help the laugh that escapes me. She tries to be so unattached. So in control but I can see how affected she is by me.

"You were listening to my conversation?" She accuses, as she steps aside for me to come in.

"Well, considering all I had to do was stand at your door to hear every-thing it was difficult not to."

I step further into her apartment and my smile widens. The space is just so *her*. From the soft rose color on the wall behind her post-it note cluttered white board, to the furniture. I can see her picking out the perfect color to paint everything. The overstuffed but worn-in big chair by the window. One corner has a divot in the cushion that tells me it's where she settles in to work or read or watch...wait.

"You don't have a TV," I state with surprise as I turn and double check I didn't miss it. She's standing in front of the door with her hands tucked behind her holding onto the knob. My eyes drink in her just-from-bed appearance; her black tank, black sleep shorts, white collared shirt unbuttoned over both, the gentle flush to her cheeks, her golden hair piled high on her head.

"Ah, no, I watch things on my laptop sometimes but usually I read at night."

I'm about to ask what she's reading but she points accusingly at the coffees and pastry bag I'm holding in one hand. "What the fuck is that?"

"Coffee and pastries." I reply slowly as I take another look at them just to make sure that they haven't morphed into something else.

"This is such a bad idea," she mutters as she steps past me. I notice that she has a pair of sneakers lined up by the door so I step back and toe my shoes off next to hers.

"So bad that it might be good," I say as I walk past her and set the coffee down on the table in front of her chair.

She huffs as she sits down in the divoted spot that I noticed before but she reaches forward and pops the lid off one of the coffees and blows on it before taking a sip. "Why did you bring breakfast, again?"

"Why are you drinking the coffee?" I challenge and instead of admitting that she got called out she narrows her eyes at me over the rim of the cardboard and takes another sip.

Those blue eyes, even when they're shooting daggers at me, are like jumping into the pool on a hot day. The cold is a shock but there is relief, joy, and anticipation.

So I dive.

In one motion I move her coffee down to the table and gently push her back against her chair. She inhales like she's going to try and say something but I don't give her the chance.

The second my lips touch hers, blood rushes like white water rapids to every last inch of my body. I feel alive. This arrangement is an incredibly bad idea, I'm already in too deep, frantically treading water trying to stay afloat. But I want more.

When Maggie pulls back quickly and breaks the kiss I panic at the sudden loss of our connection. She shimmies out of the button up and pulls her tank top off over her head and I immediately grasp her breasts and bring them to my mouth. Her head falls back and she digs her nails into my scalp, sending shivers down my spine.

"Austin," she breathes as I roll her nipple with my tongue. My hand slides down her side, over her hip, down the outside of her thigh, mapping and memorizing every spot. I pull her knee up and hook it behind my hip because I need as much of me touching as much of her as possible. My knees almost buckle when she reaches between us and cups me.

I break the kiss this time and yank my shirt off. Her hands cover my chest quickly.

"You're so fucking hot," she says against my lips.

"You're so pretty it hurts," I tell her as I kiss down the length of her neck and nip at her collarbone. She tastes bitter and sweet, like iced tea.

She pushes on my chest until I fall back against the other arm of the chair then she stands in front of me. I watch as she reaches forward and pulls my glasses off, folds them and sets them on the table. I reach forward to peel her shorts off and find her bare underneath.

"Do you sleep without panties?" I ask as she steps out of her satin shorts.

"I rarely wear underwear at all," she says and my mouth goes dry. "Gives me a competitive edge."

"I'm the one on edge, MC," I smirk as I lean back and open my fly before pulling my jeans down my legs.

"Every word that comes out of your mouth irritates me," Maggie growls as she helps to pull my pants off my feet. She's almost kneeling before me and I am rock hard. I exhale in a hiss when she leans forward and licks me from base to tip. "Seems like I know how to shut you up though," she grins.

"Careful, I'm getting some ideas about your smart mouth."

The fire that flashes through her eyes tells me that she'd be up for it but I'm craving her so as she straddles my lap, I run my fingers against her pussy and they come away slick. She watches as I pass my fingers over my lips.

She's sitting on my thighs and stroking me in a distracted way, almost like she isn't aware she's doing it. I lean forward and kiss her deeply as I wrap my fingers around the back of her neck and thread them into her hair. The kiss awakens her and she begins to wage war against my tongue.

We're each trying to keep up with the other while also battling to be in control. I decide to settle back and let her run the show for a minute but I keep my hands on her. They run up her thighs, around her waist, to her breasts and shoulders and along every sweet inch of skin I can reach. She lets out these delicious little moans and sighs as I caress her and her grip on me falters when I slide my fingers along her folds again.

I press against her clit and immediately she tightens her grip on me. I circle and she strokes then her body goes stiff. She jerks and I feel more fluid slide along my fingers.

"Did you just come?" I ask her as I nibble along her neck.

"Yes, I couldn't help it," she says, like she's disappointed.

I pull back and connect with her shockingly blue eyes. "Let's get one thing straight, MC, don't hold back with me. Got it?" She nods. "Now, let's have some fun and get you another one."

She grins before she can stop herself. Her crystal eyes sparkle as she pulls the smile back in between her teeth.

I'm not prepared for the shock her smile gives my heart. It hurt in a good way. I want to see it again so I use my thumb to free it.

When her smile flashes I use the surge of energy it gives me to flip her onto her back before planting myself between her legs.

"Austin," she whimpers as I rub my self through her folds. Instead of dipping in I pull back. "Where are you going?"

"I'm having breakfast," I respond and I kiss my way down her stomach as it bottoms out and start with one agonizingly slow lick up her pussy.

"Oh fuck," Maggie hisses and she throws her head back. As I continue to lick, her legs start to tighten around me so I push them up towards her chest.

"Hold those," I instruct and her eyes widen.

"Austin, we don't have time for all this."

"You have something more important to do this morning than get the best head of your life?" I ask with my arms propped on the top of her shins. My dick is seeking out her heat and he twitches between us. When she doesn't respond I continue, "I didn't think so but I can get your phone so you can cancel your meetings."

I stand and make my way to where I see her phone on her bedside table. Maggie jumps up and puts her beautiful naked body between me and the nightstand.

"No, that's fine, it's no problem, I don't have a meeting early this morning."

"What's in the drawer?" I ask as I see her hands slowly push it closed behind her ass.

"Nothing."

"You and I both know that's not true, but I'm going to let it slide because arguing with you is not what I want to be doing while you are standing in front of me naked."

She raises an eyebrow and tries to push me down on the bed but I catch her wrists and walk her backwards to the chair. When her legs hit the edge of the seat I gently push her down and then I hook her knees back up to her chest.

"Hold still," I instruct as I get down on my knees in front of this force of a woman.

"I like bringing you to your knees," she says in a breathy voice as I begin to eat her out again.

She has no idea.

I nip at her sensitive flesh, teasing her and I find it difficult to breathe through the head rush that her groan unleashes.

"Austinnnnnnn," she whines my name and I respond by slipping two fingers inside her. She gasps and whips her head to look at me. When our eyes connect, I pump and her head falls back.

"Oh fuck, yes," she whispers as my fingers plunge in and out of her heated core. When I slide in a third a breathy "yes" falls from her lips. Her first orgasm was so quiet, so delicate, like she wasn't sure it was happening. This one, the one I feel closing in on my hand, is all consuming.

I can't believe this is only the third time we've been together. It feels like Maggie Collins has been a part of my life much longer. Like we have a connection that is stronger than incredible sex.

I reach up to pinch one of her hard nipples and then it hits. Her orgasm rushes through her. She whines, almost pouts, as her inner walls crash down on my fingers and I lap gently around her swollen bundle of nerves at her peak. I slowly kiss up her thighs and plant one on her stomach.

"Oh god, I've-" her breaths are shallow as she regroups, "I hate how good that was."

"I can imagine your inner turmoil," I say as I step back and pull a condom out of my jeans pockets. "Ah, ah," I scold as she starts to lower her legs, "I didn't tell you to stop holding those."

The look on her face reads disdain but she pulls her knees up into her chest again.

"Good girl," I tease and I watch her eyes narrow. "Now," I place my thumb on her clit as I grip my base, "hold tight."

In one thrust I sheath myself in her to the hilt. She gasps and grips her knees tighter but her insides stretch around me.

I'm so hard this isn't going to last long but I want her to have a third so I start to strum her clit as I slowly roll my hips into her.

"Shit, Austin," she says but I can see on her face that even she doesn't know how to be upset because her mind is too clouded with pleasure.

My name on her lips has a dizzying effect.

"Keep saying my name Maggie," I tell her as I slowly pull out and thrust back in. Her whole body rocks with the movement and if her chair wasn't up against the wall I'm sure we'd have moved it across the room already.

"Why? Your ego needs to be stroked that badly?"

I pull out and thrust in again, hard. "No. I need you to hear yourself say my name when I fuck you better than anyone else ever has."

And she takes it better than any other woman I've been with but she doesn't need to know that.

"Now I'm going to not say it, you know that right?"

"I'd like to see you try," I whisper in her ear as I slide my hand off her clit and palm her ass. I've trapped her in on the other side with my hand against the back of the chair and so when I slap the skin under my hand and she loses her grip on her knee my body catches it.

"Austin!" She scolds as her insides clamp down on me.

"Do it again?" I ask as I rub her ass to soothe the sting.

"Yes," she whispers with her eyes closed.

"Look at me," I command. And as our eyes connect I lay another smack across her flesh and then hold my hand against her ass as I pump furiously in and out. Her tits are jumping beneath her knees and I begin to lose feeling everywhere except my dick. With one last slap to her ass and a pump from me, her insides flutter and roll to pull every last bit out of me. I press myself forward and rock into her a few more times as my breath shudders with my release. "Fuck, Maggie. Yes."

The urge to collapse down on her and then spend the next hour cuddling her to my chest comes out of nowhere. I'm hooked on Maggie Collins. My body is addicted to hers.

Slowly I pull out and we untangle ourselves. I help her sit up and she lowers her feet to the floor before I grab my glasses and step into the bathroom to clean up.

After I wash my hands, I look up at myself in the mirror and see a man who is well and truly fucked.

Physically, obviously, that was the best sex I've ever had.

But emotionally too. Maggie Collins makes me feel things. Our emotional connection isn't as established as what I share with TalkShopGirl but could it get there? It doesn't matter. Maggie hates me, and tells me so every day.

When I walk out into her studio apartment I find Maggie has slipped into the white dress shirt again and she's folded my clothes on the coffee table.

"So, umm, hi," she starts as I reach forward and climb into my boxer briefs.

"Hi, Maggie," I give her a side smile.

"This is going to sound weird," she starts, "and I probably shouldn't say this but maybe I've been dickmatized or something. Anyway, that was my first orgasm on my back."

I stop getting dressed with only one leg in my jeans.

"I'm sorry, come again."

She huffs out a breath, "I've never gotten an orgasm on my back. Only when I've been on top or on my stomach."

"What did you think?"

She looks at me with curiosity in her eyes. Did she expect me to make fun of her for that? Did she want me to berate any past men she's been with? Because, actually, the idea that there have been other men who haven't satisfied her brings a rage to the surface I'm not sure I can control.

I can see the internal war she's waging over this conversation. I focus on keeping myself settled because the way she's biting her lip is stirring the desire in me.

"It was intense," she finally admits. "I felt like I was falling."

My jeans are on all the way now so I step forward and run my hands up her arms. I grip her shoulders and hold her there in front of me. I've never seen her so vulnerable. I knew there were greater depths to her but this is the first time she's exposed them to me. Granted, I've only known her a week but look at all the ground we've covered so far.

"I've got you," is what comes out when the words finally reach my lips. That desire to cuddle her returns as I watch her feelings unfold across her face. Her honey blonde hair falls around her shoulders, as her sapphire eyes search mine. She might be looking for derision from me, since we've established this relationship on teasing, but all I see is bravery and strength.

When her eyes soften to show gratitude, my mind trips over the idea that maybe she doesn't hate me as much as I thought.

I pull her against my chest and wrap her in my arms. My nose lands in the soft waves of her hair and I inhale the floral scent. She doesn't respond right away but when she wraps her arms around my ribs I feel warmth travel through my body. After an indulgent beat, I squeeze her a little tighter, leave a delicate kiss in the crook of her neck, and then release her. Quickly I step over to my shirt, afraid of what I will see in her eyes if I go looking for it.

Afraid of what I might not see but want to.

"Have a good day Maggie," I manage as I get to the door and grab my skateboard.

"Um, yeah, you too Austin," she says as she crosses over to the door. She watches me walk down the hallway and I catch her still looking at me as the elevator door closes between us.

I might as well admit it to myself. I don't want Maggie Collins to hate me at all.

***

"You got here *early*?" Felix calls to me from the floor as I reach the angled section of the wall. My grip slips because he distracted me. Truthfully, I've been distracted all morning, but let's blame him.

"Fuck," I hiss as the harness catches me and I belay myself down to the floor.

"Hello to you, too," he mutters as he clips in next to me. Felix Fournier and I met at a charity event a few years ago. He had just moved to D.C. and the Renegades owner introduced us, telling Felix that I could help him navigate the world of D.C. as a wealthy young man. I shared a few of my favorite spots. When I told him that I rock climb for exercise he asked only one question.

"How hard does it hurt your balls?"

When I laughed and said that it didn't hurt any more than riding a bike he clapped his hands and said "I'm gonna be fit as fuck next season."

We've been coming to First Ascent twice a week for five years now. When he went back to training camp that first August his trainer asked him what he did in the off season to stay so well conditioned and when he said rock climbing the trainer recommended it to the whole team.

So now, instead of seeing just one professional hockey player here I usually see three or four. I've also noticed an uptick in really pretty women around the gym.

"Seriously though, why are you here so early?"

"I had an early start to the day," I say but I have to turn my head away so he doesn't catch the smirk or the fucking twinkle in my eyes that I can feel when I think about Maggie from this morning.

"Usually that makes you more grumpy, unless," he stretches the word out as he walks closer to me. I have to meet his gaze head on or he'll definitely know something is up. He leans in and narrows his eyes and inspects my face before stepping back slightly and glancing down my body. "You fucked."

"What?" I try to laugh it off. Maggie doesn't want anyone knowing about our arrangement and I've come to respect her in a way that makes me want to do dirty, dirty things to her.

"Ha! For sure you fucked," Felix says loudly, I quickly scan the gym for anyone who might have heard. "Wait, did you get with someone here?"

"No," I laugh again but then stop abruptly because the idea of being with anyone but Maggie sent a shiver of distaste through me.

"What was that?"

"What?"

"That shiver." Felix points at me.

"I just, umm, it's cold in here, right?" I ask as I also pull on my collar to release some of the heat.

"Holy shit. You actually like a girl. I've never seen you so flustered over a hookup before."

Instead of answering him I step around him and line up to start my climb again. "Stop gossiping and get to work," I grumble.

He laughs as he steps up to the track beside me. "I didn't know you were seeing someone."

"I'm not."

"But, you fucked."

"I never said that." I say as I reach for a grip but miss and end up swinging around with only my left hand and foot on the wall.

Felix's eyes go wide in shock, "And you've never missed a grip before so c'mon man, spill the tea!"

"Spill the tea?"

"It means gossip."

"I know that, I just didn't expect you to use the phrase."

"I've been trying to add to my vocabulary," he states. "I've got a word of the day calendar."

"And *spill the tea* is part of your education?"

"No, but at least I'm trying to expand my thinking."

"I invented a freaking AI news service." I say indignantly as I reach for the grip again and get it. Fuck yeah.

"Right, but you did it to prove your dad wrong."

"Well, I'm motivated by competition," I grunt as I make another stretch for a grip and get it. I'm hitting my stride as I start to feel more agitated with Felix Fournier and his questions.

"Is that why you're racing to pull a muscle?"

"Fuck off man."

"No thank you, but I will talk about who you fucked last night."

"This morning," I mumble under my breath before regretting it.

"THIS MORNING!?" Felix yells and again I look around the gym for anyone who notices. A few heads turned.

"Will you shut up!" I hiss as I move sideways closer to him. "Okay, fine, you're right, I hooked up with someone; this morning."

"Who?"

"Can't say."

"You don't know her name? Morning sex is intimate and you did it with some rando?"

"No, I can't *tell* you her name." She certainly knows mine though. I feel my palms start to sweat when I remember how she said my name. Many, many, times this morning, over the course of her three orgasms.

"Is it a secret?"

"Yeah, she doesn't want people knowing we're together. Well, not together really, it's like a sex arrangement."

"Fuck buddies, I get it." Felix nods as we move up the wall next to each other.

"Minus the buddies part, she's been very clear that we're not friends." Although her confession before I left seems like something she'd only tell me if she had put trust in me. Maybe she's starting to see me as a friend.

"But you want to be more than friends? Err, wait, no, you want to add friendship to the fucking? That's like backwards from how it usually goes isn't it?"

I shrug as best I can with my hands holding me to a wall 20 feet in the air. "Maybe, I haven't thought about it much."

"Except constantly."

I laugh, "well yeah, the sex is really good."

"So are you going to try and become her friend and turn it into a relationship?"

"I dunno," I admit as I move a little more quickly up the wall. I haven't told Felix that I signed up for SMS Connect. Both of us have commiserated over girls wanting to be with us because of our status or position instead of for who we are.

"Actually, I do know," I tell him once he catches up and we're only a few more paces from the top. "I don't think I'll do anything more than sex with Ma–, her," shit I almost said her name. "A few months ago I signed up for that SMS Connect service."

"Oh really?" Felix confirms. "And how's that going?"

"Well, you can't tell anyone I'm on it, I wasn't even supposed to tell you, but the girl I'm talking with is great. I actually like texting with her."

"Have you met her?"

"Not yet. Next week is the earliest we could meet."

The twelve weeks messaging with TalkShopGirl have flown by. It feels like we've been talking forever, like she's always been a part of my life. Even though she's not really a part of it at all.

She's in my head, that's probably the best way to describe it. When I'm alone, or on the way to the office, I find myself wondering who she is and what she's doing at that moment.

Except when I'm with, or thinking about, Maggie Collins. When she and I are in the room together at work, or better yet at her apartment, all I can think about is her. This is all a little confusing; two girls, two different scenarios but both leave me feeling satisfied and seen.

Chapter Sixteen
MAGGIE
Small Venn Diagram

THE DEBATE IS IN an hour and I've sweat through my body suit. Needless to say, I'm nervous. This is the senator's first national debate since the primaries at the beginning of the year and it is the very first time we're relying on AI Media.

I hate to admit that the practice questions we went through last week went well. The AI Media content sounded like the senator's voice and was tailored to the audience. We're on a college campus and while the audience will mostly be filled with pundits and wannabe politicians, we insisted on at least 25% of the audience being students.

The senator does well with younger voters.

She's the younger candidate, the cooler one. She's energized a new set of voters who were disengaged in prior elections. But the race is still tight in the battleground states. When I remember how high the stakes are my eye twitches.

Austin and I haven't had sex since last week. I blame myself. I haven't asked for it. But after I complimented his sexual abilities, I couldn't seem to get myself to text. The man gave me not one, but two orgasms with me on my back, and my brain has been foggy ever since.

Then when he walked into the office two days later he looked so freaking good that I could hardly handle it. I avoided eye contact or responding to him directly. I passed questions or comments off to Sam and she definitely noticed something was up but hasn't said a word.

I can tell that's about to change.

"So, last week it was clear that you were getting your needs met and that it was helping you chill out. Now?" She points at the line of boob sweat that is only growing with her attention on it, "Why aren't you using your stress reduction methods?"

I shove her hand to the side and reach for my blazer. The idea of putting more clothes on my sweating body makes me nauseous but it'll help to cover up the sweat stains. "I haven't had the time."

"Well make the time because you're making *me* nervous and I live for live television."

I laugh because it's true. Sam was born to be in the spotlight. I probably should have her do the podcast and news show appearances from now on.

"Okay, we're ready for the senator," a production assistant with a headset says to me and I nod at Sam.

"Showtime!" Sam accentuates with jazz hands as she walks towards the classroom down the hall that is serving as a green room.

I take one last look at the printed notes the senator will use and then find myself pacing two steps in one direction and two steps back.

"Chill out! It looks like you're about to go on stage. You're green!" A production assistant tells me like we're friends. Not necessary right now, random person, but thanks. I force a smile wave her off but instead I freeze because behind her I see Austin and the nauseous feeling returns.

What is he doing here?

My body stiffens and a welcome chill runs through me.

"Maggie," he says in greeting as he comes up beside me. We're both looking out at the stage and the three inches between our shoulders is thick with tension.

Can he feel it too?

"Austin," I reply and it's a mix of disdain and relief and I don't like that I find his presence comforting.

He checks his watch and I focus on the many veins in his hand and the slight dusting of hair on his arm as he lifts his sleeve out of the way. "It's a little less than 12 hours but maybe we can agree to a travel addendum to the rules."

"What do you mean?"

"I mean, I want you to come to my room tonight."

"Oh," I whisper and icicles fall down my spine. "Um, okay."

"Everything should be wrapped up by 11:00." He says as he slides a key card into my hand. I wrap my fingers around it and hold tight. "Room 1201."

And with that he steps backwards and turns away from me. My breath leaves my lungs with force because the promise of a night with Austin has already settled my nerves. When the senator crosses past me to the stage she gives me a curt nod. Sam gives me a thumbs up and heads out of the auditorium. She's headed to watch the debate from the spin room at the hotel. I stay in the wings so we can regroup during commercial breaks.

We have a full team of people ready to respond to the media during and after the debate. I have spent the last three days prepping all of them and getting them to practice certain lines. We need them to be confident and strong.

They need to spin anything negative and reinforce everything positive.

My palms start sweating more as the importance of tonight hits me again and when my fingers slide against the keycard I'm gripping, I quickly push it into the pocket of my pants and turn to find a glass of water.

***

"And the senator's response to the prison reform question was another departure from her normal stance, care to elaborate?"

My pen taps out a furious pace against my notebook as I stand off to the side of this interview. Sam is doing great but the reporter has picked up on the face that some answers were different tonight. Sam and I know it was the AI Media written responses but we can't say that on the record.

The AIM team told us they would be factoring in real-time opinion data from a select set of voters but I did not expect it to alter her positions.

"While slightly different from what Senator Quinn has been saying on the campaign trail, I see her response tonight as an evolution. She's learned new information, had more conversations, and has decided to deepen her understanding of the issue."

"By calling for reduced sentences?"

"That is just part of a comprehensive plan aimed at addressing systemic issues for incarceration."

When Sam slices her hand through the air below the seat of the chair she's in with a "cut it off" motion I jump to action. I turn to the producer standing next to the camera man.

"She has time for one more question."

He checks his watch and gives me an inquisitive look. "I thought we had five minutes, it's only been three."

"Well since your reporter is trying to do everything to catch her out I think three minutes is plenty."

"Fine, one more question," he says begrudgingly before tapping the side of his headset to tell the anchor it's time to wrap up.

When the camera's light turns off, Sam unclips her microphone and shakes hands with the anchor.

"That went quickly!" She says cheerfully as she joins me. "It felt like only a few minutes."

"I cut it short after you motioned to me."

"Oh!" She laughs, "no, I meant for you to knock off your pen tapping, it was like standing next to a jackhammer."

"Oh," I bite my lip, "sorry."

"No worries, how's the senator doing?"

"Fine, she's going back to the hotel, I don't want her taking any questions."

"Good plan, any updates from the watch data or polls?"

"Not yet," I sigh and check the time on my phone. It's not even 8:00 pm local time. Since we're on the west coast the debate started early and I've got a lot of time to kill until meeting Austin in his room.

"Wanna grab some dinner? I'm starving." Sam says as she slings her bag over her shoulder.

"Sure, just in the hotel bar?"

"That works for me."

On our walk over to the bar Sam is buzzing with energy. She's chatting and hypothesizing about results and checking her phone for official data all at once. We get a seat at the bar and order drinks and a few appetizers to share.

"So," Sam starts as she swings her barstool around to survey the rest of the room. "Think we can find some ass tonight?"

I cough on my drink and bring the cocktail napkin up to my chin to catch the dribble. "I'm not looking for ass in the hotel bar."

She turns to me with big, cartoon princess eyes, "Why not? Haven't we covered the importance of stress relief at times like these?"

"We have. I just don't need to find it tonight."

"So you already have a source?"

"Can't say," I respond over a sip of my drink.

"Can't like he doesn't exist yet, or won't because you're trying to be smug about already scoring a hook up for tonight? If that's the case, I'm impressed with your forward planning with Austin back in D.C."

I shrug and swivel towards the bartender who is clearly listening to our conversation. I give him a full once over because I can appreciate the finer points of the male form but his wink does nothing for me.

Not when I know what Austin can do.

"Alright Maggie, who are you booty calling tonight?" Sam asks, drawing my attention back to her.

"I'm not going to tell you."

"Bet I can figure it out." Sam says smugly as she drops a handful of bar mix into her mouth. "You can't keep a straight face when lying so I'll know even if you deny it."

I just laugh at her, at myself, and fish out a sesame stick.

"The bartender?"

"No."

"That producer from the last interview? He was hot."

"No."

"Ooh, a tinder swipe that you booked as soon as we landed and your location updated?"

"No."

"Hmm, you're right, it wouldn't be a stranger. You're too careful about who you hook up with." I don't deny it so she keeps going. "It probably would be someone you know, but not someone you work with because that's a line you wouldn't cross."

She's watching me as she tries to suss this out so I just shrug in response.

"I'm getting closer." She drums her nails along the side of her glass. "Who is someone we know, that is out here for the debate, but not someone you work with?"

"That seems like a pretty small venn diagram of candidates." I mutter as I cut up the flatbread that was just set down in front of us.

"Holy shit, it's Austin Thorne."

"What?" I cough because I didn't know he was in Arizona until minutes before the debate, how would Sam know? In fact, she doesn't, she just told me he was back in D.C.. Austin wasn't in the spin room when we got there. He didn't stay backstage. In fact, if I didn't have his room key in my pocket I might think I imagined him being here. When I look up at Sam, she's staring off past my shoulder. I slowly turn around and see what she's mesmerized by.

Austin Thorne is waiting by the elevators in gray athletic shorts and a navy blue tee that is like a second skin so we can see his incredibly fit torso.

"Is that a yoga mat?" Sam asks.

"He does yoga." I tell her, matter of factly.

"Down dog," Sam says in a way that makes it sound sexual. I turn to her and we both giggle a little like freshman spying on the seniors.

That's what it feels like to be around Austin. He's so put together, so in control. He feels more mature than me sometimes. I pride myself on being both mature and in control but around him my own highly evolved sense of responsibility melts away. Maybe it's that he grew up in the spotlight. More and more I'm realizing I'll need to practice my public persona if I want to be successful.

"Told you I would guess it, you're going to do him," Sam says as we watch him step into the elevator. I envision him getting ready for me to visit in a few hours. My mind goes to him in the shower, wondering what it would be like to join him. I get a little uncomfortable thinking about the way my body seemed to settle when he was at my side earlier.

"Ha, yeah." I agree with a little laugh.

"Listen, I don't know the details of your agreement with each other but based on your big distressed energy earlier I think you should see what a million thread count sheets feel like with him on top of you." Sam pops the cherry from her drink into her mouth and chews it around a smile.

I blush, violently, as the mental image of just that invades my brain. All my senses. I'm sitting at the bar, I know that, but I can feel my skin warm as his touch travels across my body. I can smell his unique scent that energizes and soothes me. My blood turns to lava as icicles crash down my spine.

"I...ah...well," I try to laugh it off again and focus on the damp sections of my napkin.

"Oh Maggie, sweet, sweet, gentle, Maggie." Sam laughs as she pats the back of my hand.

"What?" I challenge.

"You're so gone for him."

"No I'm not!" I argue but we both know it's a weak stance.

"Okay, keep telling yourself that."

"Yes, alright, fine, he's hot. And the sex makes me question the laws of physics but it's just sex. Most of the time I can't stand being around him."

Except, I can. Every time we've taken the time to talk he has surprised me with how well he listens. And oddly, that thought brings my conversations with DCFox to mind.

For the first half of our correspondence I wondered if DCFox and I could have a relationship that is physically fulfilling. Now I have the texts to prove that it is. That it can be. And, sure, I'm not *technically* sleeping with another man, but would Austin consider my sexts with DCFox to be cheating.

Before I let that train of thought out of the station I remind myself that this is just sex. That's all it is between Austin and me. Sex. Really, really good sex. Like mind blowing sex. The kind of sex that gets you hot just thinking about it.

"You're thinking about it aren't you?" Sam asks and my attention snaps back to her.

"Thinking about what?"

"Sex with Austin Thorne."

***

It's several hours later and *sex with Austin Thorne* has indeed been on my mind. I got back up to my room at 10:30 and have been pacing the small space for twenty minutes.

Do I change clothes before going up there?

Will I be spending the night with him?

Should I shower?

I lift my arm and sniff my armpit, it's not great but it's not terrible.

I step into the bathroom. My makeup looks okay, a little less sharp than when I first applied it this morning but that was eighteen hours and three time zones ago.

I fill up a glass of water from the tap and chug down the lukewarm sink water. It's better than nothing I suppose. I pull my SMS Connect phone out of my toiletry case and turn to lean against the counter before I power it up.

DCFox usually writes to me at night. Since he's back in D.C. I bet there's a message waiting for me.

I drum my nails against the back of the phone while it turns on and only realize I was holding my breath when I inhale sharply at the empty inbox.

Weird.

Reading the notes from DCFox has been a comforting way to end my day these last couple of months. He seems to understand me in a way no one else does. I've been more vulnerable with him than I have been with anyone else.

Well, except for Austin.

Austin has a way of making me feel comfortable. Even if I'm annoyed with him it feels more like a game than actual hate.

Is it possible I've come to respect my fuck friend? That we could actually become friend friends?

I double check that his room key is in my pocket before slipping my own into my other pocket and heading up to his suite.

***

"You're late," Austin says as I let myself in. He's lounging on the bed in just a pair of slate blue pajama pants. My mouth goes impossibly dry as I take in his chiseled torso. Each muscle is taught and firm and begging for my touch. He leans forward to grab the remote and it's like every muscle I can see is pointed towards his waistband and I zero in on the bulge just below it and my mouth goes even drier.

"It's one after," I respond when I can unglue my tongue from the roof of my mouth. He turns off the TV and slides across the bed to sit on the edge facing me. The smile on his face is sinister and when he slowly crooks a finger for me to walk to him my own smile grows wide.

"One minute when I could have been doing this," he says as he pulls me down to kiss him. Our mouths open and I desperately inhale through my nose as the familiar taste of him floods my senses. My fingers thread through his thick hair and my nails scrape along his scalp. He groans as he unbuttons my pants and slides them over my ass.

They pool on the floor around my heels but when I reach down to pull one off his hand stops me.

"Those, stay on," he informs me as he adjusts the glasses on his face. "Turn around."

I turn slowly and he reaches up to pull down the shoulders of my body suit. Shivers explode in the wake of his fingers as they trail along my skin.

He's savoring it.

Savoring me.

While we might just be doing this for the stress relief he's attracted to me. And I like it.

Feeling desired gives me power.

Thank goodness the election is less than two weeks away because the more I think about being with Austin the more I want to be with Austin.

The more I find him charming, quick witted, and intuitive. The more I find myself admiring him.

When the bodysuit reaches the curve of my ass, Austin stands and pulls it off my hips. I shiver and wrap my arms around myself while his chest warms my bare back.

He guides the garment to the floor and helps me step out of it before he stands up again and takes a seat on the bed.

I'm standing, with my back to him, in nothing but a pair of black pumps. I peek over my shoulder and see him rubbing his chin like he's trying to solve a problem. His eyes are dark behind his glasses. He slides them off his face and tosses them on the nightstand. My stomach flips at the gesture. When his eyes flash up to meet mine, it feels like the cage on a tiger enclosure was just unlocked. He's ready to pounce.

"What should we do first, Austin?" I ask.

"I've got a few ideas."

Austin stands behind me and I hear his pants swish as he steps out of them. The anticipation of his touch is heavy in my veins. I gasp when he reaches into my hair and unclips the tortoise shell claw there.

He gently pulls the hair off my shoulder and then wraps one arm around my chest and pulls me back into his. His other hand starts to tease my opening from behind. His thumb providing a pressure against my ass I wasn't expecting. He slides his hand further forward and begins to massage my clit and my knees buckle as electricity shoots through my veins.

His grip across my chest tightens to keep me upright as he fingers me. It feels like he has fifteen fingers moving around with how quickly he taps my clit, massages my slit, and presses into the space between my cheeks.

"Oh fuck, yes, Austin," I breathe out as my knees begin to shake.

"That's it, I've got you," he whispers into my ear before he trails kisses down my neck and along my shoulder. "I've got you Maggie," he repeats.

I hear myself whimpering as his fingers, his words, bring me closer to the edge. My eyes slam shut as I feel his erection growing along my hip. I reach for it as he works me to the brink.

"Yes Maggie, so good," he says as his forehead falls to my shoulder and I stroke him harder, faster. Focusing on him took me away from my own orgasm but when he slides two fingers into me and presses into my ass, my eyes fly open and I squeak in pleasure. Two more pumps of his fingers inside me and I freeze. I jerk forward as my orgasm hits me with such intensity it feels like the wind has gotten knocked out of me.

"Oh god, Austin," I grit out as he massages me through the peak and into the valley.

He spins me towards him, my hand still closed around his steely length, and kisses me fiercely. I feel him throb under my palm and after indulging in a few more languid strokes of his tongue against mine, I break the kiss and drop to my knees.

"Fuck yes Maggie," he whispers as I lick the underside of his cock from the base to the tip before pulling his head into my mouth and swirling my tongue around him.

Our eyes follow each other as I begin to bob my head down his length. The corners of his eyes soften as he rakes his fingers through my hair and cradles my head. I grab his thighs for balance as my own legs begin to quiver.

Seeing how turned on he is exciting. The awe in his eyes is empowering.

"This is only slightly better than when you use your mouth to argue with me," he says with a twinkle and in response I suck hard and my cheeks hollow out.

He stumbles backwards at the sudden sensation and pops out of my mouth. I grin up at him from my knees on the floor and his own is returned with a hint of wickedness.

"You think you're pretty clever there huh?" Austin asks as he slowly strokes himself and steps back up to me. "Get on the bed."

I stand and step past him. When I've got both knees on the mattress, Austin grabs me by the shoes and swings my feet to the headboard. My head hangs off the foot of the bed. For a moment he simply takes in the view before climbing onto the bed himself.

"Open up," he commands and I lick my lips before parting for him. He slowly dips himself down my throat and then he lowers his head between my legs and sucks my clit into his mouth, hard.

I try to scream but the noise is muffled around his cock. He comes back up to kneeling and looks down at me.

"Two can play at this game Maggie Collins," he says before squeezing my tits together and pinching my nipples. Again I groan with the sensation but all we can hear is a garbled sound.

He stands and slowly guides himself in and out of my mouth while holding my head carefully. The position is lewd but there is a reverence to his movements that makes me feel respected.

It is unlike anything I've ever experienced.

My hands instinctively move to my chest and I fondle my own breasts and watch his eyes zero in on the movement. The cold AC of the room hits between my legs and causes a chill to run through me as it meets the dampness there. I slide one of my hands down and finger myself.

Whenever I masturbate I either use a toy in the shower or lie on my stomach and ride my hand. I've never been laid out like this with my knees propped up in heels on a hotel comforter. My mind zooms out to what we look like together and the image sends another wave of arousal through me.

I groan again around his cock and Austin pulls out.

"How are you doing Maggie?"

"I wanna come again," I tell him because that's the only truth I can speak out loud. I can't tell him that I'm feeling things for him I've never felt for anyone else. I can't tell him I'm confused by these feelings. I can't tell him I consider him a friend. I can't tell him I'm thinking about not continuing with SMS Connect because I've met him.

"Let's get you another orgasm," he offers and then again he dips himself down my throat and leans forward. Instead of putting his mouth on me he uses his fingers to compliment the movements of my own hand. As I maneuver tight circles on my clit he sinks two fingers into me and curls them to rub along my inner walls. He holds himself up with a fist on the bed next to my waist as he continues to dip in and out of my mouth.

My knees start to shake and I know I'm close, I rub myself harder, he plunges in and out of me faster. My thighs slam together and I grind out my orgasm on our hands that are trapped between them. I whimper through the tension with Austin still in my mouth. As the stars dancing across my vision start to face and my legs relax he pulls out of my mouth and pumps his orgasm onto my breasts.

I watch him finish and admire the pure masculinity of him. The way his muscles flex, how his hand fits around himself while mine covered much less.

He leans down and helps to lift my shoulders onto the bed and then turns to the bathroom. I look down at his release on my chest. The streaks of cum slide slowly down the slope of my tits. I run a finger through the still warm liquid and bring it to my lips. My tongue darts out just as Austin turns the corner from the bathroom.

"Are you tasting my jizz?" He asks as his feet stutter to a stop.

"Maybe," I reply before sliding the finger past my lips and sucking hard. He's salty, briny, and the taste makes my walls clench around emptiness.

His gaze is pure adoration and I panic when I realize I'm looking at him in the same way. Anxiety rises in my chest, and I dart my eyes away.

"If I had known you wanted to taste it I would have shot off in your mouth," he says as he hands me the washcloth. "Would have saved me some clean up. Do you wan-" he stops when I sit up quickly and say "So I'll just go now."

"Okay," he agrees quietly as I step into my body suit. "Want me to, oh, no, okay." He finishes as I slide the garment up my arms myself and reach down to step into my pants. I have to get out o here. Feelings are happening and I'm not supposed to have feelings with Austin.

He sounds disappointed. Did he want to go again? Should I ask him? Was he going to ask me to stay? I already decided that I wouldn't. Right? Right. This is just sex.

Except, I can't escape the crash. It's happening in slow motion and in real time and at hyper speed all at once.

The emotions of wanting to stay, of the experience we just shared, of still despising him because of the business he created. I'm also overwhelmed by the awkwardness of being the one to leave.

How does he do this? Just finish sex and walk out the door. Our sessions leave me in a foggy state for several hours afterwards and right now my body is screaming at me not to leave.

It's begging to cuddle up next to Austin. To spend the night.

Instead of indulging these desires, I fasten my wide leg pants, take one last look around his suite with regret because it's really nice, and then I turn around and leave.

Chapter Seventeen
AUSTIN
Twelve Weeks Exactly

THE DOOR CLICKS SHUT behind Maggie and the sounds of silence fill the room. I slowly lower myself to the bed and cradle my head in my hands to give it time to catch up to the rest of my body.

I almost fainted when I saw her drag her finger through my cum and bring it to her mouth. Stars appear in my eyes as I remember it now. That image will stay with me forever.

She is everything I could ask for in a sexual partner and it is killing me that it's just sex.

I would ghost TalkShopGirl in a heartbeat if Maggie asked me to because it hurts far too much to watch her walk away. I spot her hair clip on the nightstand and reach for it. I pinch it open and let it clip shut on my finger. The sharp pain is welcome. It distracts me from the pain of Maggie walking out.

It's best that she did. Maggie loves her job, she's good at it. She will never be able to look past the fact that I started AIM and made her work life incredibly more challenging.

I rub my hand down my face and feel the complexities of our situation close in on me. It feels like a fucked up version of If You Give A Mouse A Cookie. Everything rolls back to the fact that I created a product that she has to compete against.

AI Media did exactly what it was supposed to at the debate. I saw early numbers before Maggie came over and the response from the target demographics were better than we had expected. The language, the slight adjustments to Senator Quinn's positions, and the additional factors we were able to sneak in resonated with voters.

The campaign lines and prepared speeches Maggie wrote did not perform as well. And it's not to say that the writing was bad, far from it, but it sounded rehearsed and prepared and people can smell planning a mile away.

It isn't Maggie's fault, it's just the current consumer landscape. People want what they want in an instant and they want it customized to them.

I was glad Maggie didn't change before coming to my room. When I saw her before the debate in that body suit my reaction was visceral. It hugged every curve and then her pants hung off the globes of her ass and flowed down to black heels. I could only see half an inch of them, leaving the rest to my active imagination. I bit my lip to keep my tongue from rolling out like a dog.

I don't think she's dressing like that to get to me. I think this is how she always dresses. Always clean cut, muted colors that compliment her complexion and let her ideas shine.

People could only say that she dresses well. There's nothing flashy or controversial. It makes a statement by not making a statement.

I wonder if it's on purpose? She's mentioned her boss getting attention for her clothing choices. Maggie strikes me as the type of person who would learn that lesson and apply it to herself.

I shake my head and toss the hair claw onto the nightstand again. Obsessing over Maggie is counterproductive. We won't get together, and thinking otherwise is insane. I move across the suite and pick up the SMS Connect phone.

Whoever TalkShopGirl may be, she likes me as a person.

Unlike Maggie who couldn't get out of the room fast enough.

I was about to ask her to stay, to have a drink, to spend the rest of the night talking before we fell asleep in each other's arms but she cut off that line of questioning and jumped back into her clothes. I've never seen a woman move so quickly to get out of my bed.

And as painful as it is knowing my potential tabloid attention is the real reason they're with me, it hurts more to have a woman I respect and admire jump ship after we share mind numbing sex.

I want Maggie Collins to like me. To respect me. To value my opinion. I want her to want me.

But since that doesn't seem likely in this lifetime I'm going to focus my attention back on SMS Connect and hope TalkShopGirl can wipe the hope of Maggie out of my brain.

DCFox: I can't seem to get you out of my mind. The figurative you. I'm almost dying here trying to guess what you look like, if your smile lights up a room like I imagine it does, if you hold your head high and speak clearly like the way your messages come across to me. If this connection we've built will engulf us when we meet in person.

So, what do you say? Can we meet in person?

Instead of turning the phone off like I usually do I leave it on the nightstand and mix a myself drink. I stare at it from near the window while I sip on my bourbon and finally throw back the final dregs of the liquor when an hour has passed without a response.

I climb into bed and stare at the ceiling until sleep takes over.

I'm jolted awake from a dreamless sleep when the SMS Connect phone pings next to my head. Sunlight is just starting to streak the sky and I grab it, and my glasses, at the same time.

TalkShopGirl: I'd love to set up a time to meet. Next week? Tuesday?

DCFox: Lapis in Adams Morgan at 8?

TalkShopGirl: See you then, I'll be wearing a red dress and I'll put this phone in a floral case on the table.

I grin from ear to ear. I have five days until I meet the woman who has built herself a home in my heart.

Chapter Eighteen
MAGGIE
Down Dog

I'm sitting on the plane next to Sam as we fly back to D.C. by way of Chicago and Detroit. We added these stops as soon as the numbers from the debate came in.

Senator Quinn did really well which is the good news. The bad news, well for me at least, is the AI Media responses were her best received lines of the night.

Another blow to my ego? It was the responses Sam crafted that did the best out of the ones we wrote. Mine performed the worst.

I'm telling myself it's okay because the AIM responses were based off of the speeches I wrote over the last six months that got fed into the database. So really, it was my work plus a little computer magic that made them so good.

Sure Maggie, keep telling yourself that.

I feel like I've done a 180. Usually I am happy with my work life and grumbling about my dating life. After sex that rocked my world last night, and after I recovered from fleeing his room, I went back to mine and ran my hands over the body he used as he wanted to maximize both our pleasure.

Then today, I started my day with a text from DCFox asking to meet.

We're getting together next week at Lapis which is in my neighborhood. Could he live nearby? Could I have passed him on the sidewalk or at the bakery or the park before and not known it? Or is he just tuned into the dining scene and knows that it is one of the best restaurants to open in the last several years.

"So when we get to Chicago, Ben wants to have a meeting," Sam reports as she returns from the bathroom.

"Why can't we have it now?" I ask as I slide my legs to let her through. I lean into the aisle and see him sitting with the other top campaign people and realize, as Head Speech Writer, I should probably be in that conversation.

"They're working on the schedule for the next few days."

"Oh, I should tell them that I need to be back in D.C. Tuesday night, by like seven o'clock."

"Why? Hot date?" Sam asks jokingly but when she sees my smile grow and catches the tiny nod I give her she squeals. "Ohmigod really?"

"Shhh, yes really. Hold on."

I unfasten my seatbelt and make my way up to where Ben is sitting in a group of seats that face a table like on a train.

"Hey, Sam said you're working on the schedule?"

"Yeah, just mapping out the campaign stops and making sure our people on the ground have what they need."

"Okay, I umm, if it works out, I need to be back in D.C. Tuesday night. I've got plans that night I can't change."

"That should be fine. If anything you could skip the Monday-Tuesday swing, you might have to fly commercial out to meet us on Wednesday. I don't think she's going to have more than one night back in D.C. until after the election."

"Okay."

Try not to read into it. This doesn't mean you're replaceable.

"Plus Sam can still travel with us right? That should be fine. With her and AI Media we should be able to cover anything that comes up."

"Okay." I reply again and mutter a "thanks" before turning and heading back to my seat. It isn't sitting right that he was so willing to give me the time off. Maybe I should reschedule this date for after the election. The team needs me.

"So, what'd he say?"

"He said it was fine. If anything, I can skip Monday and Tuesday and then fly commercial to meet you on Wednesday. Wherever you'll be then. And between you and AI Media they'd be able to cover anything that comes up."

Sam waits a beat while that sinks in. "I'm sure they want you on the trip, they're just trying to respect your schedule, too." Or maybe she's reading my mind.

"Yeah, sure, you're probably right."

"Okay, enough about that, tell me about this date! Can I help you pick out a dress?"

"I already decided what I'm going to wear, because I had to tell him how to find me. It's umm, a blind date, sort of."

"How can it be a blind date, sort of? Did you let someone set you up?" She sounds offended. "You know I've been wanting to do that for ages."

"No, well, yeah, maybe? I dunno." I take a deep breath and square my shoulders in her direction. "I'm meeting my SMS Connect guy."

"Wait, for real!?"

"Yes."

"When did this date get scheduled? Why am I only hearing about it now?" Sam asks, again sounding offended.

"Just this morning. Well, he asked me last night, I guess, but I said yes this morning."

"Just like that? I mean, gosh this is so fascinating to me," Sam mutters. She squares her shoulders in my direction, "What have you two been talking about lately?"

"Well, it has evolved into sharing about our days. I'd tell him about the challenges in mine, but not any details because you're not supposed to give away any identifying information. So I'd share the emotions behind the challenges and the wins."

I find it to be a really healthy way to discuss things I'm experiencing. The details of the matter don't really add much, it's how I feel about them. How I react to them that counts.

"You just drifted away," Sam says gently and I turn back towards her. "You really like him?"

"I really do."

"Are you scared to meet him?"

"Terrified!" I admit with a laugh. "I've told him things I haven't told anyone else. Probably because it was a faceless void. It's so scary to be open with someone to their face."

At that, my mind flashes to the morning in my apartment when I admitted the history of my orgasms to Austin. And how I felt safe telling him because of the way he honored my body. I think of the way he pushed me to new heights last night and the trust we shared.

Now that I've seen the AI Media data from the debate I'm not so sure I can trust him. If the Senator decides to rely on AIM more for the next week, I'll be left editing for a computer. I said from the beginning I wouldn't be able to do that. My reputation and pride are at stake.

Austin will essentially be in control of my job security. And after how I bolted from his room I'm not sure I can face him again. And, now that his company is poised to replace me I don't think I want to.

I pick up my phone and force myself to feel brave.

Hey.

Well, that's not brave at all. You're a professional writer. Do better.

Hey yourself.

I know we said the election was our end date but I'm calling this earlier.

You sure?

Yes. So, thanks, I guess.

You're welcome?

I can picture him laughing at me. The thought makes me laugh at myself.

This is weird. I'll see you around.

Take care MC

I exhale a deep breath. Okay, that's done. Now I'll focus on meeting DCFox and put everything I have left into getting the senator elected.

****

I thought the rule of threes only applied to celebrities dying. But it appears the rule of threes applies to the guy you've been having sex with but don't want to see anymore because you're about to meet the guy you've been texting with.

I ran into Austin on my run yesterday morning. Literally. I was coming up to a crosswalk and was looking down the one way street for any cars when I slammed into someone. It was Austin on freaking roller blades.

First the skateboard, then the yoga mat, and now roller blades. Why can't he do a normal workout like everyone else? Except, okay, his body is fit and it begs to be touched so when he swung around to get his balance by clinging to me I wrapped my arms around his torso and enjoyed the solid warmth of him. Clearly I need to pay better attention to my surroundings when running.

Yesterday afternoon I saw him at the deli near our office. I managed to keep myself hidden from view by ducking behind shelves stocked with artisanal candy and peeking through the items to keep track of him. Austin didn't see me but at one point I was so distracted watching him that I kicked over a corner display of gluten free mac n cheese boxes and then ducked for cover and watched his legs pass by through the lower shelves. Even the quick and distorted view of his gait immediately sent a volt of lust through my insides.

And now, as I make my way into a challenge-myself-to-try-something-new puppy yoga class with Sam, I see Austin leaning against the welcome desk talking to the, very pretty, receptionist.

"We can talk about this tonight," the receptionist says and I am seized with jealousy. The mere suggestion of Austin spending his night with someone else triples me. I only snap out of it when Sam elbows me in the side, hard.

"Oww!" I grumble.

"Look who it is!" She stage whispers so loud that Austin turns around and spots us immediately.

I smile sheepishly and walk up to the desk.

"Hi, I'm Maggie Collins," I say as I try to ignore Austin's form next to me. He is still leaning against the desk and I can sense how big his smile is. "I'm here for the puppy yoga at 9:00."

"Sam Gibson," Sam chimes in from behind me. Then I hear, "Austin, are you taking this class?"

"I wasn't going to, I just finished my power flow class, but now that I've got some friends here, maybe I will." He turns to the receptionist, "Can you fit me in, Elle?"

"Sure thing, Austin," then she turns back towards me. "Did you bring your own mat or do you need to borrow one?"

"I, uhh, need to borrow one."

"I brought mine!" Sam adds unhelpfully as she lifts her mat in the air behind me.

"No problem, Maggie, there are some in the back of the studio, grab one and pick a spot."

"Okay, thanks." I mutter and without looking back at Austin I turn and head to the studio. I hear Sam skip to catch up with me.

"Aren't you going to talk to him?"

"What would I say?" I adopt a dopey cartoon voice, "nice job inventing a software that is smarter than I am."

Sam blows me off with a scoff. "No, but you could at least be friendly to the man. I mean, he is helping the senator get elected which is the ultimate goal of all this, right?"

"I'll talk to him after class," I ruefully agree as I pull a mat out of the bin. "Where should we set up?"

"By the mirrors," Sam says, "I saw a video of a puppy who was so confused by the mirror and was walking into it for five minutes trying to figure it out."

"Isn't the point of this to workout?"

Sam laughs, "No, the point is to do some light stretching while puppies run around the room. The cardio comes when a fine ass man is doing down dog in front of you and your heart rate spikes."

We roll out our mats out and sit facing each other to continue chatting. I glance at each person who walks in, mostly pairs and trios of girls who look like they're going out for mimosas after this. The room fills up in clusters of friend groups and no one is directly next to me and Sam so thankfully there will be no one to witness my lack of balance and flexibility.

I agreed to do this because I admitted to DCFox that I wanted to be braver about trying new things. And then Sam wouldn't shut up about wanting to try it. She's been on a puppy kick since seeing them at the hockey game last week. It's really just a matter of time before she's trying to sneak a puppy onto the campaign bus.

At the very least, my experience with this class will make a good first date story for DCFox.

Austin walks in followed by, Elle from the front desk. She comes up to the front of the room and Austin whips open his mat right next to me.

Of course he does.

"Good morning my friends, I just need to share a few things before our puppies arrive. First of all, welcome! Raise your hand if this is your first puppy yoga class?"

I raise my hand and glance around the room, there are only a few of the twenty people here who aren't raising their hands. Austin is one of them.

"You've done puppy yoga before?" I challenge him quietly.

"Of course I have," he says as he keeps his attention on Elle and her long limbs and dark hair. Silly Maggie, obviously he's taken this class before. He clearly has a connection with the adorable instructor so I bet he comes here often.

"Next, ladies, well and I guess gentleman too," she gives a smile to Austin, "watch your ponytails. Our pups often like to bite them if they're hanging as they walk by. If this happens try not to pull because they'll think you're playing tug-of-war. Raise your hand or have your neighbor get our attention and I'll come over to help."

I turn around and see Sam putting her hair into a swirled bun instead of a ponytail and decide to do the same.

"And finally, if a puppy has an accident nearby let me know and I'll clean it up." Elle claps her hands together and turns on some music. "Who's ready for puppy yoga?"

The class whoops and cheers as Elle walks to the door at the side of the room and opens it slowly.

Immediately three puppies come bounding out and trip over each other as they race into the waiting laps of the closest humans. The room fills with giggles and baby talk. A few people make little kissy noises. A few more pups make their way out slowly and finally a brown lab puppy with adorable droopy eyes meanders out into the room.

"We're going to start in child's pose so if you have a puppy in your lap please set them to the side and move into position. We'll be going through Sun A and Sun B flow today ending with a few hip openers and a delicious savasana at the end."

I look around the room and lament that I picked a spot at the front. I think I know what child's pose is but I don't know much about anything else she said.

I watch as Austin sits back on his heels and then folds forward to the floor. His body is stretched out and I see the way his muscles wrap around his bones. Of course he would do puppy yoga shirtless. I hope he gets scratched by tiny little puppy nails.

As soon as I turn my head over and press my forehead into the mat like Elle instructed, a puppy flops down on my neck. His belly is warm and squishy and it wiggles as his tail wags back and forth. I chuckle a little bit and turn my head to the side and see it's the chocolate lab that was the last to join the party.

"Awwww that's so cute, hold still," Sam coos and then I hear the shutter of her camera.

"You cannot post that picture!" I inform her as she settles back onto her mat.

"Why? Worried it would make you look soft?" Austin challenges and I roll my head towards him and narrow my eyes.

"No, I'm worried that my boss will be upset that I'm not working, and that I brought my direct report with me to this ridiculous class." Technically she brought me but that seems besides the point.

"You know, they say the puppies seek out people who are in the most emotional distress. To soothe them and comfort them." Austin says as Elle instructs people to move into down dog. I watch him plant his hands on his mat and unfold until he's in an upside down V position.

I go to move my arms and get into the next pose, thinking the puppy will just jump off. But as I start to move I realize the puppy isn't. Then I see Elle's perfectly manicured toes come into view.

"Looks like S'mores here has fallen asleep," she says gently. "Usually when our puppies do that they've made a strong connection with the human. They've put their trust in you because they can sense you're a safe place."

"That's great but what am I supposed to do, I can't move."

"Can you breathe?"

"Yes," I respond slowly, fearful of what she is getting at.

"Then you don't move. You sink into the pose, let the pressure of your companion release the tension in your shoulders. Enjoy the forced break. Drift off to sleep yourself if you'd like."

With that Elle rubs a hand down my spine and walks away. As she instructs the class through the next set of moves I watch Austin's body flow fluidly from one position to the next. There is power and strength in his movements. Control. He's making it look easy and now I'm very glad that S'mores has camped out on my neck. If not, I'd be trying to do yoga moves and embarrassing myself in front of him.

My canine heating pad doesn't stop me from keeping my head turned in his direction though. The first time through the routine he was facing away from me so I could admire the view without fear of him catching me.

The second round has him facing me and I blush deeply every time he flicks his gaze to mine. His eyes soften as he watches me lay here with a puppy across the back of my neck like a travel pillow.

"Do you want me to move him?" He asks as he sinks into a chair pose. It looks challenging based on how his abs are flexing and he keeps rolling his toes.

"Nah, I'm good, this is the best workout ever." I say with a laugh and when I do S'mores stirs and slides backwards onto his butt and off my neck. He flops to the side and looks startled to find himself there.

I laugh as I slowly sit up and reach out to give him a good pet and scratch behind his ears.

"Start with a down dog," Austin says. "It'll feel good to stretch out your legs."

I nod and push myself up into position. It does feel good along the backs of my legs. I close my eyes and slowly sway from side to side to feel the way my muscles stretch with the movement. I'm starting to appreciate the benefits of yoga.

Suddenly there are hands on my hips and my eyes fly open to see Austin's feet planted just outside of mine. He's holding onto my hips and pulling my ass higher into the air. The stretch travels from my legs to my back and it feels so good I almost moan.

"How does that feel?" He asks.

"Mhm, good," I say even though my throat is tight. "Are you qualified to do this?"

He leans forward over me and my arms start to feel the burn from holding both of us up.

"I think we both know I'm qualified to do this."

And then he stands and returns to his mat. Cold rushes into fill the space he vacated. I spy Sam through my legs behind me and her eyes have doubled in size.

"Get a room!" She mouths to me as she points between us.

"Shut up!" I mouth back but break eye contact right away. I can't afford for Sam to see the desire he's stirred in me. I was the one to end it but try telling that to my vagina. She's crying for Austin like a kid being pulled past the ice cream truck by an overtired parent.

I look around and focus on copying what my fellow yogis are doing as Elle talks through different transitions. S'mores makes his way back over and plops down at my side as I attempt something called pigeon but I think I look more like a dying swan.

I am able to roll him over so I can lay down on my mat for the final resting pose. Yeah, this is the kind of yoga I could get used to.

As soon as I close my eyes, the pup climbs onto my shins and snuggles in. I lift my head and peek one eye open and I find S'mores lying on his back, mimicking my pose with his head balanced perfectly between my knees.

I let out a little chuckle and rest my head on my mat.

I'm not sure how long we lay there but the forced stillness to keep the puppy comfortable is more relaxing than I'd thought it would be.

My mind slows down to almost blank. I focus on the soft sounds of the music in the background. I hear puppy feet shuffling throughout the room. I feel one come and sniff at my hair before moving on.

Then I hear a "oof" exhale and peek an eye open to see a puppy walking around on Austin's stomach. The pup turns a circle and plops down for a rest.

I smile and when Austin turns his head towards mine we share a moment.

There is undoubtedly a connection between us. An understanding of what we've been to each other. My mind smiles because I can sit back and appreciate him and I can be glad for what we shared. I can let go of Austin Thorne.

Elle gently calls us back to awareness and I watch Austin's biceps fire as he picks up the puppy and holds him overhead like they're playing airplane. My eyes drink in his chiseled chest, the dip above his hip bones, the hard planes of muscle that slant into his waistband.

My head might be, but I don't know if my body will ever be ready to let go of Austin Thorne.

So how do you feel?" Austin asks as we file out of the room. Sam is busy cuddling with a puppy and pestering the handlers for adoption information.

"Oh, good, I mean it wasn't much of a workout but I do feel more relaxed."

"More relaxed than after an hour with me?" He asks quietly near my ear and my knees nearly give out as scenes from his hotel room replay in my mind.

Austin stays close as I gather my things. He holds my water bottle for me while I put my sweatshirt on. When I resurface I catch him watching me and a blush rushes in across my face and neck. I have shared the most intimate moments of my life with this man and the look in his eyes tells me there could be more if I ask for it.

The idea sends my nerve endings into a frenzy.

He holds open the door for me as we step out of the studio.

"I'll, umm, see you around," I rush the words as I hook my thumb over my shoulder. I wince when I realize I'm pointing in the wrong direction.

Apparently all my mental energy is being diverted to tampering my desire for him.

Austin's eyes dance with humor.

"I'll walk with you," he says as he indicates the correct way over his shoulder. He smirks and then pops an elbow out for me to take. It feels like the only option at that point is to latch on and hope for the best.

"So MC, what are your plans for the rest of the day?" Austin asks as we turn the corner.

"This was my excitement for the day. After this it's laundry and tidying up my apartment."

"Cleaning up the whiteboard?" He teases and I smile.

"Probably, Senator Quinn has a busy week ahead."

He nods but doesn't respond. We fall into a companionable quiet. Two blocks later the late morning sky gets darker as a storm rolls in. We agree to get coffee at Sunrise when we reach my block when suddenly the sky bursts with cold, heavy rain and Austin pulls me further down the block with him until we find a shop awning to shelter under.

He takes his phone out of his pocket and sends a quick text. "Greg will be here in a few minutes, I'll take you home."

"Oh, that's okay, I'll be alright," I tell him because the wet waffle shirt version of Austin Thorne should be on the national security watch list. It's a danger to women everywhere.

A shiver racks my body and Austin pulls me in closer. His cooled sweat scent blends with the rain and I want to open mouth kiss every inch of his skin to try and consume as much of it as I can. His hand slowly circles from the small of my back up my spine and I shiver again.

"Maggie," Austin whispers and I look up at him. Droplets hang heavy on the lenses of his glasses and it's like I'm looking at him through a window. I reach up and gently slide the frames from his face and watch his eyes slowly close and reopen to focus on me.

We study each other on the sidewalk, under an awning, in the frigid October rain. I'm searching for answers to questions no one can answer.

Can Austin be the man I need at my side?

Is my physical attraction to him tricking my brain into believing it could be more?

What do I do about DCFox?

It's the last question and the sound of a car pulling up to the curb that has me blinking and stepping back. I put his glasses into his hand and he slides them on as he ushers me to the car. The cold raindrops hit my face and serve as little reminders that I need to stick to my initial plan to end whatever this is with Austin.

When he slides in behind me he tells his driver to go to my place and with a quick nod in the mirror we pull away from the curb and merge into traffic. The trip will be short. I only have to survive a few minutes without looking, touching, or kissing him.

Totally possible.

"Maggie," Austin says and he slides his warm hand onto my thigh. I stare at the veins that create a complex topography along his knuckles and joints. The spot where our bodies connect warms like coals, not blazing and showy, but rather hot and intense.

My focus travels from his hand up his forearm, past his biceps and shoulders to his jawline and finally his eyes, the desire burning in them lights a fuse in me.

"Yes," I whisper. I'm not asking. I'm giving permission.

Before I can register what is happening he pulls my leg over his lap and positions me across his thighs. Our mouths connect and open to each other. The taste of him is familiar and exhilarating. His hands travel up the inside of my sweatshirt and then back down to where he holds my hips. He feels steady and strong and I lean into him.

My hands sink into the hair at the back of his head and I hold on for dear life when Austin starts to roll my hips against him. The friction of his bulge through my leggings makes my toes curl inside my sneakers.

He pulls me against him and I throw my head back to inhale deeply. Austin's lips find my neck and he presses kisses along the exposed skin.

"Fuck Maggie, you're perfect," he compliments as his fingers press into the flesh of my ass before he pulls my center onto his again.

I know time is running out. My hormones know it too because I am barreling towards an orgasm just from his hands on me. His mouth moves across my jaw and neck, peppering kisses along the way, charting a course on my skin.

"Austin," I whine when he bites gently.

He lifts both hands and brackets my face in them and his smokey eyes are clouded with lust that he's finding matched in mine.

The car slows and his eyes dart out the window for a split second but it is long enough to break the spell.

I cannot hook up with Austin when I'm meeting DCFox in a few days. This has to be our last moment. Responsibility prevails in the end.

When we come to a stop outside my building I don't have any words to say. Austin doesn't either. He lets me slide towards the door that is quickly opened for me.

I climb out with a hand from his driver who gives me a curt nod before saying, "Enjoy the rest of your day, Miss Collins," and I smile sadly at him. I can't look back.

The closing car door reverberates against my ear drums causing my shoulders to jump but my steps don't falter and I get inside my building. The lobby is too quiet and the silence hurts my ears. I want to hear Austin. To hear his breath, his groans, his satisfaction. I want to hear my gasped inhales when I've forgotten to breathe because his hands are on me. I want to hear my muffled moans as he captures them with his mouth.

My fingers shake as I try to get my key in the lock. My feet feel heavy, like I've just run a marathon. As I push open the door, my body is sluggish and exhausted and my heart just feels sad.

Ending things with Austin is the right thing to do. It was never supposed to include feelings. And it's gotten all the more confusing to message with DCFox. Austin doesn't want to be in a relationship. It's foolish to think that's a possibility. Plus he needs some sort of society darling on his arm, not a speech writer from a small town with political ambitions. It'll hurt more if I give in to my heart and then experience the rejection from Austin down the road. This is for the best.

I've managed to step into my apartment and close the door before the tears spill over. I slide down the wall and curl up on the floor, hugging my knees to my chest as the first wave racks my body.

The list of things I wouldn't give to have Austin here to comfort me is short. And therein lies the problem. My body chills because I'm craving affection from someone who can't give it to me.

I sniffle up my tears and take a deep breath. On a shaky exhale I tell myself I'll be okay. That on Tuesday I get to meet DCFox. The person who could very well be The One. And I'm confident our emotional connection will lead to physical feelings. Or, maybe I'll be lucky and he'll walk in and be sex in a suit.

Which makes me think of Austin.

Tears roll slowly again as I roll my head along the wall. I push air out with my cheeks and decide that I either need to curl up in my chair, lie down in bed, or take a shower. My eyes dart around my space as I think through the options. Chair, bed, shower. Chair? Bed? Shower? Chair? Bed?

Knock. Knock.

The air in my lungs vaporizes as I look up over my shoulder at the door.

"Maggie," Austin's muffled voice sounds pained.

I slowly stand and open the door to find Austin leaning against the doorframe. His head snaps up from where it was hanging between his shoulders. He lunges forward and captures my face in his hands. He steps into me and uses his thumbs to catch the tears that have spilled over once again.

"Austin?" I whisper as the battle between my heart and my head erupts. My heart beats wildly in my chest as my mind reels to reign in the thoughts that are giving my heart hope.

It is so good between us, why stop a beautiful thing?

Maybe he's here because he wants you, not just sex.

What if he's developing feelings too?

Austin closes his eyes and I wonder if he's battling the same way I am. I mentally beg him to open his eyes again, to let me in.

"Please," he whispers a moment before closing the distance between our lips.

Chapter Nineteen
AUSTIN

She doesn't know that I know.

MAGGIE'S HOT TEARS POOL against my thumbs as I dive in and kiss her. She shudders and my arms wrap around her waist. The second her toes lift off the ground, I spin into the apartment, kick the door closed, and press her up against it with my hips. She returns my kisses like they're oxygen.

"Austin, what are you doing?" She asks, breathless.

"I'll stop if you tell me to but, fuck Maggie," I rest my forehead on top of hers, "I'm not done with you yet."

Her hands slowly circle my shoulders and upper back and my arms quiver in reaction to her touch. My whole body tries to get closer to her. I don't know why she's trying to push me away when every cell in my body is on fire when I'm near her.

"Okay," she whispers on an exhale. She reaches up and slowly pulls my glasses off; her eyes fixed on the frames as she sets them on the little table near the door. I smile at her and revel in this moment of intimacy.

The sweet moment is over quickly. She frantically pulls her sweat-shirt over her head in a hurry, then her tank top, then her sports bra. I lower to my knees as I pull her leggings down.

Maggie uses my shoulders to steady herself while she steps out of the tight fabric and then she pushes my shoulders down and I fall back onto my ass. She dips and pulls my shirt off over my head and discards it behind her. She slides her hands up my chest and down my arms before sliding them into the waistband of my shorts and pulling them down. I lift my hips to help her.

I take her hands in mine as I toe off my shorts. With a quick tug she falls into me and I've never been prouder of my solid body. I would be her support every moment of every day if she would let me. The weight of her on my thighs a welcome pressure and I want more.

I twirl one hand up to my mouth where I pull two of her fingers inside and she shivers as I suck them and scrape my teeth along them as I drag them out. Maggie closes her eyes and her head falls back as I repeat myself on her other hand.

Still holding her wrists I cover her hammering pulse points with a kiss and then place them on either side of my head as I roll down to the floor.

With my hands free, I blaze a trail up her thighs to her center. My thumb applies pressure as she starts to slide on top of my dick.

"Oh fuck," she whispers as she picks up her pace.

"That's it Maggie, use me, take what you need," I coach her as I grip her ass and bring her down on me harder.

"Condom," she says on an exhale.

"Not yet, get yourself off on me first."

"Ohmygod," she chants as her movements start to splinter. I take over and rock her against me and roll my hips to help her out. She lifts up and grabs her tits and I feel a surge of arousal shoot through me. My eyes zero in on where she is rolling her nipples between her perfectly manicured fingers.

"Austin!" Maggie yells out as I feel her wetness slide across my cock.

"Now we get a condom," I tell her as I give her ass a little smack and move her off me. She stands and gets a condom from her bedside table while I give myself a few languid strokes. My palm spreads her up and down my length, I fucking love being covered in her. With my other hand I slide my glasses back on.

She turns and holds the condom out to me and I grasp it in one hand and pull her by the back of the neck into me for a kiss with the other. If she thinks it's too rough she doesn't say. I'm not sure I could slow down. My body is buzzing.

"Turn around, hands on the wall," I tell her as I slide the condom on. I lean over her shoulder and press my back into her as I cup her breasts and pull her towards me. "You going to give me two more?"

"If you earn them," she replies and my chuckle blends with the kiss I place along her neck. I slide one hand down and slip it between her legs where she is wet and waiting. My dick throbs wanting to get in on the action but I'm giving Maggie one more before he goes anywhere.

I pinch her nipple as I circle two fingers over her clit. I watch as her fingers press into the wall and her jaw flexes to keep it shut.

"Don't hold back MC, you know this feels good," I tell her against her ear. My breath is hot along her skin but then I purse my lips and blow cold air in the same spot and her knees buckle.

"Holy shit," she curses as I hold her up. I strum her faster and pull my hand down her side and around to her ass. One small smack lands and my fingers get wetter. I grip her ass and press my thumb between her cheeks and her head falls forward between her shoulders.

"Give it up Maggie, give it to me," I growl into her ear. "Come."

"Don't tell me what to do," she whines but then I watch goosebumps dance across her arms and she smacks the wall when I shove two fingers inside her and feel her walls crash down on them.

"Atta girl," I tell her as she gasps for breath. I grip her hips and line myself up. I'm going to take her next orgasm from her hard and fast. My body is thrumming with tension and with an inhale I press myself into her.

I watch my cock disappear under her ass and my eyes roll back into my head as she flutters around me. My entire reason for existence is to fuck this woman.

"This pussy is perfect, Maggie," and she whimpers in response as I pump into her at a furious pace. The room around me fades at the edges of my vision and I feel my glasses start to slide down my nose but I will not let go of her to fix them.

"Harder, Austin," she begs and I spank her ass cheek before I reach forward and cup her pussy.

"You in a hurry for this to be over, Maggie?"

"No but I need more," she whimpers.

"Flick your clit," I command before I bring my hands to her breasts. Her pert nipples grate against my palms before I clamp down and pinch them. She shrieks and I twist. I lean back just enough to see her pussy consume my cock and I feel my balls tighten.

I can feel her fingers flying across her folds and her third orgasm is close. This incredibly smart, willfully strong, and excruciatingly beautiful woman is panting before me.

With a final pinch of her nipples her knees buckle. I wrap an arm around her waist as she pulls her hand away from her clit to press into the wall again. I pump into her twice more and release myself into her fluttering center.

Shockwaves course through my veins and Maggie's body vibrates in my hands. She gasps for air as I breathe heavily into the crook of her neck while our bodies come down from the intense high.

I pull my deflating cock out of her slowly and remove the condom. I tie it off and wash up in the bathroom. When I come out, Maggie has slipped her sweatshirt on again and is leaning against her bed.

"And to think you almost walked away from that," I grin as I step into my pants.

"I think that was our last time."

I look up at her from where I was picking up my shirt.

"You think, or you know?" I ask.

"I know, Austin, I just can't. This was good for what it was. Really good. Served its purpose. The election is in 10 days, Senator Quinn is flying all over and we'll be in Kentucky for election night."

"Makes sense MC, that's fine, I've got a few things going on this week anyway." I tell her, remembering my date with TalkShopGirl who I forgot about as soon as Maggie walked into the yoga studio.

"So, okay, well, then, bye?" Maggie says as she stands and follows me to the door.

"Consider this goodbye for now," I say and I press one last kiss to her heart shaped lips before walking away.

***

"Dude, Thorney, chill out. Why are you nervous?" Felix asks me as I pace around my apartment.

He's off tonight so he had the time to come and hang out with me before my date with TalkShopGirl.

"Why am I nervous?" I ask him. "Why am I nervous?" I repeat again, louder this time. "Oh, I don't know, maybe because I'm meeting the woman I would give up the best sex of my life for and I don't even know her name!" The anxiety has ratcheted up steadily the last three days.

"Wait, who was the best sex of your life? You're not talking about your hand, right buddy, because, he's great I'm sure, but there is better out there."

"No I'm not talking about," and before I continue I stop myself because I can't share the details of Maggie with him. I can't tell anyone. I can't talk about how amazing it was to watch her melt into relaxation with puppy yoga. How S'mores is training to be a therapy dog so he definitely sensed some tension and stress coming from Maggie.

Now that I'm thinking about her, I'm wondering how it went when she got the data from the debate. How her team responded. How it's going for her out on the road right now. The senator is visiting 40 states over the next week including one or two on election day itself. I smirk to myself trying to imagine Maggie traveling that much, she must hate it.

"That girl," Felix says.

"What girl?"

"The one you're thinking about that put that love sick smirk on your face. She's the best sex of your life."

"Yeah, she is, but you'll never know who she is."

"Because it's over?"

"Because it's over." I confirm before I loosen and retie my favorite neck-tie, again; for the third time.

"Wow, man, this is weird. I've known you for five years and I've never seen you this wound up about a date."

"Well, if this woman turns out to be even remotely attractive I might propose on the spot."

"Really? Maybe I should sign up for this thing."

"You sure man? I was ready for a relationship but I honestly didn't believe that the first person they matched me with would be this great. It's been a surprising journey. And since we've made such a strong connection I couldn't imagine stringing her along for a few years until I'm ready to get married. I have to decide quickly but if she returns my feelings, she'll be it for me."

"That fast huh, maybe not."

I laugh as he swipes open his Instagram and there is a message waiting for him. Of a girl, topless.

"Want me to drive you?" Felix asks when he checks the time.

"Sure, I can always call Greg for a ride later if I need him."

"Or maybe you can take text girl for a ride!" Felix laughs as he grips my shoulders and I have to shake my head to clear the image of Maggie from the first time I offered her a ride home, well before our arrangement.

She seems to be the only person I want to ride anymore.

I'm quiet, pensive, on the way over but my knee bounces in the front seat of Felix's Porsche the whole way. He parks outside the restaurant and I run my palms down my pants to dry the sweat accumulating there.

"Time to go, bud," he says.

"Yeah, I know, but," I turn to him and he must see the desperation in my eyes because his expression turns serious. "Will you look for me?"

"What?"

"Just hop out, peek in the window and see if you see a woman in a red dress with a phone in a flower case on the table."

"You're crazy man." He says as he pops open his door.

"Thank you!" I call out after him as he walks across the front of his car. I don't know what I would do without him. The sayings are true: sometimes your found family is just as strong as the one you are born into. I know in our case, we have each other's back, no matter what.

Felix tries to be casual as he looks inside but I see a few people give him double takes. It's tough for a guy who is 6'4" and built like a grizzly bear to blend in when he has his hands up next to the glass to improve his view through the window. It doesn't help that he's wearing a Renegades sweatshirt and his signature long hair is sticking out the sides of his beanie.

I watch him scan the restaurant and hold my breath when he stops, leans in a little closer, and then turns back to the car.

"So?" I demand as soon as he opens his door.

"I saw her," he tells me.

"And?"

"She's very pretty."

"Hell yes! Fuck. Thank god." I say on an exhale.

"Yeah, good, okay, one problem."

"What? No, you know what, it doesn't matter." I decide it as I say it out loud.

"That's the spirit Thorney, the election is almost over anyways."

A rock rolls in my stomach. What does the election have to do with this? Shit, have I been texting with Senator Quinn? I scoff. That'd be wild. No, wait it can't be, she's out of town. And that rules out her team too.

"What does the election have to do with anything?" I ask as I reach for the door handle.

"You said it yourself. It doesn't matter," Felix says and then he reaches over and pops the door open for me and all but shoves me out. "Go get 'em tiger!" He cheers.

I close the door, run my hand through my hair, and walk up to the door of the restaurant. I purposefully don't peek through the windows, wanting my genuine expression to be the one she sees. I step past the lattice that blocks the door from the rest of the space and stop dead in my tracks before rushing backwards behind the screen.

It's Maggie.

The woman in the red dress with the flower phone case on the table is Maggie Collins. Her hair is down in soft waves that falls just past her shoulders. She's looking down at the menu and nervously playing with the frayed edge of the corner. I eye her through the screen for a minute until she lowers the menu to the table and folds her hands on top of it. She checks the time on the phone and then looks around the restaurant.

I swallow the lump in my throat, and pull my tie off, and stick it in my pocket. As I undo the top button on my shirt, I stride confidently to her table. I'll decide how I play this once I get her reaction.

It's immediate. I see the change from hopeful anticipation as she scanned the room to skeptical disdain when her eyes settle on me. I watch as her jaw sets into place and her eyes narrow. She squares her shoulders and drops them down into their sockets.

"Well, well, well, Maggie Collins. Fancy seeing you here."

"Austin." She says shortly.

"Mind if I?" I ask as I pull out the chair across from her and take a seat.

"Yes, actually I do mind," she hisses and then she looks around the restaurant again. "I'm meeting someone."

"For a date?"

"Wouldn't you like to know."

"Yeah, I think I would."

"You know it's a date, don't be a dick."

I shrug, "How come you never got this dressed up for me?" I lean across the table and pull a strand of her hair through my fingers.

She swats my hand away. But the tingling sensation of the silky curl lingers.

"Can you go? I'm sure you've got yoga instructors to fawn over."

"Jealous, Maggie?"

"No." She insists but she definitely looks a little green.

I make a point of checking my watch. "Is your date late?" I ask and follow it with a tisk tisk sound effect.

"I'm sure he'll be here any moment." Maggie says as she flips over the phone to check the time again.

"Wait a minute, is that?" I grab the phone from under her grasp and pull it towards me. "Why, Maggie Collins, I believe we have an SMS Connect phone here. Are you meeting your match?"

"Just, stop it. Give me that." She says as I let her snatch the phone back. She sets it down in her lap and looks up hopefully at the door as it opens.

A kid who could not be more than twenty years old strides in wearing an oversized t-shirt, baggie jeans, and Birkenstock sandals with socks.

"Think that's him?" I ask as I turn back towards her.

"No," she growls.

"So, tell me about him? How long have you been chatting?"

"Austin," she says in a pleading way. "Do we have to do this?"

"Were you talking to him while fucking me?"

"Yes, and I felt bad about it, okay. Are you happy? But we were just sex and you clearly had options with a socialite or a yoga instructor this whole time so, pot meet kettle."

"Okay, okay, fair enough," I say as the waiter approaches.

"Can I get you something to drink?" He asks.

"No, he's leaving," Maggie says while I say "The Lapis Negroni please."

The waiter nods and walks away.

"Have you been here before?" I ask as I pick up the menu that's in front of her.

"What, no, you're not staying. You can't stay. You have to go." I can hear the desperation in her voice. If she feels half as attached to the SMS person as I am, she must be panicking right now.

"You're right. Sorry Maggie," I say as I stand up. I smile at her and see relief wash over her face. And then see it replaced with confusion when I pull back the empty seat right next to her table and sit down.

"Are you kidding me? That is not what I meant Austin."

"Maybe you should be more clear next time."

"Maybe you should take a hint and actually leave!"

"Is that what you want Maggie?"

"Yes!" She almost yells. I study her as she collects herself. "Yes, I want you to leave."

I stand, push the chair in, and step up next to her. I lean down and plant a feather light kiss on her temple as I brush her hair behind her shoulder.

"You look incredible tonight Maggie," I whisper and then I stand to my full height and look down into her face that is tilted up to see me. "And, that yoga instructor is my sister."

I force a weak smile and pivot for the door. Once I'm out on the sidewalk I glance back in at Maggie and feel a wild pang of jealousy that she doesn't know what I know.

She thinks her SMS Connect date is a no-show. That he stood her up. All she knows is I randomly showed up which in a city like D.C. isn't impossible.

I stick my hands in my pockets after turning the collar of my coat up. The late October chill has settled in tonight but I need to walk this jumble of feelings off and figure out what to do next.

Usually I send my SMS Connect messages at night. But since I'm supposed to be meeting her tonight I probably shouldn't send one. I don't want to cancel while she's still out. But how will I know when she is home?

My cell phone buzzes in my pocket and I pull it out.

FELIX

> So was she happy to see you?

I huff out a sarcastic laugh and shake my head. No, I don't think she was. This is almost too much for me to handle. How on earth did Maggie and I get matched just a few months before our worlds collided?

I cannot believe how many times we've been thrown together lately. Only for this to happen. How am I going to talk to her again?

How am I going to fix this?

What if I send a SMS Connect message saying that I got caught up at the office and couldn't make it?

That's no good. The natural thing to do is reschedule. Or she'd expect me to. And what do I do then?

"You're home early," Elle says when I let myself in. "She stood you up?"

"No," I insist, "it just didn't go as planned."

"What was wrong with her?" Elle asks, knowing how I've dismissed possible dates for seemingly small offenses. She knows I don't even consider a woman unless appears to be able to handle dating me. In the past that has mostly been focused on "can she handle the media attention?" but that has left me with a bunch of girls who only want me *for* the media attention.

"Nothing, she was perfect. She is perfect, I just, I'm not what she was expecting."

"Really? Aren't you the total package?"

I laugh as I sit down on the sofa with her. I pull my tie out of my pocket and start to slide the silk through my hands. I don't want it to remind me of Maggie's hair but it does. "Some might say that, but I'm not sure this girl would."

"So she broke it off with you?"

"Not exactly."

"I'm so confused." Elle says as she stuffs a handful of popcorn into her mouth.

"I am too, Elle," I say and reach over for some popcorn of my own.

We sit in silence for a few minutes while the period drama Elle is watching plays in the background.

"What are you going to do?" Elle asks the question we both want the answer to.

"I'm not sure. At this point I'm going to sleep on it and see if an idea comes to me in the morning."

"Well, remember what Mom always told us, honesty is the best policy, except in politics."

We share a laugh and after one character challenges the other to a duel for kissing his sister, I turn to her. "You know I'm not going to die because your honor is in question."

"My honor has been questionable for a long time, you're off the hook."

I laugh and stand up, "I'm headed to bed."

It is a fitful night of sleep as I toss and turn, replaying the hurt in Maggie's face and not knowing what to do with the information that she is also TalkShopGirl.

Chapter Twenty
MAGGIE

Theories Involve Broken Thumbs

"Good to see you last night?" I read out loud because maybe I'm dreaming. "Good to see you last night? What the actual fuck?!"

I toss my phone onto my bed and flop down into the comfy corner of my chair. The SMS Connect phone is sitting on the coffee table staring up at me blankly. Taunting me with it's silence. Constantly reminding me that DCFox never showed.

Instead, Austin Thorne walked in with his sexy, stupid, glasses, hint of tantalizing man cleavage, and then texts me the next morning saying *good to see you last night* and nothing else.

"Why even bother with that text, Austin Thorne?" I say out loud. "Was it good to see me? Why did you have to interrupt the first night of the rest of my life? What if DCFox showed up while you were sitting at my table, saw you, and then bolted? And why hasn't he texted? Fuck! I just want to know why this is happening to me. I'm supposed to be writing speeches for the presidential candidate of the century but instead I'm sitting here in my PJs sniffling over a text. Aaahhh!" I scream into a pillow.

My heart stops as I hear the familiar woosh of an iMessage being sent off to the satellites. I jump up and lunge for my phone on my bed and see that my iPhone did a voice to text of my rant and sent it to Austin.

"Shit shit shit shit shit shit shit," I repeat as I try to figure out how to unsend it. Instead three dots appear. He read it. He's responding.

Then the three dots disappear.

Then reappear.

"Spit it out!" I yell at the phone.

Ping.

"I bet those PJs are hot," I read out loud as the message comes through. "UUGH! What a turd!"

I lock my screen and then stuff my phone under the pillow before heading to the shower. Hopefully between the shower running, the bathroom door being closed, and a feather down barrier, Austin won't get a voice to text rendition of my next rant.

***

A refreshing shower helps me to reset my thought process. I got a bad night of sleep after waiting at the restaurant for an hour after Austin left. I couldn't settle my mind trying to figure out why DCFox didn't show up.

Maybe he got a glimpse of me and turned around?

Maybe he saw Austin and thought he was getting set up or phished?

Maybe some sort of tragedy befell him and he didn't have his SMS phone with him so he had no way to reach me?

Then I spent the next hour lying in bed thinking of all the terrible things that could happen to a man on his way to a date.

I ran through several of these scenarios again during my shower and decide that it's best he fell down an open sewer and broke his thumbs so he couldn't operate a phone to tell me where he was.

It's better than some of the other possibilities.

After I'm dressed, I dig my phone out from under my pillow and see that I have a missed call from Sam.

I call her back as I slide my notebook into my bag and check that I packed my charger. I'm leaving for the airport in forty minutes to fly and meet the team in St. Louis for a rally before flying to the twin cities for another rally and then flying overnight to Florida.

"So? Tell me everything!" Sam practically yells because of the noise behind her. I'm guessing she's at the first event of the day in Texas.

"Nothing to tell," I say slowly into the phone so she can hear me.

"Oh shit, is he still there? Sorry, why'd you call me back! Go get some!"

"No, he's not here, he's not, well, anywhere."

"What do you mean? Did he ghost you?"

"More or less," I admit with a sheepish shrug that she can't see.

"Damn, that's rough. Did you at least have a good meal? I love that restaurant."

"No, I didn't have an appetite, especially after Austin showed up."

"Austin Thorne?"

"Yeah he walked in while I was waiting for DCFox and basically harassed me. I mean I gave as good as I got this time but still, he was the last person I wanted to see."

"Ugh, poor you," Sam says before she pauses. "So, what are you going to do now?"

"Well I'm about to head to the airport."

"No, I mean with the SMS Connect guy. What do you think happened?"

"My current theory involves a manhole cover and broken thumbs."

"Sounds plausible."

I let out a little laugh before I inhale and exhale deeply. "Honestly, I don't know. I feel like I should message him but I don't know what to say. Maybe the meeting pushed him too far too fast. But, no," I remind myself out loud, "he was the one who asked to meet up. It just doesn't make any sense."

"Yeah, it's weird. I don't know what to tell you but I do have one question."

"Oh yeah, what's your question?"

"Did Austin look hotter at puppy yoga or at the restaurant last night?"

"No comment," I say and then I hang up on her as she starts to protest my lack of response.

I stare at the SMS Connect phone on my coffee table. I decide to be the bigger person and send a message.

TalkShopGirl: Hey. Picking an opening word or line for this message seemed like an impossible feat so I went basic. Casual. No big deal. Except, I'm not in a good spot this morning. I want to ask why you weren't there last night. I want to know what happened to you. But any reason you can give me doesn't change the fact that I sat alone, waiting, for over an hour.

And the thing that hurts the most right now is that I want to talk to you about what happened to me last night. When I was at my most vulnerable point waiting for you, a person who has been a pain in my ass for the last month at work showed up and, I'm not proud of it but, I was mean to him. I let some jealousy and nerves from our meeting spill into my conversation with him. And while we aren't friends I do want this person to think highly of me. To respect me.

So not only did I miss out on meeting you last night, I drew the line deeper in the sand with a person I might be forced to work with going forward.

I'm headed out of town for the next week and I'm going to leave this SMS Connect phone at home. Maybe we pushed it too far too fast. Maybe you got scared. Or maybe your thumbs are broken because of some terrible accident. But regardless, your silence speaks volumes and I need some space.

Chapter Twenty-One
MAGGIE

From Bad to Worse

"And I anticipate four years of prosperity and...and?"

"Growth?" Sam suggests with a shrug.

"That's the same as prosperity." I say as I rub my face before remembering I've got makeup on. My fingertips come back brown with eyebrow pencil and sparkly from my eyeshadow.

"True, okay, umm, peace?"

"We can't promise that."

"Right," Sam mutters as she lays with her legs propped over the arm of the sofa. We're in the Senator's hotel suite on election day. She jumped on the plane to make one last appearance in Dayton, Ohio and Sam and I stayed back to finalize her acceptance speech. The concession speech has been done for weeks. It's not considered a bad omen to have that one ready plus it's short and sweet to write. "Thank you, I've learned so much, enjoyed the process, and look forward to the future under president blah blah blah."

In order to avoid all manner of tempting fate, the acceptance speech cannot be written before election day. It definitely cannot be read by the candidate before the results are in. So in-line with tradition Sam and I are drafting it now.

My pen taps incessantly on the top of my notepad. The thump, thump, thump, doing little to calm the chaos in my mind.

"Why is this so hard?" I grumble as I toss my things on the coffee table between us in frustration.

"That's what she said."

"Lame." I deadpan but I can't help how I smile anyway at the dumb joke.

"Let's take a walk and let the physical movement shake some words out of us." Sam suggests as she swings her legs around and sits up.

"Alright, where to?"

"Wanna go check out the ballroom?"

"Okay, and then get a coffee on the way back up."

"Sounds like a plan."

***

The walk, the flurry of party preparations, the coffee, none of it worked. We ended up with a different line in the speech. I have a feeling *prosperity and* is going to keep me up at night.

The sun set hours ago and we're now in the suite together with the senator's family, close friends, and the entire team.

Including Austin.

I'm using my spidey sense that's tuned into his frequency to avoid him. If he walks into the dining area where I've been writing at the table, I stand up and move to the sitting area. If he walks closer to the kitchenette that dead-ends into the wall, I make a beeline for the second bedroom in the suite that has an alternative exit through the bathroom. I'm like an undercover agent always scouting out the closest escape route.

I have tried to push last Tuesday night so far out of my mind that the pressure of keeping it tucked away takes up more mental energy than just feeling the horribleness of it. Anytime I try to figure out what I'm feeling about being stood up by DCFox it morphs into the frustration of seeing Austin instead. How his presence doubled the pain of the moment. That

I was escaping the challenges of my professional life by going all in on personal endeavors only to get burned. So here I remain, holding hands and skipping down the sidewalk with denial, trying to focus on the election results as they come in.

At this point in the evening we are waiting on results from Ohio and Arizona. If one of those goes our way along with a few other states that we expect to fall for us then we've done it. If not, then we haven't.

It's humbling. After the countless hours of work, the months of analyzing every word choice, and reviewing countless data sets, it still feels like a game of roulette. We're just spinning around and around waiting to see where we'll fall.

"I got a heads up from the news director at Thorne Media Corp, he said they're about to call Ohio and he expects the other networks are going to call it soon too." Someone shouts out.

"Change it to TMC." Ben shouts above the chatter.

I watch as Austin slides backwards into the crowd. He's never used the fact that his father owns the largest media company in the country to his advantage, in this arena, or any that I can think of. He's never mentioned it, he's never once tried to use his connection to the senator with the AIM contract to promote any of the TMC brands.

It's either highly suspicious or highly demonstrative of his superior character.

I laugh at myself because there isn't much evidence of that superior character anywhere. None that I can see, nor care to find. Especially when my failed date at Lapis comes to mind. I hate that he was there, I hate that I engaged in conversation with him.

Moreover, I hate that in the moment I *liked* talking to him. I always do. But as soon as I step back and take in the full picture I'm reminded that he is driven to succeed. He only cares about the bottom line.

The few blips when he put me first, or showed me kindness, and seemed to be a caring and compassionate man flash in my memory but I dismiss them. Remembering the few moments he's been the man I think he can be will not help me stay firmly in the I Hate Austin Thorne camp.

With a shake of my head to dislodge the thoughts of Austin actually being a nice guy, I turn my focus to the TV. The anchors are sitting in a wide semicircle, there are six of them. Two hosts and then two commentators on each side because balance and fairness are the themes of the night.

"TMC's election data team is ready to make a call on Ohio," the first anchor says.

"That's right, and they're calling it for Senator Quinn."

The whole room erupts in cheers and hugs and high fives and claps and fist bumps. Joy. Simply put, the room explodes with joy.

I hug Sam, I hug Ben, my smile is so wide it almost hurts.

Then my eyes shift to Austin who is standing in the back and smiling at me. Just watching me. Our eyes lock and instead of the hurt and anger I was expecting to feel, his graphite eyes are soft and comforting. And I feel, well, loved.

The activity and jubilation in the room fades as I connect with him. We don't need words. We did it. He breaks eye contact first when someone steps up next to him for a congratulatory handshake and I snap out of my trance. I blink heavily and try to decipher if my heart is racing because of the results or that interaction with Austin.

Sam calls me over to the table to make sure we get the speech loaded into the teleprompter correctly and to do one final pass through.

When we're satisfied we tell Ben that it's good to go and sit back to wait for the confirmation from Illinois and Minnesota before sending the senator out on stage.

***

"And so, it is with immense pride and an overwhelming sense of relief that I accept the position of President of the United States. I look forward to four years of prosperity and stability. I believe we can accomplish a great deal together and I cannot wait to get started."

I'm clapping from just off stage with a smile pasted on my face because there are cameras everywhere but I'm furious.

That wasn't my speech.

I don't know who wrote it but it wasn't mine. Sam has a look of confusion on her face next to me which tells me she is just as surprised as I am.

"What the hell was that?" She whispers out of the side of her mouth as she continues to clap.

"I have no idea." I admit with a shrug as I also continue to smile and clap. We might look deranged.

I look past the senator and the crowd on stage and see Austin standing in the wings directly across from me. He's leaning over an iPad with Tyler and they're both nodding. When he looks up his eyes catch mine and I want to rip those glasses off and stomp on them.

He smiles, shrugs, and slips his hands into his pockets.

So it was an AI Media speech.

Fuck my life.

Chapter Twenty-Two
MAGGIE
What's Worse than "Worse"?

"Maggie, it's as simple as us trying to stay current with the trends, to use all the technology available to us. It isn't personal. It's politics."

I'm nodding and willing the sting in my nose to evaporate so I don't cry in front of the president-elect and her chief of staff.

Two people that I have given everything to this last year.

Two people who are telling me I don't have a job in their administration because they're going to use AIM for speech writing.

"We appreciate everything you've done with us, for us, and will help you get settled anyway we can," Ben says and the urge to kick him in the shins is strong.

"I understand. Is there anything else you need from me?" I ask slowly so I don't disturb the tears that are threatening to spill over.

"That's all for now," the president-elect says and she stands up and offers me a hand to shake. I return it but it feels like I'm floating away from my body. Like I'm watching myself shake her hand. Like maybe this is all a terrible dream.

How is it possible for me to have absolutely nothing left?

No job.

No plan.

No partner.

No prospects.

I slide my bag on my shoulder and hand my security badge over to the agent at the door. The tears slam into the backs of my eyes as I envision walking int my empty apartment. So, instead of going straight to the metro station I decide to walk. It's warm for a November day and I am banking on the fresh air being good for me.

As I wind my way past the Smithsonian. I take in the scene around me. The walls of these buildings have seen so much history. I'm certainly not the first person to be strolling down these streets feeling dejected and rejected. There have been plenty of political analysts scorned in this town. When I reach the edge of the tidal basin, in the shadows of the Washington Monument and Lincoln Memorial, the water makes me think of home.

It's the last place I ever wanted to be but I know no one in my small hometown will care about all the things I've come to worry about here in D.C.. They'll be proud that I helped get the senator elected. They will think it's normal not to be working for her anymore. Or, they won't know any better, at least.

I could spin it so it seems like I was the one who left. Like I wasn't the one who was stood up on a blind date. Who didn't fall for the mystery person writing the words on the other side of a small e-ink screen.

They'll think my clothes are fancy; my big city habits exotic; my connections to people they see on TV mesmerizing.

I sit on a bench and look out over the water and call my mom.

"Well, hello, big shot!" My mom cheers as she answers the phone. "Charles, come here, Maggie's on the phone. Come say hello before I tell her what Dawn was telling me about The Inn earlier."

"Hey Mom," I say, sounding every bit dejected as I feel.

"What's wrong?" Her tone is more first responder than concerned parent.

"I, umm, I've decided to step away for a bit."

"You got fired?" Dad supplies.

I suck in a breath between my teeth. "I wasn't included in the restructured team."

"Oh, honey, I'm so sorry." My mom coos into the phone. Her sympathy doesn't help the tears I feel gathering.

"What do they think they're going to do without you?" I hear my dad say. His voice starts louder, grows fainter, and then comes back to full strength which tells me he's pacing a few steps away and back. The same thing I do when I'm processing new information.

"I dunno Dad. So, yeah, this is not ideal, but, umm, can I..." I stop to sniffle up the tears that are now flowing freely. "Can I come home for a bit?"

"How long is a bit?" I hear my dad ask from a distance while my mom says, "Of course."

I smile and let my mom talk to me about town gossip and projects she's working on while I walk to a bus to get back to my apartment. Going back to upstate New York is more than a few anxious paces but I need the change of scenery while I try to put my life back on track.

***

Three days later, I'm in a rental sedan with two suitcases, an assortment of boxes filled with books and notebooks, and my preferred bed pillow, piled in the back seat. I've already paid my November rent so my apartment can just sit there. I'll decide about December after Thanksgiving.

Mom is thrilled to have me home in Lakeville. My little sister's wedding is New Year's Eve and now that I'm unemployed she has enlisted my help. I should start to tally the number of times she says "silver lining" or "when one door closes..." and adds a noncommittal shrug. Every time she does, my mind briefly flits to Austin and then I re*consider*.

Dad said he'd be thrilled to have me home for a month and I could hear the unsaid *and only a month* loud and clear. He's the parent who believes in kicking the chicks out of the nest when he thinks they're ready, not when they actually are.

My parents are both retired now, after putting my older brother through med school, me through law school, and my younger sister through undergrad. Academic performance is highly valued in the Collins family. Every phone call with them or visit home was peppered with questions from Dad about grades, job prospects, and salary projections.

Dad has always expected big things from my siblings and me. It started in childhood. Good grades, good effort on the teams we joined, good attitudes around the house when it came to chores.

And there were lots of chores. While my mom handled the laundry and my dad took care of the yard and the bathrooms, us kids handled everything else. Dishes, dusting, vacuuming, wiping down tables, washing windows; there was a routine and we followed it.

Not for an allowance mind you, no, this contribution was simply expected. We would work hard, as a team, and all achieve excellence, together.

None of us really understood how much we subscribed to this notion of Collins excellence until Liz lost her job and moved home. She started working at the coffee shop in town and would put up photographs she'd taken on the walls. Some sold and people around town asked her for portrait sessions, and then a year later Dad helped her finance a photography business. He used the money he had set aside for her advanced degree but, in a smart move, he didn't mention that when he gave it to her.

Liz's career pivot served as a turning point for him. He softened a bit about expectations, not that he'd ever really go easy on us, but he did start to sprinkle in personal questions when we talked instead of just 401k inquiries.

At first I felt jealous of Liz and the handout she got. I toiled through law school and she was just handed cash to start her dream business. Once that initial reaction passed I realized that going to law school was my dream because it led me to the career in political communications that I had always wanted.

It stung because it felt like, as the baby of the family, Liz, once again, just had things handed to her. When she was born, everything in our house shifted to make sure she was taken care of. CJ picked up some of my chores so I could help Mom take care of the baby.

In high school we'd take turns driving Liz around.

Memories surface of stopping for ice cream on the way home, or taking her to her friend's houses on the weekends. The time we got stuck in a snow storm and had to walk to get help. As I exit the freeway towards Lakeville, I see the welcome sign commemorating our Guinness Book of World Records entry for longest domino chain re-action with anything besides dominos. I wasn't born when it happened but the story is taught to Lakeville's young right after we're taught the story of Adam and Eve. Our town lined up books from one end of downtown to the other and set them all tumbling down. Then we opened up the first library in city history with the books, T.H.E. Library named after Tessa Harper Edwards who led the world record efforts.

I decide to drive through downtown before heading to my parent's house. The coffee shop has a new sign, Liz's photography studio next door has a beautiful painted design on the window. Lewis Hardware glows under the fluorescents inside and I spot the lights flickering on in the apartment above.

I turn the corner and see a new space for my sister's friend Angie's interior design business and next to it the bake shop her friend Maeve opened.

I haven't been home for more than 24 hours in years. Always flying in just for the holiday and then flying out again to get back to work. I still know the latest news because Mom keeps me up to date on all the gossip and notable events. A lot has changed in the years I've been gone but it doesn't feel different. Just renewed.

The next generation is putting their mark on the town. My generation. The people I grew up with who stayed, or left and came back.

I pull into the driveway, put my car in park, and look up at my childhood home. My hands are still on the wheel as a tsunami of feelings hits me. Disappointment, sadness, embarrassment, fear, loneliness, insecurity, and oddly, relief.

What's that doing there?

Ending up back at home as my life hits rock bottom is not supposed to feel right. It's supposed to make me feel frustrated and twitchy and anxious.

I can see people walking around in the house. The porch light is on. With a deep breath, I climb out, grab my purse and one suitcase, and complete the solemn march back to my childhood home.

"MAYBE!" my little sister Liz yells out as she storms through the house to meet me at the front door. "You're home!"

"Hey Lizzard," I laugh at the nickname she bestowed on me as a toddler because she couldn't say her G's clearly. Liz wraps me in a hug and I look over her shoulder to see her fiancé, Kyle, standing century behind her.

"How are the lovebirds," I laugh and give Kyle a quick hug too.

"We're good," Liz says as walks back into the kitchen. "But even better now that you're here and Mom can channel some of her energy your way."

"What do you mean?" I ask as Dad comes up from the basement. He gives me a hug, a quiet "good to see you," and then gets a beer and heads back downstairs. He gives Liz and I a smile and says, "I'll let you girls catch up."

Liz pulls out a bottle of white wine and starts to open it. Kyle makes his way to the cabinet and pulls down two glasses and sets them on the counter.

"I mean, she is absolutely bonkers about this wedding. I get at least four new ideas a day. With seven weeks to go she's still got way too much time on her hands to add projects. You need to reign her in."

"How do you expect me to do that?" I ask as she slides a glass of wine over the counter to me.

"Be practical. Tell her no." I laugh but Liz's face is stern. "I'm serious, Nora has tried. There are lists galore and budgets and plans but she won't stop looking for new things to do."

If Nora Heely, my sister's best friend and most organized person I've met, can't get control of Mom, I'm not sure I'll be much help.

"Is that where she is now?"

"Probably. I don't know who introduced her to Facebook Marketplace but she is absolutely obsessed with it and checks it constantly."

"Is there a theme?" I ask.

"Winter wonderland," Kyle chimes in as he pops the top off a bottle of beer.

"Seriously, the possibilities are endless," Liz adds after a sip.

"I'll see what I can do." I mutter as I take my glass with me to the sofa. Liz and Kyle follow. Thank goodness they were waiting for me at Mom and Dad's. It will be nice to ease into being home without incessant questions about why, or how long, or what happened.

"So, I want to know all the stuff you haven't told Mom," Liz says as she sits down with me. Maybe not such a calm reentry. Kyle perches himself behind her on the armrest.

"I hate to ask this but, do you already know everything I've told Mom?"

"Well, I'm not sure if it's everything but, Mom blew up the book club chat right after you called her."

"You're a Tome Raider?" I ask with an eyebrow raised because the book club group chat is notorious for being more about town gossip than about the books they're reading.

"I was tired of having to use Mom as my source." Liz says with a shrug. "There has been some exciting shit happening around here, I mean nothing as glamorous as a presidential campaign, but Angie and Jimmy's TV show is pretty fancy."

"You don't have to tell me, I bet Lakeville life is twice as exciting as D.C.," I mutter quietly.

"I doubt that, but is boredom the reason you left? Mom said you lost the job, sorry about that by the way, I know how much it sucks."

"Thanks," I give her a salute with my wine.

"But, if you want to get another job, why wouldn't you stay?"

"D.C. isn't as small as Lakeville but it has its moments," I say and Liz's eyes grow wide.

"You've got an ex!" She proclaims and turns her body to fully face me on the sofa, tucking her legs up under her criss cross applesauce style. Her wine sloshes dangerously close to the edge of her glass with the movement but it doesn't spill over.

Kyle laughs and stands, "I'm gonna go watch whatever game your dad has on in the basement."

He kisses the top of Liz's head as he walks away. I feel a sharp pang of jealousy. It's similar to the kiss on my temple Austin gave me when he crashed my date but I didn't realize until seeing it here that I want that type of affection from a partner.

"He's not an ex," I say, getting straight to the point. If my mom is a bull dog for gossip my sister is a wolf. "I had two different situationships going I guess."

"Two?"

"Well, one was real. Or," I let out a frustrated puff of air. "Okay, I started a sex arrangement with someone I was working with. Just sex. No feelings. I actually hate his guts."

"Go on," Liz prompts with excitement in her eyes.

"And the other was," I look up at the ceiling and pull my lips in between my teeth. I close my eyes, turn back to Liz, open my eyes and say, "just texts."

"Just texts?" She repeats to confirm.

"He was a guy I was texting. I don't even know his name. I don't know who he is or what he does or what he looks like but I know that I am," I pause and regroup, "Well, I *was* developing feelings for him and I miss talking to him every day."

"You didn't want to meet him?"

"No I did, and I thought he did too. We set a date and then he didn't show up. And actually, my annoying sex exchange partner made an appearance and that made the whole night worse."

"And then you lost your job?"

"Because of Austin Thorne's new software."

"Why do I know that name?"

"He's sometimes on the TCM gossip sites, his dad owns TCM and Austin oversees the AI Media side of things."

Liz slides her phone out of the thigh pocket on her leggings and with one thumb she starts googling. I know she's going to find a picture of him and tell me how hot he is.

"Whoa, Maybe! He's a fox. Wait," She continues swiping and typing. "Is this him?"

She turns her phone to me and it's an Instagram post. Austin is walking out of a bar with Felix Fornier.

I sigh, "yeah that's him."

Austin and all the things we did together live rent free in my mind and I don't need a picture to bring memories of him in a suit to the forefront.

"Wait," she says as she continues sleuthing, "He's the guy you did the podcast with?"

"Yeah," I say because the way she asks this it's like she knows who he is.

"You two had some really good banter going, good chemistry. We could hear it through the audio."

"We?"

"The Tome Raiders. Mom sent it out when it was published because she was proud of you but all we could talk about at the meeting was how you two sounded like you were ready to pounce on each other."

I bite my lip thinking back to that day. My anger as I first realized who he was. How he had deceived me at the office earlier. How I knew, even then, he was a threat to my livelihood. How we started working together. The first kiss that felt like he'd branded me. The first time we were together and it felt like he met me in stride. The next time we were together and I was vulnerable and opened myself up to him, emotionally and physically.

"You pounced on each other didn't you?" Liz's question pulls me back to the present.

"He was my sex for stress-relief partner."

"And the guy who spoiled your blind date?"

"Yeah, and who put me out of a job."

"Yikes, well then it's a good thing he's hot because he doesn't have much else going for him."

I think about how attentive he was at, and after, yoga, about the way he held doors open for me, about the emotion in his eyes when the election results came in.

If he hadn't been the reason I lost everything I think I'd want to know him better.

"Anyway," I transition because I'm not ready to examine those feelings. "I know Mom is going a little crazy with your wedding but are you excited?"

"Yes, so excited. My dress is beautiful and I can't wait to wear it. And I know we already live together and have been together for years but there's something about actually getting married that feels big."

"It is big," I tell her as I take a sip of wine. "To commit to spending the rest of your life legally bound to another person? That's huge."

"Legally bound," she laughs, "is that what you think marriage is?"

"More or less," I admit. "I know Mom and Dad had this amazing partnership and worked together as a team so Mom could keep working and we could all do the things we wanted to do but I think what they have is rare. I think people are too selfish to really put someone else's needs before their own for an entire lifetime."

"It's not about putting their needs before your own. It's about knowing that both of you have needs and figuring out how to best meet them. Yes, sometimes I do the thing Kyle wants to do but it isn't because I'm putting his needs before mine. It's because supporting him fulfills me and ends up benefiting us both."

I pause as I let her words sink in. I have believed for a long time that I'd need to find a partner that was willing to sacrifice for my career. Someone without ambitions of his own. A man that was willing to be at my beck and call.

But maybe when a person, who has their own thing going on, sets it aside for a moment to support you they're showing a deeper kind of love.

A respectful kind of love.

And if it's a two way street, with each of you working on your own things side by side but leaning on each other along the way, that kind of love can last a lifetime.

I sit back on the sofa as this new perspective settles in. I'm so used to jumping to action when something needs doing. I'm accustomed to setting aside my task to complete the more urgent one. Or the one being asked of me. I can feel Liz watching me as I run through different scenarios, reframing them with this new support-not-sacrifice lens. I had never thought of it in this way.

I saw it as everyone sacrificing for the others. My mom with her laundry schedule and color coded calendar, sacrificing her free time for the family. My dad with his grocery list up on the fridge and expectations that we kids help out sacrificing a full night's sleep so he could leave early and be home to help with dinner. Us kids having to keep up with the chores together, often covering for each other if there was a big exam or project, a game, or social event, sacrificing our childhood because our parents needed help.

For the first time I'm seeing these things as love instead of resentment.

"Well, I like the way you put it but it doesn't matter. Austin hates me, I hate him, and the SMS guy isn't talking to me." I shrug and take a gulp of wine. "Should we go watch whatever sports game is on with Dad and Kyle?" I suggest. "I feel like if we're out of sight when Mom gets home from whatever errand she's running we'll be spared helping with a craft project."

"It's cute you think you'd be spared but yes, let's go." Liz says and we head downstairs together.

***

"Margaret Geraldine Collins, get downstairs and help your father!" My mom yells from somewhere on the first level. I pull the covers down from my ears and blink my eyes open. With a quick lift of my head to peek out my window I can confirm that the day after Thanksgiving dawns with a fresh blanket of snow on the ground. It looks to be about three inches, nothing for upstate New York, but still enough to light up my chest with excitement.

I love snow. Well, I love snow the day after a holiday when you've got nowhere else to go.

Snow in D.C. is a nightmare. Everything turns gray and slushy and the metro platforms are slippery with the snow melt puddles left behind by everyone's boots. You have to carry a spare pair of shoes with you and the radiator heat in the office is always four degrees too warm to be called comfortable.

I hear my dad shoveling the front walk and I pad down the stairs to the front door.

"Morning Dad," I say as I step out onto the porch and wrap myself in my puffer coat.

"Morning Mags, beautiful day isn't it!" He cheers.

"Need some help?"

"You can choose between shoveling or helping your mother pack away the china until Christmas." He levels me with a stare that tells me he agrees shoveling is the better end of the deal. "She's delirious with happiness and activity. It means a lot that you're home," he adds.

I scoff, "How do you figure? The way I see it I've failed in every possible way."

Dad stops shoveling and leans on the handle. "Accepting change, or admitting things didn't go according to plan isn't failure. It's strength. It's a skill. You'd never tell a friend or a colleague to look at this as a failure so stop telling yourself that nonsense."

"Yes, Dad," I say like a teenager but his words hit me in the solar plexus.

"Put on some sensible footwear and help me." He says before he scoops up another line of snow and tosses it off the path.

"Yes, Dad," I repeat but with a smile on my face. I see him smile before I turn around for the door. I slide into my snow boots from high school and walk out to the garage for the other shovel.

The two of us make quick work of clearing the walkway and the drive and as we're sprinkling salt and sand down to prevent ice, Liz and Kyle pull up.

"Tree time!" Liz calls out as she steps out of their car. She and Dad wrap each other in hugs and Kyle gets a handshake before they reach me and we hug our hellos too. The front door opens.

"Finally! Everyone is here, let's get out to Cole's before all the good ones get picked."

"Katherine, that boy has enough trees for everyone in Lakeville to have two, it'll be fine."

"But they're all different sizes and shapes and we need the perfect one because it is the kick off to wedding month!"

My dad shakes his head with humor but he grabs the keys and I pile into the backseat. Liz and Kyle drive behind us on our way out to my old high school boyfriend's farm. Cole MacDonald was a star first baseman for Lakeville H.S. and he inherited his family's farm a few years ago.

Every year, my family treks out to MacDonald Farm for our Christmas tree the day after Thanksgiving. We then spend the day decorating it and eating leftovers. Wish lists are discussed over turkey sandwiches and Christmas music plays from the speakers in the kitchen. I haven't been a part of the festivities since undergrad when I had the entire week off.

We pull down the road to the farm and it feels smaller than I remember. Everything about Lakeville felt small to me when I lived here. I couldn't wait to move on to bigger, and better, things. Then once I lived the life of the bigger cities and more important things I barely spent enough time here to feel the smallness of it all. In the last week I've gotten waves from people as I pass them, been stopped and asked how I'm doing anytime I'm not in my car, and I was even invited to the next Tome Raider meeting.

I passed.

In D.C., occasionally, I'd get a wave from Joanne of Sunrise, but I didn't know my neighbors. I worked with people but we rarely discussed anything besides work. Even Sam, who I would call my closest friend, and I haven't talked since I left.

As we turn into the parking lot I feel tears well up in my eyes.

I'm lonely.

I swallow down the tears because I do not want to set off my mother's alarm bells and when we step out into the cold I inhale the biting air and pull myself together. I send a quick text to Sam wishing her a Happy Thanksgiving even though the actual day has passed. Better late than never they say.

Liz and Kyle meet us at the edge of the field and my throat grows thick with emotion seeing them walk up holding hands.

"The Collins family! Merry Christmas!" I would know that voice anywhere, Cole MacDonald is headed our way. Slowly I turn and muster as much excitement as I can because if I didn't want my mom to see me cry I definitely don't want to break down in front of Cole.

"Cole MacDonald, how are you, darling?" My mother coos and I don't miss the quick look she sends my way. Yes Mom, I'm aware, he's attractive, he's local, he's single. Too bad none of that is doing anything for me at the moment.

Greetings and hugs are shared and while I'm wrapped up in Cole's familiar embrace my phone starts buzzing in my pocket.

"Sorry," I smile up at him. ""'m going to take this," I tell him when I see Sam's name on the screen. "Hello?"

"Maggie! I was so happy to see your text. How are you?"

"Hey Sam, I'm fine," I say unenthusiastically as I take a few steps away from the group.

"I've got some news to share," Sam starts.

"Oh yeah?"

"I got a job as Director of Content Strategy for Forever Home! That app that brought the puppies to the hockey game!"

Sam's excitement is palpable. It reverberates off the cold cinderblock of aimlessness at my core.

"What?"

"I start in January. I had an amazing interview with this guy Wes who of course remembered me from the campaign stop," she continues rambling excitedly as I spiral further and further down into despair. I start shaking my head quickly back and forth before my feet begin pacing an oval in the snow. She just got another job?

"How?" I ask, interrupting something about her being the most senior woman on the team.

"What do you mean? I needed a job."

"But it's not in politics. It's a tech company. It's, it's…" I don't know how to form words. I can't process making a switch or veering off my career course.

"Listen," Sam interrupts, sounding more serious than I've ever heard her. "I know we got caught on the shit end of the stick after the election. But after the last several months of working my tail off I'm doing something that will be fun. I get to play with puppies all day and help them find their families. I get to coordinate events and help roll out the app in new markets. I wasn't on Senator Quinn's team for the politics. I was in it for the experience. All I want to do is use my words for good."

My vision blurs as I look out at the pine trees. It isn't tears, it's a earth shattering thought causing a dizzying effect.

What if I'm not in politics anymore?

My instant reaction to Sam's words makes it feel like the walls are crumbling down around me.

Maggie Collins, not in politics?

If I don't want to continue in the field that I've spent my entire life working to get to the top of, what do I want to do?

Oh god, where do I go from here?

I'm almost 40, sure in the world of politics that's pretty young, but it is way too old to start over. I'll never make a name for myself in a new field at this point.

"Maggie, are you done with your call, love?" Mom calls out. "Cole said he'd help us cut down the tree," she adds in a sing-song voice.

I look quickly at Kyle who is an Eagle Scout and more than capable of cutting down a Christmas tree. It looks like he's about to share that tidbit too but Liz cuts him off with a whack to his chest.

I guess I'm the match-making target today. I roll my eyes and end the call with Sam promising her that I'll call her again soon but feeling hopelessly lost in my thoughts and farther away from my friend than ever.

"Yep, let's go," I try to muster as much enthusiasm as I can.

We fall in line together, two by two. Mom and Dad, Liz and Kyle, and Cole and me at the end.

"Well, well, well, Maggie Collins is back in town," Cole jokes and I laugh with him. "How long are you staying?"

"Not sure," I admit with a shrug and I can feel his stare on me.

"That's odd," he says.

I turn to him, "What do you mean?"

"You've had a plan to get the heck out of Lakeville since grade school."

I laugh a little in agreement.

When I don't say anything, Cole continues, "I remember us in high school. Man, I sure loved you," he laughs and I turn to him in shock. "But

I kept telling myself that Maggie Collins wasn't going to stay in town for anyone. She was going out to rule the world."

"Ha, I didn't even come close," I scoff.

"No?" I feel Cole turn to look at me. "Your mom said you wrote speeches for President Quinn. That's about as close to running the world as someone can get!"

"I guess so," I shrug, "but I don't do that anymore."

"What happened?"

"They fired me," and replaced me with a robot.

"Their loss," Cole says with a quick lean in to bump my shoulder. I force a smile to hide how distraught I am. In one conversation with my high school crush I'm revisiting all my shortcomings and if he asks me what I'm going to do next there's no way I could keep myself together. "You staying until the wedding?"

"Probably," I shrug again and Cole stops walking. He reaches out and grabs my hand so I stop too.

"Maggie, I can tell you're lost. It happens to all of us. Try to remember what's important to you, why you made all the career and life choices you did so far. It's not that they led you astray, they led you here." Cole reaches up and grabs hold of my shoulders, he lowers his head so we're eye level before he continues. "And you can always start fresh from here," he says and then he turns my shoulders so I'm forced to turn around.

Behind me is a view of Lakeville I've never seen before. There is a clearing where last year's trees were harvested and I can see down the rolling hills to the lake, I can see Sunfish Park, I can see the buildings in town with their Christmas decorations already shining.

It's beautiful but I don't have the heart to tell Cole it also makes me itch to leave. As far as places to be from go though, Lakeville ranks pretty high up on the list. I just wish I knew where I was going from here.

Chapter Twenty-Three
AUSTIN
Meanwhile in D.C.

"Okay everyone, it is 9:00 and I am calling this meeting of the Thorne Media Corporation Board to order."

Today is a great fucking day. I get to present the first earnings report for AI Media. We have crushed it. The product has been live for nine weeks and we've already cleared our initial investment. From here on out, there will be some maintenance costs, but it's essentially pure profit.

Not only do I get to show strong revenue numbers, I get to share that we are not being sued. We were able to prove that the speeches AIM wrote and the news articles it created for users were based on articles created by TMC only and from content uploaded by users under contract.

Basically we aren't being sued because Maggie and her team uploaded everything willingly.

It sucks.

But it's true.

And it's been eating away at me.

I try to stuff the uneasy feeling down and focus on the activity in the room. This is the last board meeting of the year. Next year Dad turns 65, the widely accepted retirement age. I expect him to announce his succession plan today.

I need a win. I've been in a funk since learning that Maggie and Talk-ShopGirl are the same woman. The perfect woman in fact. One that I've both had and lost.

It was painful to be in the same room on Election Night. I watched every emotion dance across her face and wanted to share them all. The anticipation as results came in. The high of the win. The low of when she realized AI Media had written the speech.

That one hurt the most.

After our missed, but actually realized, connection at Lapis I've started to carry the SMS Connect phone around with me. It's a pathetic attachment to hope. Delusional even. But my logic is if she messages me I want to be there for her right away.

When I watched her face fall during the acceptance speech I desperately wanted to comfort her as DCFox. I tried to give her a reassuring smile from across the room as I clutched the little phone in my pocket.

It wasn't enough.

A week after the election, I got an email telling me Jorge would be our contact for President-Elect Quinn's team. I emailed him and asked where Maggie was. Jorge told me after she and Sam were fired, Maggie went back home to upstate New York. So, all the times I found myself walking around her neighborhood hoping to catch a glimpse of her were for nothing.

I haven't responded to her SMS message from that night. I don't know what to say. She left it final. In truth I don't have a way to explain what happened. What could I possibly say? But I still carry this thing around, still paying the monthly fee, in the hope that she'll reach out again. And I will hold on to the hope a little while longer because TalkShopGirl, Maggie, hasn't given up on me, either. I would have been notified by SMS Connect so while the odds aren't with me, I haven't lost all hope.

In the last few weeks I've thrown myself into work. I've hired several additional developers to review our code and look for biases. We're also working on a new tab for the app that would show users articles that other people are seeing. Instead of a "for you" page, a "for them" page. I don't know if anyone will use it but it's a way to try and open the user's eyes to help prevent them from getting stuck in their own algorithm.

That can't be bad, right?

Would Maggie be proud of it?

Of me?

I shake my head as the Secretary of the Board wraps up his report. I'll be up soon. Maybe an announcement from Dad to the board will bolster my confidence. Make me feel like the tycoon I've been raised to be.

"Let's quickly work our way through divisional reports. The investor meeting next month during earnings season will be where we discuss details so let's keep things at a high level here. We'll go in our typical order. Board Members, please reserve your questions and comments until the end."

I sit up a little straighter in my seat. Show time.

Newspaper is first, sad.

Podcasts is next, not bad.

New media is next. I'm not the president of the division but I've been allowed to operate on my own while developing AIM.

"I'm excited to share that our division is reporting a profit with only ten days left in the year." I lift my chin, expecting to have the conversation passed to me because I'm the reason for the influx of cash. "Our digital news production is a major contributor but the other assets in our division are also performing well. We expect performance to continue into the new year."

The division president for publishing starts sharing his summary and I blink rapidly while looking around the room.

Nothing?

Absolutely nothing about AI Media or the lawsuit I rescued us from.

I stare at my father at the head of the table and mentally beg him to look at me. Maybe he'll call me out separately. He's never done that before but I only received my voting seat a year ago so, there hasn't been much opportunity.

The division presidents wrap up and the meeting moves on without a word about my product. No acknowledgement. No recognition.

He's really playing this one close to the vest.

I reach into my pocket under the table and run my thumb along the SMS Connect phone. It's become a sort of talisman. It's what brought me to Maggie in the first place. Never mind the fact that it's the reason Maggie isn't currently talking to me.

""Before we adjourn and go into end of year mode I wanted to share something." Dad starts and I grasp the device like it's the top hold on the wall. "Next year marks a milestone for me and we'll be celebrating throughout the year. As many of you know I'll be 65 and because of that we'll spend the year marking my 30th year at the helm of my family's corporation. It has been the work of my lifetime to get to this point and I am excited to continue in this position for years to come."

The room fills with polite applause. I'm slow on the uptake but I join in. I tow the line to be polite but inside I am furious.

Grandpa left the company when he turned 65. Dad was 35 at the time.

Now, 30 years later, I expected the tradition to continue.

What do I have to do to prove myself to him?

Why doesn't he want me to succeed?

What do I do now?

***

A few days later I'm dressed in a tux at the family Christmas Eve party. Don't picture Norman Rockwell, tonight is a high society affair. It's about

250 people at my father's estate in Mclean, fully catered, with a pianist playing soft music in the corridor. Everyone is in black tie and the multiple trees throughout the first floor have been professionally decorated according to the theme. This year it is winter wonderland so there is fake snow along the baseboards, crystal snowflakes hung with fishing line from the ceiling, and twinkle lights covering every other surface. It looks like frosty the snowman threw up all over my father's home. Elle and I arrived together but she quickly disappeared and now I find myself stuck between Dad's head legal counsel and one of his golf buddies.

"The numbers out of AI Media look good. And the way you maneuvered to dodge that lawsuit? Bravo, son."

I give him a closed lip smile because I'm not proud of how I dodged that lawsuit for Dad. In fact, I'm not happy with my dad at all. I haven't spoken to him since the meeting.

Before that meeting I was able to throw myself at work to escape the misery of my Maggie situation. Work is no longer an oasis.

Basically, I'm miserable everywhere, all the time.

I bow out of the conversation they were having and walk slowly around the party sipping my old fashioned. I look at all these people who would rather spend their Christmas Eve trying to impress my billionaire father than be with their own families. Most of them are Dad's age or older, their children would be my age now, but when I was younger I don't remember other kids being at these parties. So did they spend Christmas Eve with nannies? With their grandparents?

More and more these days I'm questioning the way I've done everything my entire life.

I turn the corner and find Elle standing near the doors that lead to the terrace. When she spots me she waves me over.

"Bro, get a load of this!" She pulls my shoulders in front of her so I can peek out the window of the french doors.

At first I don't see anything but then I squint and can make out two figures that are wrapped around each other.

"There is nothing remotely sexy about this party. What is wrong with people?" I say as I turn back to Elle.

"Well, for one, they're each married to other people," she grins.

"I see you got the Thorne gene for endless gossip."

She punches me in the shoulder. "C'mon, even you have to admit that is scandalous. I wonder if Dad has a photographer on call ready to document this. I feel like he's a House rep or something."

"Well, either way, Dad will find a way to profit off of this."

"He always does."

"Should we find the man and take the obligatory family photo?" I ask as I dump the last drops of my drink down my throat.

"Sure, better do it now before I get too drunk and start to look it." Elle says as she stands up from where she was leaning. "Let's find Mom."

I hold out my elbow for her to hook her arm through. Then the two of us try to find Laura in the crowd. When we were little she came to the parties with us and would pose in the photo with Dad. She bragged about us to his colleagues and their wives.

When I got older I'd hear the whispers about her. They'd be questioning why she would attend the party. Was she trying to get him back?

They called her desperate and pathetic. And they'd give Elle and I pitying looks.

As a teenager I got angry about it. One time I lashed out at a woman who called her a tacky, gold digger but Elle was next to me and she pulled me away before I could get more than "Hey, you don't know anything" out.

I don't know why Mom still comes to these parties.

We cross into the den and find her sitting on the end of the sofa. She's chatting quietly with a friend she brought with her this year.

"Hey Mom," Elle says and she steps ahead of me.

Laura turns towards us and when she smiles widely I'm reminded of the woman who was my nanny and then my step mother for the rest of my life. The woman who made me lunches for school. Who took me shopping for new clothes. Who bandaged my knees and got me a glass of water before bed.

"Elle, darling!" Mom extends her arms and wraps Elle in a hug. I feel a distinct pang of sadness that these two, the most important women in my life, don't know Maggie. And might not get the chance. "And my Austin, come here."

I cross over to her and she pulls me down for a kiss on the cheek. She gives my shoulder a reassuring squeeze. When I don't step back she lets out a little sigh and gives me a hug.

"Your father is short sighted, can't see past the bottom line." She whispers into my ear.

"Yeah, umm." I say as I struggle to figure out how she would know about what happened at the board meeting.

"Is it family picture time?" She asks brightly. Elle rolls her eyes and I search the bottom of my empty glass for more. Finding none, I set it on a side table and then hold out both elbows to take them each by the arm.

"I know it's not New Year's but do you have any resolutions for next year?" Mom asks us.

"Ugh, Mom." Elle chastises. "Can you not be your usual upbeat self right now? We're on the death march to take a photo with the man who is a glorified sperm donor."

"Eloise Elizabeth," Mom dishes right back. "I'll be the first to admit he is not the traditional midwestern dad but you've done just fine and he loves you in his own way. Answer my question about resolutions and then we can gossip about his new girlfriend."

"Deal. Okay, so for next year, I dunno. I'm loving my work at the studio but I also feel like there is more I can do. Or figuring out how to open up the classes to more people. We have such a bougie clientele."

"Hey, I'm not bougie!" I protest as we make our way into the entrance hall where Dad stations himself for most of the night. He stays here so he can greet everyone who comes in and watch to see who leaves early. Plus, I think he likes that his voice echoes off all the marble.

"You're right, you're the least bougie billionaire I know." Elle says with a chuckle.

"I'm not a billionaire, yet," I tell her but she levels me with a look that says I'm pointing out a useless technicality.

"Like I was saying," Elle starts with an eye roll and an exhale. "I've been thinking of ways to make people happy. Like your friend who came in for puppy yoga, she looked so stressed when she walked in but when she left she was relaxed and I even saw her smile."

I remember that smile.

And I remember the car ride to her place.

And the desperate feeling that compelled me out of the car and to her door.

"Is there a girl in your life?" Mom asks me, hopeful.

"Eh, not really."

"He had two." Elle says like she's tattling.

"Austin Thorne! I've raised you better."

"No, it's not like that, and it wasn't really two people."

Both women look at me for more information as we stand in the receiving line that snakes around the hall. Waiters pass by with hors d'oeuvres and more circulate with champagne. At least we'll be well fed while we wait.

And maybe I can use eating as a diversion from this line of questioning.

"But, you were seeing someone before the election, right?" Elle asks before popping a stuffed mushroom in her mouth. She immediately reaches out to snatch a crab cake off the next tray.

"Yeah, I was. Sort of."

"Explain," Mom demands quietly. It's her mom voice and I don't stand a chance. Felix knows everything, I should let the two most important women in my life in on the secret.

"I enrolled in SMS Connect over the summer."

"Austin, that's wonderful," Mom coos.

"Yeah, I really enjoyed texting with her, it felt significant."

"She's the one you tried to meet?" Elle asks, suddenly way more interested in my failed love story than she was a minute ago.

"You two met?" Mom asks excitedly.

"We met." I say flatly.

"What did you do?" Elle asks.

"Nothing!" I defend. Really, all I did was start fucking her in real life a few weeks before, make her work life a living hell, and not tell her that I was also DCFox. So, maybe not nothing. "It just didn't work out."

Mom gives my arm a gentle squeeze.

"Well," Elle starts, "since you *still* won't explain exactly what happened I'll just say this; it's Christmas and people are a lot softer around the holidays so maybe you should reach out to her and see if she's willing to talk to you again. Like *Love, Actually* teaches us; at Christmas you tell the truth. Try it. With yourself and the girl."

"That's right, as I always say, 'honesty is the best policy,'" she smiles at us.

"Except in politics." We finish together.

I chuckle and give them each a kiss on the cheek.

As we inch forward through the line, all I can think about is Maggie and what I should do next.

All I have to do is write a note to her.

Is it really that simple?

***

Several hours, and several drinks, later I'm lying in my bed staring at the ceiling. I slide my glasses off and rub at the bridge of my nose before sliding them back into place and sitting up.

In one swift move I swipe the SMS Connect phone off my night table, stand up, and start to type out my message.

DCFox: My friend, Merry Christmas, or Holidays, or whatever you might celebrate this time of year. I have to admit I don't feel much like celebrating. The reason is simple. I can't begin to feel excited about anything after losing your companionship.

I'm sorry. I'll start there. It was never my intention to hurt you or for you to be put in a position you weren't prepared for.

If you get this message and ignore it, I'll understand.

But if you read this and feel the least bit of empathy for me and want to start talking again, know that I'll be a faithful correspondent.

You're still the best woman I've ever had the pleasure to know and I hope that I have the chance to know you even better.

I hit send and flop down on my bed. It would be pathetic to just sit here holding it and waiting to see if she responds. It's almost 2:00 a.m. so there's no chance she's up now anyway.

I set it next to my cell phone and climb under the covers. I don't expect to sleep but I need to try.

Chapter Twenty-Four
MAGGIE

Like Christmas Morning

A ping wakes me up.

I look at the alarm clock I've had since high school and see that it's 1:54 a.m. Without turning on the light, I pad my hand around on my nightstand for my phone.

My iPhone has no notifications. Weird. I shut my eyes and flip on the lamp, letting my eyes adjust to the light through my eyelids for a moment before squinting them open all the way.

The SMS Connect phone is plugged in on the little desk in the corner of my room. Call me pathetic but I couldn't just leave it in D.C. Then when the renewal reminder came through for this month I couldn't get myself to shut it down. I never got a notice that DCFox had returned his. I wasn't going to quit until he did. With everything crumbling that little gray rectangle represented hope.

That hope starts jumping on a trampoline in my stomach.

It feels like I'm tempting fate with each step.

I'm one step away when the thought that he could be ending it in the message hits. Time freezes but then the little light at the top flashes red.

A promise?

Or a warning?

With trembling fingers I unplug the phone and bring it with me back into bed. I reach up and turn off the light before opening the messages.

As I read, a tear rolls down my cheek. For a moment, instead of focusing on his words, I focus on how my tear starts out hot when it first leaks out of the corner of my eye and by the time it drops to my chest it's cold. With no one to catch my tears they turn icy as they fall. This thought makes the tears fall faster and I slide down to my side and curl into my pillow.

I think back to the last time I was with Austin. The way he was there to wipe my cheek, catch the tears, and kiss me. Kiss me like I was all he needed.

Please.

That one word was all I needed to hear. But where did that leave me?

After the tears slow, I roll to my back and stare up at my ceiling like the answers I'm looking for will appear.

You're still the best woman I've ever had the pleasure to know and I hope that I have the chance to know you even better.

Why couldn't he have ended it? That would have been easier.

Eventually I close my eyes because I'm tired of trying to find solutions in the dark. As I drift to sleep the questions keep coming.

Do I want to keep talking with him?

Can I trust him?

Why didn't he tell me where he was?

What is he hiding?

What if I get burned again?

Am I willing to take the risk?

Chapter Twenty-Five
AUSTIN
What am I missing?

ELLE AND I ARE watching the Renegades away game when my phone rings. I slide it out of my pocket and see Kevin's name on the caller ID.

"Hey Kev, what's going on?" I ask.

"We're fucked, that's what's going on," Kevin nearly screams.

"Whoa, whoa, what do you mean?"

"Turn on CNN," he says and a bowling ball hits me in the gut. This can't be good.

"Elle, hand me the remote," I demand and she looks at me with wide eyes.

As I change the channel all the possible "we're fucked" scenarios run through my mind. We are under nuclear attack. AI Media or TMC got hacked.

CNN comes on and I keep the phone to my ear as I listen to the anchors and try to read the scroll at the bottom of the screen.

TMC'S AI MEDIA CAUSES MASS PANIC IN CERTAIN PARTS OF THE COUNTRY.

What the fuck?

"Kevin, what is going on?"

"I'm on my way into the office but when I logged in at home I saw one article had gone viral within the app. It was a natural disaster piece we summarized from TMChatter and about half of the people who had our summary on their feed shared it."

"Okay, but why is this causing mass panic?"

"Because our article said all these disasters were going to happen this next year."

"Shit," I say as I stand up. Elle is waving her arms at me trying to communicate something but I ignore her.

"A lot of shit." Kevin clarifies, "From what I can tell the article went viral within our app but people also shared it to other social apps. Clearly they didn't realize it was incorrect information."

And from there people decided the information was true because their friends said so. It's exactly what we wanted to happen. It's what the entire model is based off of. But we never accounted for the original information being incorrect or misleading.

"Fuck!" I yell out. "I'll see you at the office in twenty."

Elle is now standing and looking at me with concern in her eyes. "Is there anything I can do?" she asks.

"No, this is going to be a mess and I have to get it handled before Dad knows."

"You think he doesn't yet?"

"Shit, you're right. I bet he's already at the office."

***

"Sir. *Sir.* He's not taking meetings right now," I hear Elizabeth say outside my door. I lift my head from where I've been reading the content analytics report from the last 24 hours to see my dad storming into my office.

"What the fuck Austin?" He demands as he comes to stand over my desk.

"I'm sorry, Mr. Thorne," Elizabeth says to me at the door as she reaches for the knob to close it.

"It's fine, thank you Elizabeth." I give her a weak smile and turn to face Dad. "I'm not sure how to answer your question. Could you be more specific?"

I know I'm being childish but I'm tired and annoyed and it's how he sees me anyway so why bother to summon maturity?

"Why has our stock plummeted to half its value overnight?" he roars.

Money, it's always about the bottom line.

I sigh and slide my glasses from my face. I press into my temples as I gather my calm and reply. "From what we can tell it was from one story that went viral. Unfortunately, the story had misinformation and instead of people calling out the issue they shared it as real."

"Help me understand how your little computer could fuck up this bad."

"Well, as with all technology, humans have to teach the computers what to do. We can give machines the tools to learn but ultimately they rely on human input. TMC shared content yesterday with the top ten natural disasters of the last twenty five years and when AI Media created the summary to share to our users it said the disasters were going to happen next year."

"Why am I losing money?" Dad demands as he walks over to the window in my office.

"Because half of the internet figured out the mistake but the other half didn't. Those people, instead of sharing the original story, started to post that they were going to stock up on food and toilet paper, and their friends picked that up and told all their friends they were doing the same."

"Can you see which people started the rumors?"

"We can see who read the article and who shared it." I tell him before I realize why he's asking.

"Then I'm suing them. Fucking idiots don't know how to tell fact from fiction and they're going to pay me back."

"Seriously? You can't sue people for misinterpreting something?"

"Watch me!"

And with that he storms out of my office. Elizabeth comes to the door and looks at me for instructions or next steps but I'm frozen. I can't believe Dad would go after our subscribers like that. Sure the stock dropped but it bounced back once we were able to get a clarifying story out.

Kevin and Tyler had a chat with the original writer of the TMChatter story and explained the importance of putting a "history" tag on any content that covers past events so AIM knows how to summarize it. And they started to build a guide that we'll distribute to all staff writers for how to properly categorize their content.

All things considered this was a good lesson for us to learn. No one really got hurt, sure some people might have a year's worth of toilet paper now but they'll use it eventually.

"Mr. Thorne, Kevin is here to see you," Elizabeth says. She sounds as tired as I feel. I've been at the office for eighteen hours. She has too.

She was arriving at the office when I pulled up. Greg sent her a message that I was headed in. She stayed up all night with us and helped keep us organized. Greg offered to pick up team members so they wouldn't have to take the metro or get a ride share in the middle of the night. I don't know what I've done to deserve their support and loyalty but I'm grateful for it.

We first removed the story as best we could. After that, we had to issue a statement explaining the situation. Then, we spent the next several hours hounding news outlets to print the statement or at least summarize it but the damage was done.

Shares opened at about 50% of their previous value. The good news from where I sit is they've bounced back to 95% over the course of the day.

But that's still not 100%. Or better.

"Thank you, Elizabeth, and thank you for being here overnight and all day today, but please, head home. I don't want to see you in the office until next year." I tack on a cheesy smile and it works. Elizabeth is just delirious enough to laugh.

"Of course Mr. Thorne, Happy New Year."

She steps back and Kevin walks in.

"Why did I get a request from our legal team for the usernames and data of the people who shared the story?" He asks as he sits down across from my desk.

"Because Dad is going to sue them." I state matter-of-factly. It's so absurd to me I don't even feel like I have to joke about it.

"Really?"

"Yes, or he's going to try." I take off my glasses and toss them on my desk. As I rub my temples I continue, "I don't see the point, I mean, yeah they caused the stock to waiver but it's basically back and we've fixed the issue. It just feels vindictive."

"What's his case? Emotional damages?" Kevin laughs.

"That and defamation. He's building a case for both libel and slander against them. I wouldn't be surprised if he and the lawyers ask for a lot more data. I also wouldn't be surprised if he went after the other networks that reported on the story."

"I can't say I blame him," Kevin says and I slide my glasses back on to see if he's serious. "I'm a little mad I didn't buy low this morning knowing we were on our way to bouncing back."

"That's called insider trading Kevin," I tell him.

"Eh, no one really has time to investigate that these days," he says as he stands and heads towards the door. "I think we're good here tonight, thanks for coming in and helping us get this fixed."

"Yeah sure," I mutter as I watch him leave.

I am dumbfounded. Flabbergasted.

Am I the only one who thinks suing people over a misunderstanding is wrong?

Chapter Twenty-Six
MAGGIE

Alone at the Head Table

"Heck of a wedding right, Mags?" I look up from where I'm reading an article about AI Media to see Cole MacDonald walking towards me.

"It is a really good party." I say with a smile. When Cole reaches me, I stand and he leans in for a hug. He's sweaty and there is a faint trace of farm animal on him. Occupational hazard, I suppose. His hug feels warm but void of the heat I would feel with Austin. I can't help but compare. Cole looks good, rugged, but his suit fits a little loose on his frame and I miss the way Austin's clothes were tailored to him. Urgh! I can't get him out of my mind.

"Have you met Levi Jackson? We call him Jack. He's new to town since you left us for bigger and better things," Cole smiles and I know he's teasing but that doesn't change the sting of pain I feel. I'm sitting here, unemployed, going into a new year, single, at my younger sister's wedding. What was the point of leaving and trying to make a name for myself if I ended up right back where I started?

"I haven't yet. Hi Levi, I'm Maggie Collins." I paste on a smile as I hold out my hand to shake.

"Seriously call me Jack, I barely reply to Levi anymore." He smiles and it lights his entire face, but it doesn't set butterflies free in my belly like Austin's does. "It's great to finally meet you!" He says as we shake hands.

"Finally?"

"Yeah, I've been following the campaign and election closely with the seniors this year." He says as he pulls out the seat next to me. Cole leans against the side of the table and crosses his arms to follow the conversation.

"You're a teacher?" He nods. "I can only imagine how much there was for them to learn this year."

"The kids were really engaged. Some of them cast their first vote." I was already into politics as a teen but I think I'd have been even more into it if he was my AP Gov teacher. "But I think the biggest thing was knowing someone from Lakeville had a hand in history being made." He smiles again and Cole playfully punches my shoulder.

I blink deliberately because I wasn't expecting that.

I guess it makes sense that people back home would know about my job and my involvement in the campaign but it never occurred to me that they'd tout a local connection.

"I umm, honestly don't know what to say," I give a little shrug. Still not believing strangers would be proud of me.

"Well, you're a writer, not an improv comedian, and I put you on the spot." Jack laughs, "Are you going to be in town for a few more weeks?"

"I think so, why?"

"Well, the kids come back at the end of next week. I'd love to have you visit and tell them about working on the campaign."

"Oh? Umm." How do I tell him I got replaced by a robot? That I got fired. That I have no career momentum and wouldn't make a good role model for impressionable kids.

"Think about it," Jack says as he stands. He and Cole are being called to the dance floor. "It doesn't have to be a big deal, I mostly want to do it so I can get out of creating one lesson plan."

He winks and I let out a little nervous laugh.

I watch the two of them join Jimmy Lewis and Holden Monaghan, also high school friends of mine, and they start to line dance to a Nine Inch Nails remix.

I can't remember the last time I participated in dance floor antics like that. Maybe college? Even then it was rare.

I've been career focused for the last half of my life. And look where it got me.

I nod at my older brother CJ as he comes to sit down next to me while I take in the whole scene. Liz and Kyle's wedding is what dreams are made of. The ceiling is covered in white twinkle lights with holographic snowflakes hanging down so when people move around the lights twirl and little refractions dance on the tables and through the room.

The tables themselves have beautiful evergreen, white rose, and berry branch centerpieces that I was up until midnight putting together with Mom. The place cards are in mini snow globes that people can take home and put their own photos into.

Flameless candles are everywhere creating a romantic vibe that even the coldest hearts have to appreciate. The party has been rocking for hours. Liz and Kyle appear to be relishing every moment of their special day, as they should.

"Was it a mistake to leave home?" I ask CJ after we sat through three songs in silence.

"Hell no," he responds and shifts so he's facing me. "You and I were both destined for bigger things. I'm the head of the Emergency Department in a sizable metropolitan area. You're a sought after speech writer who just worked on the winning presidential campaign. That's huge. Way too big for Lakeville."

"Does that make us bad people? Getting out? Wanting to get out?"

"Again, no. It means we can appreciate where we came from and know there is more out there for us."

"I'm making a New Year's resolution to talk to you and Liz more." I tell him as I watch my sister get twirled around by her husband.

"I'll make a resolution to respond to you when you reach out," CJ elbows me in the side. I laugh even though I recognize that he just put the full responsibility for building a friendship on my shoulders.

"Is it weird to be home?" I ask him.

"Yes and no," CJ says with a shrug.

"Explain."

He laughs, "I guess it is but I think the weirdest part is how disconnected I feel. Like going home is fine, that's family dynamics and I can handle about a day of it before I want to get back on my own terms. But I don't feel much of anything as I drive through town."

"Yeah, I think I get that." I don't admit that being home for so long without a clear end date has actually turned me onto the place. The town is cute, the people are friendly, and I appreciate slowing down a little bit. "Do you like your job?"

CJ looks at me, "What's going on with you Maggie?"

"I dunno, I need to figure out what to do next. I've been working for years to get to where I was and the rug got pulled out from under me and I'm in free-fall."

"Well, as a medical professional I can tell you that you're handling this prolonged anxiety attack way better than most people."

I can't tell if he's joking. "Thanks?"

"You're welcome."

"But you didn't answer my question," I say as I bump my shoulder with his. "Do you like being a doctor?"

"I love it."

"Really?"

"Yeah Maggie, I get to help people through tough shit. Sometimes that's serious wounds, heart attacks, or severe dehydration. Somedays it's the lonely old lady who is inventing pain so she can come in and talk with us. But no matter what, I provide care. I'm there for them."

"I didn't realize you were such a teddy bear."

"Don't tell anyone, I've worked hard on my arrogant doctor persona." He laughs. "But seriously, when I'm on the floor nothing else exists. I'm working, and I'm helping people."

"Was it rewarding when you got promoted?" I ask.

"Honestly? I couldn't care less what my title is. As long as I get to be a doctor I'm satisfied."

CJ's love of his work, not his job, sticks with me through the rest of the night. As I kick my heels off and walk up the carpeted stairs to my childhood bedroom, I try to hold the existential crisis at bay. I can feel my breathing speeding up and there is a distinct pinch in my chest. I rub at the spot.

I have never felt this completely lost in my entire life.

As a kid, every day was about helping my family.

In high school, I focused on getting into an Ivy League school and remedying injustices for my peers.

College was to get to law school.

Law school was to get a job.

That first job was to get the next one and so forth.

Each chapter of my life has been a stepping stone to bring me one step closer. But to what?

I slump down onto the floor and my bridesmaid dress bunches up around my waist. The fabric constricts my breathing which is shallow already. I'm just tipsy enough to have this conversation with myself.

What is my purpose?

What am I supposed to do now?

CJ is happy being a doctor.

Liz is happy being a photographer.

My mother is happy being a busybody.

My dad is happy supporting her.

But I'm not happy.

I shudder a deep breath and on the exhale I lift my gaze to the ceiling. Spiraling isn't going to help. I need to pull myself together.

C'mon Maggie, ask yourself the question.

What will make me happy?

Was speech writing work I could do every day until the end of time like CJ?

Is it the type of work I'd try to do in my spare time like Liz did with photography?

No. Not really. I enjoyed it. I was good at it. But I wasn't writing speeches for fun when I had time off. I thought of it as a job, not my life's work.

I think back to when the college kids came in to learn from Sam and me. Seeing their eager faces and answering their questions was energizing. Even after I had noticed Austin in the back of the room. I was able to focus enough on leading the discussion that I remember having fun.

The trip down memory lane has calmed my nervous system. My heart rate is back to normal, the pain in my chest is gone, and my breathing is even. On weak but steady legs, I stand and change into my pajamas.

When I climb into bed I reread DCFox's Christmas message, like I have every night since he sent it, and wish I could ask him what to do.

Chapter Twenty-Seven
AUSTIN
My BroFF Eeyore is done.

I WAKE UP ON New Year's Day hoping TalkShopGirl, a.k.a Maggie, has responded. And, again, like every morning for the last week, the message from me is the last thing on the screen.

With a frustrated exhale I get out of bed and get ready for the day. Felix is playing in an outdoor game today at the D.C. Monumentals stadium and I get to watch from behind the glass. I think I've got better access than most of the player's families today. They're all up in 200 level suites.

They'll be warm and fed, but I'll be where the action is.

And I need the distraction.

***

The Renegades won in a shutout. The frenzy at ice level, and throughout the stadium did exactly what I needed it to do. It's only now, that I'm waiting for Felix outside of the dugout that Maggie returns to mind. I remember how exciting it was to see her after the season opener. How the pupils in the center of her ocean blue eyes grew wide as we spoke. The flush that I watched climb her cheeks.

I feel the heat drain from my face as I remind myself she might never speak to me again.

"Thorney!" Felix hollers as he claps his hands down on my shoulders.

"Hey bud, great game."

"Tell me how you really fuckin' feel man. That is not the level of enthusiasm I was expecting from my BroFF after that game."

"BroFF?"

"Bro Friend Forever." Felix says like it's obvious.

I laugh at him. "Is that another entry from your 'word of the day' calendar?"

"Nah man, that's just common slang. Keep up."

"I don't think you've got that exactly right, but I'll go with it for your sake." I tell him as we walk through the stadium concourse to the parking lot.

"What are you doing tonight?" He asks as we reach the cars.

"Probably just heading home and preparing for the earnings call in a few days."

"I liked you better when you didn't care about work so much," he jokes. It hits harder than he intends though. I used to enjoy my work. I loved developing the AIM product and getting it off the ground.

"I did too."

In the last few weeks, since the board meeting especially, I have dreaded even opening my work email. Elle has complained about my mood but when I remind her she's living with me for free she shuts up.

Not that I've seen her much though. If I'm not at work I've been working out. Or walking. I've dragged my feet around the city to the places I saw Maggie. It's sad, I realize, but I'm hoping I can catch a glimpse of her sunshine hair and that it will cheer me up.

"So, you wanna grab dinner before you go back to being sad?"

"Yeah, sure." We get into his car and twenty minutes later he pulls up outside of Lapis.

"You know, I still haven't eaten here," he says like it just dawned on him.

"Funny, no, I'm not going in there."

"Ah HA! I knew it. This Eeyore act is because of that girl. The blonde I saw at the game and then waiting for you here on your SMS Connect date."

"Maggie." I say quietly as I look at the table where she sat that night.

"So she has a name." Felix says quietly. "Well, I'm fucking starving so let's eat and if you want to tell me all about it I'll listen. But you're buying."

I laugh, "deal."

***

FELIX

Good luck at the meeting today buddy.

Thanks man.

When we went to dinner last week I couldn't get myself to tell him about Maggie. It hurt too much. Instead I explained everything going on at work.

How I expected Dad to start transitioning the company to me.

How well AI Media is doing.

How much I hated the fact he filed a lawsuit against people who took action on bad information.

How going into the office every day is physically and emotionally exhausting.

And in the days leading up to this meeting it hasn't gotten any better.

Elizabeth walks in with the ginger ale I asked her for because my stomach is sour.

"Thanks, Elizabeth."

"Of course. Mr. Thorne, are you taking the call here or are you joining the senior team in your father's office upstairs?"

If the last meeting had gone the way I'd expected it to, I'd already be up in the room. But, there is a significant chance I get burned again during this meeting. I don't think my poker face is good enough to pull off that bluff.

"I'll be taking it from here." There, decision made.

"Excellent, do you want me in the office or dialing in from my desk to take notes?"

"From your desk please, I'd like to be alone."

"Of course, Austin," she says and I look up at her. She called me Austin without me asking her to. She smiles at me with her eyes. If Felix noticed my sour mood and I only see him once a week then Elizabeth must have a swollen tongue from biting it. I'm grateful she never brought it up, it allowed me to retreat into work and use it to numb the pain.

When she has stepped out of the office and closed the door behind her, I dial into the call. I lean back in my desk chair and feel for the SMS Connect phone in my pocket.

Still nothing from Maggie. It's been two full weeks since Christmas Eve.

Two more weeks of carrying this little phone around.

Two more weeks of starting my day with disappointment.

I zone out for most of the call, the view from my office window of the winter skyline proving to be more fascinating than earnings reports.

"Most of this revenue is from AI Media. The strong fourth-quarter finish because we cleared our costs in the first month." I perk up because I'm expecting the credit here. It wouldn't take me long to get upstairs and accept the accolades in person. I stand and button my suit coat.

"The liability of the product is correlated to the share price drop right before New Year's." I pause.

"Things are progressing with the lawsuit and I'm expecting us to win. But the lawyers suggested, and I agree with them, that in an act of good will we're going to close the product down." Dad says and I feel faint.

I grab the side of my desk and the room spins as Elizabeth comes in. She reaches me and helps me sit in my chair. She leaves the office quickly before returning with a brown paper bag for me to breathe into.

The crinkle in and out is so loud I can't hear the call but it doesn't matter. Dad just canceled my product. He basically just fired my entire team. My inbox alerts fire off at an alarming rate as messages flood in. Elizabeth reaches forward and closes my laptop.

Now the only sound in the room is my fractured breathing. I look up at her and find a steely look on her face.

"I try to stay out of it Austin, I really do, but your father simply doesn't respect you. And my advice, unsolicited as it might be, is to get out." Elizabeth says steadily. I pull the bag down from my chin and stand.

Acting on instinct I reach out and wrap her in a hug. She's rigid at first but when I squeeze a little tighter she wraps her arms around me in return.

"Thank you, Elizabeth," I tell her softly.

"Of course, Mr. Thorne, allow me to call Greg for you." She steps out of the office and picks up her phone. I look around my office and decide this is the last time I'll be in this building. In this room.

I'm done.

Done trying to impress a man who refuses to be impressed by anything.

Done making decisions based on the bottom line alone.

Done toiling away day-in and day-out to get nowhere.

Chapter Twenty-Eight
MAGGIE
Hot for Teacher

"Alright class, focus up, Ms. Collins is here and we want to make the most of the time she's giving us," Jack says as he leans back against his desk. It's clear he's the "cool teacher". "Alright, put your hands together for former Lakeville High School student body president, Cornell graduate, and presidential speech writer, Ms. Maggie Collins!"

Jack starts clapping loudly and I can't help the giggle that escapes. His face lights up with a grin that makes the corners of his eyes crease. It's a megawatt smile that does nothing for me. But some girl, some day, is going to fall hard for it.

"Hey everyone," I wave awkwardly.

"Before we let the kids ask their questions. I've got one for you; was it more difficult winning the presidency for the LHS student body or the United States of America?"

I laugh, "it was harder to win LHS but the presidential election was a lot more exhausting!"

He smiles, and it is warm and wonderful. I catch a few girls sigh at the site. I wish it inspired the same reaction from me. "Why don't you tell them what it was like to work with President-Elect Quinn on her campaign."

"In a word, it was awesome." I smile because I mean it. For the last week I've spent my time reflecting on my career and trying to figure out where to go with it next. And while I hate how it ended, I loved working for Senator Quinn.

I learned so much from her. I appreciated how she shared openly with the team. How she was able to keep her focus while speaking to thousands of people. And, even though it lead to my ultimate demise, I admire her for using AI Media to her advantage.

I spend the next forty minutes answering questions and chatting with the kids. Explaining how I applied for grants as student body president to get the programs we lost paid for. We brainstormed ideas for how they could fundraise to support a trip for the senior class.

When the bell rings I'm disappointed our time is up.

"Thanks so much Maggie, that was great." Jack says as the kids file out of the room.

"Yeah, for sure."

"I'm a humble civics teacher, but part of my job is to help my students find the best version of themselves. I don't know what you're going to do next but you really connected with those kids."

"Yeah, I had a lot of fun." I smile and slide my coat on.

"Are you going to join your sister at Trivia next week?"

"Eh, I'm not sure I'll still be here next week."

"Oh, sure, of course."

I smile at him and head out the door as his next class starts to file in.

"Take care Jack, thanks for today."

It isn't a long drive home but I accomplish a lot of deep thinking. By the time I pull into my driveway I've considered, and dismissed, a career as a teacher, a motivational speaker, and going back into the courtroom as a prosecutor.

Even without an answer I'm feeling energized as I park in the driveway. Liz's car is in the driveway too. She and Kyle got back from their honeymoon in Aruba yesterday.

"Mom, we got married like eleven days ago!" Liz says as I walk in the front door.

"But you've been together for almost six years! It is time to have a baby."

"Mom, stop." I say as I walk into the kitchen. "Liz is a business owner who's busiest time of the year is nine months from now with senior portraits and family sessions." Liz points in my direction and nods vigorously. "You shouldn't start to badger her for a grandbaby for at least six more weeks."

"What?!" Liz yells.

"Fine." Mom huffs.

I smile and slide onto a stool next to Liz at the counter.

"You're in a good mood," Mom leads as she mixes up cookies for the book club meeting tonight. "Did you enjoy your day with Jack?"

"You spent the day with Jack!" Liz spins to me. "Gosh, I haven't been gone that long! But apparently it's long enough for you to get hot for teacher."

"I went and spoke to his class about working for President-Elect Quinn." I correct her. I don't bother telling her he invited me out to join them at trivia.

"Well that's less sexy." Liz says as she plucks a bit of dough from the bowl. "Who knows, maybe I would have gone into politics if he was my civics teacher. He's hot."

"Elizabeth, you're married." Mom scolds.

"Yeah but I'm not blind." She says as she licks her fingers.

"It's fine, I'm not looking for a relationship right now," I admit and Mom stops what she's doing.

"You're not? That's new." She says trying to suss out where this is coming from. Since it's a departure from past versions of me.

"Uh, sure. I just want to get my job situation figured out."

"That makes sense," she says. "What do you think you'll do next?"

"I'm going to head back this week and start having some conversations. I'm not sure exactly what I want to do but I have a few ideas."

"Well, you've always seized opportunities when they present themselves so I can't wait to see what you'll do next."

***

Turns out Mom didn't have to wait long. That night as I started to pack up, my phone alerted me to a new email.

Dear Ms. Collins,

I'm Emily Brady, a student at Georgetown. We met back in the fall when your office hosted an event for students. You spoke about the craft of speech writing and also shared your thoughts on the AI Media announcement.

What you shared that day stuck with me. The semester just started and one of our mandatory seminars is a media literacy class. When we arrived in class today we were told the adjunct professor had taken a job overseas and would no longer be available. They were going to cancel the class if a replacement couldn't be found quickly.

I imagine you're too busy working for President-Elect Quinn but do you know of anyone who could teach this course? I'll put the department head's number below.

I appreciate your help. If this course gets canceled I'll have to make it up in the summer.

My course load is packed every semester between now and graduation so I can triple major in poly-sci, public relations, and leadership. I'm hoping to attend law school and follow your path to become a speech writer.

The ultimate goal will be for my words to become a part of history, like yours.

Hope to talk soon,

Emily

Chapter Twenty-Nine
AUSTIN

What is this, an intervention?

I OPEN THE DOOR to my apartment to find Elle and Felix standing at the island waiting for me. They are both giving me looks that make this feel like this is an intervention.

Or that my fly is down.

I check quickly and it isn't so this might be serious.

"Thorney, sit down," Felix says and he pulls out one of the counter stools for me. I walk over and sit between them after hanging up my coat.

"What's going on?"

"We're concerned about you," Elle says.

Intervention. Nailed it.

"Why? I'm fine," I say and I reach down to pick up Brinkley. He glares at me as I try to situate him in my lap so I let him pounce to the floor instead of risking a left hook.

"You're not fine," Felix says and then he pulls a piece of paper out of his pocket.

"You prepared a fucking statement for this?" I chastise.

"I have things to say!" He yells as Elle hollers "Let him speak!"

"Fine, go ahead, let's hear it," I say as I cross my arms and settle in. This is going to be ridiculous.

"Austin, my dear Thorney," I roll my eyes, "I'm here tonight to tell you that I am concerned about you. We have been friends for a long time and I have never seen you so lost."

I look between him and Elle. Felix is focused on his speech and Elle is nodding in encouragement.

"We used to enjoy the finer things in life together, beers on the sofa while watching a game, rock climbing so we're fit as fuck, inviting girls into VIP sections," Elle rolls her eyes but I smirk, "and trying to outperform the other in any competition we could think of."

He takes a break and looks at me dead in the eyes. He's taking this so seriously I try really hard to contain my smirk.

"C'mon man! Don't laugh! I'm serious," he looks at Elle, "He's laughing at me!"

"Finish your words, he's listening, he's in denial."

"I am not," I protest but she just raises an eyebrow at me.

Point taken.

"Okay, where was I, oh yeah," Felix regroups, "in the last two months the Thorney I have come to know and love has been gone. You've been moody and dismissive and have been working out way too much."

"Can you really work out too much?" I ask as I flex my bicep and kiss it. Okay, I can see it, I'm being a jerk.

"Austin, seriously, what is the matter with you?" Elle complains. "You've been off since the fall. It got worse before Christmas, and even worse after all that AI Media bad story stuff at New Year's. I thought it would get better when you finally quit being a corporate monkey jumping around for Dad. Instead you've been working out, taking sad walks around the city, or spending your time holed up in your room."

Elle throws her hands up in the air in exasperation.

She's not wrong.

I expected my mood to lift after I left too.

But it hasn't. The cold has settled into the city and my heart.

Everyday I wake up without a response from Maggie it freezes a little more. I feel hollow without her in my life. But I'm not about to admit how low I actually am to these two after they organized this little ambush.

"Why is it so bad that I'm working out so much?" I ask instead to deflect from the numbness inside.

"Well, it's not bad exactly, it's just not, like, mentally healthy. You're borderline obsessed with it. I'm the professional athlete in the room and I think you're training more than I am."

"It feels like you're avoiding something," Elle says gently. "And," she glances at Felix who nods, "you haven't mentioned your girl recently."

"What girl?" I ask as my foot slides off the bar under the stool.

"Maggie," Felix says with a smile. And I don't miss the eyes Elle shoots to him and then to me. She's going to be pissed I told him her name before I told her.

"I don't know what to tell you guys." I admit. Even if a part of me really wants to tell them everything. And, it doesn't matter anyway.

She's gone. I missed my chance. It's been almost a month since my message to her and no matter how hopeless the outlook is, I can't let go of her yet.

"Well, I said my piece," Felix says as he folds his paper back up. "I'll only add that you'll be joining me and the boys for our All Star break trip in two weeks. Your attendance is mandatory. I'm fuckin' pumped. Puerto Rico, here we come!"

***

"Don't forget to reapply!" Felix says with a smack to my back. Sunscreen bottles start flying between the group as we all lather up again. Five dudes with little else to do besides swim, play pickleball, and try to set up ping pong ball trick shots throughout the house.

Our triumphant moment was when one bounced off the ceiling fan, into a funnel and then down into the cup. When it dropped in we all stood in silence for a beat and then erupted in whoops and hollers like we'd scored a game seven, overtime winner.

Not that I know what that feels like, but the other guys do.

There were hugs and cheers and I spied Felix wipe a tear from his eye.

It's been three days of these kinds of shenanigans.

Tonight is our last night and Felix has booked us a private room at a restaurant in town. It's Valentine's Day too, so of course, he has bags of cheap party supplies, decorations, and wearables for us. One thing about Felix is he is a sucker for a theme. He loads up on cheesy party supplies and makes sure anyone and everyone feels the experience from all aspects.

"Any excuse to celebrate right?" He jokes as he slides a glitter heart necklace over my head.

"Did you invite any girls to this dinner? Or is it just going to be five dudes celebrating Valentine's Day together?" Duncan Paisley, affectionately known as Dunc or Pays or Vera, after the bags girls made famous at high school sleepovers, asks as he slaps a heart sticker to the back of his hand.

"I thought we could visit the bar at the resort before heading to dinner. We've got the whole room, it wouldn't be difficult to add a few chairs. And even easier if you have your girl snuggle up on your lap!" Felix laughs and gives me a slap on the back that feels personal. "You gonna pick up a girl tonight?" He asks.

"I dunno," I respond with a shrug.

"C'mon man, it's time," he pauses his work of unraveling a heart garland. "Why are you so hung up on this girl from the fall?"

"It's hard to explain."

"You've never even tried." He sounds hurt.

"No, I haven't," I admit as I think back to how angry Maggie was at dinner. She still doesn't know that I'm her SMS Connect date; she just thinks it was a bad coincidence. "I messaged her on SMS Connect at Christmas and I haven't heard back."

"Ouch." He says with a wince like someone is cleaning a cut on his knee.

"I'm just not ready to move on yet." I admit.

"That makes sense, but are you going to do anything about it?"

"Like what?"

"Well you can always fuck around to get her out of your system. That has never failed in the history of manhood." Dunc calls out from the sofa.

"I think you need to check your facts." I tell him as I point my beer in his direction before taking a sip.

"Fine, but I don't see how pining for her and not taking any action to fix it is any better." He shrugs.

He has a point.

***

It wasn't hard to find girls at the bar. In fact, as soon as we walked in, a group approached us. One of them, Charity, I think, or maybe it's Cassidy, attached herself to me and is now sitting next to me.

Well, it's more like she's perched on the edge of her chair trying to be as close to me as possible because I wouldn't let her sit on my lap.

She is playing with the hair at the back of my neck and I have to keep reminding myself not to swat at it thinking it's an insect.

Because she's definitely a pest.

Felix is a happy camper at the head of the table and the other guys seem to be doing fine with the attention as well. I wouldn't be surprised if all these girls came home with us. And it would be awkward if I sent Chelsea, maybe that's it, home alone while her friends were otherwise engaged so, it seems I'm stuck with her.

"So Austin, what do you like to do for fun?"

I turn towards her and try to appreciate the green of her eyes and the brunette of her hair but, even though she is pretty, she's not Maggie.

"I like to exercise," I respond coolly.

"I bet you do," she giggles and squeezes my bicep.

Maybe I enjoy the chase, the challenge, because fighting with Maggie was a thousand times more arousing than having this girl throw herself at me.

I can see it now, sex with this girl would be mechanical. Going through the motions. She'd of course mew and writhe and do all the things women are somehow taught to do so men feel like we're pleasuring them, but it would be an act.

Maggie never acted with me.

And, shit, I'm only thinking about sex with Maggie. It's been months and I still haven't wrapped my mind around the fact that she is also my SMS Connection and that we share this incredibly deep emotional bond.

"I'm sorry, Chloe," I say, taking a stab in the dark.

"Cady," she corrects, trying not to show her annoyance.

"Right, Cady, I'm sorry but I'm just not in the mood tonight." I point across the table to Duncan. "He has been known to enjoy having two girls in his bed so you could try your luck there if your friend is willing to share."

"We've shared before," she shrugs and stands up from the chair with little finesse.

I stand as well because I'm not going to sit here and watch four other guys and five girls get themselves riled up. I walk to the door, slip some cash to the waiter who is standing nearby, and decide to take the car service back to the house. He'll turn around to gather the guys later.

"Austin, wait up!" Felix calls.

"I'm gonna head out," I tell him, stating the obvious.

"You okay? What's going on?"

"I'm just not in the mood for all this. I don't want a random hook up. It won't make me feel better. I want Maggie."

"Then, go get her." He says like it's the most obvious statement in the world.

"It isn't that easy." I remind him. I'm still stuck in the spiral of how interconnected our lives became. We had one of the hottest weeks of my entire life, one that I wanted to put everything else in my life on hold for. But then I ruined her first date with the guy she was expecting to fall head over heels for, who also happens to be me. Oh, and let's not forget the small little fact that I put her out of a job.

"Well, I don't know what to tell you, but sulking like you've been doing isn't going to get the job done. You gotta figure out how to win her back."

"Back?"

"She's the girl you were fucking in the fall, right?"

"You knew?"

"Ever since I met her after my game. You had hearts falling out of your damn eyes man. It was obvious."

"Huh," I mutter out loud. "So, what now?"

"Well," Felix brings his hand to his chin in thought and stares off into space for a minute, clearly milking my vulnerability. I want to punch him in the gut. "I think it might be time for The Big Guns."

"The Big Guns?"

"Oh yeah," he says with a sly smile. "Wait here."

Felix leaves me standing by the door and goes back into the private dining room. I can hear him clap his hands loudly and tell the girls that something came up and we had men's work to do.

He comes bounding back to the front of the restaurant and claps me on the shoulders before walking me out to the curb. "This is going to be great. And FUCK YEAH," he yells and I jump, "so much better that it's on Valentine's Day. This should have been my plan from the start."

"What are you talking about?"

"You said you didn't know what to do so we're going to watch the best romance movies of all time and help you come up with a plan."

"That's ridiculous." I laugh.

"No, it's genius. Ah, look here's Rico with the car."

Turns out the big guns are Tom, Matthew, Michael, Leo, Dermot, and Darcy times two.

"See how he notices the way she is trying to hide her fear?" Emmett Turner, or E.T., says as we watch Kate Hudson walk into the ballroom. Her hair is the same color as Maggie's, which is what I'm focused on. "There are so many emotions in everyone's face. Sometimes they're not even aware they're making the expressions that give them away."

Oddly the guys have been super insightful about this. We started with *Sleepless In Seattle* and I thought it was outrageous that a woman would travel across the country based on a radio show. Felix proceeded to tell me it was no more outrageous than to fall for someone over text messages and to shut up and watch.

Apparently this isn't the first time these guys have called in The Big Guns, as they call it. They have been on the team together for three years and have coached two guys out of the singles group through these movies.

It gives me hope.

"There's always some deception or miscommunication. In this one, they have opposing goals. In *Sleepless* they had distance. But ultimately, love conquers all, there's nothing that can get in the way." E.T. says.

We watch the rest of the movie quietly. Scoffing at her boss when she limits what Kate can write about. Cheering when Matthew catches her cab.

The credits roll and we all stand up to stretch. Felix had Rico stop at a market so we picked up plenty of junk food and candy to fuel our marathon. My stomach hurts but I'm enjoying myself for the first time in months.

"Any ideas yet?" Felix asks as I get some water from the kitchen.

"Well, considering I don't own a motorcycle I'm not sure I can chase her down through Dupont Circle."

"OH! I know which one is next, Dunc queue up Mr. President." He hollers into the next room. "And no, I don't expect you to do exactly what happens in any of these movies. It would be lame to just copy them. You've gotta use them for inspiration."

"Inspiration."

"Yeah, like see if any of the characters remind you of Maggie and not just appearance because I saw you staring at Kate. Think about her work, her struggles, her values, and see if our MMC meets any of those needs."

"MMC?" I ask, perplexed.

"Oh, Thorney, you have a lot to learn. Male Main Character." He responds. "But don't worry, one thing at a time."

"Okay, I've never heard of Mr. President, what movie is that?"

"It's a classic, *The American President*. Michael Douglas is a single dad in the White House and Annette Bening is a consultant trying to swing enough votes in her direction that the president will sign some bill. He doesn't want to sign it or something. I dunno, the politics aren't the point. They're enemies but they fall for each other, he is smitten from the first time they meet." Felix chuckles, "she actually insults him pretty good and he still wants to take her out."

"Could be promising."

Because that sounds a lot like Maggie and me.

***

We stayed up all night watching seven romcoms. After watching one more together on the plane back to D.C., I have a plan.

Chapter Thirty
MAGGIE

Hello Old Friend

"You'll need to papers your turn, I mean, turn your papers in at the beginning of class next week. Remember I'll be looking for your sauces, I mean, sources, so please note them correctly. Okay, that's enough from me, see you next week."

I shake my head as I start to pack up, I've never had so many blunders in a lecture before. I'm sure the students are wondering if I'm drunk.

Part of me feels intoxicated.

I woke up to a message from DCFox this morning.

It's been two months of silence since Christmas Eve and a soft ping from inside my bedside table drawer stirred me awake.

It was short, sweet, and even though he cracked me into a thousand pieces by not showing up back in November I felt like sunshine seeped in through those cracks and warmed my soul when I read his words.

DCFox: My friend, hello, good morning? I know you used to respond to my messages in the morning and I have long savored the idea that reading my notes was how you started your day.

I've been thinking of you a lot lately and if you read this please answer just one question; are you in?

Am I in?

In what?

With him?

In trouble?

Because, yes.

I brought my SMS Connect phone with me to campus today. I wanted to feel close to it. To him. I run my thumb down the side of the phone while I read the message again. I haven't responded yet but based on the physical reaction I got to this text I think I need to be honest and tell him that yes, I am in.

All in.

With my gaze down staring at the message, and my head in the clouds deciding how I'll respond, I don't see the person standing right outside the classroom door. I bump into them hard.

"Oh, Excuse me. I'm so sorry, I wasn't...Austin?"

"Hi Maggie."

Every muscle in my body simultaneously freezes and goes up in flames. I think I'm standing up straight but with the way the earth is tilting I have to lean towards him.

Austin Thorne is standing in front of me and looking like a wet dream. His hair is longer than it was in the fall, but not too long. I like it. His glasses are perched on his nose and the scruff he's sporting adds a sexy new dimension to him. His eyes are dark and rich like a cherry wood desk but they sparkle like he's picturing doing me on it. I'd be into that.

Way into it, I think as I look down. Did he get more muscular or did my memory fade over the last few months? He's in a suit but no tie, the top of his shirt is open and it's almost indecent. His shoulders are round and curling towards me because his hands are behind his back.

Desire takes over. I want to rub my nose along the spot where his neck meets his chest. I want to inhale him. I want to feel his heat inside and out.

I want him.

"I heard you were teaching and I wanted to see how you were."

"How did you hear I was teaching?" My question comes out at half strength because I'm not confident I'm breathing.

"Sam told me."

"Sam never said she talked to you."

"Checking in on me MC?" He smirks and I feel myself blush.

"No, but I heard about the program being canceled and I may have looked into it a bit further" I deny but I can hear how flat it falls.

"I'm starting to work on some other things. But I didn't come here to talk to you about my work."

"Oh, no? What did you come here for?"

"I wanted to get your thoughts on something."

"Yeah, what?" I say with a little more sass. His vague sentences are starting to annoy me, I can feel my breath returning and my insides are warming up for a fight. Our old dynamic is back and I don't hate it. I feel alive.

"I wanted to see if we could be friends."

"Friends?"

"Friends. You know, two people who talk about things, hang out occasionally, drive the other to the airport, that sort of thing."

"Don't you have a car service on retainer?"

"Well it would be you using my car service if you needed it I guess. That still counts I think. I'll have to check the rulebook."

I hate myself for it but I laugh. He's charming. And now that I'm coming out the other side of my job loss I can separate Austin from the product he invented.

"You really think we can be friends?"

"I do, now that we're not competing, I think we have everything we need for a storybook friendship."

"You might have to work a little harder than that," I reply as my hand floats up to his bicep. Might as well own it; I am flirting with him. I didn't mean for it to happen but the eyes, the scent, the muscles, just the proximity to him is doing things to my brain.

"I plan to," he says and then he pulls a bouquet of flowers out from behind his back. "I'll see you around, MC."

I take the soft white and pink tulips wrapped in kraft paper and twine and look up at him as he takes a step backwards and turns.

He's just going to walk away? Suggest we become friends and then leave?

"Okay, sure," I mutter mostly to myself because Austin is already halfway down the hall.

There's a bench outside of the building and I sit down in a daze. It isn't even afternoon and my day has been one surprise after another. I reach for my phone and dial.

"Hey, big sis!" Liz answers on speaker phone, I hear a dog bark in the background. "Do you mind chatting while I take Mitsy's portrait?"

"Uh, no, that's fine."

"What's wrong?" Liz asks. She is becoming more and more like Mom. The way she can read into my mental state immediately is unsettling but incredibly helpful.

"He texted."

"Foxy man?!"

"Yes, he texted and asked if I was in," Honestly I could recite the entire message for her, it is imprinted on my brain.

"So, are you?"

"Well, I was, I mean, I am, I," I exhale and regroup. "Austin showed up after class with flowers and asked to be my friend."

"Wow, good for you!"

"Liz, that's not helpful, what do I do?!"

"Why not say yes to both? Does Austin want to be friends or *friends*?"

"I think just regular friends, we kinda flirted but that's just how he is." I admit. But, do I want to be more than friends with him?

"Okay, and would you give DCFox another chance if he asked to meet again?"

"Yeah, I'm still drawn to him and wildly curious about who he is."

"Then reply and say you're in and let friendship with Austin be whatever it is."

"You make it sound so clear cut," I tell her.

"Well, it can be. You don't have to pick between them, yet." I hear Liz's little giggle. "Seriously how do you go from being the pickiest dater in history to having two guys falling at your feet?!"

"If I knew I'd tell you," I mutter as I twirl the SMS Connect phone in my hand.

"Dang it, no Mitsy, no!" Liz yells out. I hear rustling in the background. "I gotta go."

And the line goes dead.

I stop spinning the little device and open the thread.

TalkShopGirl: I'm in.

***

"Good morning, Maggie Collins!"

"Holy shit!" I yelp as I skid to a stop outside Sunrise. "Austin?"

"The one and only, well, not really, but the one you know and, well I was about to say love. That isn't really true is it? The one you know and..."

"Despise?"

"Ouch," he pulls a hand up to his chest like he's wounded. In the arm that is still by his side I see a little box.

"What's that?" I point to it.

"A gift for you," he says as he hands it over to me.

"You can't buy my friendship, you know," I say with a smile as I pull open the ribbon on the small square package. Austin looks delightfully disheveled this morning in jeans and a gray t-shirt. The soft cotton frames his broad chest that looks firmer than I remember. While my eyes notice the physical changes in Austin since the fall, my heart is stumbling over the flowers and now the surprise present.

"I've got money to burn so I'm going to try."

I roll my eyes as I open the box. It's a gift card to Sunrise. I pull it out of the tissue and look up at him.

"A gift card to the bakery on my street?"

"I want to buy you breakfast," he says with a small shrug. He takes a barely noticeable step forward but I can feel the electric charge of his body through the post-exercise heat of mine. "And since I probably can't do that after spending the night, this is a way for me to buy you breakfast every morning. There's five grand on the card."

"Five thousand dollars?!"

He throws his head back and starts laughing. It's a rich, sexy sound. If I wasn't livid with him for this gift I'd probably throw my arms around him and kiss him to try and swallow the sound for myself.

"No, but oh, shit, that was worth it," he wipes at tears in his eyes. "I put fifty bucks on it," he holds up a hand. "Scouts honor."

I push his shoulder hard and he stumbles backwards with another giggle. I turn and start walking to my apartment and I hear him grab his skateboard and jog to catch up to me.

"Aren't you going to buy me breakfast? It's what a friend would do."

I roll my eyes. "I'm starting to wonder what kind of friends you have."

"I've got great friends," he defends. "I'm trying to add another one to the mix."

"Well this friend has a seminar at 10:00 so she's got to go upstairs, shower, and get ready."

"Can a friend help another friend with their shower?" He asks as a devilish grin spreads across his face.

"No." I say sternly. But Little Maggie between my legs screams yes. I open the door to my apartment building and then pause before going all the way in. I turn back to him, "thanks for the gift card, I hope you have a good day, *friend*."

"She called me friend!" He yells as he lifts his arms victoriously and spins in a circle. A laugh bursts from my mouth. A woman with a stroller walks past and he turns to her and reports, "She called me friend!"

"Ohmygod, get out of here," I laugh as I close the door.

The smile doesn't shrink from my face as I shower, as I get dressed, as I pack up my bag.

There wasn't a message from DCFox when I woke up this morning but I check the phone before I leave anyway because I've quickly become re-addicted to messaging with him.

There's a new message.

DCFox: I don't understand women. I know that's a broad statement but time and time again I find myself questioning their logic.

Nails for example. I don't know if I've ever given one thought to a woman's nails but I hear women talking about their nails constantly. What shade. What shape. The trends.

Am I supposed to notice a woman's manicure? Compliment it?

Would it be terrible to admit that I think it's a waste of money?

I laugh and look down at my almond shaped chrome manicure that I got refreshed over the weekend. Since I started teaching I've been branching out into different shades and it's been fun.

TalkShopGirl: I don't think it's terrible to admit but never say it to a woman's face. Her nails are a means of self expression. A way to admit her into the in-crowd or to set her apart. Men may not care but other women notice it.

I once heard a woman say that crazy girls have chipped nail polish and I've never been able to forget that. So, each week, I dutifully get my nails done. I used to do the same shade that was basically skin tone but, recently I've tried new colors. I'll admit it is fun to try something new but it is also agonizing to try and pick a color.

Even if it is just for a week, red nails say one thing, purple says another. Designs and art is another world I have yet to explore.

I hit send and slip the phone into my bag. I lock up, and by the time I reach the corner there's a new message.

DCFox: Okay, but now I have to know, what does red nails vs purple say?

TalkShopGirl: I don't know but it says something. It's a vibe.

DCFox: See, this is why I don't understand women. Explain it to me!

TalkShopGirl: Have you ever had your nails painted?

DCFox: No.

TalkShopGirl: Well, when you do, you'll understand.

DCFox: So since I'm too manly to have my nails painted you won't explain a color vibe to me?

TalkShopGirl: Is it manly to be closed minded about trying new things?

Chapter Thirty-One
AUSTIN

The green one?

"WHAT THE HELL ARE you doing?" Elle hollers as she walks into the apartment.

"I'm painting my nails but it is fucking impossible!" I yell back even though she's standing in front of me. I've been sitting at the kitchen counter trying to paint my own nails for over an hour and have more paint on the towel I put down under my hands than on my nails themselves.

"Why on earth are you doing this? And, oh gosh, no!" Elle swoops in with a paper towel to start wiping up. She plucks the brush from my hand and screws it back onto the bottle. It's a shade I picked from the stash in her room. It's a little bit pink, a little purple, a little orange, it reminds me of the sunrises I saw when I was at Maggie's apartment early in the morning.

"Someone told me to try it." I shrug.

"Someone or *she* did?"

"She who?" I ask sarcastically. It's obvious I'm doing this because Maggie suggested it.

"Ohmygod, come here." Elle says exasperated as she soaks a cotton ball in the remover. She holds my hand and starts to clean off the polish. "I mean the she who you have been trying to impress."

I look up at her and she just shrugs.

"I heard you and Felix talking about it."

"Well then, the cat is out of the bag. I'm trying to get my SMS Connect girl back. Or, get her for the first time, kind of."

"I still don't understand all the moving parts of this but whatever bro. Now, go wash your hands, dry them with a paper towel and come back, I'll paint them for you."

"No, I'm good actually." I say as I wash my hands. "I was going to take it off tonight anyways, I just wanted to try it, not actually run around with sunrise colored nails."

"Sunrise?"

"It's what the color reminded me of." I shrug.

"I can't wait to meet her." Elle laughs.

"What's funny about that?" I ask.

"Well, the girl who has Austin Thorne painting his nails and comparing the color to nature has got to be someone special."

"I have a feeling you two are going to get along splendidly."

***

Today I'm going to trail Maggie. It isn't stalking, I'm not going to do anything, I just want to see how she spends her day.

I've got a meeting tomorrow morning about a new venture. It was inspired by the night the boys brought in the *big guns* and some compelling data I was able to dig up. Plus, I think Elle would be great at running the whole thing and I could be the CFO and let her make strategic decisions.

But, today, I'm on Maggie watch.

Sam has been helpful, she told me where she is teaching and then it was pretty easy to find the classroom and time online. That day I met her after her class, Greg and I sat in the car and watched her walk off campus towards Adams Morgan so I think she walks to and from Georgetown.

It's like an hour long walk so I was also surprised to see her out for a run the other morning.

I had gone to Sunrise for the gift card and was waiting for Maggie to leave for work when I just happened to look up the street as she came jogging down in my direction.

Jumping out at her probably wasn't the smoothest of moves but I couldn't let her get by without stopping her.

It worked out perfectly. The way she smirked as she walked into her building? Heaven.

And then the back and forth with me on SMS Connect? I could hear her smiling through her words.

Felix keeps reminding me to be patient, to wait until I'm sure she's fallen for me.

Austin me.

She has to be so smitten with Austin Thorne that she wishes DCFox is me.

I have to be careful with what I say as DCFox, I don't want to tip her off but I don't want to throw her too far off the trail.

The goal of following her today is to find the places she visits often so I can pop in and be there. That's my current strategy. Be there.

It's not complicated, it's not sophisticated. It's simple. Straight forward. Show up, be there, and be myself.

***

"So what did you find out?" Felix asks as we crack open beers in his kitchen.

"I found out she walks to and from work. She listens to something while she's walking and I don't think it's music because she never sings along. She carries this purple water bottle with her but I never see her take a drink of it. And her purse slides off her shoulder, a lot."

"Interesting, so what are you going to do with that information?"

"I asked Elle to recommend some bags and I'm going to buy her one."

"So your strategy is to buy her affection with gifts?"

"Maybe, I think she likes it. You should have seen how her face lit up when I gave her the bakery gift card. Plus, I want to treat her, surprise her, spoil her. Let her know that I *know* her and what she needs, maybe even wants. It's not like I'm spending it on anything else."

"True, but before you go buying her a Birkin, I'd make sure she doesn't have an attachment to her current bag or that she's not a minimalist or something."

"Good point," I say as I pull out my SMS Connect phone.

DCFox: Do you think it's possible to form an emotional attachment to an object? I ask because there is one pillow on my sofa that for some reason calls to me in a way no other pillow ever has. I get jealous when someone else cuddles it or stuffs it behind their back. I get especially angry when someone throws it on the floor.

"Are you just lying to her to try to get her answer?" Felix asks as he reads over my shoulder.

"No, I have a pillow I feel this way about."

"Which one? No wait, let me guess, the green one?"

"No," I respond in a way that probably tips him off that he's correct.

Felix laughs as he pulls the meal prepped food from the fridge. He has a chef come in once a week to put everything together for him so he doesn't have to worry about what to eat every day.

The phone pings and he abandons the stir fry on the stove. "What did she say?!"

Chapter Thirty-Two
MAGGIE

No Takesy-Backsies

TalkShopGirl: I imagine it is possible, although, I have to admit I don't share your devotion to your throw pillow. I have a preferred bed pillow I guess. But for the most part, I see my things for the purpose they serve. There are a few mementoes around my apartment, pictures mostly, but I've never been one for collecting things.

I've heard of people collecting key chains or snow globes everywhere they travel but for me a picture does it. As soon as I see an image, I'm thrown back into the memory.

I sit back against my headboard and look out the window. It's a rainy night and I'm glad to be home and snuggled under the covers.

Things have felt different these last few weeks. First, the messages from DCFox have been frequent. And light hearted. I mean, emotional attachments to pillows? C'mon. But, then there's also Austin asking to be my friend. Him showing up and being endearing and looking delicious. It feels different, new, and it feels good.

There is a lot of history between us but we've only known each other for six months. We've managed to cram in a lot of drama in that time.

The Austin of this past week has been different. He's been goofy. He's been immature. Like the serious and pulled together version of him from last fall was work-hard Austin and this is the play-hard version.

I don't know what to make of it. I feel like I did right before the election where I had to choose between DCFox and Austin. Not that Austin wanted to date me back then but now that he's my friend I guess it feels like we could possibly move from friendship to something more. I know we're good at the sex part of something more.

But still that leaves me wondering what to do with DCFox.

I snuggle in and reply to students. I told them I'd be willing to talk about career paths and planning for their early careers. I was surprised at how many kids reached out asking for guidance. I'm also surprised by how much I enjoy working with them. I might not have the famous kind of notoriety but I can tell I'm making an impact on their lives.

At the top of the screen a text notification comes up.

I click over to my messages and see one from Austin.

> **Can I walk with you to campus tomorrow, friend?**

I snuff out a laugh because "friend" feels like an inside joke.

> **Sure, friend, I leave at 8:15.**

> **It's a date, friend.**

***

At 8:15 there's a knock on my door. He's right on time, as usual.

"Good morn-" I'm cut off as I open the door fully. In front of Austin's face is a Saks Fifth Avenue shopping bag. "What's that?" I ask.

Austin lowers the bag and seeing his face is like dunking my head in ice water. It's a shock and refreshing all at once.

"Open it and find out," he says as he steps into my apartment.

"You're really trying to buy me, aren't you?" I joke as I set the shopping bag down on the coffee table.

"I'll do whatever it takes, MC."

I gasp as I feel the little flutter in my stomach when I hear the nickname. He hasn't used it since the fall. When there was so much more between us. It's sweet, and personal, and, dare I say it, *friendly*.

I pull away the tissue paper and uncover a beautiful tan leather Prada bag. I know immediately that it will fit my laptop and the notebooks I've carried with me for years. I slowly lift it out and my breath gets caught in my chest as my fingers brush against the butter smooth leather.

"Austin, this is too much," I say as I sit down with it on my lap. It's beautiful. For the first time I understand DCFox's attachment to an object. I would go to war for this bag.

"Okay, then I'll return it."

"Nope, no takesy-backsies." I hug the bag to my chest and turn away from him to protect it.

He laughs and I feel it between my legs.

"Wanna use it today?" He asks.

"Yes, I think I do."

He chuckles again and hands me my old bag. As I start to transfer everything I pick up the SMS Connect phone and slide it into place.

"Is that an SMS Connect phone?"

I freeze. "Hmm?" I ask like I didn't hear him.

"I asked if that was an SMS Connect phone you slid into your new bag."

"Oh, ha ha ha," this is awkward. "It, umm, yes it is an SMS Connect phone," I admit as my shoulders slump. New laid-back, college class teacher Maggie still can't think on her feet.

"Are you looking for love, MC?" He asks gently, there's a hint of a tease but more respect to his tone than mirth.

"I might be," I admit. "I signed up last year and have been talking to one guy."

I stand and slide the new bag on my shoulder and make my way to the door. Austin follows and steps out into the hallway. He doesn't say anything, just waits for me to lock up, drop the keys into my new bag after attaching them to the built-in lanyard, and I realize he's waiting for me to continue.

"He, uhh, actually, was the person I was waiting for when you showed up at Lapis."

"Ah, that explains the hair then."

"What?" I laugh.

"You had your hair down. At work it was always up. I got to let it loose when we were together but I'd never seen it done like that. I almost didn't recognize you."

He holds open the door for me as we head out to the sidewalk.

"So, what happened after that night?" He asks.

"Nothing," I shrug.

"What do you mean?"

"Well, he never showed up that night, then I sent him a message saying I needed space. Which he gave me until he sent a message at Christmas. I didn't respond to it."

"Wanted to give him a taste of his own medicine?"

I let out a little laugh, "Maybe. But mostly, I just didn't know what to say. I didn't know what I wanted."

"So tell me about him, *friend*," Austin says as we cross the street. He grabs my arm to pull me back as a bike comes zipping around us. Sensations travel throughout my body from the spot where his fingers graze my skin. His touch, however innocent, is making it hard to think. I am overwhelmed by the memories of what it felt like to be in his arms and feel his touch everywhere.

"Thanks," I mutter finally while my mind wanders to what holding hands with Austin Thorne would be like.

"Wouldn't want to see that new bag covered in tire marks," he jokes as we continue our walk.

"Right, the bag," I bite back my smile as it tries to grow. He wanted to protect me.

"You were about to tell me everything about your digital soulmate," he says as we cut through the park.

I laugh, "I was?"

"Yes, as your friend, I need to approve of this guy."

"We're that close of friends that you get boyfriend approval rights?"

"Absolutely. And who would be a better judge than me? I'm the total package. Since you have turned me down, if I'm not good enough then I am the only one to judge a man who is better than me."

"You're unreal," I laugh. "Okay, let's see, he's thoughtful."

"In a philosophical way or in a I noticed your work bag sucked and got you a new one way?"

"Philosophical," I retort and narrow my eyes at him.

"Okay, fine," he responds and lifts his hands in the air in surrender.

"He's open, he tells me about his feelings towards things."

"What things?"

"Oh gosh, I don't know. We've talked about music, books, I know he likes to cook but not clean up after himself."

"So, he's lazy."

"No," I chuckle, "he's honest, it's sweet."

"I see," he says thoughtfully. We pause at a corner and I turn to study Austin's face as he watches traffic. His eyes move as he follows different cars or pedestrians, jumping every so often to the next thing. He's perceptive, I never really noticed that about him before. If I'm honest it feels like he can read me like a book.

But then again, DCFox has too. "There are times when it feels like he knows me better than I know myself." I admit right before the light changes.

I start to move into the crosswalk but after a few steps I turn to see Austin still standing on the sidewalk.

"Austin?"

"There's no way to compete with that," he says soberly and then blinks quickly like he's coming out of a trance. "C'mon, time's running out."

And he reaches down for my hand and pulls me quickly through the intersection before the light changes because now it's my feet that are stuck in place.

Chapter Thirty-Three
AUSTIN

For The Record, Again

"The start-up costs are personnel, the first few author advances, and production people. Printing is outsourced and quickly off set once the copies start selling."

"And you're confident these would sell." I ask as I thumb through the presentation.

"Absolutely, the romance genre is the fastest growing and highest selling subset on the market." Meredith tells me, which I already knew. She's an editor for TMC's book review section and has been working on the side to put together a business plan for a romance focused publishing house for me and Elle.

"Talk me through who I would need to hire." I say as I set the presentation down and look at Elle.

"Well, you two would be the C suite. CEO," she points to Elle, "would be in charge of directional choices and big picture thinking. Then Austin, as CFO you'd manage all the finances. To start you'd need a couple of agents, editors, designers, and marketers. But it is pretty easy to find independent authors on social media since they all use hashtags to get discovered."

"And what's that put us at for salaries, five million?"

"Probably. It depends on how seasoned the candidates are but figure 150-400k per hire including benefits."

I jot the numbers down. "Okay, thanks so much Meredith. Elle and I need to chat but I'm fairly confident we'll be moving forward. Elizabeth, can you schedule a time for us to follow up in a few days?"

"Thank you Mr. Thorne, Ms. Thorne," Meredith says with a nod in both our directions before she stands up and leaves the office with Elizabeth escorting her out.

"Mr. Thorne?"

"Ms. Thorne?"

Elle and I both roll back with laughter.

"That's rule number one of this new company, no Mr or Ms's. Unless we're publishing a regency romance and then we could all use titles to get in the mood." Elle says as she stands and gathers up the presentation papers.

"So you're on board with this?"

"Yeah, it's not something I was seriously considering but when Meredith shared the data about women's sexual liberation through smutty romance novels, I was on board."

I knew she'd like that part of it. When I walked out of TMC two months ago I didn't know what I was going to do next. When I came across an article about how the romance genre doubled in size over the last three years the idea hit. I had Elizabeth, who also left TMC, contact Meredith and get her working in the background.

"Is it going to be an issue that we're brother and sister?" I asked. Something about my sister saying the words "sexual liberation" makes me uneasy.

"We just won't let you read any of the books. Your little sentimental heart couldn't handle it."

I laugh, "I think there might be some stories out there inspired by me."

"Ew, no. Nope. We are not talking about your sexploits being inspiration for romance novels."

"Fine, but I could be and you'll never know." I inform her. Maybe this is going to be fun after all.

"You will not be reading any of the submissions." Elle says.

"Submission sounds nice."

"GROSS!" Elle yells and then she storms out of the room. I laugh because she makes it a little too easy.

Just then my SMS Connect phone pings in my pocket. I pull it out and read the message from Maggie.

TalkShopGirl: I'm not sure if I told you this but I lost my job back in November. It was a job I had been working towards my entire career and one I thought I would do for years to come. When I was let go I felt really lost.

I went home for a while and tried to figure out what to do next. Right around New Year's I was offered a new job that would last until March. I've never taken a short term role before but I wanted to get back to D.C.

Now this job will wrap up soon and again I find myself questioning what I should do next.

But this morning I woke up to an email from someone who I didn't think even knew who I was, someone with a lot of influence and resources, someone who has been aligned with people I didn't want to do business with. He offered me something I don't feel great about but the paycheck is big. Like eyeballs bugging out of your head big.

So now, as I sit here in my chair, I find myself wanting to talk with you through the details. I want to get your opinion. I want to know if you think I should take the money and run or turn it down and trust something else will come my way.

It's funny, everyone else in my life that I could ask about this is predictable. I know what my parents, my siblings, and my friends would say. But I don't know what you would say.

I finish reading the message and am dying to know what offer she got. The urge to text her as Austin and say "so anything new?" is strong enough to have me pulling out my iPhone. Instead of sending a note to Maggie, I place a call to someone we both know. Time for phase two.

***

"Welcome back to the podcast Austin Thorne, we were excited when you reached out to us."

"Thanks for having me, Charlie."

"We've got a lot to cover, so let's dive right in." Charlie says and then he turns towards me. "Give us an update on AI Media."

"Well, as you probably know, initially it was well received. The users loved the customized content and our readership levels grew steadily."

"How did you measure readership?"

"We tracked daily users, the amount of time they spent on the app, and the number of articles they swiped through. There's a formula that uses those factors to determine the number of words read each day."

"Care to share why the product was shut down?"

"It wasn't my call but the product was deemed a liability following the incident at the end of the year."

"For our listeners, AI Media was engulfed in controversy over an article it summarized and distributed with misleading information in it."

"It was one little mistake with a compound effect. We worked to correct the error as quickly as possible but the damage was done. I empathize with the families impacted."

"And empathy is important to you?" He asks.

"The most important. Without it we view every human we come across as a threat, as someone who might take everything from us. Instead, empathy allows us to think about how our advantages or disadvantages are different from others. Not better or worse, simply different."

"That's a very philosophical thing to say. This podcast audience might be in over their heads." Charlie says with a little laugh.

"Well then, they'll learn some empathy for the desk chair philosopher I am."

"Good point," Charlie says with a laugh. "Alright, let's get back to AIM and this other feature the public is only now learning about."

"Right," I say before I clear my throat. This was a quick decision I made after getting Maggie's SMS Connect text yesterday.

It was time for the world to know that she didn't lose her job because she was bad at it, she lost it because AI Media cheated. We used her words against her. And I haven't felt good about it for a long time. When I called the producer for this show I explained to her that I would be revealing an exclusive to this podcast.

"Well, when we first released AI Media back in the fall the public knew about the custom news features of the app. But what they didn't know was that we were also using the software to generate speeches."

"Speeches?"

"Yes, political speeches, debate scripts, media responses. That type of content was being written by our software to appeal to the target audience."

"So instead of custom news, people were hearing custom speeches?"

"No," I correct before the world spins out thinking the speeches weren't live or something. "The speeches would be delivered as usual, it's just that the wording was customized to who was in the audience."

"Kind of like how politicians always say "Go local sports team!" when they're on the road?"

I laugh, "sort of like that."

"This is interesting," Charlie says. "We're going to step away for a break but we'll be right back with Austin Thorne of TMC's AI Media."

Because this isn't a live show all he does is look to the producer through the window who counts down 5, 4, 3, 2, 1 on her hand before he picks right back up. "Welcome back, listeners. So Austin, you were telling us about the speech writing capabilities of AIM."

"Yes, this technology was utilized by political candidates in the fall."

"Can you tell us who?"

"No, I'm not at liberty to say."

"Fine." Charlie says with a little pout. "I want to ask about the lawsuit AI Media issued against some of it's users."

"Sorry Charlie, I cannot comment on ongoing legal disputes."

"Man," Charlie laughs, "You called us to be on the show! You're not sharing anything. But actually, if you're not going to share who the speeches were for or what the lawsuit is about; can you tell us why you're sharing this information now."

"Well, a person I respect and admire lost their job because AIM was being used to write speeches. This person believes in elevating the discussion and the goal for AIM generated content was to find the lowest common denominator.

"I often disagreed with this person because I focused on the bottom line of this product. How more people would use it if they felt the news agreed with them. And, I was right, for the record, but I also saw in the data that people's opinions started to skew even further from the middle. They get stuck in an algorithm that took them further away from common ground. And that concerns me."

"How so?"

"Well, this country takes all sorts of people to make it work. It does best when diverse groups of citizens come together for the good of everyone. It feels like that is slipping away from us now. That we only want to interact with people who think like us. And while that might be easier, it's fucking boring."

He laughs, "You seem to feel passionate about this, Austin."

"Yeah, I do, I am, because I've found a person who challenges me and makes me think deeper about issues. She pushes me. She's the person I want to talk to about things. We come from different places. We have different opinions. We hardly ever agree." I let out a chuckle as Maggie's face comes to mind. "And even though she frustrates me to no end, I'm grateful she's in my life."

"Who is this lucky lady?"

"Again, I'm not at liberty to say," I reply with a smirk.

"Well you know we always get to dating on For The Record, so does this mean you, Austin Thorne, are off the market?"

"I hope so."

Chapter Thirty-Four
MAGGIE

For The Record, Again Pt 2

"I CAN'T BELIEVE I'M calling you about a political podcast," Liz says into the phone.

"I can't believe you're calling me about a political podcast either." I tell her as I swing my legs under me and settle into the corner of my chair. I switch the call to speakerphone and set it down on the armrest while Liz continues.

"It's that one you went on last year, when you got in a fight with Austin Thorne."

The way she says his name has me picturing her wiggling her eyebrows at me.

"Yeah? For The Record. What about it?"

"Austin was on it again, yesterday."

"He was?" I ask as I grab my phone. I pull up the podcast's website and scroll to find the latest episode.

"So you haven't heard it yet?" Liz asks.

"No, I don't follow it as closely anymore."

"Well, this one might be worth a listen."

"Okay, I'll listen when we're done talking," I promise. "What photo sessions do you have booked this week?"

"One family session, a newborn, and, oh, what's that? Sure thing, be right there," she calls off to the side of the phone. "Gotta go, call me when you listen to the show! Bye!"

I doubt anyone was really calling her considering she spat that all out in one breath and she works by herself. With an eye roll I press play on the podcast.

My mind pictures Austin sitting in the same studio we were in together. Did he sit in the same seat? Take mine? I didn't see another guest's name so he is on this one alone.

He starts with some updates on AIM and I like hearing what happened from his side. I get the sense there is more to the story than what he's sharing. I can picture his emotionless business face.

He continues with the news that AIM was used for speech writing. Which I certainly knew all about but no one outside the senator's, well the president's, inner circle knew.

My mind drifts to that old team. I think most of them are still working together, at the White House. Part of me is jealous.

Part of me is glad I am not strung out working eighteen hours a day.

I refocus on the show and then all the air leaves my body.

I've found a person who challenges me and makes me think deeper about issues. She pushes me. She's the person I want to talk to about things.

Could he mean me?

I hit the pause button and process what I just heard. Austin coming to my defense. Austin admitting the AIM speeches worked, but they may have worked too well. They didn't ask or require people to think.

Which was the hill I died on.

That and *prosperity and.*

This whole podcast has been in defense of *me.* It sounds like he's speaking directly to me. I hit play again after I manage a deep inhale and exhale.

But we come from different places. We have different opinions. We hardly ever agree.

He laughs in a quiet way and I picture his handsome face and the way his smile probably leans to one side.

And even though she frustrates me to no end, I'm so glad she's in my life.

I have to hit pause again because tears are streaming down my cheeks. I use the backs of my hands to mop them up. With a juicy sniffle I hit play again.

Who is this lucky lady?

Again, I'm not at liberty to say.

Well you know we always talk dating on For The Record, so does this mean, you, Austin Thorne, are off the market?

I hope so.

I hit pause again and the tears turn into wails.

I want Austin Thorne. He's the man I can spend my life with. We will disagree about almost everything but it'll be exciting, fun, challenging. It'll be a partnership.

My stomach falls out when I hear my SMS Connect phone ping. With shaking hands I pick it up and read the message.

DCFox: I understand if the answer is no, but, could we set up another time to meet?

With tears still in my eyes and my mind reeling, I drop the phone like it burned me. I don't have to respond. I don't have to agree to a meeting. Part of me wants to because I'm dying to know who he is. Part of me thinks I should just let it go and see if Austin is actually interested in me or if he was talking about someone else.

I listen to the rest of the podcast but all he talks about is what he wants to do next.

When the podcast finishes I text Liz.

Whoever the lucky girl is, she's got a good thing going.

You don't think it's you?

> We're just friends. He says it like every other sentence when we hang out.

My phone vibrates but it isn't a message from Liz. I go back to my inbox and see it's from Austin.

My palms start to sweat as I open the message.

> Hey Friend! Wanna meet me for a run tomorrow morning? I'd offer our old morning routine but that would be a different kind of friendship, friends with benefits, and we're not that.
>
> Right?

I laugh despite myself and reply.

> Right. And sure, meet at 7?

> I'll be there.

I'm about to move back over to my messages with Liz when my SMS Connect phone pings again.

DCFox: Tell you what, I'll be waiting for you next to Stumpy the Cherry Tree at the basin at 6:00pm tomorrow evening. The sun should just be setting and it'll be beautiful. Meet me if you want to, or don't, but I'll stay until 7:00.

Chapter Thirty-Five
MAGGIE

Run It By Me

BY THE TIME AUSTIN shows up in the morning for our run I've already logged two thousand steps from pacing my studio apartment. The nervous energy is coursing through my veins.

Should I bring up the podcast?

Should I pretend I haven't heard it if he brings it up?

What would I even say if we started talking about it?

I yelp when the soft knock comes at the door.

"Nervous MC?" Austin asks as he pushes off the doorframe and steps into my apartment.

"No." Yes.

"You shouldn't be, you're the one who runs all the time, I just rock climb and do yoga."

"Well, then, I should challenge you to a race." I joke as I grab my phone and keys. I slip the gift card for Sunrise into my leggings pocket, maybe I can treat him to breakfast, on him, after our run.

He holds the door on our way out and when we reach the corner he turns to me and says, "so do we just start?"

"Yes!" I grin and take off at a sprint. I hear him grunt behind me and I start to laugh. I'm so nervous that even at full stride I can feel the jitters coursing through me.

"Hold up!" He yells and I slow my pace a bit to let him catch up. When he reaches me we fall in step next to each other and run quietly for a few blocks. I listen to the way our breaths match each other's. It is a true struggle to keep my thoughts focused on the run or even in a category appropriate for a public location.

When we stop at a light he props his hands on his hips and turns to me.

"Good thing I didn't want to talk to you today," he huffs out between breaths.

"We do fine when we're not talking," I tell him and I start off again when the light changes leaving him standing on the corner. I didn't wait to see if he understood my meaning. I'm not sure I did. I did not plan to spend this morning flirting with Austin Thorne but now that I've started, I don't want to stop.

He catches up and our feet pound into the pavement in sync. His legs are longer than mine so he's adjusting his pace to match me but I think it's a challenge for him anyways.

"Was that an offer to add benefits to our friendship?" He asks as we turn a corner.

"Honestly, I don't know."

"Are you seeing someone?"

"No, but I'm still talking to that SMS Connect guy."

"That's right, Foxy Boy."

I laugh, "DCFox."

"Same thing," he shrugs. "Have you met him?"

"Not yet," I pause. Do I tell Austin? Would it make him jealous? Do I want him to feel jealous? I think I might. Maybe I'll figure out how I feel if I can figure out how he feels. "He messaged me to say he's going to be somewhere tonight and I could meet him if I wanted to."

"So he's putting the ball in your court. That's a bold move."

"Confident," I amend.

"Cocky. But hey, maybe you're into that kind of thing." He's quiet for a few paces and then asks, "What have you two been talking about lately?"

"I dunno, mostly surface level stuff. We still don't talk about details in our lives. There was something I wanted to discuss with him, get his perspective on."

"Yeah? What is it?"

"I umm, I got an offer to do a book, actually from TCM."

"My former employer."

"Former? Since when?"

"January." I knew AI Media was shut down but I didn't realize he doesn't work there anymore. "I'm investing in something new that's a little different from what I've done in the past."

"Care to elaborate?" I ask as we turn another corner.

"Not right now," He tosses a quick grin in my direction. "What was your offer from TCM?"

"To write a book about the campaign. I think they want the scorned former staffer angle and that's just not who I am. I know things didn't end up the way I wanted but I still believe in President Quinn and want her to do well."

"That's admirable, Maggie." He says and he looks at me for a few paces. I turn to him and smile quickly before focusing back on the path ahead. "It sounds like you've already decided not to write it."

"I think I have."

"But?"

"Well, I kind of wanted his opinion on it." We come to a stop at a light and I cover my face with my hands. "Is that crazy? I mean he's a stranger, I don't know him, but I value his opinion. I feel like he'd know me well enough to help me decide what to do. It's hard to pass up, it's a good paycheck."

"A good paycheck for bad work is a backwards way to live if you can help it." He says, and I look over at him. He's looking across the street at the signal but his eyes are off even further in the distance.

There is so much about Austin that I don't know. I dismissed him initially because he was my nemesis. Then because I didn't think he was capable of substantial conversations like the one we're having right now. Since coming back into my life a month ago he's proven himself to be a good friend. Reliable, insightful, generous with his time and, I think back on the Prada bag sitting on my coffee table, his resources.

I watch the side of his face and am desperate to know what he's thinking. Am I the girl he was talking about on the podcast or not?

I'm about to ask him why he left TCM, which feels like a safer topic than if he likes me, check yes or no, but he starts running away. It takes me a beat to realize that the light has changed and it is our turn to cross. I hustle up to him and match my pace to his.

"What's on your mind, MC?" He asks.

"Why did you leave TCM?"

"It's a little early for those questions don't you think," he tries to deflect. I can see vulnerability flash through his eyes.

"No, you made me talk about DCFox and the book deal. Tit for tat."

"Tits are on the table?"

I playfully shove him sideways, he laughs as he smoothly recovers his stride.

"Alright, no tits. But, for the record I'd be game if you were." He says like it's a question. I shoot him a sideways glare because as much as my body wants that I want his answer more. "Fine, fine. I left TCM and AIM because I didn't believe in the work I was doing."

"Really? I'm surprised. You were such a big fan last fall."

"Well, I saw how easily humanity could get lost in the shuffle of it all. My next project is about slowing down."

"What's your next project?" I ask because part of me thinks I want to be a part of it.

"I'm going to publish romance novels."

I bark out a laugh. "You're going to write romance?"

"What? You don't think I'm romantic? I charmed the pants off of you, literally."

"That's not how I remember it," I chuckle and shake my head.

"Well, I remember you not being able to keep your hands off of me."

"Because I wanted to strangle you."

"Hey, whatever you're into is good with me," he winks when we pull up to a stop. "How much longer are we running?"

I check my fitness watch and tell him, "It's only been 20 minutes, usually I run for at least 45."

"So we're about to turn around?" He asks hopefully, having done the halfway there math.

"Sure, we can turn around," I placate. We pivot and start heading back the way we came. "Okay, enough evasion Austin, are you seriously going to write romance novels?"

"No," he laughs and I feel the sound warm me from my belly out to my limbs. "My sister Elle will be the CEO of our publishing house, I'll be the CFO. We're going to find independent romance authors and sign them. The industry is growing at an exponential rate and we want to be a part of it."

"It isn't the worst idea."

"Thank you for your vote of confidence," he deadpans. "Elle is excited about it, and it's our own thing so we answer to ourselves."

"Is that a nod to why you left TMC?"

"My dad just doesn't see things the way I do. I thought for a while he was grooming me to take over but I don't think we have the same priorities and I get the feeling he wants to run the company until he dies."

"He doesn't have much of a life outside of work?"

He barks out a laugh, "No. None at all. He rules that company with an iron fist and somehow makes not adapting to change work for his bottom line."

We let that idea sit between us as we snake our way back to my apartment. I don't think to ask if he wants to run all the way back with me, he just does.

As we pull up outside of Sunrise I turn to him, "Can I interest you in breakfast you've already paid for?" I ask him lightheartedly while flashing the gift card his way.

"Always," he says with a smile and we jog up the steps together.

After we order our coffee and pastries we take a seat by the window. I hold my chin in my palm and watch Austin as he settles in.

"What?" He asks.

"I'm realizing I don't know much about you."

"Oh, yeah? What is it you want to know?"

I think about the repertoire of "first date" questions that normally don't interest me at all but with Austin, I suddenly want to know everything.

"Where do you want to travel that you've never been before?"

"Antarctica." He says before a sip of coffee.

"Bullshit."

"You're right, but I haven't had a chance to visit the southern tip of South America and once you're down there you're basically at the South Pole so it makes sense to just tack on a day trip."

I laugh, "I don't think Antarctica is a day trip sort of destination."

"No? That's too bad. I bet they could do a lot more in tourism revenue if it was."

My giggle escapes before I can catch it and he grins. The smile he gives me is warm and friendly, open and sexy, and triggers all the things my nervous system is supposed to do when I am on the receiving end of smiles from cute boys.

I clear my throat and busy myself with the corner of the napkin. As the weight of this crush and impossible situation weighs down on my shoulders.

"Same question to you," he says after I'm able to regulate my breathing. The pastries get set down between us and I rip off a corner of my croissant before answering.

"I studied in Florence in college and I love everything about Italy. I got to see a lot of western Europe during that time. It might be fun to go back not on a college kid's budget but I've never been to Japan and I think it would be amazing."

"Japan is amazing. I'll take you sometime, friend. Unless Foxy has a problem with you traveling halfway around the world with a handsome billionaire."

"He's humble too." I laugh and Austin points a finger at me to indicate a good point.

"What else are you up to today?" he asks.

"Probably some chores, laundry, then figuring out if I'm going to meet him and what to wear when I do."

"Well, if you go you should wear your hair down. You're always pretty but when you have your hair down..." He mimes a chef's kiss. "Perfection."

I blush and mutter a thank you.

"What about you?"

"I'm not seeing anyone." He says quickly and pins me with eye contact that I feel in my bones.

"No, I, umm, meant what else are you doing today?"

"I think I'm going to take a long shower because this run was brutal. I'll probably have lunch with Felix. Then I'll head out for the evening. It's a Saturday night after all."

"So, it is."

"Maggie, can I ask you something?" He asks as he looks out the window.

The way his voice softened makes me nervous. "Sure," I whisper back.

"Well, do you think," he turns to face me and I feel the weight of his question before he even asks it, "if we had just met and never been pitted against each other or done the stress relief arrangement; do you think we could have been more than friends?"

"Austin," I interject but he holds his hand up to stop me.

"No, wait, I don't want to hear if you're going to let me down gently. I've been with women in the past who only wanted me for my last name and my tabloid potential. You've been the first woman to know the real me. And even if you hated me at first, I think we've gotten somewhere good. So, if you go and meet this guy tonight and fall in love, just, I don't know, think of me from time to time."

He offers me a closed lip smile and glances out the window again. His words are what I want to hear but I feel like I owe it to myself to meet DCFox. Things with Austin feel wonderfully easy but he also caused me a lot of grief. DCFox did too but I'm finding it easier to forgive him.

"That's Greg." Austin nods to the car that just pulled up to the curb. "Take care, Maggie Collins," he stands. I watch as he steps next to me, plants a gentle kiss to my temple, and then walks out without looking back.

I watch him climb into the backseat of the car. Watch the car pull away. Follow it to the end of the block and then watch it disappear around the corner.

The spot where he kissed me tingles and I touch it gingerly. I remember seeing Kyle kiss Liz on the head like that. It is such a gentle show of affection. It's a tenderness I've now come to expect from Austin.

One that I crave.

One that I'm not sure I'll find anywhere else.

Chapter Thirty-Six
MAGGIE

Wild Horses and Fire Breathing Dragons

I SHOWER AND THINK of Austin.

I dry my hair and think of Austin.

I get dressed and think of Austin.

I do my makeup and think of Austin.

And at every step I think, what if he's the one standing at Stumpy tonight? It would certainly make everything easier! I wouldn't have to choose.

And then I have to tell myself that it'll be a disaster if I have to recover from my disappointment by expecting or hoping for one person and another is there.

I guess I could always try to leave before DCFox sees me. I didn't tell him if I'd be there or not. I didn't tell him what I was wearing.

So I guess that is my plan. Head over there, spy and try to figure out if it's Austin or not and make a game time decision. Not that I've gotten any better at making those in the last year.

Everything with Austin over the last few weeks has felt easy and natural. And, since we've taken sex off the table I've learned to be in a room with him and not immediately jump his bones.

I still want to, very much so, but I've been able to control my baser urges.

My body is still buzzing with anxiety by the time I've changed outfits three times and landed on the red dress from our first attempt at meeting that I had started with. I fluff up my hair and check the clock. I have an hour until DCFox said he'd be there. It's about an hour walk down to the Tidal Basin. And it's a pretty route that takes me past the White House and through the mall.

I pile my things into the Prada bag and head out the door. It feels like Austin is with me as I carry this bag. It's comforting. Sam and I chat every so often now and I've gotten used to the regular check-ins with Liz and CJ, but Austin is probably my closest friend. Him, and then DCFox.

I never would have imagined such a strong bond with Austin and I really hope that DCFox and I share a connection in person.

But do I?

Because then I'll have to pick one over the other and I don't think I'm prepared to do that.

Outside the White House I see Ben leaving the grounds.

"Ben!" I yell in greeting, "Hey! How are you?"

"Maggie Collins! Hey. I'm good, exhausted. I'm headed home for the day finally."

"But it's Saturday?" I ask, and as soon as I do I realize how far out of the political elite loop I am.

"Is it?" He sighs. "You look nice, where are you off to?"

"To see the cherry blossoms."

"Ah yes, they're reaching their peak bloom this week I think. It'll be beautiful."

I smile warmly, "Yeah it will."

We part ways and I continue towards the water. It's funny, I never thought losing my job would have been a good thing but it forced me to change.

It forced me to let go of plans I had clung to. Expectations I was stuck to. It felt scary to let go of my fifteen year plan but in the last few months I haven't thought much about the future.

Not in a bad way, but in a, *I'm happy with the present* way.

The connection I've built with my students is rewarding. One asked for a recommendation letter for a job this summer. I don't know if I can get another teaching job but there are leadership development organizations I can join. Honestly, I could start my own firm and teach seminars, coach people through career decisions, and provide the kind of support I never really found early in my career.

The ring of cherry trees looms larger with each step I take and the nerves settle back in. Although, I don't feel anxious exactly. I feel excited. It's anticipation.

These next few moments will alter my life path. And it's a path I couldn't have planned if I tried.

As I slowly make my way closer I realize that I am comfortable taking this risk. If it all goes wrong I'll still be fine. I'm okay walking up to the little stump of a cherry tree with one branch left in bloom not knowing who is standing on the other side.

I've come back from losing everything I had ever worked for, and am happier than I could have imagined. The addition of a partner is the cherry on top. If this doesn't work out I can still count on myself to recover.

Not just survive, but thrive.

When I approach the tree there are a few people taking pictures but I spot a figure sitting by the edge of the water.

His back is to me as I walk up but his hair is dark. His arms are propped up on his knees so I can't tell how tall he is but his back and shoulders look strong, sturdy.

A branch crunches under my foot and I glance down at it.

"Maggie, you came."

My head snaps up.

Time stands still.

Tears well in my eyes and I start shaking my head. This can't be. This is too much. This is what I wanted. This is impossible.

Austin stands and shrugs, bunching up the jacket of his steel blue suit, and steps over to me.

"You're late," he scolds and the tears spill over onto my cheeks. I go to wipe them with the back of my hand but I bump into his thumbs as he brushes them away.

"Don't cry MC, don't cry." His touch grazes across my cheeks. "This is a good thing."

"I know it is," I wail and then we both start laughing.

"Sorry, I wouldn't dream of telling you how to feel."

"How long have you known?" I ask. Needing to know the answer while also dreading it.

"Since Lapis. I showed up and it was you and I panicked."

"Am I the girl from the podcast?"

"You heard that?"

"My sister sent it to me and I'll explain to you later why that's a stretch."

He laughs, "I can't wait to know everything about you. And, yes, you're the girl from the podcast."

I sniffle and he intertwines our fingers bringing them between us. Then he wraps his hands around mine and holds them tight. His bourbon eyes burn me as he holds my gaze.

"Thank god you're here. I was so scared you wouldn't come." He exhales. "You make me better. You make me want to be the best version of myself. I want you to be proud of me. I want you to rely on me. I want to support you in everything you do. You're incredible and amazing and all the other adjectives you can think of."

I let out a laugh because he knows me well enough to know that I'm wordsmithing even as he declares his love for me.

His *love* for me!

"You're perfect, Maggie Collins and I can't pretend I don't love you for one more minute."

"Oh, Austin," is the only phrase I can get out before his hands dive into my hair and he pulls my lips to his with the hunger of a starved man. My arms wrap around him and I hold him to me.

This man has been a pebble in my shoe since we met. Always there in some way. Sometimes annoying, sometimes arousing, but always present.

He knows my deepest thoughts, he knows my body in ways no one else does. He knows my aspirations.

"I'm so glad you showed up tonight," he says again as he pulls me to his chest and holds my head against him. I can hear his racing heart beat through his jacket. Mine is pounding at a matching pace; again we meet each other in stride.

"I'm so glad it's you. All day I kept hoping it was you."

"I'm so glad you don't hate me anymore."

"I don't think I ever, really, hated you." I admit as I pull back to look up into his eyes.

"Because I'm so handsome?"

"And humble," we laugh.

He reaches up and cradles my head in his hand before slowly lowering down and kissing me gently. Reverently.

My body melts into his and the warmth of his embrace spreads through my body. My fingers thread into his hair and he inhales sharply at the contact. His hand slides down to grip my ass and visions of fucking against a cherry tree have me lifting my leg to wrap around him.

Austin breaks the kiss and smiles at me.

"Hold your horses MC, I've got plans."

***

"Really?" I look at Austin as the car pulls up outside of Lapis.

"I didn't get to eat last time," he says over the rim of his glasses which goads me into an affectionate eye roll. "Plus," he reaches out and interlaces our fingers, "I wanted the chance to redo our first date."

A blush blooms up my neck and settles in my cheeks as my smile widens. Greg opens the door for us and Austin climbs out first and then reaches back for me. I look up at the restaurant and then glance through the window to see that the table I sat at all those months ago is adorned with a large bouquet of flowers and a bottle of champagne.

"I can't believe I get to see that smile whenever I want," Austin says as we sit down at the table.

"You better love my scowl too because I have a feeling you'll be seeing plenty of that." I retort as I lift my menu.

"And your O face," he adds with a finger pointed in the air.

I can't help myself. I laugh.

The messages with DCFox always made me smile. I think back to the first one I received. He said he researched a list of questions to ask on a first date and found a post with 150 listed. He said he read them all and then picked his favorite to ask me.

If you won the lottery, what would you do with the money?

I replied that I'd need to know if it was the Mega Millions Jackpot or a lucky scratch off ticket from a Christmas stocking. If it was a scratch off I'd just stick the cash in my wallet and probably forget it was there. If it was a big one I'd set up some automatic donations to national public media and maybe fund a journalism scholarship.

The memory makes me chuckle.

"What's so funny?" Austin asks as he picks up his menu.

"Nothing, I was thinking about the first text you sent with the 150 first date questions. I told you I'd donate to public media but I obviously had no idea who you were or who you worked for."

"Yeah, I loved that. It made me want to talk to you more."

"I'm glad you did," I smile and then shake my head because I simply cannot believe I am sitting across from Austin Thorne on our first date when we've been talking since last summer and spent the fall together in a sex marathon.

Austin leans forward resting his forearms on the table and folding his hands together. "Alright, should we go through the 150 questions now...or..."

I laugh and he grins. "Did you really bring the list?"

"No, but now that you've brought it up I think we should just go through it item by item. Get it all out on the table."

"Sure, look up the list, let's see what you've got."

***

"No way!" I say with a laugh as Austin nods enthusiastically. "There is no way you actually believe that."

"All I'm saying is that I've been in a room with all those guys and I can't say for sure that it isn't true."

I laugh and shake my head as we settle down from our boy band conspiracy theory debate. Austin picks his phone up and scrolls for the next one.

"Oh, this is a good one. Do you consider a hot dog a sandwich?"

"No," I state immediately. "Well..."

"Tricky one isn't it. I say no. It's more in the burger category than a sandwich."

"But what about a torpedo?"

"We're talking about sandwiches, MC."

I laugh, "Yeah I know, a torpedo sandwich, it's on a bun like a hot dog."

"Wait, you mean a hero?" Austin asks.

"What are you from New York City or something?"

"No, my stepmom is though. And I'm just teasing, I knew what you meant."

I smile, "so we agreed, hot dogs are not sandwiches. Now, I've got another important question. Pineapple on pizza?"

"Absolutely."

"What?! No Austin! No, no, no, no." I shake my head with mirth.

"Yeah, the guys give me shit for that one too but the sweet balanced with the spicy pepperoni and umami of the cheese? Yeah, I love it."

"We have to move on from this. Maybe a less controversial topic, what Chinese Zodiac year were you born?" I ask before taking a sip of my champagne.

"1990..." he drags it out while he searches but I no longer care what year he fell into.

"You were born in 1990?" I asked because never once did the possibility of Austin being two years younger than me cross my mind.

"Yeah," he laughs and sips his cocktail. "Why? When were you born?"

I swallow the lump in my throat, "1988."

He grins and I have a feeling I'm going to be annoyed by what he says next.

"Robbing the cradle Maggie Collins? Is 1988 the year of the Cougar?" He can barely contain his snicker.

"Dragon." I reply flatly.

"That makes a lot more sense." He nods solemnly and I kick him under the table. He's saved from further harm because our food arrives.

I've never been on a date like this before. The ease of conversation between us is comfortable. The genuine laughter. We continue talking and asking random questions while we eat and I am really enjoying this casual side of Austin.

I saw a hint of it as we became *friends* these last few weeks. At first I wasn't sure if I believed it but after tonight I can see that this goofy, light-hearted man is the truest version of Austin Thorne I've seen yet.

***

"This is the best first date ever," Austin says as our plates are cleared and he reaches across the table for my hand. I give it to him and watch as he brushes his thumb gently across the tops of my fingers. My gaze travels up his arm, over his shoulder to his neck, and the 5 o'clock shadow covering his square jaw. His whiskey eyes burn into me and I feel like I can read his mind.

"So, what do we do now?" I ask playfully.

"I can think of a few ideas." Austin says in a low voice.

"No, not that, are we...well...dating?"

"Yeah MC, we're dating. But we won't be for long."

"What?" I cough out a laugh.

"I'm not going to be able to wait very long to make you my wife. I need you at my side."

"Does this mean we're a power couple?"

"There's something powerful happening here, that's for sure." Austin says with a pump of his eyebrows.

"Ohmygod you're insatiable," I joke.

"Maggie, you have no idea. I am buzzing with desire to take you somewhere private and cash in on the benefits of being your boyfriend."

"Are we tossing out the no sleepover rule?"

"Oh, we won't be sleeping but you and I will start our morning together tomorrow. Greg has a bag for me in the trunk."

"No he does not," I laugh and Austin laughs too. He never disputes my statement, he simply stands, and pulls me up with him. He plants a kiss at my ear that sends shivers down my spine before guiding me ahead of him toward the door by the small of my back.

As he opens the door for me I pause next to him.

I look up at the man who has proven himself to be exactly what I need. "Can I catch a ride with you?"

"Always."

Chapter Thirty-Seven
AUSTIN
Mr. Maggie Collins

"I'm nervous!" I say as I wipe my palms on my shorts. Maggie is stepping out of my shower and reaching for a towel. She wouldn't let me shower with her this morning because we're on a schedule. We tend to ignore the clock when we're in there together.

Try as I might, she just won't accept the simple fact that I own my company and she owns hers. This makes us the bosses and we make the rules, or at least we can not punish ourselves for being late. But my Maggie likes to stick to her routine.

My Maggie.

I still smile a little every time I think it.

It's been an adjustment to get used to waking up early when she leaves for a run. After our first date we went back to her place and in the morning I told her to pack a bag. I was tempted to whisk her across the globe to Japan but I settled for a night at The Ned.

Getting us together was a feat of patience and determination but as soon as we accepted our devotion to each other things have flowed.

Felix met her and instantly knew she was the one for me. They gang up against me whenever they can. Maggie because she naturally disagrees with me, Felix because he knows it irks me. We get together a lot more than we used to because Maggie and I just moved to a house that's about five minutes from his in NoVa.

Elle was happy to take over my condo and even though Dad was upset I left Thorne to go into business with her, he honored her trust fund access agreement. Dad grumbled about it being a waste of our time but I've made a point to not agree with the man. Together we opened Girl Fox Publishing and will be putting our first book out in a few weeks

Maggie turned down the book deal and formed a consulting company where she works with female policy makers on their tone and wording. She's been talking with Ben from President Quinn's administration about contributing to the state of the union address next year.

"You don't have to be nervous. My family is pretty chill," she can barely say this with a straight face. "Maybe chill isn't the right word but they're normal enough."

"You have to realize I've never been around normal people."

"This is true, it's a wonder you turned out as okay as you did."

"I'm more than okay and you know it."

"I know it!" Felix chimes in and Maggie yelps before slamming the bathroom door shut.

"Dude, boundaries!" I yell before ushering him downstairs to the kitchen. "Don't make me change the door code again."

"You wouldn't," he says, astonished. "That was the worst three days of my life."

"And it should have taught you a lesson not to walk in on my wife in her towel."

"Not yet," he wags a finger at me.

"Close enough."

That's right, I'll be proposing to Maggie this weekend. We're headed up to Lakeville for the town pontoon parade and summer festival. Float Fest they call it. And when Maggie told them we were coming up over Facetime a few weeks ago her sister started gyrating her hips, her mom clapped at a furious pace and her eyes doubled in size. Her sister's husband nodded and her dad tipped his beer in my direction.

I snuck her dad's number out of her phone and called him on my own the next day. I told him that I wanted to make Maggie my wife and was hoping to have his family involved in the proposal.

As much as she gives her family grief, there's a deep affection there.

Felix helped me pick out the ring. Well, actually all he did was look over my shoulder and make unhelpful comments as I inspected each one. The ring box has been burning a hole at the back of my sock drawer for a week and anytime Maggie calls to me from the bedroom I break out in a cold sweat.

"Are you all packed?" I ask Felix because once he heard Maggie describe Float Fest he said he wanted in. She can't say no to him so he'll be riding up with us today.

"Yeah boy, I'm so excited. Upstate New York is so close to home, I wish my parents were still there, I'd swing by." He pops some grapes from the counter into his mouth. "Are you going to pay Greg time and a half?"

"Greg isn't driving us," Maggie says and we both spin towards her as she walks down the stairs.

"What do you mean Greg isn't driving us?" I ask as she rolls her suitcase into the foyer.

"I mean, I talked to him about it and said we'd get ourselves there."

"I don't think I've ever actually driven the Tesla," I say as I rack my brain, I didn't even drive it when I bought it, just picked up the keys and tossed them to Greg.

"Oh, we're not taking the Tesla." Maggie laughs. "No way. The good people of Lakeville would have a field day with that car. No Foxy, we need a normal car."

I'm confused but I still smile inside at the use of her nickname for me.

"I've got a normal car!" Felix chimes in. "I've got four normal cars. Well, I guess we won't all fit in the Ferrari so that one is ruled out."

"No," Maggie shakes her head. "Your cars are too flashy and far from normal for the good folk of Lakeville."

"What about the Rivian? That's a pick up truck!" Felix pleads. "It's a car of the people."

"It's an electric pickup. Doesn't count." Maggie says as she pulls a drink out of the fridge. "Guys, I got it. Stick with me."

As if on cue the doorbell rings and Maggie smiles. She walks to the front door and opens it up to a kid who doesn't look old enough to drive wearing a car rental polo and khakis standing at our door.

"Ugh, hello, I've, umm, got a car here for Maggie Collins." He rushes through the sentence.

"Yes, thank you," Maggie smiles at him. Felix grabs his duffel and steps into the foyer behind her. I grab both our bags and join them.

"Wait, you're Felix Fornier," the kid says.

"Hi, nice to meet you."

"Big fan but what happened at the end of the season?" The kid asks and I see Felix's grip on his bag tighten.

"We didn't win the cup, that's what happened," he grits out and gives the kid a tight smile.

Maggie comes to the rescue. "Do we need to drop you off at the office or are you able to get picked up by a colleague?"

"Ugh," the kid looks back at her, "The contract says I'll be picked up by a colleague."

"Fantastic, I'll take the keys, and I really appreciate you bringing the car over to us today." She smiles to end the conversation and we step out the front door and walk to the driveway.

Parked there is a giant, black F150.

"How is this less flashy than my car?" I protest as she uses the key fob to unlock it.

"It'll fit in much better, trust me." She pats my back after I lift our bags into the back seat. "You want to do the first shift?"

"No," I say and I shake my head. "I haven't driven in years, I'm not even sure my license is valid."

"Ugh, excuse me, ma'am, the contract only has your name on it so you are the only authorized driver for the length of your rental agreement." Kid chimes in from where he's taken a seat on our front stoop.

"Shotgun!" Felix yells and he tosses his bag on top of ours and rounds the front of the truck.

"No way, you do not get to sit in the front seat while Maggie drives, that's clear boyfriend territory."

"Thorney, the rules of shotgun are very clear. And, I've got witnesses who will corroborate I said it first, and clearly."

I slide my glasses off my face and pinch my nose. Maggie steps into my side and kisses my jaw.

"You can call shotgun for the next leg," she says and I deflate because I kind of expected her to overrule shotgun.

***

"There it is!" Felix yells from the back seat. "What do I get for seeing the sign first?"

"Nothing," I grumble.

"In our house, the first one to spot the sign gets a five minute late start on dishes. It was our biggest bargaining chip growing up," Maggie says as she signals to change lanes. "Do you guys want to drive through town or go straight to my parent's?"

"Town!" Felix yelps and Maggie smiles. She looks over to me for confirmation and I nod.

Lakeville is the quintessential small town. The square downtown with locally owned businesses lining the street, beautiful landscaping, and friendly waves even to the unfamiliar truck slowly moving down the street.

Although, I do spot three other black F150s and we've only been in town for a few minutes.

"That's my sister's studio," Maggie points out the window, "and be careful what you say in that coffee shop. It's owned by the matron of town gossip."

She comes to a stop at the corner and in front of us is the park and the lake. The setting sun sparkles off the water and while DC is beautiful there is an urban grit to everything that I can see hasn't tainted Lakeville.

After Maggie makes the turn I reach over and slide her hand into mine. She's sitting up a little straighter in her seat and I can tell she's nervous. We wind down the road away from town with the lake to my right.

"This place is really pretty," Felix says from the back seat. I can't see him but it sounds like his face is pressed up to the window.

"It is, I'm lucky to have grown up here," Maggie says with a small smile at me.

She pulls her hand away to turn the truck into a driveway. There are already two other trucks parked there. We're barely out of our seats when the front door opens and the screen slaps shut behind a blur of blonde headed our way.

"MAYBE! Congratulations!!" The ball of energy yells.

"Hey Lizzard," Maggie and Liz wrap each other in a hug. I slide my hand into my pocket. "What are you congratulating me on?"

Liz steps back and has a wide eye look of unease on her face. "Ummm, congratulations on making it up here safely?"

Maggie narrows her eyes at her and turns her head towards me but keeps her eyes on Liz. "This is my boyfriend, Austin."

"Hey Liz, great to finally meet you," I say and I step forward. Her eyes somehow get even bigger when she wraps her arms around me in a hug.

"Have you not proposed yet?" She whispers in my ear and I start to cough in shock.

"No, he hasn't," Felix says and I have to close my eyes not to lose my shit.

"What is he waiting for?" Liz asks Felix before extending her hand, "Liz Collins Sutherland."

"Felix For–"

"Oh, I know who you are." Liz says as she pulls her hand back from the shake.

Maggie has, thankfully, moved further from this conversation to give hugs to her family members on the porch. Liz leads Felix and me over to the group. A woman who looks like Maggie but thirty years older steps down off the porch and wraps me in a hug.

"I'm so excited to have another son-in-law!" She squeals and I stiffen.

"Mom," Liz hisses before she starts slicing across her throat with her hand.

"Why can't I call him my son-in-law? He will be soon enough right?"

"What are you talking about?" Maggie asks as she joins us.

"Why didn't you tell us yourself, Maggie dear?" Her mom asks.

"Tell you what?"

"That you're engaged to Austin!"

"I'm not engaged to Austin." Maggie says with a quick shake of her head.

"Well, not yet," I give her a sheepish smile and a shrug. I feel Felix's hand on my shoulder so I bend down to one knee. No time like the present I guess. "Maggie, you are the best thing in my life and I never want to spend another day without you as my partner. You're my ride or die and I need you at my side." Maggie's eyes are wet with unshed tears and everything else I wanted to say about looking forward to fighting with her, about the light she brings to my life, about how I took a risk by signing up for SMS Connect but our relationship was a bigger reward than I could have imagined disappears. "Will you marry me?"

She nods and reaches for me. My arms wrap around her and I press her to me while our lips crash together.

"Is that a yes?" I say against her lips.

"Yes Austin, it's a yes. I'm in!" Maggie says as I use my thumbs to catch her joyful tears.

"She said yes!" Felix yells from behind me and Maggie startles. I hug her tighter before we break apart and accept hugs from our friends and family.

Later that night, as we sit as a group in the Collin's back deck, I'm holding Maggie's hand under the table and my cheeks hurt from laughing. I help clean up the dishes with Maggie while Felix enjoys his bonus five minutes from seeing the sign first. I sneak kisses every chance I get and at first Maggie is embarrassed but she has started to lean into them so I keep going. We start the dishwasher and instead of joining her family on the deck again she pulls me up the stairs behind her.

We step into her room and I take in Maggie's high school choices. Political posters alongside movie stars and post it notes are all right on brand for her. She closes the door and then she jumps into my arms.

"I'm sorry my family ruined your proposal," she says after a few kisses.

"They didn't, I was going to do it this weekend but I didn't know when, it was perfect."

"You were?"

"Yeah, it was one year ago tomorrow that we started texting on SMS Connect so I felt like the timing was right."

Maggie curls into me and I cradle her against me. One year ago I was completely oblivious to the deep connection that was possible between two people. My conversations with TalkShopGirl opened my eyes to true companionship. My attraction to Maggie Collins the first time I saw her was undeniable.

And, as awful as those winter months were, I think we needed to break apart in order to come back together. Because of everything we endured, we're stronger than ever.

***

Want to attend Maggie and Austin's engagement party thrown by Felix? Check out the bonus content!

Acknowledgements

Holy shit that was fun! I hope you enjoyed reading Maggie & Austin's story as much as I enjoyed writing it!

Thank you times a million plus infinity to Liza Illuzzi who is the best developmental editor and book bestie an indie author could ask for. Seriously thank you for holding my hand through the entire process. I don't think I'll ever get over how perfectly the last chapter came together.

Thank you to Priti Das for bringing the characters to life on the cover.

Thank you internet for your support during the process and of the book itself. It was amazing to get to know the many ARC readers and I am floored by the enthusiasm for this book. Autumn Dee and Justine at Bookish Bubbly PR and Shay and Lindsey at Good Girls PR made ARCs and promotion so easy and I look forward to partnering with you all again and again!

To Bekah and Nikki at Method Agency thank you for all the ideas and answering all the questions I come up with!

My kiddos, here's another one that you can't read yet but someday when you do I hope you'll understand how much your unconditional love means to me when I am in my story world.

Danny B, you and me together, we can do anything.

About the Author

Erin Marie Bassett is a geriatric millennial, wife, and mother of two living in Chicago. (A mile west of Wrigley Field but she, like her husband and kids, are St. Louis Cardinal fans). When she's not reading or writing romance, Erin helps small businesses and local organizations use the magic words to connect with their communities. She volunteers hard at her kids' school and she believes in the power of S.L.O.W. Living.

Her doctor tells her not to but she drinks a lot of coffee. Like, a lot.

Connect with Erin online & Take the Book Boyfriend Quiz to get on the Tuesday Night Newsletter List!

erinmariebassett.com

@erinmariebassett

Also by Erin Marie Bassett

For details, to order a signed paperback, or to take the book boyfriend quiz visit erinmariebassett.com.

D.C. Renegades Series

Unmasking Love – Aiden's Story
Unrivaled Love – Bryson's Story
Unlaced Love – Crosby's Story
Unstoppable Love – Duncan's Story
Unforgettable Love – Emmett's Story
Unfrozen Love – Felix's Story

Standalones

The Thorne at My Side

The Howdy Holidays Series

A Forrest for the Holidays
A Holiday in Ashes

A Still River Holiday

The Lakeville Trio

<u>Here For It</u>
<u>Upstate Expectations</u>
<u>Don't Call It Puppy Love</u>

Breaking Barriers Series

From the Sidelines by Rachel LaBerge
Beyond the Court by Stef C.R.
Quite the Pair by Kathryn Kincaid
<u>Over the Line</u> by Erin Marie Bassett

The Thorne at My Side

AUSTIN THORNE IS A media conglomerate heir who has invented an AI speech writing software.

Maggie Collins is a political speech writer working on a presidential campaign.

Her boss hires him, and the two are now forced to work together, having very different ideas for how that work should be done.

The stress of the campaign is getting to Maggie so her friend suggests she bang it out. So Maggie picks Austin with is slutty little glasses, and the two are now engaged in a highly successful sex for stress relief arrangement.

Now, at the same time the two are texting each other on an SMS only dating service meant to foster deep connections where you don't know who they are, what they do for a living, how much money they make or what they look like.

Austin discovers the secret first, and it doesn't so well for either of them. Things get worse for Maggie, and she has to build herself back up before realizing it's been Austin all along.

(Awww, I know, but 95% of the spice is in the first half of the book.)

It's basically a spicy retelling of You've Got Mail.